CONTENTION
AND OTHER
FRONTIER STORIES

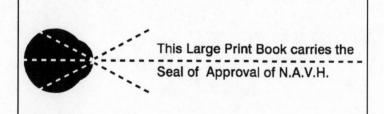

This Large Print Book carries the
Seal of Approval of N.A.V.H.

CONTENTION AND OTHER FRONTIER STORIES

A FIVE STAR ANTHOLOGY

EDITED BY HAZEL RUMNEY

THORNDIKE PRESS

A part of Gale, a Cengage Company

GALE
A Cengage Company

Farmington Hills, Mich • San Francisco • New York • Waterville, Maine
Meriden, Conn • Mason, Ohio • Chicago

LIBRARY OF CONGRESS CIP DATA ON FILE.
CATALOGUING IN PUBLICATION FOR THIS BOOK
IS AVAILABLE FROM THE LIBRARY OF CONGRESS

ISBN-13: 978-1-4328-5469-0 (hardcover alk. paper)

Published in 2019 by arrangement with Five Star, a part of Gale, a Cengage Company

Printed in Mexico
1 2 3 4 5 6 7 23 22 21 20 19

Dedicated to Richard S. Wheeler
1935–2019
Writer extraordinaire and
a dear friend to many.

TABLE OF CONTENTS

8

■ ■ ■ ■

CONTENTION
BY JOHNNY D. BOGGS

■ ■ ■ ■

I didn't know the Widow Kieberger from Adam's off ox, but she came up to me inside a Yuma grog shop, sat down, introduced herself, and told me her hardships, which were plentiful. Though she wasn't hard to look at, I had pretty much stopped listening and started cogitating a polite way to get away from her, maybe suggest that she find a deputy U.S. marshal, contact the Pinkerton National Detective Agency, or perhaps I'd mention a couple of buckets of blood where she could find men who killed cheap. Having just gotten out of the Hellhole, I had little desire to go back behind those walls. Or hang. That's when I happened to catch a few words she whispered.

Setting my glass on the table, I cleared my throat, and she stopped talking.

"Did you say . . . baseball bats?"

Her face paled, and she stared at squashed

scorpions on the floor. "Yes." I barely heard her.

I killed my bourbon. "Let me get this straight. This major, he breaks into your house, with eight other ballists, and they proceed to beat your husband to death?"

She didn't look up.

"With baseball bats?" I added.

"Forty inches," she whispered. "White ash. One was flat."

I nodded. "For bunting."

"Or pounding a sleeping man's head to mush."

"Baseball bats." I waved at the barkeep, who sent a strumpet over with more Chicken Cock and another glass. Once the barmaid left, the widow added, without looking up, "Then he ran me out of Contention City as a . . ." Her eyes lifted toward me. I understood.

"Baseball bats," I repeated, then killed half of my fresh bourbon and felt that heat rising, turning my ears red, like they were prone to color when some umpire made a bad call or Hank Fuller swung at a pitch a mile over his head.

"That ain't right," I said.

She had to tell me the story again, but this time I listened. When she finished, I asked, "Isn't there any law in Contention?"

"The town marshal is the right fielder. He came with them that night."

My head shook, trying to comprehend this outrage. "Folks in town let this go on?"

"When's the last time you've been to Contention City?" she asked.

I shrugged. "Haven't been anywhere, ma'am, for three and a half years."

"They love their baseball," she explained. "And Major Perry has never lost a game."

I pondered. This Major Perry fielded one of the best baseball clubs in Arizona Territory. Undefeated in six years. Throttled teams from Tombstone and Tucson. Even beat the boys from Bisbee, which had some mighty fine ballists. But when they weren't dominating a baseball diamond, Contention's First Nine kept the workers under control. So, when some revolutionary like Mr. Kieberger started talking about improving conditions at the stamp mills, Major Perry and his ballists, including the town's law dog, would bust into a darkened bedroom and bludgeon the man to death for being an anarchist — with forty-inch batsticks.

Gives ballists like me a bad name.

"So . . ." I hesitated. "What do you want of me?"

When she told me, I sighed. "I haven't

13

played in years, ma'am."

"You played with the prison guards," she said. "I saw you in a couple of games. I found out about you. That's what gave me the idea."

My head shook. "The guards needed a catcher. It got me out of shoveling caliche or getting tossed into the Snake Den. And we lost plenty of games, even to those velocipede riders on that train to California."

Her green eyes hardened. "I said, I *found out* about you. *You* could get a team. *You* could beat Major Perry's murderers."

That gave me pause. I squinted. "What exactly is it you want me to do?"

She told me.

"And . . ." I put this kind of delicate. "What's in it for me?"

She told me that, too.

The next eastbound Southern Pacific took me to Lordsburg, New Mexico Territory, where I caught a stage to Silver City and met Hank Fuller in the Copper Tarnish Saloon. Last time I saw Hank, he was a hundred and seventy-seven pounds of baseball prime and on his way to sign with the Louisville Colonels. Now, he topped two-fifty and played for the Fat Fellows. The bib

14

front of his uniform pictured a foaming mug of beer. His meaty right hand held an empty mug, which was getting refilled, again. The Fat Fellows were celebrating their 20-to-6 victory over the Slim Jims. That's how far Hank Fuller had fallen. He'd gone from playing professional ball to playing for kegs of beer.

Since the Fat Fellows had won, the Slim Jims bought the beers — and all were drunk — I didn't have to spend any of the Widow Kieberger's greenbacks. After the crowd thinned out, or passed out, Hank asked what I wanted. I told him. He asked how much it paid. I told him that, too, which sobered him up right quick.

"What do you want from me?" he asked.

"To lay off any pitches a mile over your head," I said.

We traveled to Tombstone and sat high up in the grandstands, watching the Contention Millers wallop the home Tigers.

"Who's the big guy?" Hank asked.

I swallowed my peanut. A first baseman who tops two hundred and fifty pounds was asking about a "big guy." That ought to tell you something about Contention's baseball team. Only none of Contention's First Nine carried his weight in his belly. Those boys packed solid muscle, and every time their bat-stick crushed a ball, I envisioned the Widow Kieberger's unfortunate late husband.

"That's Major Perry," I answered. I knew him because the Widow Kieberger said he played center field. He played it pretty good, too.

"The third baseman is Caleb Cartwright," Hank said.

"You know him?"

"I played against him when he was with the Pittsburgh Alleghenys. He played last season for that Kansas City club in the National League."

"The team the National League kicked out?"

"Yep. For hooliganism."

The Contention Millers didn't need to resort to hooliganism or beating men to death on this Saturday. Tombstone was awful. The Tigers lost, 35-to-1, but this Major Perry wasn't the nicest fellow I'd ever seen on a diamond. I mean, the jackass berated his fellow ballists when the third baseman made an error in the eighth inning, allowing Tombstone to score its only run.

They taunted the poor Tombstone ballists. Major Perry screamed insults at his opponents. His teammates laughed when the

Tigers made poor plays. Considering how bruised and bloodied Tombstone's players looked after the game, you would've thought Contention's First Nine used brass knuckles or billy clubs on the players in the field — which they might have.

After the slaughter mercifully ended, the Millers tore apart the visiting team's bench, laughed, and headed for the depot. The Tigers of Tombstone just stared. Nobody protested. Hank drained his beer. "We've got to beat *this* team?"

Me? I sat there fuming at what I had just witnessed, and I had taken part in some inappropriate behavior on baseball fields. I told Hank, "The Contention Millers have forgotten A.G. Spalding's prime rule for our sport: 'To make baseball playing respectable and honorable.' "

Hank shook his head. "They forgot another rule, too, Skip: 'Thou shalt not kill.' "

Rounding up ballists in the Southwest isn't hard. It's not even tough to find baseball players who lack ethics. But finding exceptional ballists willing to risk a stay in prison or having their faces pounded to jelly by forty-inch timbers of white ash proved about as taxing as trying to tag out King Kelly when he's sliding into home. I had to meet up with the Widow Kieberger in Tucson to get more money, but she didn't put up any fuss. Her husband had been dead for pushing two years now, and she was eager to exact her revenge on Major Perry and his murdering thugs.

I didn't ask where she came by such money.

Finding a *Spalding's Base Ball Guide* proved a mite difficult, but that only set me back ten cents in Phoenix, and I needed to bone up on the rules since I had been out of circulation for three and a half years. Prison guards, you see, made up rules they thought appropriate, and didn't give a fig how the National League or American Association played the game.

Once I had hired all my accessories — I mean *ballists* — we practiced just across the border, away from prying eyes. We probably could have swept a three-game series against the territorial prison's guards, and maybe even whipped those California velocipede riders. But we certainly were not undefeated after four barnstorming seasons.

Yet that's what the *Tucson Enterprise* reported, of course, since I paid the inkslinger one of the Widow Kieberger's double eagles to print exactly that: that we were undefeated. It's also what the posters the Widow Kieberger paid to have printed announced, too. I made sure Contention City got some of those posters.

Sure enough, when the American Zephyrs — Hank came up with that handle for us — played the Tucson Base Ball Team (there's an original name for a club) on a Friday afternoon, Major Perry arrived by train to see us play.

"Congratulations," the major said after our 20-to-nothing victory. He held out his massive right hand.

"You'll forgive me if I don't accept your hand, sir." I kept shaking to get the feeling back into my stinging hands. "Masterson wasn't at his best today, but even his worst hurts like blazes after nine innings." (Kent Masterson wasn't at his worst, either, but nigh his best, and my hands remained swollen and numb after catching him.)

"You don't wear a mitt, sir?"

Some catchers did — so did infielders and outfielders who could take the heckling — even in the professional leagues. But you try wearing a mitt playing for and against prison guards. They'd have thrown me in the Snake Den. I shook my head.

Major Perry praised our pitcher, and lauded Hank's hitting — Hank hadn't swung at one bad pitch the whole game —

19

and then the major got down to business. Why, his team down in Contention City was undefeated, too, and he thought a game against us would bring in quite the crowd.

"We don't play for beer, sir," I told him. "We get half the gate and an appearance fee."

"What's the fee?" the major asked.

I told him.

He wasn't smiling, but he said that could be arranged. Had I known that a baseball team could charge that kind of money to play a game, I might've avoided forty-two months in the Hellhole.

Then I got greedy. "And it's customary for a little wager between the teams."

"What do you propose?" he said.

I grinned. "How about your bat-sticks and all your equipment? We put up the same."

He paled, but nodded. A man like him, with an undefeated team, can't back down from a wager. I was pleased. After we clobbered his team, the major wouldn't have any bat-sticks to make another anarchist's wife a widow.

"How about next Friday?" Major Perry asked.

My head shook. "Sir, we have to be in Los Angeles in a few days." I excused myself, found my grip on the bench, opened it, and pulled out a book, which I opened and stared at a blank page. "I'm sorry to say that we're booked for all this month," I lied. "Let's see. We're playing the White Stockings on Saturday the twenty-third before going to Detroit the next Monday."

Major Perry's eyes widened. "The White Stockings?" His words come out like a gasp. "In Chicago?"

"Yes, sir," I said. "Cap Anson's a real nice man. And a fine ballist." The last sentence was the only truthful one I spoke.

"And Detroit?" Perry asked.

"The Wolverines," I said.

"You . . . play . . . ?"

My chuckle silenced him. "Sir," I said, "those are just exhibition games. The National League, you must be aware, doesn't start its season till later that week. We Zephyrs are just a traveling team of ballists — like the Red Stockings of '69." I smiled. "They went undefeated, too, you know."

"And you've beaten the White Stockings . . ."

Closing my book, I waved my hand. "Oh, I'm sure if we played Cap's boys in a full series, we wouldn't still be undefeated. In fact, Detroit played us close last year. If Hank had not homered in the last inning, well, our record might be a hundred twenty-three and one."

I opened the book to another empty page. "I guess, though, if you really want to risk your perfect season, we could squeeze you in . . . would Friday the thirteenth of May work?"

"Sure," Major Perry said weakly.

I closed the book. "We do require half of our appearance fee in advance, sir."

He paid that, too — by check, but the bank cashed it without argument — and walked, a mite unsteady, out of the baseball park.

Inside the nearest saloon, Hank said, "Maybe we should just take that money and skedaddle while we're ahead."

"What about the Widow Kieberger?" I asked, and when Hank just sipped his beer, I added: "Is that what you want to do?"

"No," he said. "I'd like to beat those Contention killers."

"So would I," said Masterson, who had pitched for the Boston Beaneaters till the National League found out about his relationship with gamblers.

"Then we better start practicing," I said. "And find us a southpaw hitter."

Naturally, we did not take the train to Los Angeles. Nor did we travel to Chicago and

Detroit. I did go to Denver, where I signed up Skyrocket McSorely, who played right field with a center fielder's speed and batted left-handed. By the end of the month, we were back across the border, practicing every day for our date with the Contention Millers.

While celebrating a real fine practice on the third of May, we all got knocked off our feet. The earth shook. Hank lost six pounds. Masterson lost his breakfast. Skyrocket McSorely confessed all his sins, which sounded considerable. I cried out for my ma.

The rumble didn't last that long, and the Almighty did not open up the earth and drop us down to Hades. The next morning, another little shake rattled our nerves, and after we found our scattered horses, I rode to Bisbee to see what had just happened.

What had happened, of course, was an earthquake. The telegraph lines were all down, so I spent some of the Widow Kieberger's money on a stagecoach ride to Contention City.

Not that I was drunk, but what I saw and heard sobered me.

Roofs had collapsed, the whistles at the mine and mills kept blaring, and the baseball diamond lay in utter ruins. Somehow, amid all this commotion, I managed to find Major Perry. Seeing me, he shook his head, and waved at the mess behind him.

"We cannot play," he told me. "Not on this."

Ever seen photographs of Atlanta taken after Sherman's boys marched through? That's what the Contention City Base Ball Field resembled. It's what a lot of Contention looked like. I quickly thought of this: "But you do understand that there is no refund on the deposit of our appearance fee."

"I don't give a whit about that, sir!" he snapped.

That earthquake was a godsend — for me.

"Why don't we reschedule our game?" I suggested.

"Next month?" Major Perry said.

"Next year," I said.

Yep, that was a gamble. But I had seen Contention play and my boys practice. We couldn't beat the Millers, not with the ballists I had lined up. I also saw just what a boomtown Contention City was, and figured once she got fixed up, there might be more money to earn. I am greedy. Which, along with my temper, had cost me forty-two months in Yuma. And was why even the Beer and Whiskey League wouldn't let me play on their teams anymore.

"You'd do that?" Major Perry asked.

This was no lie: "Major, it'll take you a year to get this diamond, and your city, back in shape."

I can't call the Widow Kieberger understanding. When I met her up in Benson, she did not sound like the meek, frightened, revengeful woman I had talked to in Yuma. But eventually, reason prevailed. If we were to beat the Millers, if she was to get what she wanted, then patience, and practice, came first. She also conceded, after a second brandy, that she had yet to find a man suitable for her purposes. Turned out, I knew a fellow who would be out of Yuma in November.

After paying off my middle infielders, two outfielders, and a backup hurler, I let the rest of the boys find baseball clubs for the upcoming season whilst Hank and I took off to Galveston . . . New Orleans . . . St. Louis . . . Cincinnati . . . and even Laramie, where a couple of ballists I knew were getting out early on good behavior. From those towns and a handful of others, I sent telegraphs to newspapers in southern Arizona, letting their readers know that the American Zephyrs had won another game, making up a few details and a final score, and hoping no editor would ask for confirmation from another source.

By late October, the mercenaries that made up the American Zephyrs reconvened in Bisbee, and we crossed the border again. In early March, I sent a telegraph to Major Perry, suggesting a date to make up our ball game. He happily agreed to the date and our original terms.

Even the Widow Kieberger looked happy. I had rounded up a pretty good bunch of ballists, and that fellow I'd told her about proved mighty handy at cracking safes.

The game pitting two undefeated teams would be played on Monday, April 30. The payrolls would arrive in Contention City on the evening train on April 28. Contention's miners and millers would not be paid until May 1.

I didn't think another earthquake would postpone our game this time. As long as it didn't rain . . .

We arrived on the same train as the payrolls, and the armed guards, including Contention's right fielder/marshal, greeted us at the depot. Turns out, some of Major Perry's ballists — when not beating town teams or clubbing some anarchist to death in his bedroom — also protected Contention's money on its way to the bank for safekeeping till payday.

Caleb Cartwright, Contention City's third baseman, grinned a broken-tooth smile and directed us to Mason's Western Hotel.

That rundown adobe structure wasn't much to look at before the earthquake, but a year ago, the windowpanes had glass, the adobe walls didn't show straw, and the roof covered the entire hotel.

"Criminy," Skyrocket McSorely whispered as we walked down the deserted street. "I thought you said Contention City was a boomtown."

"The key word in that sentence," our shortstop, Professor Anderson, said, "is *was*."

The Contention Millers had won all twenty-two games last year, but every contest had been played on the road after the earthquake had destroyed their field. Though I had briefly seen the town after the earthquake, I never really appreciated the extensiveness of the damage.

After settling into our hotel rooms, we walked to the Contention City Base Ball Field to practice. On our way, a little waif sprinted out of a ramshackle *jacal*. He didn't wear shoes, and I doubt if the urchin

27

had seen a washcloth in months. "Are you the famous Zephyrs?" The boy held out a baseball.

Silent Cobb, our third baseman who hated everything and everybody, took the ball and stared at it. "Uh," he said, "yeah" — more words than he'd spoken in two weeks of practicing.

"Gosh." The boy snatched back the ball. "A Zephyrs ballist touched my baseball. Nobody but me will ever touch it again. Even if you beat my team Monday."

"Your team?" Cobb just doubled his dialogue.

An old man arrived over from the other side of the street. "About all we have left in this town now," he said, shaking all of our hands, "is our baseball team." He said it was a pleasure to have us here, that a team with the national reputation of the American Zephyrs would be a great test for the Millers.

"We'll see if we can compete against something other than other town teams," said a woman in a parasol who stepped off the boardwalk to welcome us to Contention City.

"At least you're honorable players," said a gent in sleeve garters. "Unlike the Tigers of Tombstone."

"They burned our bench the year before last," the urchin informed us.

"And abused our womenfolk," said the old man.

"We hate Tombstone," said one of the bunch of folks greeting us.

Hank Fuller shot me a glance, and I knew he was wondering if maybe Tombstone had deserved that abuse and beating we witnessed last year.

I didn't dwell on that, however, because a woman brought us cookies. Another resident, bless his soul, carried buckets of bottled beer. But that was nothing compared to what we saw at the Contention City Base Ball Field.

Our practice, I realized, was the first time we had played in front of spectators, excepting, just before we left Mexico, the Widow Kieberger and her safecracker and a few other rogues she'd hired. I'd played real games before smaller crowds.

"Wait till tomorrow," one man said. "The whole city will be here. Everyone in town!"

Which is what the Widow Kieberger had said when I first met her in Yuma.

Even though we were just practicing, everyone cheered us. They whistled. It felt great, like it used to feel when I was playing years ago. A long time had passed since anyone had hollered encouraging words for me at a baseball field. I sure never heard anything like that whilst catching for Yuma's guards.

Then I remembered what brought us to Contention.

Just nine years back, this city had boomed after the discovery of silver. Miners found pay dirt in the hills around the town, but Contention thrived because of the stamp mills — hence their baseball team's nickname, the Millers. The San Pedro River provided water, which most of the mining towns — including Tombstone — didn't have. Two stamp mills had been established, the railroad arrived, the team kept winning, and life looked fine in Contention City.

We learned all this as those poor folks treated us to supper and beers after our practice.

Of course, nothing lasts forever, someone pointed out, to which Kent Masterson leaned toward me and whispered, "Like the Millers' undefeated streak," and grinned.

Folks, we learned, found a way to get water to Tombstone. The mines around Contention got flooded. So did the two mills, especially after that earthquake. One mill had already closed this week, and its miners were waiting to collect their last pay before moving on. Everybody knew the other mill's days were numbered, too. The railroad had reached Fairbank a few miles south, meaning fewer folks needed to travel to Contention. The Bisbee stage line had already stopped running to Contention. Since the earthquake, folks had been leaving for better jobs, or any jobs. Once, you could hardly find an empty spot at the Contention City Base Ball Field when the Millers played. These days, the grandstands could seat twice the town's current population.

The team had struggled, as well. Once, the Millers had an outstanding First Nine, a Second Nine that could beat most town teams easily, and even a Muffin Nine that played solid baseball. Now, they had ten players total, and last year they won their twenty-two games by an average of one-point-nine runs. Four of the games went extra innings. One game they won by forfeit. Such things never happened in the glorious days before the earthquake.

When we got back to the hotel, I had to remind the boys, even Cobb, why we came to Contention, what those thugs did to the widow's husband, and what we could take home after beating the Millers to a pulp.

The last day of April dawned bright and sunny with no wind. We had the Millers whipped before the umpire, an Army chaplain from Fort Huachuca, called us out to flip a coin. The Millers won the toss and elected to be the home team. Masterson snickered, "That's all they will win today."

Indeed, it looked that way. Masterson struck out the first six batsmen he faced. We scored two runs in the first inning, and three in the second. The crowd looked like they were attending a funeral.

But, by grab, how they cheered in the bottom of the third. That's when Caleb Cartwright singled up the middle. He didn't get past first base.

We led 9-to-2 in the sixth inning. I could hear sobs coming from the little waif whose baseball Silent Cobb had briefly held. Major Perry hit a little grounder to third, and Silent Cobb's throw had that brute out by a mile — till Hank Fuller dropped the ball.

"Safe," the chaplain said.

Masterson then hit the next batsman with a pitch.

"Take your base," the chaplain said, and I muttered an oath. Giving a batsman first base when he got hit had just become a rule in '87. The soldier boys at Fort Huachuca knew their baseball.

The next Miller got hit, too, loading the bases, and sending me out to calm down Kent Masterson. Hank Fuller waddled over, too.

"Relax," I told my pitcher, who wasn't throwing as hard as he could. "Your arm hurting?"

"No."

"Well, Hank muffed a play. It happens. Forget it."

"I didn't muff that ball, Skip," Hank told me.

Masterson said: "And I know what I'm doing."

I pulled off my cap to scratch my head.

"We can't beat this team," said Silent Cobb, who trotted over to take part in our discussion.

"We can beat the tar out of them," I said. "Which we've been doing."

The chaplain hollered: "Hurry up!"

Seeing my teammates' faces, I put my cap back on. "You can't throw this game, boys." I felt sick.

"You did," Silent Cobb said, and I wished he would turn mute again. "With the Brown Stockings in '82."

"And the Buffalo Bisons in '79," Hank

recollected.

My ears reddened, and Hank hadn't swung at a ball over his head this afternoon. "You . . ." I jabbed my swollen finger at Hank's fancy lace-up shirt that the Widow Kieberger had paid for. "You remember how these Millers played ball that time we saw them. Played like hooligans."

"You heard what the Tigers did here," Hank pointed out.

I countered: "I *heard*. But I *saw* how this team played. Like hooligans."

"Just like I played with the Maroons in '86," the professor said. He had walked over, too.

"And ain't that why you got sent to Yuma?" Masterson said. "Beat up the umpire with your bat-stick in Prescott for calling you out on strikes?"

"Fool deserved it," I said. "Ball was a foot outside, and low."

"Do you want to gossip?" the chaplain yelled. "Or play baseball?"

"They beat a man's head in," I told my Zephyrs. "With bat-sticks. That's why we're playing them."

"We're playing them," Hank said, too honest for his own cheating good, "for what the Widow Kieberger, that safecracker you knew in Yuma, and those gunmen she hired are doing right now."

"Because," I argued right back, "of what Major Perry, the town marshal, and the rest of these murdering ballists did to her husband."

"The Millers aren't the point," Masterson said. "I can't beat them . . . for their sakes." He nodded at the practically empty stands, filled with the last of Contention City's lovers of baseball, pretty much everybody in town.

I made the mistake and looked. I saw the little urchin, the old man, the lady with the parasol, and that redheaded strumpet who brought us all the beers we could drink at the cantina we had been frequenting. I saw their faces. The chaplain yelled again, but what struck me was the crowd. Any other city, any other team, and the spectators would be shouting louder than the umpire for us to quit chattering and play ball. They just sat, respectful, patient.

"Don't be suckers, boys. We're professional ballists, or once were. Let's get out of this inning," I said. Then I slapped the ball into Masterson's hand and trotted off to my spot.

Caleb Cartwright hit the next pitch over McSorely's head, and all four runners scored. It was 9-to-6.

35

It stayed that way till the bottom of the ninth inning. With two outs, and the Contention City faithful resigned to their fate, Major Perry singled. The professor let Contention's marshal/right fielder's hard roller go between his legs, and Major Perry wound up on third. Masterson then threw five consecutive balls to the Millers' second baseman, who ran down to first base.

"It takes seven balls before he can take first," I pointed out.

"That was in '86, Skip," the chaplain said. "And it was four strikes instead of three last year, and they counted walks as hits. Who knows what the rules will say next year."

Course, I figured if the umpire knew the rule about hitting a batsman, he'd know how many balls it took to send a player to first. It was worth a chance, though. Sometimes, you get umpires who don't know a thing. Not in Contention City, though. They used smart umpires.

I asked for time and went out to talk to Masterson. When my infielders started to join us, I yelled at them to stay put. I didn't need my boys teaming up against me.

"Walk Cartwright," I told Masterson.

He blinked and beamed. "You're with us!"

"No. I want to win."

Confusion masked Masterson's face. "You

want to put the tying run on second base, Skip?"

"Yeah, because Cartwright has power. Their shortstop hasn't hit all game. All we need is one out."

Masterson grinned. He thought he could outsmart me. "All they need is four runs. I could walk or hit Cartwright, the shortstop, and everyone else."

"You can try to walk that shortstop, and he'll still strike out. You can try to hit him, and he'll dive out the way like the coward he . . ." I stopped. It sort of struck me curious that a member of the Millers could be such a coward on the baseball field and a rapscallion who beat men to death in bedrooms. But Contention wasn't the same Contention anymore.

Something else, something better came to mind.

"You can walk in all the runs, let Contention win," I said. "And you'd not only be a sucker, you'd be a heel. You'd be cheating all these folks here. You'd crush them. Kill them. They want to see the Millers win. Not the Zephyrs blow it. You let those boys win with walks and hit batsmen, and you'll just disappoint everyone left in Contention City. So go ahead. Do it your way. Shame these poor folks. Walk Cartwright. If that shortstop after him can tie the score, good for him. That's baseball."

Knowing I had Masterson — because I'd just, for once, told the truth — I walked back, squatted, and waited for Masterson's pitch.

It came, faster than he had thrown since the first inning. Straight across at Cartwright's belt. Cartwright swung. I cussed. The ball once again sailed over McSorely's head, but this one went even farther. Three runners crossed the plate, and Cartwright was coming home. The crowd stood, screaming, cheering, but the chaplain started yelling something, too. I kept waiting for McSorely to get the ball, but he just stood at the fence. I didn't think Cartwright had knocked the ball over the fence. It couldn't be a home run. Could it?

"Double!" I heard the chaplain. "That is a ground-rule double. Back to second, Cartwright. You —" Our umpire pointed at Contention's second baseman. "You must return to third base."

Now, Contention's faithful in the stands booed the Army chaplain. Major Perry came from the bench to argue.

"Sir," the ump said, "there is a new rule this year that states if a fair ball bounces over the fence, and that the fence is not more than two hundred and ten feet from home plate, then the hitter must remain at second base."

That Army man knew everything. The crowd stopped booing. The old man said, "The umpire is correct."

"So," I said, just to make sure I understood everything. "The score is now 9-to-8, with two outs?"

"Yes."

I grinned. The chaplain let McSorely climb over the fence and fetch the ball, and I got ready as Millers shortstop Rotten Willie took his place inside the batter's lines.

Again, I trotted to talk to my hurler. "Hey," I argued. "They gave us a good game. Those folks won't be disappointed now. This'll be a game they'll remember, and there won't be shame in the Millers losing. So don't be a softhearted sucker."

Masterson nodded. I went back to catch him.

The crowd roared. Masterson threw a pitch at the waist that the chaplain called a strike. I had to dive to snag Masterson's next pitch — that's how bad it was — and heard the ump yell, "Strike two."

I dusted myself off. Rotten Willie had swung at that pitch? It made me laugh.

Masterson bounced the next one in front

of the plate, but Rotten Willie did not swing. The crowd fell silent. Sweat poured down Rotten Willie's cheeks. Masterson began his windup and fired another pitch. This was a ball, too, way off the plate. Rotten Willie swung. And somehow, his bat connected and sent the ball over Silent Cobb's outstretched hands as he leaped toward his left. But the professor was running on contact, backing up Cobb, and he snagged the ball in shallow left field on the second bounce.

Contention's man on third touched home, turned, and waited. That tied the score, but we could win in extra innings. All I had to do was catch the professor's throw and tag Cartwright out. Winning meant a lot to me. So did the money the Widow Kieberger was stealing.

I saw the baseball clearly. Then, out of the corner of my eye, I spied that little urchin, who still didn't have shoes, still looked dirty, and still clutched that ball he had let Silent Cobb hold the day we got in. I caught the professor's throw. The Contention player behind me yelled for Cartwright to slide. Cartwright slid. I saw the face of the woman with the parasol. I heard the kid yell, "Slide, Cartwright, slide!" I glimpsed the old man. And I imagined seeing a woman and some men leaving the alley that ran alongside

Contention City's bank. I had real good eyesight and imagination. You need that when you play catcher. I brought the ball down.

"Safe!" the chaplain yelled. "Safe! The runner is safe. The Millers win!"

The place turned into bedlam. Major Perry and his boys exploded off the bench and poured beer on Rotten Willie's head. The folks in the grandstands cheered and sang and sang and cheered. And they cried.

I couldn't argue. Cartwright's toe touched the plate just before I tagged his knee. I made certain of that.

As we shook hands with our valiant opponents, those folks in the stands cheered us, too. A few of us cried, as well.

Even when Major Perry collected our bats, balls, and equipment, my Zephyrs just smiled. A wager's a wager. We weren't welshers. I handed Major Perry a hundred-dollar note, too.

"What's this for?" the major asked.

"Well, some of the folks in this town look like they could use it."

Tears welled in his eyes. "Our citizens will need this money far more than we shall need your bat-sticks and baseballs, sir, for our future . . ."

That's when somebody shouted about something going on at the bank.

So, there we sat, waiting for the train to take us up to Benson, sipping hot beer and trying to keep the dirt sifting down from the roof from turning our drinks to mud. Caleb Cartwright came inside, nodded at us, downed a tequila at the bar, and said that the robbers had made off with twenty-three-thousand dollars.

"That'll finish Contention City," the barkeep said.

"I've already found a job in Globe," Cartwright said. "Baseball team's not that good, but it's baseball." When Cartwright pulled out a coin, the barkeep said, "No, it's on me. Loved watching you play these past few years. Maybe I'll get a job in Globe, too."

As he walked outside, Cartwright told us we played a fine game, said he thought he was out for sure when he had started his slide.

Twenty-three-thousand dollars. The professor ciphered in his head. "Ninety-two-hundred dollars for us. That takes the sting out of losing."

"When do we meet the Widow Kieberger?" Hank asked. He spoke too loud 'cause the barmaid was bringing us another round.

"Joyce got married?" Her face beamed.

"Joyce?" I said.

"Joyce Kieberger. Is that who you was talkin' 'bout? I used to work with her. She got married?" The rest of what she heard saddened her. "And her new husband up and died?"

I needed that bourbon. "The Widow . . . Joyce . . . Missus Kieberger. She wasn't married . . . while she was . . . working . . . here?"

Hank drank his beer and Skyrocket McSorely's, too. Both looked as sick as I must've.

The barmaid lowered her voice. "Goodness. Girls in our line don't get married. Not in the towns where we ply our trade." She started to leave, turned, and said, "If you see Joyce, tell her Dixie says congratulations — and more congratulations if her late husband was real rich."

When she stood back at the bar, I muttered something that the professor told me was anatomically impossible.

The urchin stuck his head in what once was a doorway to the saloon. "Train's coming in," he said. The whistle affirmed his statement.

"You think that widow will pay us?" McSorely asked.

I gave him the look I give Hank when he swings at pitches a mile over his head.

"You think," the professor asked, "that she might somehow let word out that we were in on this heist?"

"A few telegraphs," Hank said, "and they'll figure it out themselves."

We made a beeline for the depot, passing the Contention City Base Ball Field. Hank, McSorely, Masterson, and I took a detour, but we got on the train all right, and soon were steaming as far away as we could from Major Perry's ballists, especially Contention's right fielder.

As we tried to relax in the smoking car, Masterson sighed. "The thing is, we could have beaten those boys. Had them beaten."

I shook my head disgustedly. Masterson had been among the first to go soft.

"Won't get another chance now," Hank lamented. "Contention City's done for. That team will always be remembered as going undefeated in seven seasons and one game."

Cobb leaned toward me. "And you owe us our dough. You said we'd be paid win or lose." That silent third baseman never shut up.

Hank pointed this out: "The deal was

we'd get paid when the Widow Kieberger paid Skip."

"When we get to Tucson . . ." I began, the idea coming over me and making me feel as good as that urchin and those other Contention City folks must have felt after watching their team win that game. "Why don't we try to play Tucson's town team?"

"With what?" the professor said. "Thanks to your bet, we lost our bat-sticks, balls, and all our equipment to the Millers."

Hank chuckled. So did I.

"No," I said. "The marshal and major led that posse off as soon as they heard about the bank being looted. Most of the Millers rode out with him."

Hank added: "Left their equipment and ours, too, at the field. We picked it up. All of it. Put it in the baggage car."

"Major Perry won't be using those bat-sticks to club anyone to death ever again," Kent Masterson said.

"Like that ever happened," Skyrocket McSorely said. "I'd like to use my bat-stick on that widow's noggin."

"Now, now," I said. "You don't want to wind up in Yuma. And I'm serious. Let's play Tucson's team when we get there."

"Hey," Masterson said. "Maybe Benson has a team, too."

"Most towns do," Silent Cobb said. "We could also play Tombstone."

I pointed out: "After we beat Tucson, we should leave the territory. Unless you want to play prison baseball."

"I bet," Hank said, "we could play the Fat Fellows in Silver City."

McSorely said: "And there are plenty of town teams in Colorado."

Cobb and the professor didn't look so angry now. Cobb even admitted, "We do have a good team."

"We might even best the Millers' record," McSorely said.

Masterson grinned. "The American Zephyrs. For real, this time."

"No," I said. "We use that handle, the major and marshal would undoubtedly find us, and even if those boys didn't beat anarchists to death with bat-sticks, they surely would stove in our heads."

We thought.

Long before the train pulled into Benson, we had our name.

The American Suckers had a nice ring to it.

Johnny D. Boggs is a seven-time Spur Award winner. The Little League baseball coach, umpire, and former sportswriter lives in Santa Fe, New Mexico, with his wife and son. His website is JohnnyDBoggs.com.

■ ■ ■ ■

EDDIE AND THE
STRANGER
BY VONN MCKEE

■ ■ ■ ■

Sheriff "Fat Jack" Jennings didn't even look up from his newspaper when two cracks of gunfire echoed from up the street. The man seldom heaved himself out of his chair unless things got truly ugly. It was said there'd been seventy-two murders in Pioche, Nevada, before the first death by natural causes occurred, and already the cemetery was the fastest growing part of town.

Pioche was young and cocky, swarming with glinty-eyed speculators who laid claim to swaths of Treasure Hill outside town, hoping for a piece of the silver mining action. For every investor, there were hundreds of threadbare laborers, risking their lives in the creaky shafts underneath the mountain for a dollar or two a day. Common thieves, claim jumpers, and general troublemakers rounded out the town's population.

Hearing three more gunshots, Fat Jack

51

huffed and slapped the paper on the desk. He shoved his chair back. "Spence, I s'pose we'd better go check on things. Sounds close. Lynch's Saloon, maybe."

Deputy Spencer Melton had just finished passing out plates of cabbage and beans to the inmates. The Pioche jail hadn't been empty since the day it was built. "Well, if there's any left standing, I don't know where we'll put 'em," he said, hanging up the oversized key ring.

"Just shoot 'em. That's my creed."

Indeed, Fat Jack had lead-poisoned plenty of men since he took office. And he had taken bribes from plenty others who could buy their way out of his jail. He was called "Fat Jack" for the bulk of his wallet and not necessarily his middle-aged paunch.

"You'd think these hell-raisers would eventually all shoot each other dead," said Spence, grabbing his hat. "Wouldn't be nobody left to bury 'em, I guess."

"Wouldn't that be nice?" said Fat Jack, slamming the door behind them.

The sheriff guessed right. Two men carried a blood-soaked body, boots first, through the doors of Lynch's Saloon and crossed the crowded street to the undertaker's office. A man, surrounded by a ragtag group of miners, sat on the edge of the boardwalk with his head in his hands.

"Who's the shooter?" Fat Jack asked, to nobody in particular.

"Him," said John Lynch from the doorway, pointing to the hunched figure on the boardwalk. The saloon owner looked disgusted, maybe even a little pale. "The two of 'em got in a tussle over something. Couldn't hear what about. They'd had a few . . . well, too many, I reckon. This one turned mad out of his head. Grabbed somebody's pistol and shot the fellow twice in the face. Then . . ." Lynch wiped his brow and blew out a deep breath. "Then he stood over the man, who was done dead, for sure. Shot him a few more times square in the chest. Out of control, he was. Just kept shooting. Biggest damn mess I ever saw. And I've seen some." Lynch motioned over his shoulder. "How the hell I'll get that floor cleaned up, I don't know. Then there's the bullet holes."

Fat Jack and Spence stood at each side of the crazed killer, who was no more than a small heap.

"What's your name?" Fat Jack grabbed the man's shoulder and straightened him up so he could see his face. He was a miner, slightly built — probably a Basque — wearing a shabby flat-crowned hat. His face, coat, and overalls were embedded with dark reddish mine dust. His eyes were squeezed shut and he didn't answer.

"Maybe he don't speak English," said Spence, turning to the other miners. "Who is this fella? Somebody speak up."

The laborers looked sorrowful, until one said, "That's Eddie. He would not . . . it is not like him to do this kind of thing."

"I did *not* . . ." The quavering, pitiful protest came from Eddie. "I did not . . . I did not," he continued weakly. His small grimy face was streaked with tears.

"Well, Shorty, a saloon full of men say you did." Fat Jack grabbed Eddie's arm and dragged him to a standing position. The miner couldn't have stood more than five feet tall. "Keep your gun on him, Spence. He looks like a tough one."

Fat Jack grinned, revealing a gap between his front teeth. The sheriff somehow managed to maintain a frown, even when smiling.

Edarto Luken — or Eddie — was by far the quietest prisoner in the Pioche jail, except for when he had nightmares. The first night, he woke up the whole place with his thrashing and babbling.

It would be a pretty cut and dried conviction, Fat Jack thought, although it would be over a week before the next court date. The sheriff was always a little peeved when he had to follow legal procedures. If the little miner had put up a fight, there would have been grounds for putting a bullet in him and ending the matter.

"What came over you, Eddie, that you went and killed a man?" asked Fat Jack, locking up a cell after the release of a sobered-up drunk. Eddie had a cell of his own at Deputy Spence's request. He didn't think the little man would last long with any one of the current cellmates.

Eddie sat on his narrow bunk. He'd washed up — his face, at least — and Fat Jack guessed him to be about twenty. "Sheriff, I did not commit this terrible act."

"Yeah, you keep saying that. If you didn't, then you wanna tell me who did? You were the only one standing over that fella with a gun in your hand."

Eddie rose and walked to the cell door. He wrapped his fingers around the bars and looked imploringly at the sheriff. "Sheriff, I will be needing — what do you call? One who argues the law." Fat Jack cocked an eyebrow.

"A lawyer? You wanna get a lawyer? You think you got a prayer of getting off with murder?"

"You must believe me. I was not the one responsible! It was . . . someone else."

"And just who might that be?" The sheriff was interested to see where this was going. Eddie swallowed hard.

"It is hard to explain. Sheriff, I am not a man who would do this. You may ask anyone at the mines."

The sheriff recalled hearing the miners outside the saloon saying more or less the same thing. Surely, Eddie did not believe he was innocent! He let the man keep talking.

"I do not myself touch strong drink. I do not believe in harming another. I am a religious man, Sheriff Jennings."

Fat Jack was getting impatient with the little man. "Five shots, you liar. At close range. That man's face and chest were shot to a pulp when you got through with him."

Eddie buried his face in his dirty sleeve, choking back sobs. After a minute, he looked Sheriff Fat Jack Jennings straight in the eye. "I am not the one who fired the shots. It was . . . it was the stranger."

Fat Jack had heard a lot of wild tales. A man behind bars would say about anything to save his hide. This was a new one. "The stranger? Didn't hear anybody mention a stranger."

56

Eddie gripped the bars again and wedged his face between them. "The stranger is a terrible man. He has done terrible things. Things I would never do. I swear this to you," said Eddie, placing a hand over his heart, in oath.

"Okay, let's say I buy your story so far. Where do you reckon this stranger is now?"

A look of misery washed over Eddie's face. He slowly moved his hand from the left side of his chest to the right.

"He is here," he said.

The sky outside the sheriff's window was gray with the approaching dawn. Water for coffee heated in a pot on the woodstove.

"Gawdamighty, Sheriff. Can't you do something about this little Turk, or whatever he is? It's hard enough to sleep on a board without some fool jabbering in his sleep." Hobie Smith was a frequent guest at the Pioche jail due to his love of a good brawl. He gingerly rubbed a swollen eye with his big paw.

Fat Jack was good and tired of Eddie's nightmares and the complaints from the other prisoners. He grabbed a fire poker and stalked to the back, then slammed the poker a couple of times against the bars of Eddie's cell. "Wake up! Enough of that caterwauling!"

Eddie jumped up from his bunk and looked around wildly. Like a storm cloud swallowing the sun, his face turned angry and his eyes sparked hate. He rushed to the cell door and poked his skinny arms through the bars, reaching to grab Fat Jack by the throat. His small hands were locked into rigid claws. "Get over here, you coward! I'll squeeze your fat neck to mush."

Fat Jack took a step back, the iron poker hanging forgotten in his hand. "Eddie?"

Eddie strained to get a grip on the sheriff. His hair stuck up in messy spikes, framing his frightful countenance. Profanities in at least two languages spewed from his mouth. Apart from Eddie's tirade, the jail was dead silent. Fat Jack's brow furrowed as he considered his next move. Eddie continued to claw the air between them. The sheriff propped the poker against the wall behind him. He lowered his head and charged toward the cell door, with his big fist drawn back. He connected neatly with the bottom half of Eddie's face, but not before the miner grabbed his shirt. The jail echoed with the sounds of ripping fabric, the smack of the punch, and Eddie's body sprawling heavily onto the bunk behind him. He lay motionless, eyes closed.

Fat Jack picked up the poker and walked back to his office. He sank into his chair, waiting for his heart to slow down. On the stove, the coffee water boiled vigorously. Spence came in the door, ready for breakfast duty. He froze when he saw Fat Jack, shirt ripped, staring at the pot clattering on the stovetop.

"You all right, Chief?"

Doctor William Kent sat beside Sheriff Jennings at the Capitol Saloon bar. He was not a frequent patron at the Capitol, or any saloon, but Fat Jack invited him there to ask his opinion on something.

"It's the damnedest thing I ever witnessed." Fat Jack wiped the beer foam from his mustache and clunked the empty glass onto the counter.

"For two days now, this Eddie fella has been switching from a meek little lamb to a bull madder than hell. I want him out of my jail. When he's quieted down, he swears his other half should be charged with the murder. Have you heard of such? Says *the stranger* makes him commit acts against his will . . . that ain't part of his genuine nature." Fat Jack shook his head, rubbed his temples, and ordered another drink.

Doctor Kent's brown eyes were alive with interest. "Now isn't that something?"

"He got worse day before yesterday. He was in the middle of a nightmare, twisting around and hollering. I just meant to wake him up by banging on the door, but he jumped up ready to choke me. Maybe tear me to pieces. It's like having two different men in the cell at different times. He's Eddie for a few hours, then — poof! — that *stranger* comes outa nowhere. They's something wrong with that boy, that's for damn sure. You got any idea what it might be?"

"That is truly puzzling," said Doctor Kent. "It does remind me . . . . well, have you ever heard of Doctor Benedict Morel, Sheriff?"

"Nope. Was he an Englishman, like you?"

"French, actually. I read some of his papers while I was studying medicine. Morel observed patients in asylums who exhibited similar behaviors."

"Well, maybe Eddie was one of 'em."

"It's doubtful. His findings were from studies conducted over twenty years ago."

"Hmm. Before Eddie was born. And what did this Morel fella make of it?"

The doctor pressed a finger to his temple, conjuring a memory. "Blast it, what was that term? Morel had observed declining mental capacity in older patients but this was a phenomenon he saw in younger ones. Dem . . . ah! *Démence précoce!* That's it!"

"Oh, well, I could have told you that." Fat Jack laughed at his own joke. He was losing interest in the discussion and waved at someone across the room.

"At any rate, it means *precocious dementia.* Not terribly specific but at least he understood that it was a unique disease of the mind. Sheriff, would it be all right if I observed Mister . . . what did you say his name is?"

"Luken. Edarto Luken. Known as Eddie . . . or the stranger. Depending on the time of day, I reckon."

Doctor Kent shook the sheriff's hand. "I'll drop by in the morning. Thank you for tonight's invitation."

As the doctor left the saloon, Fat Jack realized the man hadn't touched his beer. "Well, no use in it going to waste." He slid the glass over and raised it to his lips.

At Doctor Kent's request, the sheriff again awakened the fitfully sleeping Eddie. However, he only called out his name rather than using the poker to arouse him. He wasn't sure his heart was up to another confrontation, even if he knew it might be coming.

Eddie tumbled out of the bunk, irritated, but at least not bent on murder.

Fat Jack whispered to Doctor Kent, "This here is the stranger we're talking to. I can tell by his eyes."

After fifteen minutes of interrogation, Eddie said, "I've had enough of your questions, limey." So far, he'd given mostly rude responses.

"One more, if you'll allow me. Your mother and father . . . did they have any . . . peculiarities? Unusual moods?"

The stranger that was Eddie looked suddenly stricken. Fat Jack thought the man was about to break down and cry.

"Mother . . ." he mumbled. "My mother." His lower lip trembled and, sure enough, tears welled up. Before Fat Jack and Doctor Kent's eyes, his demeanor changed. His hands slid down the bars and he seemed to melt into a frail child crouched on the floor. When he looked up, he wore the same expression as when he'd been arrested — sorrowful, crushed.

"I am so terribly sorry, Sheriff. And you . . . are you a doctor? You look like one."

Hiram Newkirk stopped outside the sheriff's office to adjust his collar and flatten his hair on top for the tenth time. His wiry strawberry hair was a constant bother. Suits never hung well on his gangly frame and, no matter how he fiddled, his tie and Adam's apple were always at odds. At least, no one judged his fashion sense harshly here in the west. If anyone looked askance, it was solely because he was wearing a suit. He collected his thoughts and opened the door.

"Sheriff Jennings? I'm the lawyer you sent for. Well, not the one you sent for precisely but . . . Mister Hodge is away in California. I'm Hiram Newkirk."

Fat Jack sized up the tall, awkward young man. "Obliged," he said, shaking hands. "You, uh, new in town?"

"I am, sir. Not so new. I've been here for three months. From Indiana."

"Might've seen you at the courthouse then. Well, three months. You're a regular old-timer, by mining town standards anyhow. You're taking some heat off of Hodge, are you? There's lawsuits flying around this town like locusts."

"I am aware of that. I've handled a dozen claim disputes already. Mister Hodge has kept me busy. But you wanted to speak to me about representing someone in a murder case?"

"Yes, murder. It should be simple, what with having several witnesses. But, well, it's taken a peculiar turn. Ah! Doc Kent just rode up. Maybe he'd better explain it."

"So, you're really going to court today and arguing that Eddie can't be held responsible for the actions of another part of who he is? This is making my head hurt." Fat Jack plucked the key ring off the hook and turned to Hiram Newkirk and Doctor Kent, who both looked like excited puppies.

"Yes, Sheriff. It sounds preposterous but if you think of it logically, it makes perfect sense," said the doctor. "Mister Luken has a distinct and separate entity within himself who seems to surface when he is under strain. I have interviewed both of these 'persons,' if you will, and found them to have remarkably opposite values and character traits."

"All right, Doc. Save it for court. And you think you can pull this off, Newkirk?"

The lawyer nodded. "I'm looking forward to making the case. Why, there's never been such an argument presented in court. We could very well set a precedent. In fact, we shall do so simply by bringing it before a judge, whether we win or lose."

"Well, winning or losing when you're the same person doesn't sound like good odds to me. What are they gonna do? Hang half of him?" Fat Jack puffed out his chest, sure that he'd made a valid point.

Newkirk frowned. "No, Sheriff, that's not my strategy. I hope to convince the judge to absolve Mister Luken from the crime and commit him to a doctor's care. This, per the M'Naghten Rule of 1843, which states *'at the time of the committing of the act, the party accused was laboring under such a defect of reason, from disease of the mind, as not to know the nature and quality of the act he was doing; or if he did know it, that he did not know he was doing what was wrong.'* "

Fat Jack rolled his eyes. "You lawyers. Spence! Go get Eddie and take him to the courthouse. The three of us will be there in a few minutes."

Spence fetched Eddie and fastened a manacle onto the prisoner's narrow wrists, which were crossed behind his back. The heavy iron bands were made for much bigger men, and Eddie straightened as the weight of them pulled down on his arms. The deputy herded Eddie out of the sheriff's office and through the door. The miner looked exhausted. He had intentionally kept himself awake to avoid slipping into the stranger's terrifying grasp.

Spence didn't hold out much hope for the prisoner's chances in court. The judge was

65

an irritable man, and generally ruled on the harsher side of the book. Spence checked the manacle lock and gave Eddie a gentle pat on the shoulder.

"We're just walking to the courthouse and going in the front door, Eddie. Looky here what a beautiful day we got." He usually transported prisoners through the court-house's back entrance but the door and frame were being painted. Somehow the job required two boys, each with a bucket and brush. It was nearly eight thirty, and the morning ore train whistle drifted down the street, three short blasts as it backed up to receive a dozen cars of raw ore. After chug-ging twenty miles to Bullionville, it would return to Pioche at the end of the day.

Eddie trudged ahead, shoulders drooped. They passed a fence with a scraggly rose-bush entwined in its pickets. Eddie stopped and bent over to sniff one of the forlorn blossoms, then smiled. Spence cleared his throat. "Let's move on."

A crowd had gathered in front of the courthouse, waiting for admittance. News of Eddie's trial had attracted a lot of local interest. Spence motioned for the onlookers to step back and let them pass.

Later, the deputy would say the movement was like that of a rabbit bursting from under a bush. With one quick shrug, Eddie pulled one of his hands free from the large manacle, and broke into a sudden, blurred flight — skirting the crowd of people and bolting across the street. He vanished between two buildings and Spence took off in pursuit just as the ore train blasted twice and its wheels began moving forward. Fat Jack's voice boomed from behind. "He's headed for the train! Catch him, Spence! Shoot him!"

The deputy caught glimpses of Eddie as he darted low and fast from one block to the next. He angled toward the edge of town, like he meant to intercept the train as it gained momentum and left Pioche. When Spence ran past the livery at the end of the street, he saw Eddie in the clear. He had shaken loose of the other iron cuff and slung the manacle aside. The engine was picking up speed, its pistons chugging faster and faster. Soon, it would be in the open and Eddie would be up-track to meet it with time to spare.

"Eddie!" Spence, still running, yelled over the sound of the approaching train. He was sure the miner couldn't hear him but he didn't want to shoot him in the back without a warning. Eddie reached the edge of the railroad bed and turned around. He looked directly at Spence, who was only fifty feet away, holding a Colt at arm's length. They stared at each other for several seconds as the engine rounded the building, steam billowing from its stack. The deputy had a clear shot and they both knew it.

Spence aimed high on the torso and thumbed the hammer. Another second passed, and another. Fat Jack would be catching up soon. Eddie didn't move even a finger — just kept staring. Spence began lowering the revolver, inch by inch, and uncocked the gun. Standing ten feet from the tracks, Eddie held up a hand in solemn thanks.

The space between Eddie and the train narrowed. Spence still held the Colt straight down at his side, waiting for the miner to crouch and jump onto a passing ore car when the time came. Instead, Eddie scrambled up onto the tracks. He laid himself down and stretched his body along the top of the rail farthest away, face up, arms and legs spread wide. The engineer sounded the steam whistle frantically.

"No! Eddie, no!" Spence shouted, and sprinted toward the tracks, knowing he couldn't reach Eddie in time. The ore train's brakes screamed against the rails, but too late to make any difference. A wall of hot air and dust pushed Spence back as the train thundered past.

Doctor Kent joined Fat Jack at a corner table in the Capitol Saloon. It was mid-afternoon and the place was quiet. "Well, Sheriff. So ends the remarkable story of Edarto Luken."

"Yep. Didn't end the way anybody figured. Crazy son of a gun. Knew I shoulda shot him first off. Might've spared him some misery."

Both men stared at the table, coming to grips with the aftermath of Eddie's last act. They would not soon forget the horrendous image. The ore train had accomplished what Eddie intended — rendering him, more or less, in half. For the first and final time, he had separated himself from the stranger.

"I hope he finds peace in the afterworld," said Doctor Kent. "Poor chap deserves it."

Fat Jack nodded. "I reckon he does at that. Say . . . I bought you a beer. You gonna drink it this time?"

The doctor smiled sadly. "Yes, I believe I shall. To Eddie . . ."

Fat Jack clinked his beer against the doctor's. "To Eddie."

Vonn McKee, Louisiana-born and descended from "horse traders and southern belles," has worked as everything from country singer to riverboat waitress to construction project manager. Now based in Nashville, she turns her experiences and love of history into stories of the West.

■ ■ ■ ■

THE DESERTER
BY LOREN D.
ESTLEMAN

■ ■ ■ ■

The hot Texas wind struck his face when he heaved open the door on its rollers, actually a relief after the oven hell of the freight car. Wind and streaming movement took his clothing in their teeth and shook it, the bandanna around his neck snapping viciously. He threw out his rucksack, then his saddle, and while they were still bouncing, braced himself with both hands, bent his knees, sucked in a gust of lung-searing air, and jumped.

He tucked himself tight, struck hard on his shoulder, and rolled, seeming to take on speed as he went, until he thought he'd go on rolling, flaying himself for a mile against stones, sand, and cactus until he plunged into the San Antonio River and drowned. When at last he fetched up in a ditch, he remained still, waiting for his breath to overtake him. He moved each of his limbs in turn, checking for broken bones. Reassured, he lay looking up at bright-metal sky. Given the choice, he'd have waited for the train to slow down some more before leaping, but he had not deserted his father's ranch during the calving season, hopped a homely freight in motion, and roasted and starved all the way from Del Rio to be beaten by railroad bulls and turned over to a road gang so close to his destination.

At last he stumbled upright, took inventory of his rips and bruises, and hobbled back to reclaim his worldly goods. He found his hat and saddle, then the rucksack twenty yards west. Both were sound, the sack's contents unspilled. Hoisting the saddle onto his shoulder and carrying the sack, he hiked toward the Cradle of Texas Liberty, regaining his footing with each step.

He was coming late to the ball, he knew. The first volunteers had arrived by horse, train, and shank's mare weeks before, greeted by the brass band of the San Antonio Volunteer Fire Brigade playing a rousing version of a tune popular in the minstrel shows back east:

When you hear dem bells go ding-a-ling,
All join 'round, and sweetly you must
    sing,
And when the verse am through, the

chorus all joins in,
There'll be a hot time in the old town
    tonight.

No trumpets, drums, or cymbals greeted him at the station platform, where stood the train he'd left, hot and oily and panting like a winded buffalo bull. A gang of teamsters lugged kegs of powder, crates containing rifles, uniforms, and boots, cases of tinned goods, and sack after sack of grain from the freight cars.

A lounger in a straw boater and seersucker jacket stood aslant against a porch post, picking his teeth. Hicks asked him for directions. The lounger took out the splinter of wood, studied the masticated end, and pointed it at a wooden plank nailed to the station wall, painted with uneven letters. The sign read, THIS WAY TO CAMP OF ROOSEVELT'S ROUGH RIDERS. The newcomer touched the salt- and sweat-stained brim of his hat and followed the arrow painted at the bottom of the sign.

As he walked, shifting his burdens from arm to arm and back to relieve his muscles, other signs wrought as if by the same inexpert hand hung below more formal placards directing him toward Riverside Park, on the banks of a swift waterway winding through the biggest city he'd ever visited.

Another sign of recent manufacture, mounted on tall posts and straddling a lane worn by the tread of many feet, told him he'd arrived at Camp Wood. A tent large enough to shelter a circus sideshow stood at the far end of the lane.

Here, Spencer Hicks lowered his saddle and rucksack to the ground and took hold of one of the posts supporting the sign, as if to test its solidity and assure himself he hadn't dreamt the whole odyssey.

"Well, I'm here," he said. "Now which way's Cuba?"

"Delighted to meet you, son." A burly young man in a buff uniform that fit him too well to have been issued by a quartermaster seized Hicks's hand and wrung it till he thought blood would spit out of his pores. The man seemed to have more than his fair share of teeth behind thick mustaches. Gold-rimmed spectacles straddled his nose. He struck the Texan as a popinjay, but before he could form a solid opinion, the officer — for he wore the epaulets of a lieutenant colonel — turned to the man at his side, who looked younger even than he. "Leonard, this is the young man I told you about. His father ran my ranch in Dakota.

He was awarded the Distinguished Service Cross in sixty-three and *his* father fought with distinction in the Battle of New Orleans. His *grand* father served with Washington at Monmouth. We can expect fine things from this lad."

"Perhaps. Heredity isn't everything, Theodore. Isaac Newton's father was an illiterate tradesman."

Hicks said nothing; the wise course, in view of the fact he had no idea who Isaac Newton was. He stood at more or less attention, facing a desk in the sideshow tent that seemed even bigger than it had appeared from outside because it contained no other furniture except a homely crate on the floor. They were all standing.

Theodore, the man in glasses, adjusted them, registering slight annoyance at the other's remark, though he said nothing; it seemed Leonard, the younger of the two, was his superior. Nothing about this war resembled the stories Hicks's father and grandfather had told him. "Young man, tell me in as few words as possible what you have to offer this regiment."

"Marksmanship."

The other officer spoke. "Perhaps a few words more."

"Name the thing and the distance and I'll

shoot it."

"With what?" Theodore looked at the rucksack and saddle at Hicks's feet. "You've brought no rifle."

"I had to leave my daddy's Winchester behind. We got a coyote problem."

Theodore grinned. It didn't seem possible for so many teeth to fit in one man's mouth. "Fortunately, we have more rifles than coyotes." He bent to the crate on the floor.

The firing range was a level area that still bore signs of having been used for racing horses, and probably would be again when the regiment shipped out and the park returned to being a fairgrounds. Bales of straw stood some hundred yards' distant, spaced out at ten-foot intervals, with paper targets fixed to them. The carbine he'd been handed, called a Krag-Jorgensen, was heavier than the repeater he was used to and required reloading after every shot. He swung it up to his shoulder, then down to his waist, then up again, accustoming himself to the heft and balance. The bolt-action loading mechanism was simple; from his pocket he drew four finger-length cartridges he'd been given, slammed one into the breech, and planted each of the other three between the fingers of his left hand. With the two officers standing behind him, he took quick aim on the first bale to the left, fired, ejected the spent shell, replaced it with a fresh cartridge, aimed and fired at the next bale to the right, and repeated his actions rapidly, hesitating only to sight in, spending the rest of his ammunition on the next two bales in line. He lowered the smoking weapon.

Theodore stepped forward, squinting through his glasses. "Leonard?"

The other officer remained where he was. "Four bull's-eyes in ten seconds." His voice displayed no more excitement than if he were tallying cows.

"Bully!" Theodore seized Hicks's free hand and pumped it. "We have our sharp-shooter."

"Thank you, Mr. — uh, Theodore."

The grin vanished. "Lieutenant Colonel Roosevelt, soldier," he said. "Sir, when brevity's more convenient."

"Yes, sir!"

"The same goes for you, Lieutenant Colonel," said the other officer. Looking at Hicks: "Colonel Wood, private. Sir at all times. If this war is to be won, it must be waged with dispatch."

Military life required sacrifice. He was forced to trade the stock saddle he'd carried all the way from Del Rio for a McClellan supplied by the War Department, a nutpincher from the look of it, with its oval-shaped hole plumb in the center, and for a cowboy born to the stirrups, all that marching on foot was pure-dee humiliating and dumb to boot, because they always ended up where they'd started. But he liked most of the men he bunked with in his barracks tent — the tenderheels especially, who held him a hero for his horsemanship — and even the Yankee saddle turned out to be as comfortable as a parlor chair when you adjusted the stirrups low so that you rode damn near standing up. Even the leather-tough recruits whose wilderness experience had inspired the creation of this cavalry admired his performance on the firing range. The Rough Riders had cured him of homesickness by becoming his second family. At the end of his first week of training — sore, sunburnt, and tuckered from hair to heels, Spencer Hicks lay on his bunk with his hands behind his head, humming "There'll be a Hot Time in the Old Town Tonight" until he slept.

The second train ride of his life was a damn sight more pleasant than the first. He got to sit on a cushioned seat, and to sleep with both eyes closed without having to watch out for the bulls. Even so, the griping of his fellow troops was a constant annoyance. Invasive coal-smoke from the stack didn't discriminate between stock cars and passenger cars; the air sweltered worse as they rattled closer to end-of-track in Tampa, Florida; and a two-day trip for most trains ran double the length for all the stops they had to make to unload, feed, and water the horses. The frontier veterans were as bad as all the rest, and even the welcome interruption of patriotic townsmen and -women who came aboard at major stops to ply the heroes with homegrown treats were met with poor grace by the owners of the more blackened faces.

And in Houston, New Orleans, Mobile, Tallahassee, and dozens of whistle-stops along the southern route, what seemed to be the same band of brass, strings, and percussion stood on platforms playing that same minstrel tune.

"I'll give 'em a hot time up the ass next time," grumbled a man late of the Arizona Rangers.

Hicks did his best to make up for such rude behavior. He feasted on hot apple and mincemeat pies, fresh tomatoes, steaming hunks of bread, and ripe pears, washed them down with milk, and touched his hat to achingly pretty girls in hoop skirts and wide-brimmed straw hats. They blushed for the lantern-jawed boy without a whisker to his name and curtseyed, leaving him with a memory of décolletage that he reckoned would see him through many a sultry Cuban night.

Fortunately for his heroic status with the public, no civilians were on hand to hear his opinion of the seagoing life. He shared an armed troop transport, an ugly black ironclad christened the *Yucatan,* with men, horses, and lice, sleeping in a hold as dark as a root cellar but a hell of a lot more close. It stank of manure, urine, oil, sweat, and tobacco spit, and though the ship was bigger than four barns, the ocean was bigger, pitching it up and down and from side to side, sometimes all at once, until the stench of puke overwhelmed all the others.

"Is it always like this?" he asked a crewman, who smoked a corncob pipe while Hicks unfolded himself from the topside railing, wiping bile from his lips.

"Just till the sea gets rough."

They dropped anchor at last in Santiago Bay and rowed to shore in boats. The march to Santiago was torturous. Swarms of mosquitoes seemed to swim in the sopping heat, gorging themselves on human blood. The jungle foliage, penetrable only on foot, was suffocating, closing in tighter and tighter until the troops could proceed only in single file. When it opened, they gazed at what appeared at first to be a line of boulders at the top of a steep ridge; stone breastworks built to conceal rifle pits. Hicks barely had time to digest this information when something that was not a mosquito whined past the column of men and whacked into a palm trunk. By the time the report came, every man was on his face.

Smitty, the man sprawled closest to him, swore. "The sarge wasn't kidding about them Mausers. You're dead before you hear the shot."

Hicks didn't reply. He was shaking so bad he was sure anything he said would come out gibberish.

The men under attack returned fire; all, it seemed, except Hicks. He let his carbine slide to the ground and buried his face in the dirt. Compared to the dreadful buzz of the Spaniards' high-powered slugs and the crack of the enemy reports, the thudding of the Krags struck him as primitive, and woefully inadequate.

What good were bullets against stone forts? The Mauser fire came down the face

of the slope like a hail of comets. He felt
Smitty jump; they were huddled that close.
He lifted his head and saw a boy with his
mouth open as if he'd been picked on in
class by his teacher: It formed an *O,* with a
smaller *O* in the center of his forehead.
Then the face was gone, down in the dirt to
stay.

Someone grabbed his shoulder. He
shouted, sure he'd been hit. Colonel Wood
was there, his face inches from his. He
hadn't heard him crawling his direction. The
calm unflappable commander of San Antonio was gone. He looked enraged.

"Look alive, Hicks! That sharpshooter to
the far left is worse than the whole damn
Spanish regiment put together. He's cutting
us to ribbons."

He knew he was supposed to say "Yes,
sir." His jaw fell open and wobbled there as
if it was broken. Nothing came out.

Wood's hand mangled his shoulder. "Get
hold of yourself! Show these bastards some
of what you showed us in San Antonio!"

The man was giving him some kind of
order; the tone was unmistakable, but the
words meant nothing.

"Hicks!" He shook him. The man's fingers
seemed to meet in the flesh of his shoulder.

Hicks tried to swallow, but it was as if a

rock were lodged in his throat. Somehow, he got his fingers around the grip of his Krag and dragged it up to his shoulder, the motion shaking himself loose of the officer's grasp.

"Colonel! Colonel!" A high-pitched voice: Roosevelt's. The colonel twisted his head that way, looked again at Hicks, and gave him a push as if he were throwing the man away. He reversed directions and crawled toward the source of the shout.

The sharpshooter on the ridge showed himself whenever he took aim. He wore a ridiculous tall hat with a plume; in another mood, Hicks would be tempted to pluck it off his head. He managed to swallow this time, nearly choking, swept a sleeve across his eyes, which stung with sweat and tears, and lined up his sights on the smear of face beneath the tall hat; but his eyes blurred and his hands shook.

And still the bullets came, singing like gleeful witches in a terrifying bedtime story. He heard the noise when they struck flesh, heard men grunt and gasp as if from simple surprise. He thought of the unbelieving expression on Smitty's face, and in his blindness, was sure the man on the ridge was drawing a bead on him. He let go of his weapon and buried his face again in the earth, sobbing.

But the relentless fire from the Rough Riders broke the Spaniards' lines. They retreated behind the ridge and their rocky trenches fell into American hands. Hicks, encouraged by the silence from the other side, retrieved his Krag and struck a vigilant pose with the stock against his shoulder, offering the promise of cover to those cavalrymen bold enough to lead the charge on the run. (Troops trained to horse, but attacking on foot: No, nothing about this war confirmed the anecdotes he'd heard.) He waited until the first wave had taken the ridge before rising and trotting along at the rear of the column.

Luck was with him yet. Roosevelt's summons to Wood had spared Hicks the humiliation of being seen to wither before the enemy. As far as the colonel knew, he'd traded shots with the sharpshooter above, and perhaps had even killed him. The wisest course was not to boast; even, if asked, to profess ignorance of the results of his efforts and be thought modest.

And await the moment when no one was watching and his path to survival was clear.

With the sun setting, the force pitched tents on a patch of level ground beyond the ridge, and with sentries posted, ate their rations and set coffee pots boiling on flat rocks provided by dismantled breastworks. Those who had not lost friends in the skirmish amused themselves recounting the details, playing jew's-harps and mouth organs, burning the soporific mosquitoes with their cigarette ends, and swapping plugs of chewing tobacco.

Taps sounded. Hicks unrolled his bed and crawled into it. Men were still winding down. Their voices rode like dogwood blossoms on the night air.

"Hear about Isbell?" he heard someone ask.

"Nope. Who's he?" someone else said.

"Half-breed injun cowboy with Fish's Company L. Shot him a spick and afore he could duck got hit seven times."

"Dead?"

"Not yet. But if he pulls through, his wardancing days are sure enough over."

"I heard Fish bought it."

"Straight through the heart, they say."

"That's the ticket."

"Amen, brother."

Others shared Hicks's tent. He stuffed his blanket in his mouth and blubbered silently into the coarse wool.

When he was wept out, he lay still as

death, listening for quiet. The last of the voices had ceased, wood crackled and hissed; the embers dying, the snoring began. Yet he waited, forcing himself to count to a thousand, then slid from under his covers, testing the earth for loose pebbles with the sole of a boot before trusting his weight to it. Standing, he lifted his carbine. His kit could stay behind, but if he were seen without his weapon, his intention would be clear. If challenged, he could say that he was going to the latrine and if the direction was wrong, that he'd gotten turned around in the dark of Cuba at night. Holding his breath, he ducked out through the flap.

"Hicks, isn't it?"

He almost cried out. A bulky figure blocked the stars in a human-shaped patch just yards from the tent. What light there was made perfect circles of the man's spectacles.

"Yes, sir!" He saluted.

"Belay that, Trooper." Roosevelt's recently departed position as Assistant Secretary of the Navy had adulterated his army vocabulary. "I don't want to have to remind you in broad daylight not to salute me. One of your Spanish counterparts would take it as a license to shoot an officer."

"Yes, sir."

"Colonel Wood told me of your performance today."

His heart thudded. He thought it would
burst through his chest.

"We were all shaken at the start. Quite
natural in one's first engagement with the
enemy. He says you gathered yourself together despite that. Were you as successful
at shooting Spaniards as straw bales?"

"I — I'm unsure, Colonel. It was all a fog."

A tropical bird made a sound like hysteri-
cal laughter. All else was silence. Then: "It
was indeed. Nevertheless, every man did his
duty. What brings you outside?"

"Um, I have to make water."

"Be alert as you do so. I'm told the Spanish sharpshooters like nothing better than
to station themselves within range of our
latrines." Something brighter than the lenses
of his spectacles flashed in the starshine:
Roosevelt's famous grin. "Carry on,
Trooper."

He stood there minutes after the officer
moved away, then ducked back inside. When
he did have to urinate, he would do so in
his bedding. If anyone noticed anything in
the morning, he'd pass it off as sweat.

Opportunity came, ironically enough, when
he was back in danger.

With the greatest reluctance, Roosevelt had been forced to agree with Wood that horses were useless in jungle fighting. They were left behind, and from then on the Rough Riders would walk.

They crossed the San Juan River — really not much more than a creek, ankle-deep as it was — and up yet another steep slope, with a blockhouse at the summit, pierced at regular intervals with firing ports. Directly the Americans moved within sight of it, the volley began. The terrible hornet-like Mauser bullets shrilled, clipping the leaves of trees and bringing pieces down all around like snow. Again, the foot cavalry dove to earth. On a sudden inspiration, Hicks wrapped his carbine in his arms and rolled, putting the decline to use, taking himself away from the fire and his regiment. It was like his leap from the train all over again outside San Antonio a hundred years ago; only now he was rolling away from glory rather than toward it. And like that leap it ended abruptly, in a jarring halt, this time against a fallen trunk.

Once again, his lungs were empty, but instead of waiting while they refilled, he ran, gasping for breath, in the general direction of Santiago Bay. He ran as if in a dream, or underwater, his legs churning in exasperating slow motion. He lifted his carbine to his chest with both hands, to throw it away and rid himself of the weight.

"*¡Yanqui! ¿Que pasa?*"

He stopped, swinging in the direction of the shout. A Cuban irregular, fighting with the Americans, stood eight feet from him, dressed all in white with a palm-leaf sombrero and bandoliers of ammunition crossing his torso in an *X*. The man was armed with one of the old-fashioned Springfield rifles the War Department had distributed to the rebels, but it was not raised. It dangled at the end of his hand.

Hicks's reflexes were accelerated by the madness of fear. He swung his Krag by the barrel, striking the Cuban across the left temple with the flat of the stock. It made a sickening crunch and the man pivoted at the knees and fell to his side. The American broke back into a run, leaping over the fallen man and stumbling down and down the hill in the opposite direction the Rough Riders were charging. Down and down.

He stood exhausted, starved, mosquito-bitten, and drenched with sweat on a rise overlooking Santiago Bay, where troop ships lay at anchor showing rust stains in bands above the waterlines, which had changed with the unloading of horses, mules, artillery, small arms, and ammunition. Some of them, he knew, would be steaming home with casualties, including the wounded and the slain, the latter sealed in boxes stacked in the holds. His perspiration chilled him like a jacket of ice at the thought that he could have been one of them, blinded or maimed or stretched out in eternal darkness.

A clapboard storage shack had a single window to illuminate the interior. He studied his reflection in a pane. Having shed himself of his carbine, tunic, and campaign hat, he could pass for a civilian — he hoped; one of the nonmilitary American residents recruited as laborers during the expedition. He hadn't enough of the tongue to communicate with the natives, so passed several Cubans at work or smoking cigars on a break and came finally to a beer-gutted Yankee with a red face and a tobacco bulge in one cheek, sitting atop a piling and drinking beer from a brown bottle.

"I got a message for the next ship heading to the states," he said. "I forgot the name." He put on an anxious expression.

The man belched and looked at him with red rheumy eyes. "You ain't the only idiot caught up in this mess. If them Spanish was half-smart, they'd of won this war in a week."

"Please, do you know which one's about to leave?"

"That'd be the *Savannah.*" The neck of the bottle pointed at a craft wallowing a few hundred yards offshore. "Sails with the tide."

"How can I get out there?"

The bottle pointed a different direction. "That dinghy's headed out with a fresh load from the troop hospital. You can catch her if you don't stumble."

He was prepared to repeat the messenger story, but a squad of medics was too busy helping the walking wounded and carrying others in stretchers down a flight of steps to notice when he slid into the sixteen-foot boat and took a seat in the stern.

This time the motion of the waves exhilarated the passenger. He was heading in the right direction, away from pestilential vermin, relentless heat, blistering marches, and the grave. He knew the awful *zeu zeu!* of Mauser rounds would be with him always, haunting his nightmares for the rest of his life, but it was life!

Cargo nets were employed to hoist the nonambulatory patients aboard the *Savannah.* In the commotion, he clambered up a rope ladder and followed others who were able to walk down a companionway to where an infirmary had been organized, with cots and hammocks provided. He sat on the deck in a corner out of the medics' way, next to a sallow-looking trooper.

"When's tide?" he asked the man.

"Hell, it's here. They wanted to get one last load in before weighing anchor." He paused after each word to gather breath for the next.

"Some war, ain't it?"

"I wouldn't know. I never got into it."

"Why not?"

"Yellow jack."

"What's that?"

The man grinned. His face looked like naked skull. "The flag. Didn't you see it?"

He had, now that he thought of it. He'd been too busy congratulating himself on his escape to take notice of the yellow pennant flapping from a staff topside.

"What's it mean?"

Just then the ship's whistle blasted three times. The captain was preparing to put to sea.

"Hell, kid. Can't you smell it?"

He did then; the sour stink filled the hold. Again, he'd been too concerned with himself to pay attention to details. What did the

Cubans call it? *El vomito negrito:* the black vomit, pooling on the deck and spreading the miasma of death. It was a quarantine ship, filled to the gunnels with dying men.

"It's the devil's own plague," said the other. "Faster than a Mauser round and it hits its mark every time. I won't make it home. None of us will, I guess. Not aboard this poison ship."

"Yellow fever! Jesus!" He started to scramble to his feet. Just then the deck lurched. They were in motion, pulling away from shore toward open sea.

"Just sit back and enjoy the ride," said the other. "Like it's your last."

His laugh was sharp and high-pitched, like a bullet fired from a high-powered rifle.

Loren D. Estleman has published more than eighty novels and two hundred short stories in the areas of mystery, western, and mainstream. He has received more than twenty national honors, including four lifetime achievement awards.

■ ■ ■ ■

A FULL MOON
AT NOON
BY MARCIA GAYE

■ ■ ■ ■

The tapping of the telegraph filled the dusty office. Linwood Whitaker bent over his desk as he interpreted the incoming dots and dashes. He read over what he'd written and made a second copy.

"Listen, Cog, this is what you do. Take this telegram over to Mister Festus at the bank. You know Mister Festus, don't you?"

"Sure I, I do, Mister Whitaker. Mister Festus needs, needs a haircut. I seen him put slicker in his hair but it don't help. Ain't, ain't that right, Duke? That Mister Festus has him a wild head, head of hair. Ain't that right, Duke?" Cog looked at the red rooster tucked under his arm as if he expected an answer.

Whitaker stood and patted Cog on the shoulder, even though he had to reach up to do it.

"That's fine, Cog. It's important this telegram gets to the bank, and right away."

The telegrapher slipped the paper into Cog's free hand. "Off with you, now, boy." He pulled at his beard and limped toward the sheriff's office at a good pace for an old man.

Duke pecked at Cog's hand, tasting the paper.

"Oh, no you don't, you old sneak." Cog set the rooster on the ground and stuffed the paper in his pocket. "Now, come on, we got to hurry. I got to earn my two, two bits this week."

The rooster cocked one eye. With a ruffle of feathers, he stretched out his legs and trotted off. Jumping onto the edge of a horse trough, Duke scooped a beak full of water and lifted his neck to let it pour down his gullet.

"Now you've done it, you old feather bag! Get on back, back here." Cog chased after the bird for a street and a half in the wrong direction before the cagey fowl was caught and secured in the arm of a stranger coming around the corner.

"This your rooster?"

"Yes, sir. He took, took a mind to skip out on me. It's a game he plays is all. Ain't that right, Duke? I'll take 'im, and, and thanks."

Duke received a firm scolding and a soothing stroking.

■ ■ ■

"Slow down, Whitaker. What's the telegram say?" Sheriff Boggs unfolded the paper.

"Read it for yourself, Sheriff. All I know is what's there."

"How long ago did this come in?"

"Just a minute ago, Sheriff. I rushed right over. I've already sent word to Festus. I should think he'd close the bank and post extra guards."

"Good. Go on and get back to your machine. Let me know if anything else comes in."

Sheriff Boggs leaned through the door and whistled to a group of young boys playing marbles in the dirt. "One of you boys run over to the church and ring the bell. Ring it loud, five times. Then count off exactly one minute and ring it five times again."

The boys jumped up and tangled themselves all in a knot trying to run and talk at the same time. "I'll do it, Sheriff!" and "Me, too!" and "Why, Sheriff?" spilled over the yard.

"Because I said so. You ring it just like I said and then hightail it home, you hear?"

A dust devil kicked up from all the feet scrambling away. Despite the gravity of the situation, Boggs smiled behind his mustache. These were good boys, not scalawags or budding train robbers. He planned to keep them that way.

The sound of the signal bell brought a half-dozen men gathered for instruction. Sheriff Boggs put it this way:

"Some men robbed the eastbound train out of Eureka this morning. It's suspected they're headed through here on horseback. A passenger overheard talk of a rendezvous down at Little Fork. We're going to protect our own. Keep an eye out. Any stranger bears watching."

"Ain't anybody getting past us, Sheriff," spoke Doyle Richards, to a nodding consensus. Boggs held up a hand. "Mind now, Richards, I don't want any gunplay or blood in the streets. It's business as usual until it isn't. You all just keep your eyes open and let me know if any stranger comes into town. That's it. Keep your families at home. We don't want women and children in harm's way."

Handing Duke over, the stranger in an open-crown Stetson glanced up and down the lean young man before him. "What's your name?" he asked.

"I'm Cog and this here is Duke. That's

what everybody calls me. On account of I lost a cog out of my head when I was, was a boy. A horse, horse kicked me and a cog rolled right out of my ear. That's what they say. I've looked and looked but I ain't never found one that, that I could fit back in. It don't hurt none, though. I carry a note that holds my real name. Part of it is Burns. Ain't that right, Duke? If you hold, hold onto Duke, I'll find it. I can't read it but, but maybe you can."

Cog proffered the rooster but the man in the hat shook his head.

"Doesn't matter, son. If your friends call you Cog, then that's good enough for me."

Cog wriggled his fingers into his pants pocket, coming up empty. A reach into his shirt brought out a folded note.

"Hey, here it is. Read it, mister. What's it say my, my name is?"

"This isn't . . . Well what's this now?" The man muttered as he scanned the paper.

"Oh, that's for, for Mister Festus at the bank! I got to give Mister Festus the news. I need to earn my, my keep. I need that paper back, mister."

"Well, Cog, how about I give you your pay now and I take care of Mister Festus? Here's two bits for your trouble. You and Duke can go on home."

"If I go on home early, Miss Pa-Patricia won't know what to do with me. She'll say I'm a puzzler, again. Reckon she might give Duke a bis-biscuit, though."

The stranger thought this over. "Well, then, maybe you'd rather work for me this afternoon. How about that?"

At the close of day, the mercantile was empty of customers as it had been all afternoon. Doyle Richards locked up and waited upstairs in his living quarters, his rifle trained out a front window open to view the riders coming in. There were two of them, silhouetted by the lowering sun. The riders paused at the edge of town, turned a circle, looking each way, then dismounted and walked between their horses, out of sight, down the alley behind the mercantile.

Cog, squatting on his haunches below the window at the far side of the store, cupped a hand over Duke's head to keep him still. He raised his other hand to his new friend, Reuben, who crouched in the tall grass beyond. Boot steps echoed across the width of the loading ramp.

"Hello? Shopkeep? Anybody here?" called the shorter of the men.

"Place is clear," said the other. "Best get

to it. Grab food tins and tobacco. I'll check the cash drawer." He kicked open the supply door and they hustled inside.

Reuben rushed forward, carrying a small torch. He broke the window and Cog handed him one of their homemade smudge pots. Reuben lit it and tossed it in. Cog gave him another to light and toss. The shop filled with black smoke.

The thin, shaky voice of Doyle Richards sounded from far across the room. "You boys give up or you'll never get away alive."

Two soot-blinded robbers stumbled around, kicking up a ruckus, knocking displays over, tin cans and two-penny nails rolling across the floor, jumbling everything into a confusion.

From outside, Reuben threated, "Throw down your guns and get on out here before I cut you down where you stand," though nobody could've targeted anything in that smoke.

He lit another pot and handed it to Cog. "Run around back and put this at the door. We'll flush them out through the front."

Reuben ran to the storefront and broke the glass so he could reach in and unbolt the door. Sunlight streamed a dim path from the boardwalk. Reuben drew his pistol and made a quick sidestep out of the light, slipping behind the thieves.

"Move on out, you rotten cowards," he said. "I've got you covered."

Coughing and sputtering, the robbers stumbled toward the light. Grabbing one of them by an arm and using the barrel of his pistol to prod the other one along, Reuben shoved both men into the street.

Looking around, he took notice of a rifle barrel in an upstairs window. He called out.

"Hey shopkeeper, I got these robbing thieves caught in the act. C'mon down!"

Rifle shots snapped at his legs, twisting him halfway around. More shots, some into the robbers, some into Reuben's back. He fell and the sun went down with him.

"Cog wouldn't hurt a fly, Sheriff. You know that."

Cog tapped the woman on her arm. "But I would, Miss, Miss Patricia. I can snatch a fly, fly right off Duke's back and squish it good. I, I done it lots of times."

"Hush, boy. That's not what I mean."

Sheriff Boggs glanced at the rooster tucked in the elbow curve of Cog Burns's arm. Round yellow eyes looked about as confused as the sheriff's own. Neither was quite sure what to make of it all. The smoke had cleared, three strangers lay dead, and here stood the town's errand boy covered in soot, holding that dad-blamed rooster. Except for the bodies in the street, it was almost comical.

"Now, Cog, what do you know about this mess?"

"Well, sir, Reuben said did I want, want some work, and I needed a biscuit for Duke so I said I sure, I sure do, and he gave me two bits. We made smudge pots and Reuben knowed how, how to light 'em. When the fellers came, we made 'em smoke like Hades itself."

"Reuben, you say? Who's he?"

"My friend there, layin' beside those robbers. Probably the best friend I ever had. Well, 'cept for Duke and Miss, Miss Patricia. Duke's my, my best friend. You're my good friend too, Sheriff, and old Mister Whitaker pays me, that maybe means he's my, my friend too. Reuben said, 'We got work to do,' and we set to puttin' wet hay and cow pies in cans. Reuben said, 'and nobody'll get hurt.' " Cog lowered his eyes to the heap of men blackened with soot, dust, and blood. "I reckon Reuben was wrong about that part."

Boggs sighed and turned to the owner of the mercantile. "What happened, Richards?"

"I was waiting upstairs, Sheriff, after what you told us about staying on the lookout, and sure enough two strangers came along and broke right into the store, calling me out. Then there was a racket, a hollerin' and scramblin'. I started down the stairs with my rifle but thick smoke stopped me. I thought they'd set my store afire. Seems I was trapped. But I wasn't about to let them get away, no, sir, and that's what I told them. No matter if I perished in the pursuit. As they tried to make a getaway, one of them waved a pistol, yelling up at me. I aimed from the window and squeezed off some shots." His eyes shifted up and down the street before he leaned close to Boggs's ear. "You suppose that's all of them, Sheriff?"

Sheriff Boggs looked over the damage and nodded. "I do suppose. Seems they're ready for the undertaker."

The one called Reuben moaned and moved his lips, trying to speak, but then passed out cold.

"Deputy McGrew, that one's alive. Get him to the doc. Make sure he's cuffed to the bed. Don't take any chances."

Satisfied of no further danger, Richards hooked his thumbs into his vest pockets and turned to the people milling along the street, raising his voice to be heard. "Taking down rovers ain't difficult for a man with my aim. Consider it my gift to the town. I'm turning them over to you with my compliments."

Cheers and whoops of admiration filled the dusky evening as the townsfolk patted Richards on his back and shook his hand.

Cog followed as Reuben's limp body was toted to the infirmary.

"Reuben. Reuben, can you hear me? Can't you wake up?"

Duke strutted around the bed and crowed a loud cock-a-doodle. Reuben's eyes fluttered.

"Cog? What happened? Did we get those robbers? Did we get them?"

"Yes, sir, Reuben. They's shot dead. Mister Richards shot, shot you too. Are you hurt bad, Reuben?"

"Shot me? Why'd he go and do that? I had them boys well in hand." He ran a dry tongue over his lips. "Got any water?"

After a sip from a tin ladle, he lay back, exhausted. "Now I remember. That storekeep. He wouldn't listen. I told him no need to fire. I told him *I got 'em, it's all over.*"

Deputy McGrew, standing guard, spoke up. "You saying you're not part of the gang?

Then who are you?"

Reuben gathered his breath. "Name's Monroe. With the bank sewed up tight. I staked out the mercantile. Made smoke to blind them. Flush 'em out. Turn them thieving louts over to the law."

"You didn't set out to kill them?"

"No. But I reckon I was a well-wisher to it."

A coughing fit took over for a minute before he could continue.

"Been trying to catch up to them since they robbed my mama awhile back. Knew they were in this vicinity but lost their trail. I came here to buy supplies, then heard they'd robbed again and were headed this way."

Reuben lay quiet. Cog shook him by the arm, and he drew a shallow breath.

"Those cowards don't have gumption to rob a guarded bank. They prey like coyotes on old women. Sneaking into a store to steal supplies, now that's a simple plan they thought they could handle."

"But why didn't you tell the sheriff? He'd have helped capture those vermin."

His eyes opened to stare at the ceiling. He made an effort to gather his strength. "Reckon I wanted to be a hero. Mama told me it'd be my downfall. She said, 'Don't try to be a hero, son, just live the life of a good man and that's praise enough.' Like the Good Book says, *pride goeth before a fall.* I have a prideful streak. I confess that I ain't proud of it."

Cog's brow furrowed. "That's a puzzler, Reuben. How can you be, be proud but not proud?"

"I'll be," exclaimed the deputy. "Cog, run get the sheriff. He needs to hear this."

Cog shook his head. "I got to, to stay here with Reuben."

"Aw, Cog, why you got to be contrary? Suit yourself. I'll be right back. Try to keep him alive until the doc comes." The deputy loped out the door.

Cog put a hand on his friend's arm. "Are you dyin', Reuben? I wish you, you wouldn't."

"Well, if I do, Cog, there's something I'd like to ask of you. Think you can do me a last favor? However they send me on my way to Glory, I want to make sure Richards gets the respect he deserves."

"Sure, sure I can. Favors is what friends do, ain't that right? What is, is it, Reuben?"

Duke flapped up onto the bed and swiveled his feathered neck, putting an eye on first one friend, then the other, as they worked it out.

Two open pine coffins leaned on end at the railing in front of the jail. Each held a stranger, now identified as notorious brothers Doug and Jack Thompson, their heads back and eyes closed. The flash of the photographer's light popped, recording the day for posterity. Then the lids were nailed on and the coffins loaded on a buckboard headed for twin newly dug holes in the cemetery.

Four men carried a third coffin made of solid oak by its wrought-iron handles. They slipped it into a waiting funeral wagon.

"Now that's a fine wagon. Look here, I can see myself in the shine." Sheriff Boggs whistled as he tipped his hat back for a closer look.

The long-bedded hearse glinted in the sun. Two brass lanterns hung on either side, round glass windows set high behind the driver's bench. A matched pair of black horses hitched in front stood straight still except to flick at a fly now and then. No one gave any notice to the town errand boy nuzzling the far horse, nor heeded when he and his rooster slipped out of sight.

Deputy McGrew nodded. "Well, all considered, a proper send-off back to his mama is the least we can do. I'd say we owe Reuben Monroe better than a pine box."

A snap of reins started the team. As the hearse turned onto the road out of town, the back panel fell open and there stood Cog Burns. Grinning at the crowd of townsfolk, he called out. "Mister Richards! Reuben said to give, give you this goodbye!" Cog turned his back, bent over, and dropped his drawers. Sunlight gleamed on his bare behind, shining like a full moon at noon.

Duke stretched his neck and crowed.

Marcia Gaye writes poetry, prose, memoir, and songs. She is published in many genres. Her work has won numerous awards, including first, second, and third prizes for the Showcase Award from Ozark Creative Writers. She has lived all across the United States, collecting characters and stories along the way, and currently resides in St. Charles, Missouri, with her husband, Jim.

■ ■ ■ ■

THE MEDICINE
ROBE
BY MICHAEL ZIMMER

■ ■ ■ ■

The government man shoved his chair back from the kitchen table and stood. Rémi knew he was still watching him. Staring down at the top of his head, waiting. The government man's uncertainty hung in the air between them like the ticking seconds following a heated argument, but there had been no harsh words. Only silence. That and Rémi's refusal to acknowledge the government man's demands, to even lift his eyes to meet the younger man's gaze.

Let him stew, Rémi thought. Let him wonder if he was getting through to this old mixed-blood hunter with the wrinkled skin and wild white hair and arthritic knuckles, a relic from a time so far in the past it probably didn't even seem real to a government man not yet out of his twenties.

After a minute, the government man cleared his throat. Rémi tried to remember what he'd called himself when he knocked at the cabin's front door shortly after noon, but the name eluded him. It didn't matter. His message had been clear enough.

"Do you understand?" the government man persisted, repeating a question he'd already asked half a dozen times. "You have to move."

"Yes," Rémi finally relented in a voice that rumbled from deep within his broad chest. "I understand."

"I hate that it has to be this way, but we've already started construction and we'll be moving in this direction by the end of the week."

Rémi nodded and continued to stare at the kitchen table's scarred top. But he understood. He had watched the bulldozers move in last week, less than a musket ball's flight from his front porch. Their grating roar and the stench of their exhaust, the shouts of men in hard hats and the whine of cables, were an incessant reminder of what approached. What awaited him no matter where he went.

Glancing around at the cabin's sparse furnishings, the government man said, "Do you have anyone to help you move?"

"I won't need anyone," Rémi replied. Then he stood abruptly, joints cracking, and came around the table, and the government man backed away.

"You should go now," Rémi said in a voice that belied his years, and the government man nodded and looked relieved.

"Yes, I'll do that."

Picking his briefcase up off the floor, the government man started for the door. Then his gaze fell on the tattered robe draped across the top of Rémi's old wooden trunk and he stopped.

"That's . . ."

He paused as if searching for a word that wouldn't offend.

"Large?" Rémi supplied.

"Yes, very," the government said and gave a short, half-embarrassed laugh. "You were a buffalo hunter, right? Back in the old days." He didn't wait for confirmation. "Is that a buffalo robe?"

"It is a grizzly bear's robe," Rémi replied.

"Grizzly bear? I thought your people — the *Métis,* is it? — hunted buffalo east of here, in the Dakotas."

"My people, the *Bois Brûlé* of the Red River Valley, hunted buffalo wherever the buffalo were. But the grizzly was killed on Lakota land."

At the government man's puzzled expression, Rémi added, "The Dakotas."

"I've never heard of grizzly bears in the

Dakotas."

"Now you have," Rémi replied, then pointed to the door. "You should go now. I have much to think about."

"Yes, of course. You know about the new town of Fort Peck that we're building north of the old town, don't you? If you have any questions, I have an office there. Anyone can tell —"

"I won't have any questions," Rémi interrupted, and the government man nodded and left without further comment.

Standing in the cabin's door, Rémi watched him drive away in a carriage without horses and thought that Old Joe, who had died many years earlier, had been wrong in his belief that the automobiles of the white men would someday vanish, and that the buffalo would come back to replace them. Rémi had known even then that the great herds would never return, but he'd held out hope that the automobiles would eventually disappear, allowing the return of the horse and the ox.

When the dust of the government man's auto began to settle, Rémi moved back into the cool dimness of the cabin's interior and shut the door, muting the sound of heavy equipment tearing at the soil downstream. The government that the government man said he represented was going to build a dam downstream from his cabin, and when it was completed, Rémi Caron's home would sink from sight beneath the surface of progress.

The first eviction notice had come six months ago. Others, too many to count, had followed. They had made fine starters for his morning fires. But now there would be no more notices. Now the government man insisted if Rémi did not leave of his own will, he would return with sheriffs and guns and move him out by force.

On creaky knees, Rémi shuffled back to his chair behind the kitchen table. He tested his coffee with a callused finger and was pleased to discover it was still warm. Wrapping his hands around the tin mug, Rémi sat back to contemplate his options. They seemed few and bleak, and he wondered how it had come to this, that he should allow a government man barely able to raise a scrawny mustache to dictate his future.

His eyes roamed the cabin and the memories it generated, and in time they settled on the grizzly bear robe, as they always did. A smile broke through the grim countenance of his face. The hide was old and had been with him since his youth. Its hair was slipping now, and the once supple leather had turned nearly as stiff as rawhide. Probably to someone like the government man, it looked shabby and worthless, but Rémi knew its value. So had Old Joe, before the cancer took him.

Closing his eyes, Rémi let the currents in his mind take him back to the day he'd killed the giant beast.

The day he had become a man in the eyes of the *Bois Brûlé*.

They had left their homes in the Red River Valley in June for the summer hunt, pushing southwest onto the wild, rolling plains north of the Missouri River in search of the buffalo they hunted not only for their own sustenance, but for the meat and robes they would take north into the Grandmother's land to sell to the forts of the Hudson's Bay Company. More than two hundred men, women, and children accompanying nearly a hundred infamous Red River carts — greaseless axles squalling like lost souls, the dust rising thick overhead, oxen bawling, children laughing, the men pushing ahead on their best buffalo runners. Everyone eager and excited in spite of the dangers they would inevitably face as they ventured into the homeland of the Sioux.

Among them had ridden Rémi Caron. All of fourteen summers that year and determined to prove himself worthy of the title of *Bois Brûlé* — the people of the burnt wood — named for the dark color of their flesh.

The buffalo had been elusive that year, and the hunters' rambling search had taken them farther west than they had ever before traveled. It was in their second month that they crossed the Missouri, coming in time to the *mauvaises terres,* the badlands, where the Little Missouri flowed north into the Mother River.

In his mind's eye, Rémi saw the barren, lifeless knobs and ridges of the badlands take shape before him, as real as the growl of tractors beyond his door. He saw the valleys, little more than deep, broad coulees twisting like something in pain, and bands of tinted earth that seemed too perfect in their mutations to be natural.

The caravan had stopped at the eastern edge of the badlands to make camp. The next day was Sunday, a time to rest and worship for those who wished, or to hunt and explore for those too young and wayward to slow down.

Rémi had been among the restless ones. Filled with a young man's boundless energy, he and some of the other youths of the camp had ridden into the badlands to explore its wonders. They rode their wild-maned ponies with the ease of natural horsemen, born to the flat, buffalo hair-padded saddles the *Métis* preferred, laughing and telling stories, and once in a while mentioning this girl or another who traveled under the watchful eyes of their mothers.

It was in a wide, flat-bottomed valley several miles into the badlands that they dismounted to smoke their pipes, while their ponies grazed on the rich grass carpeting its floor. Rémi had been riding a handsome gray stallion his father had purchased the winter before, but which was still too young and undisciplined to be a runner, a mount trained to take its rider into the midst of a stampeding herd of bison. To bring him close alongside the surging buffalo until the hunter could empty his smooth-bored musket into the animal's lungs.

It was the gray that scented the bear first. He threw his head up and whinnied loudly, his small ears perked toward the far end of the valley. Rémi immediately dropped the clay pipe he had been loading with tobacco and scrambled to his feet, pulling his musket up to check the priming. The others followed his example, and one of them, he couldn't remember who, had whispered,

"Sioux!" in an awed tone. But Rémi knew it wasn't their age-old enemies who lurked nearby. The gray wouldn't have reacted so violently to another human's presence.

All the ponies had their heads up now, nostrils extended as they sucked in the scent of approaching danger. Rémi quickly bridled the gray and swung into the saddle without using his stirrups. Mounted, they all felt a little braver. When the bear finally lumbered out of a distant draw, their relief was almost overpowering. It was a sow, they would discover later, the first grizzly any of them had ever seen. Too young to remember when grizzlies had roamed the Hair Hills bordering their Red River Valley homelands, they knew only what the elders of their villages told them of the giant bears' swiftness and ferocity.

Some of the older men, the better hunters — and for that reason the ones they admired most — sometimes used summer bearskins as sunshades over their carts. Such skins were considered a coup, a badge honoring their skill and courage.

"Let's kill him," Rémi had urged tautly.

The others instantly agreed. Only Louis Girard voiced caution.

"We can't rush it," he said.

"Why not?" Rémi demanded.

"You've heard the same stories I have. A grizzly can outrun a horse, and it can kill one as easily as a fox kills a rabbit."

"We're not rabbits," Joseph Demer taunted, and the others laughed and mocked Louis for his cowardice. Only Rémi remained silent, absorbing his friend's warning without comment. Of them all, he knew Louis best, and he knew Louis was not afraid of the bear. But he was smart, and that was why Rémi listened.

"How do we do it?" Etienne Bouchard asked.

"Carefully," was Louis's advice, and Rémi quickly seconded it.

By now their ponies were moving nervously under them, sensing the boys' fever but also growing more frightened as the bear ambled in their direction. At Rémi's command they spread out to begin their advance, five young men reaching for manhood. Four of them carried ancient smoothbores, the fifth only a bow with a dozen iron-tipped arrows. Their ponies balked when the boys tried to force them forward, but they had been horsemen even then, and kept the animals in check. The great bear came on in her lazy, rolling gait, her nose dipping into the tall grass every few feet. Rémi knew that, like buffalo, a bear's eyesight was poor at best, and with caution they managed to get within eighty yards of her before one of the horses whinnied and caught the bear's attention. Rising deliberately to her rear legs, front paws hanging down and toward the center of her massive body, the great bear sniffed the air suspiciously, then issued a warning grunt — a sharp *wagh* that caused two of the ponies to go berserk.

Rémi's gray wheeled and tried to bolt, but he sawed back on the reins and kicked the side of the stallion's neck with his moccasined foot until he forced the skittish mount around. The bear was still on her hind legs, still snuffling and squinting almost comically in their direction. Her massive frame tapped some of Rémi's enthusiasm. He had expected something smaller, closer in size to a black bear. Even in the shade of the sow's belly, he could see the long curve of her claws, the rippling muscles of her legs, and he knew what she was capable of. His father's voice came belatedly, a warning issued almost casually some weeks before they pulled out for the buffalo range.

"They are the offspring of the devil, boy. Meaner than a moose and faster than my best buffalo runner. If you see one, ride the other way."

Rémi knew he should, but something within him, some vague sense of invulnerability, refused to let him flee. The gray was nearly crazed with fear, tossing his head and fighting the bit, but Rémi resolutely held him back.

"Let's go, Rémi," Simon Quesnelle pleaded, and there was no longer any mockery in his voice. His eyes were wide, his mount near to bolting.

"No, I'll stay," Rémi replied stubbornly.

"Only a fool would stand against such a creature," Etienne Bouchard insisted.

Rémi remained unswayed. He tried to force the gray closer, but it seemed a hopeless task. For every step gained, the gray would take one sideways or half a dozen back before Rémi could get him stopped. It was the bear that started to close the gap between them, coming forward on her hind legs, nose wrinkling as she tested the air. At fifty yards she suddenly *waghed* again and slapped the air with a short, powerful swing of her forearm — a warning, Rémi knew, and his scalp crawled.

The gray threw its head up, almost smacking Rémi in his face, and backed off rapidly; it wheeled and danced and raised a cloud of dust in the grass until he and the bear were again separated by nearly eighty yards. It was then that Rémi discovered he was alone, that the others had either made a run for safety or been unable to control their mounts. He should have felt fear. Instead he felt, suddenly and inexplicably, wonderful. Like a warrior with every nerve ending drawn to the surface and set tingling. He and the gray and the giant bear, a dragon from his father's storybooks waiting to be slain, an enemy conquered. And he thought, too, of the young women in camp and how they would look at him when he returned with the bloodied robe. The valley was his arena, the bear his trial; lifting the musket, he sighted down its long barrel and squeezed off his shot.

The grizzly woofed and slapped at her belly as if stung. Rémi saw the puff of dust erupt from the lighter colored hair covering her stomach and knew his shot had been good, if not exactly true. He wedged the musket's butt between his foot and the stirrup and hitched his powder horn around, filling the antler-tip measure as he blew his moist breath down the barrel to extinguish any lingering sparks. He poured the powder down the barrel as the bear dropped to all fours, unmoving yet, her head held low in pain. The gray had skipped back another twenty paces or so and now stood trembling and taut. Rémi capped the musket's muzzle with a thin square of antelope leather and placed a thumb-sized lead ball over that. He quickly skated the musket's metal ramrod free of the thimbles holding it under the barrel and rammed the patched ball home. He filled the musket's huge pan with a finely ground powder from the flattened priming horn he carried in his shooting bag and closed the frizzen.

Then he waited. Waited until the grizzly finally lifted her head and started forward, abandoning her former swaying shuffle for a trot. The gray tossed its head and started to back away. He sensed the change in the sow's attitude. So did Rémi. The grizzly was coming toward them now with a deadly deliberateness.

At fifty yards Rémi again raised his musket, sighted as best he could from the saddle of the nearly frantic gray, and fired. The ashen cloud of powder smoke obstructed his view for several seconds. Then the breeze swept it clear and he saw the bear lunging to her feet, her right foreleg sheened with blood. With a terrible snarl, the grizzly began to lope toward them, and the gray took the bit in his teeth and fled while Rémi hauled back uselessly on the reins.

Behind them, the bear increased its pace as well, running effortlessly despite her wounds. Panic swelled in Rémi's breast, squeezing until he felt he couldn't breathe, and at last he gave the gray its head and let him run.

Within a quarter mile, the valley pinched down to a sandy draw, its steep walls U-shaped, the dirt soft and crumbling. It was the same draw they had followed coming in, and he saw the tracks the others had made leaving, the loose soil churned darker than the red-hued dirt around it. It was a twisting route, he recalled, its banks low enough in places to put a horse over the top if he wanted to. Rémi considered it, attempting to hide rather than try to outrun the wounded grizzly. But instinct screamed for him to run, and he did as it commanded.

In time the winding draw would lead to the plains, and the *Bois Brûlé* camp only a few hundred yards from its mouth, but the bear was gaining rapidly. Even wounded, it was obvious she was faster than the gray. Bent low above the gray's neck, Rémi imagined he could hear the angry, snuffling breath of the wounded animal. Often she was within sight when the draw straightened for brief periods. He tried to gauge her speed, to match it against the distance yet to be covered, and knew it was too far. They would never make it.

Rounding a bend, Rémi saw the south bank of the draw swoop low, the land sloping upward beyond, rising toward a series of broken, spiny knobs with passable ridges between, and he jerked savagely at the reins. The horse took the bank in a single, terrified leap, but its rear hooves snagged the lip, slipping in the loose dirt and sliding back. Rémi shouted and lashed the gray with the ends of his reins. The stallion's rear hooves churned in the loose soil. Then the grizzly appeared. Spotting the gray just yards ahead, it lunged forward. The gray squealed in terror and kicked clumsily over the top of the bank just as the bear pounced. Above the gray's shrill whinny, Rémi heard the wet, ripping sound of torn flesh. Glancing back as the gray stumbled away from the bear's blow, he saw a swath of shredded hide on the stallion's hip, the torn flesh raw and furrowed, running blood. The grizzly was only a few feet away but still at the bottom of the draw. She had one bloody paw upraised yet, and her lips were pulled back to reveal huge teeth, yellowed near the base, a fury of pain and rage in her small, piggish eyes. She wanted to kill, Rémi saw, and began to beat at the gray's croup with the barrel of his musket.

The sterile, bony knobs had seemed close when he first spotted them. Now they looked a hundred miles away. The gray lunged up the steep slope, hooves gouging at the loose soil. The grizzly had lost momentum in taking her swipe at the horse, giving up nearly a dozen yards, but she quickly scrambled over the bank to resume pursuit.

A saddleback opened before them, the knob on the right only head high to a mounted man, but the one on the left towered nearly thirty feet into the blue summer sky. Dropping over the far side, Rémi jerked the gray to the right, guiding him deeper into the labyrinth. There was a trail here. Or at least he thought it was a trail. He reined the gray onto it, pounding the horse's ribs with his heels. The maze grew close. Rémi could never see more than twenty or thirty feet ahead of him at any time. He couldn't see the grizzly either, but he knew it was still following them. He could hear her growling and coughing, and so could the gray.

Rémi wished he'd reloaded his musket after his second shot. He hadn't even thought of it at the time, and now, with the gray twisting and dodging, it was all he could do to stay in the saddle.

When they rounded the last bend and found themselves boxed in, he wanted to cry out in frustration and anger. He had looked forward to this hunt for so long, and now it had turned against him. Through his mind flashed the image of the cabin along the Red River where he had been born. And he remembered his mother and how he'd so foolishly rebuffed her affection only days before when she'd offered him a tidbit from the kettle; how he longed for it now, the quiet comfort and safety he'd always felt when she was near.

The walls rose slick and trackless around him, too steep for the gray to climb. Maybe too steep for him, too, without time to carve grips in the hard earth for his fingers and toes. And he knew there wouldn't be enough time for that. The grizzly's wet, slobbering snarls filled the tiny cul-de-sac, smothering him with its promise of destruction.

Rémi was unable to hold the gray back when the stallion wheeled and plunged back down the trail, which had apparently never been anything more than a track for runoff. Rémi let him go, pushing off with his hands and allowing the horse to run out from under him. He landed against the slope and tumbled down in a heap. Even before he stopped rolling, he heard the abrupt, terror-filled shriek of the gray, the fearsome roar of the grizzly. And above it, once more, the awful sounds of ripping flesh, the brittle snap of bones.

The gray was dead, Rémi was certain of that. The question was whether the bear would stay with the horse or come on. Did she know it was Rémi who had shot her? Or in her small, dim mind did she equate horse and rider as one?

Fingers trembling, Rémi pulled his powder horn around and unplugged it with his teeth. He poured a massive charge down the barrel, then dropped an unpatched lead ball down the muzzle and slammed it home with his ramrod. Tipping the frizzen forward, he sprinkled a hefty charge of priming powder into the pan. He checked the flint with his thumb, cutting it and drawing a thin line of blood, then pulled the hammer back to full cock and brought the stock up between his arm and ribs, bracing the butt against the steep pitch of the ridge.

He could hear the grizzly ripping at the gray's flesh just around the bend, venting its fury on the helpless beast. Then a silence so abrupt and deep it sent a chill down his spine. He closed his eyes for only a second, and when he opened them he saw her standing before him, no more than ten feet away.

Even on all fours she seemed as big as a buffalo. She was working her jaws and tongue against some pink meat lodged in her teeth, her mottled gums red with the gray's blood, the hair around her muzzle matted with it.

Rémi took a deep breath and slowly lifted the musket's barrel toward the bear. His finger curled around the trigger. Now that the moment had arrived, he felt strangely calm and in control, his fear dissipated. The huge grizzly took a tentative step forward, then another, and Rémi smiled coolly. She was watching him curiously, perhaps wondering why he didn't try to flee. Then her eyes met his and fogged in rage. With an earth-tilting roar she lunged forward, her dagger-like claws slicing, jaws yawning, slobbering. Rémi felt the tip of her claws touch his chest and slide across his belly like rolling embers as her mouth closed on the musket's iron muzzle just as he pulled the trigger.

The weapon's report was muffled in the bear's throat, but he could see the look of surprise that crossed her face as the back of her neck and head exploded. She reared back on her haunches, her closed jaws dribbling powder smoke. But she was still slapping, her claws whistling through the air above him. He could never recall exactly how long she pawed at him, but at the time it seemed to go on forever — five minutes, ten?

Probably not, he knew. Probably she hadn't cuffed the air more than a few spastic times before she keeled over dead.

Rémi shivered in the cool dimness of his cabin as he relived that day. He could still feel the tight skin of the old wound across his chest and stomach, and sometimes when the weather was especially cold or damp, there was a little pain, like a distant burning. The grizzly's claws hadn't gone very deep, but they'd left wide, wicked-looking scars from his left shoulder to a spot just above his belt, over his right hip, like furrows turned over by a plow.

"Big medicine," Old Joe had said when he heard the story.

And Rémi had agreed.

He was sitting on the cabin's porch when he heard the automobiles approaching through the cottonwoods bordering the Missouri River. He couldn't tell how many there were, but thought there was more than one. Maybe two or three.

He had been expecting them for several days, going out at dawn and waiting patiently until dusk. He had the grizzly's robe draped over his shoulders, taking comfort from its warmth, strength from what the tattered badge represented. Pulling it close, he struggled stiffly to his feet. He wanted to be standing when the government man arrived, not tottering like a stem of autumn grass until he got his knees locked, his balance steadied.

The first car into the clearing was driven by the government man. Close behind came a second vehicle, this one with the county's insignia on the door. Rémi recognized the driver through the windshield. Ed Clark had been around a long time and was a good man, although Rémi had no doubt that he would do what the law required of him.

Rémi didn't know the man riding in Clark's auto, but he'd seen him around, tall and lean with hard eyes and an immutable smirk — a bully always on the prowl for his next victim. Rémi had once watched him pistol-whip Tom Standing Bull for public intoxication and resisting arrest, although Tom had barely been able to stand when the deputy cornered him in an alley behind the Hi-Line Bar.

The government man drove straight up to

the cabin and parked with his car's nose pointed toward the front door. Clark stopped some distance away, where the dust from his wheels wouldn't drift forward onto the porch. The government man was first out of his car, gripping a sheaf of papers in one hand so tight he was crumbling the sides. His expression was one of parental exasperation crossed with anger. He started talking before he even got his door slammed shut.

"You were supposed to be gone by now, Caron. What the hell is the matter with you? I know you can speak English, you just don't seem capable of understanding it."

Rémi didn't reply. His gaze moved to Deputy Clark, climbing the gentle slope toward the porch. Clark was looking at the government man with disgust but didn't try to interrupt his tirade. The other deputy was close behind, his familiar smirk solidly in place. The government man turned to Clark and thrust his papers toward him.

"Here," he said. "He's been warned more times than I can count, and I'm fed up with it." Clark took the papers, and the government man turned back to Rémi. "These are eviction notices, Caron. You're being evicted . . . *today.* Do you know what that means?"

"Easy, Mr. James," Clark said. "We'll handle it from here."

Clark advanced several more strides, until he was standing at the foot of the porch steps. The other deputy stood beside him, his smirk turned up in a taunting grin.

"How are you, Mr. Caron?" Clark said.

"This is my home," Rémi replied. "I have nowhere else to go, and no desire to go wherever this man wants me to go."

"All I want is you outta here," the government man — James — snapped.

"You understand what's going to happen here, right?" Clark asked Rémi.

Nodding solemnly, Rémi replied, "You are a good man, Deputy Clark. I am sorry you are the one they sent."

"Now, don't do anything foolish," Clark replied, but it was already too late.

Rémi's shoulders heaved and the ancient grizzly's robe flew back against the cabin's wall. One corner hooked on the door's latch, but it didn't matter where it landed. Drawing an old Colt revolver from the waistband of his trousers, Rémi eared the hammer to full cock. His thumb screamed in protest, but his hand remained steady. He wanted to laugh at the look on the government man's face as he dived into the dirt in front of the porch. Clark was holding up a hand and telling him not to shoot, and Rémi nodded his approval. Clark understood, and would not pull his own weapon unless Rémi lowered the Colt's muzzle toward him.

But the other deputy, the one who, finally, was not smirking, didn't understand how these things worked. He didn't understand what Rémi was saying when he drew his Colt. He was already snatching his service revolver from a Western-style holster on his hip. Although Clark yelled at him not to fire, the deputy didn't listen.

Rémi saw the service revolver spit a thin cloud of pale blue smoke toward him. He heard the first bullet as it passed his shoulder, but he didn't hear the second one. He felt it, though. Like a carnival strong man's hand pressed flat against his chest, then pushing suddenly. The force of it took the wind from his lungs.

Rémi's shoulders hammered the cabin's door and his feet flew out from under him. He fell hard to a sitting position, and as he did the bear's robe came free of the door's latch and settled across his shoulders. In the yard, Clark was still yelling at the second deputy, whose face now registered fear, and the government man named James was still in the dirt with his arms pressed tight over his head.

Then the scene faded and Rémi looked to his right, where his name was being called with urgency.

"Rémi, come on."

"Etienne?"

The boy grinned. "Come on, we've been waiting."

Rémi looked past his boyhood friend to where Simon Quesnelle and Louis Girard and Joseph Demer waited with eager expressions. They were all mounted, and Simon was holding the gray's reins in his hands.

"Let's go, Rémi. There are buffalo over the horizon, a big herd, and we want to get there in time to join the hunt."

Laughing, Rémi rose to his feet and strode swiftly across the porch. He left the medicine robe where it lay, draped over the shoulders of someone he no longer knew. In the cabin's yard, he was aware of white men arguing, but their words no longer mattered. He accepted the reins Simon handed him and swung lithely into the buffalo-leather saddle atop the gray's back. Mounted, he shoved his feet into the wooden stirrups, then reached out to catch the old smoothbore musket Louis tossed him.

"This way," Etienne shouted, and Rémi

drove his moccasined heels into the gray's sides.

They rode fast, as true horsemen should, like the wind flowing through the cottonwoods toward the distant horizon where the buffalo still ran free.

Michael Zimmer is the author of seventeen novels, including *The Poacher's Daughter,* winner of the prestigious Wrangler Award from the National Cowboy and Western Heritage Museum. His novel, *City of Rocks,* was chosen by Booklist as a Top Ten Western for 2012. Zimmer resides in Utah with his wife, Vanessa, and their two dogs. His website is www.michaelzimmer .com.

■ ■ ■ ■

MARY, MARY,
QUITE CONTRARY
BY KATHLEEN MORRIS

■ ■ ■ ■

Kansas, 1876

If they came back tonight, I'd kill them both.

I brushed the hair off my face, dirt mingling with the blood from my cut lip, and stood up. The front door to the cabin hung open, but at least they hadn't burned the place. They hadn't killed me, either, and that was a mistake they'd come to regret. It had been dusk and I was cleaning up after dinner, the sun like a big sunny-side up egg, low enough it was sinking into the prairie.

Ray went to the barn to check on the horses when I heard the shots, then the laughter, which near froze me on the spot. I peered out the window and saw two men, both still on their horses, and then Ray, on the ground beside the open barn door, unmoving, a crimson flower blooming on his white shirt and spreading beneath him. I grabbed his Colt from the holster where it hung beside the door and crouched beside the stove.

"Little Missus, we come by for some dessert," said the first one, ducking his head as he came through the door, while his friend, a bit shorter, followed close behind. "We was thinking some pie?"

"Jesus, Seth, you kill me," said the short one. "Pie. Huh." He fingered his mustache and peered around. It was a small cabin and it wouldn't take them long to see me. I shot the big one but he'd turned at the last minute and the bullet winged him, rather than hitting his heart. He screamed like a gutted pig anyway.

Before I could get off another shot, the other man hit me in the face and the Colt clattered to the floor, with me right beside it. He moved quicker than I could've believed and picked up the Colt, pointing it at my head.

"Get your bitch ass outside."

I had little choice, and while Seth banged around inside, smashing things and presumably bandaging up his arm, his friend hit me enough to keep me down before he unbuckled his pants. By that time, I couldn't move much except my eyes, but that was enough to see Ray's eyes, only a few feet away, were open too but never going to shut again. I could feel the grit and little pebbles in the grass embedding themselves in my back as the man shoved into me again and again.

"Ruben, you ever going to get finished?"

The short man grunted and stood up, hauling up his pants. "Your turn." He kicked me hard in the side. "A little pay-back."

"My damn arm's hurtin' too bad to worry about that," Seth said. "Let's just get those horses and get out of here." He held up the tin box I'd hidden under the mattress. "What I got here and what's in there," he jerked his head towards the barn, "is worth more'n her."

Bastards. I watched as they stepped over Ray on their way into the barn. The two horses we'd saved so long for were inside, the mare and stallion that we'd bought to start our quarter-horse ranch. We'd brought them back from Dodge City two days ago. All I could figure is they must've seen us at the auction there and followed us back here, thinking we'd be easy pickings.

I crawled closer to Ray and took his hand, still warm. The men came out of the barn, leading the two horses they'd tied with rope halters, and turned towards their own mounts.

"What you want to do with her?" the one called Seth said.

The shorter one gave me a glance. "Shoot her, I guess. She wasn't much of a lay." He got on his horse.

Seth pulled out his pistol but a snarling blur of black fur barreled into him, jaws locking on his wrist and knocking the gun from his hand. The dogs and their constant companion, the wild colt I'd tamed, had been out on their evening ramble. Susie, always faster than the other two, had arrived first, but we all heard more barking and the thunder of hoofbeats approaching fast.

Seth was screaming again, Susie pulling him down, when Ruben shot her.

"Goddamnit, Seth," Ruben yelled, "get on your horse, more's comin'."

Seth kicked the dog, picked up his gun, and vaulted into the saddle, turning back to fire a final shot at me. The bullet tore through the grass inches from my head but I couldn't move. The last thing I remember was their hoofbeats as they galloped away, towing their bounty. It was full dark when I came to, the quiet broken only by the sound of whimpering, both mine and a dog's.

Dawn was breaking, pale streams of rose

and gold tearing through the curtain of night. Poe whined and scratched softly at the dirt I'd just tamped down over the grave. I patted his head and sat down, dropping the shovel. I'd chosen a spot on the hill behind the cabin, under the only big tree we had. I'd buried Ray and Susie in the same grave. I didn't think either of them would mind and he'd appreciate the company, sort of like those Egyptian kings that got put in a tomb with their pets and food for the journey into the afterlife. Some preacher might not like it, but then I didn't much care for their interpretations of what God might like anyway, and there was no time for that.

"Safe journey, my love."

I picked up the shovel. Poe and the colt, the three of us the only mourners, made our way down the hill. At the cabin, I stripped off my clothes and threw them in the fireplace, watching as the dying embers razed the pain and hurt from the cotton. I scrubbed head to toe, trying to do the same for myself. I put on an old pair of Ray's pants and one of his shirts, braiding my long hair into a single plait. Pulling on my boots and cinching up the pants with a leather belt to which I added Ray's Bowie knife, I headed to the barn.

Rather than building a bigger house yet, we'd made a magnificent barn, at least by Kansas standards. The idea was to breed the best quarter horses and riding stock in the state, and the two stolen horses were the beginning of that dream. Our four other horses were still inside, nickering softly as I came in. I opened the stall doors and sent them into the pasture, then filled their water troughs and tossed out enough alfalfa and hay for a few days and left the door open to the corral. The colt I'd ride myself. He was a tricky little devil, but with a sure step and a stamina that the others would never match, and we worked well together.

I threw extra feed to the chickens and the two pigs. They'd all get along fine until I got back. That I wouldn't get back was not a thought I was willing to entertain.

In the tack room, I opened the wooden box disguised to look like a bench on the back wall. Ray had thought of the barn like a fort, much more defensible than the cabin. Here we kept the Sharps rifle Ray had used as a buffalo hunter, wrapped in oilcloth, and I knew he'd cleaned it just a week before. The walnut stock gleamed near as bright as the barrel. It wasn't a practical weapon around the ranch, but like the barn, a last line of defense. Kansas had its share of outlaws, both white and Indian, and showing off a Sharps over the mantel was an invitation to trouble. A box of .50 calibers sat beside it and the .22 pistol I'd carried back in the day when I was a whore in Dodge City, just in case of an over-enthusiastic customer. Both weapons triggered memories we'd rather forget and storing them in the barn had helped with that. I've never been ashamed of my past, because that's how Ray and I met. I hadn't been in the game long, and he was just a kid, too, hunting buffalo. Neither of those professions were particularly palatable, but we'd both done what we had to. Both of us hard luck orphans, when we found each other, we found family we'd never had. We threw in together and never looked back.

I stuffed the .22 in my boot and the box of bullets into one of the saddlebags, filling the other one with hardtack, biscuits, water, and a flask of whiskey. I whistled for the colt who seemed happy to be saddled, at least for the moment. Poe danced about beside the colt, sure he was going as well, and he was right. Poe and Susie were orphan half-wolf cubs, near death when I found them. Ray had laughed and hugged me, saying, "Mary, you take in any stray you can find, just like you did with me."

Now, at close to 150 pounds, Poe was the gentlest, smartest, and most loyal dog I've ever known, just like his poor sister. I didn't bother to pack food for him, as there wasn't a rabbit born Poe couldn't have for dinner.

One look was all I allowed myself, the sun rising behind the little cabin, lighting the worn timbers, and glistening on the dew of the grass. I sought solace in the only way I could and I was going to find it.

They'd gone south, by their tracks, which even I could see and Poe had no trouble scenting. They were probably headed for Oklahoma, not back to Dodge, thirty miles east and full of people who knew those horses had just been sold to us. They'd had a long head start and it was likely I wouldn't find them today, even though I could travel faster. They were sloppy, the tracks ranging to and fro, as though the stolen horses knew they were being taken away from a safe haven and sought to turn homewards.

Even though it was only May, by noon the sun was burning through my hat and my hair was soaked with sweat. I stopped and chewed on some jerky underneath some cottonwoods and let the colt have a long drink from the creek. Poe wandered a bit, but when I got back in the saddle, he trotted up, ready to go. I loved that dog, and I'd loved Susie, too, like the children I didn't have. I couldn't allow myself to feel anguish over Ray or her, because I needed that hard ball of hatred that had centered in my chest to be my guiding star. Any other emotion would only slow me down or stop me from doing what I had to do. I thought of *Hamlet,* which Ray and I had just finished reading, Shakespeare being our only book, one I'd bought for a dollar from a peddler in Dodge. We'd had a Bible, but found Shakespeare to be a better guide to the human condition and truly the ways of the world and the things that could happen to people. "Revenge should know no bounds" was the line that kept repeating itself in my head, and a mantra that I now had set my course upon. Although it wasn't simple revenge I was after. It was justice I sought.

By sunset, still having seen no sign of Seth, Ruben, or my horses, I decided to stop for a while, even though the colt was showing little signs of fatigue and was sure-footed even in the dark. I'd sleep for a time and perhaps go on in the night, catching them when they least expected it.

When I woke, the sun was already up and both Poe and the colt, hobbled but anxious, were bent over me. I'd been exhausted, by

155

physical exertion and grief, both of which had taken their toll. I comforted them both, splashed water on my face, breakfasted on a hard biscuit and a swig of water, and we started on. So far, I hadn't seen another human soul, only the hawks and ravens and an occasional coyote. Hopefully that would change soon, but there were only two humans I wanted to see and I hoped no one else would get in my way, from stray Indians that could kill me to settlers that would slow me down.

The day passed without either of those events and I decided to stop early. I hobbled the colt and didn't bother to light a fire, falling asleep as soon as my head rested against the saddle I used as a pillow, Poe beside me, warm and snoring softly. This time when I woke, it was full dark and I saddled the colt and headed south, hoping to see some signs of a campfire in the darkness of the prairie night. This was my wish, as I didn't want to come upon them during the day, which would be much to my disadvantage.

An hour later, Poe barked softly and I peered across the rolling hills, the nearly full moon giving me good access further ahead. A half mile away, near a rising knoll of rock outcroppings, there was the glow of a campfire. We crept closer, slow silent going, the horse, the dog, and I, and stopped on the rock-strewn hill above.

The horses were hobbled, four of them, including the two I sought, off to the side, while my two adversaries sat in front of the fire, passing a whiskey bottle back and forth. While conventional niceties dictated a dawn attack, I didn't see any reason for niceties of any sort and no reason to get any closer. Besides, the firelight illuminated them just as well for my purposes. I took the Sharps from where I'd tied it to my saddle, set it atop a good-sized rock to use as a mount, and loaded a bullet. Ray had taught me well, hours of practice shooting the rifle just in case I'd ever have need to. He'd finally pronounced me proficient enough and now I hoped he'd been right.

Their voices carried in the still, clear night.

"We can sell these beauties for enough to set us up for months, Seth. I told you the minute I saw those two farmers walk away we were in clover, didn't I?"

"Yeah, you were right, as usual," Seth said. "But you ain't the one with an arm tore up by some monster dog and a bullet from that bitch, Ruben. I need more than a half share, since I'm the one took the hurt gettin' it."

Ruben took a drink from the bottle.

"Don't make no difference. Thing is, it was my idea. I just took you along for the ride. You hadn't shot the guy right off, we coulda killed them both in bed."

I sighted the Sharps on the middle of Seth's chest, took a deep breath, and pulled the trigger. He went down hard, the shot echoing off the rocks like a thunderclap. My shoulder felt like I'd been kicked by a horse but I reloaded and stared down at the campfire. Ruben had vanished, like a snake that crawls under a rock, and that was worrisome. Still, I hadn't expected he'd sit there and be the next target. The easy part was over.

They couldn't have known where the shot came from, but after a few minutes I got uneasy. There was no movement in the camp below but Ruben wasn't going to wait to get picked off. He could be anywhere and the back of my neck prickled. The urge to sneak down there, finish things, and get my horses was offset by plain sense. I'd have to wait until dawn and I couldn't do it exposed up here. I scrabbled backwards along with Poe. Taking the colt's reins, we made our way further down to the flat, taking cover in some rocks and brush. Poe would tell me if Ruben was nearby. Lord, I was tired. Killing's a weary business.

I surely was not expecting the shot when it came, buzzing just over my head. I flattened myself onto Poe's back, his deep growls resonating through both of us, and the colt had wisely skittered away. Pale light filtered through heavy clouds and I looked around frantically, not raising my head, but I couldn't see Ruben.

"Stay." I wasn't going to lose anyone else I loved. I took off my hat and Poe stared at me but didn't move. I crawled on my belly behind the biggest of the rocks to get some cover with a better vantage point, the Sharps clutched in my hand.

Another bullet cracked off the rock near my head. Where the hell was he? I ducked down and then I saw him, perched not far from where I'd been last night. It was way too close.

"Hey!" I yelled. "I just want my horses. Leave 'em and we'll call it a draw."

"Well, well. Little Missus." He laughed. "Seth always had bad aim. I don't." His next shot sailed over my head. I should've killed this one first. He was a little smarter.

"What'd you shoot poor old Seth with anyway, a buffalo gun? Half that boy was gone. I'd like to have that Sharps, Missus. Maybe we can make a trade. 'Cause, by the time you miss me once, before you can reload, I'll have you and your gun anyway."

"What kind of trade?"

"How about I let you leave, and you give me the rifle? The horses don't figure anymore, girl. You shot my partner, after all. I call it a good deal."

I waited for a minute before I answered, my voice trembly. "All right then, mister. Deal." I put the Sharps down in front of the rocks and retreated behind them. Poe remained motionless and I patted him on the head.

He came down the hill, a grin on his face, holding Ray's Colt at his hip. "Come on out, honey, and we can shake on it."

So I did. I shot him in the face with the .22 and watched as his blood leaked into the stony ground and until his heels stopped beating a rhythm to go with it. He wasn't smart enough.

I left them both where they lay. Neither of them warranted my efforts at a burial, decent or otherwise, and I doubted anyone would miss them. Things can happen to people out here. I shooed off their horses and took my two. We were home the next night, all five of us, all safe in our respective beds. I take care of what's mine.

Late summer, the prairie grass turned

golden and the sunsets were something special. I sat beside Ray's grave on the hill behind the cabin, Poe's head on my lap, watching my horses in the pasture below. The mare was pregnant, and I'd had two stud offers already for my stallion. Word got around. I lay down on the soft grass and put my hand on my stomach. The baby kicked for the first time and I smiled. Ray had always wanted a boy.

An aficionado of Western history, **Kathleen Morris** lives and writes in the desert Southwest. Her novel, *The Lily of the West,* the untold story of Mary Katherine Haroney, known as "Big Nose Kate," was published by Five Star. For more information, you can visit her website, www.kathleenmorrisauthor .com.

■ ■ ■ ■

DARLINGS OF
THE DUST
BY JOHN D. NESBITT

■ ■ ■ ■

The man named Dunbar came to the town of Westlock, Wyoming, on a snowy November day. I was loading groceries into the wagon to take back to the ranch, and I first saw him when he was about three-quarters of a mile away, on the road that led from the north and became the main street in town. As I went back and forth from the store to the wagon, the rider came closer and became more visible. He was riding a blue roan and leading a buckskin packhorse, both dusted in snow as he was. The horses' footfalls made but the faintest muffled sound on the carpeted ground, and with the snow swirling around them and the powder rising from their hooves, one had the illusion that the horses were not connected to the earth in the usual way but came roiling, with their master, out of the maw of the frozen North.

The rider drew up next to the wagon as I

hefted a fifty-pound sack of beans into the bed. The air was cold — about ten degrees, I thought — and the thin, dry snow gathered on his black hat, his dark mustache, his brown canvas surtout, and his dark brown chaps, as well as on his saddle and on the canvas packs on the buckskin horse. Reaching up with a gloved hand, he brushed the snow from his mustache.

"Good afternoon," he said.

"And the same to you."

His dark eyes took me in. "Can you tell me where the Paradise Valley Ranch is?"

"Yes, I can. It's about ten miles southwest of here."

He blew a puff of breath through his mustache. "Might be a bit late in the day for me to find it at that distance."

"Could be," I said, "but the foreman's right inside here. What do you need?"

"I heard they might have work."

"You'd have to ask him."

"Of course." He studied me. "I would almost guess that you work there, too."

"Good guess. I'm the cook. But maybe you figured that as well." I pointed with my thumb. "The foreman's name is George Clubb. He's the fellow with blond, wavy hair, warming his hands at the stove."

The newcomer smiled. "And your name,

if I might be so bold?"

"Cyrus Fleming," I said.

"J.R. Dunbar." He swung down from the saddle, passed the lead rope from one hand to another, and held out his hand to shake. "Thanks for telling me what you know. Some people aren't that helpful."

I suppressed a smile. "I didn't tell you much." At the beginning, at least, I had prided myself on not telling him any more than he asked.

He gave me a look that expressed confidence and humor together. "You told me more than you had to, and more than you said outright."

I wondered what I had told him without saying — that George Clubb didn't mind letting someone else do the work? That the Paradise Valley Ranch was not a good place to work? That the ranch did not keep hired hands for long, and that was why a stranger might find work in November? I imagined that all of those truths were inherent in what I did and did not say to Dunbar.

I said, "I'll be happy to tell you more, by saying even less."

"You're doing well," he said. He tied his horses and went into the store.

I found out soon enough that Dunbar was

not shy about asking questions, at least of me. As we were bringing in firewood the next day, he began with a statement.

"The big boss seems to keep to himself."

"The owner? I suppose he does. He leaves quite a bit to his foreman."

"His name is Wardell, isn't it?"

"Yes, it is. Prentice Wardell."

"How long has he been here?"

"Four or five years."

"Did he name this ranch?"

"Yes, he did. The ranch and the valley both, though the ranch had previous owners."

Dunbar cast a glance toward the ranch house. "And what about the two girls he has working for him?"

He caught me off guard for a moment. Common bunkhouse hands did not ask about the girls, and I did not volunteer comments. But I had seen them — two sisters who swept in silence. In summer it seemed as if they spent all of their days with a broom and a dustpan, sweeping the ranch house, the veranda, the steps, and the stone walkway. Now in the cold part of the year, they swept the dust of winter inside and the dust of snow outside.

"They're sisters," I said. "Lucy is about thirteen, and Ophelia is about fifteen."

"I could guess that much. Where do they come from?"

As I pictured the girls with their dusky complexions and straight, dull black hair, I wanted to say, as I had thought, that I imagined them as having materialized out of the dust. But I said, "According to the boss, he found them in New Mexico Territory. He picked them up off the street in Albuquerque, where they were abandoned, and he and his wife took them in."

"Adopted, or just used as inexpensive domestic help?"

"I don't know. I've never asked. All I know is what I've heard." After I pause, I added, "Are you interested in them?"

Dunbar put one last piece of firewood in the crook of his arm, smiled, and said, "All things human are of interest to me."

"Or, as the philosopher says, 'Nothing human is foreign to me.' "

"I think that might be the way I first heard it. But time, and the company of cattle, dulls the memory."

"I know what you mean," I said. "An hour from now, I won't remember we had this conversation."

George Clubb, Dunbar, and I were drinking coffee at midmorning. The two had done the morning chores of pitching hay to the horses and breaking ice on the troughs, and now they sat without saying much to each other. Rather than try to make conversation, I kept my own counsel as well.

A cold draft of air swept into the bunkhouse as the boss stepped inside. He closed the door behind him and paused, as if he needed to take stock of the room. He was wearing a fox-fur cap, a long coat made of coyote pelts, and a pair of padded leather gloves. He clapped his hands together, took off his gloves, and walked over to stand next to the foreman's chair.

"George, you need to bring in more hay. We're bound to get more snow at any time, and we can't afford to run out."

George nodded. "I was thinkin' the same thing."

The boss drew himself up to his full height. He was taller than average, and I had formed the impression that he liked to lean and loom over his men. Now he turned to Dunbar and said, "I'd just as soon you didn't talk to my working girls anymore."

Dunbar regarded him with a calm expression.

The boss waited a few seconds, and getting no answer, he said, "What business did you have talking to them, anyway?"

170

Dunbar's dark eyes held steady. "I had the impression I had seen those girls somewhere before."

The boss's eyes tightened for a second. "I'd be surprised if you did. At any rate, you can leave them alone." Turning back to the foreman, he said, "Bring in about three wagonloads. Go to the farthest haystack first."

George gave a look of displeasure but said, "Sure."

I knew that the summer crew had put up half a dozen haystacks at various places, each stack with a fence around it. The farthest one out was quite a ways from the ranch.

The boss continued. "I don't think you'll have time for more than one load per day, and you'll want to carry a lunch." He shifted in position to speak to me. "Cy, make them up something to carry with them."

I pushed my chair from the table. "I'll do that."

As I rose, I heard the boss say, "What did you say your name was?"

Dunbar said, "This bein' the first time I've spoken with you, I didn't say. Not to you, at least. But as I told Mr. Clubb, my name is Dunbar."

"Do you always give smart answers?"

"No."

"Well, do what George tells you." The boss nodded to his foreman, and putting on his gloves, he walked back out into the cold morning.

The boss came to the bunkhouse before sunrise the next day while the men were finishing breakfast. They had not gone out to do the chores yet, and they still had to unload the hay they had brought in at dusk, so I wondered why the boss appeared so early. In the cold part of the year, he did not venture out in the gray of morning.

Dressed again in his raiments of fox and coyote, he loomed over the table with the hanging lamp casting his face in shadow. He stood in a position that allowed him to face the foreman while he gave his shoulder to Dunbar.

"George," he said, "I've decided we'll put this first load up in the hay mow."

George stopped with his fork a couple of inches up from the plate. "We haven't done that before. Are you sure we even have the right equipment?"

"Of course we do. Everything came with the ranch. There's an old set of tongs out where the field tools are. Everything else is in the harness room."

"Do you know how to do it?"

"It'll take all four of us. Two teams of horses — one on the wagon, one on the hoist. We have one man with each team, one man on the load, and one man up in the loft."

"I'd think you'd want to have two men in the loft."

"I thought you'd never done this before."

"I haven't."

The boss took a calm breath as he pressed his gloved hands together, interlocking his fingers.

George spoke again. "Why do you want to go to all the bother, anyway?"

"I told you yesterday. I want to get in a good stock of hay."

"Three wagonloads will fit where we always put it, on the ground floor."

"For God's sake, man, do you have to argue with me at every turn? I say we're going to put the hay in the loft, and that's what we're going to do. So as soon as you get your grub in your bellies, get out there and feed the horses. Then get the tools together, and grease the track that the pulley runs on. By the time you're ready, the horses'll be fed, and we can get to work."

He turned and walked away, without having taken off his gloves. A draft of cold air rolled in as he closed the door behind him.

George had resumed eating. With fried potato in his mouth, he said, "Seems like a lot of trouble to me. Have either of you done it this way before?"

I said, "Back on the farm, when I was growing up. The winters were wetter there, so we tried to keep as much of the hay inside as we could."

"Build a good stack, and it sheds water." He turned to Dunbar. "How about you?"

"I have some familiarity with it. But people do things differently from one place to another. We'll see how Mr. Wardell does it."

As I walked out into the ranch yard after putting the kitchen in order, a cold wind was moving the dust around above the frozen surface of the earth. The sky was gray and cheerless, and not much sound carried on the air. At the peak of the barn, George Clubb stood in the open doorway to the loft while Dunbar seemed to hang from the gable by one hand. On closer observation, I saw that he had one foot in a loop of rope hanging from the pulley as he held his left hand on the steel track that ran overhead. On his right hand he wore a gray wool mitten with which he was smearing dark grease onto the track. George held the can of grease with one hand and the door post with the other. When Dunbar needed another gob, he reached over while George leaned out with the can.

The boss's voice sounded in back of me. "Don't fall down and break your neck."

I assumed he was talking to George, as he avoided Dunbar. Besides, I didn't think he would have minded if Dunbar did fall and break his neck. He might even have wished for it.

George called back, "We're almost done with this part."

I turned to acknowledge the boss. He was wearing a knit wool cap, a coarse wool overcoat, and wool gloves — all in drab tones of gray. He reminded me of a painting I had seen of Russian soldiers trying not to freeze to death during the Napoleonic war. I thought he might be overdressed — not because of his fondness for matching outfits but because I had learned not to wear my warmest clothes in the early part of the cold season. Even in the dead of winter, one had to remember that the weather could always get colder.

"Cy," he said, "I'm going to have you hold the reins on the wagon horses. You don't have to do much. Just sit on the seat and keep 'em in place."

"You don't want me to pull them forward each time you raise a load?"

"No need to."

"My father always did. In case the load spills. If it lands on the wagon, it can spook the horses."

"No need to. We're not going to drop anything."

I wondered if he or someone else was going to stand in the wagon, but I didn't ask. I would see soon enough. I followed him to the barn and stood outside as the men finished the task above. Dunbar tossed the mitten into the loft and held onto the rope with both hands. I saw now that the rope was doubled. With another rope attached to the pulley, George tugged and disappeared, moving Dunbar into the loft like a quarter of beef or a block of ice.

At ground level, I stood by as Dunbar wiped his hands on a cloth. Neither of us spoke. I watched Dunbar in an absent-minded way as the boss and George talked in an undertone a few yards away.

As Dunbar finished wiping his hands, I noticed something I had not seen before. In the palm of his right hand, he had a dark spot that looked as if he had been burned there. He did not seem to make an attempt

176

either to hide it or to show it. Rather, he waved his hand as people do after washing and drying their hands.

The moment passed, and George spoke as he walked toward us. "Cy, you'll work the wagon. I think you already know that. The boss will be in charge of the other team, and I'll be in the loft." Then, as if he, too, would prefer to avoid Dunbar, he turned partway and said, "You'll work the load. Make sure you get a good grab each time, and stay out of the way."

I felt a sense of dread building as George and Dunbar brought out the horses and hitched the first pair to the wagon. I did not think that the boss and his foreman had conspired to dump a load of hay on Dunbar, but I knew something could go wrong. George was not familiar with the process, and I was not convinced that the boss knew much about it, either. Dunbar had suggested that he knew something, but the boss wasn't going to put him in charge. Neither was he going to put me, an old gray-haired man with ruddy cheeks and a round girth, even though I had more experience with the work than at least two of the others.

Before long, I discovered how much the boss did not know about raising the hay. He wanted to use the second team of horses in front of the barn in order to lift the load. Dunbar looked on and said nothing, but I had to speak up.

"Excuse me," I said, "but I've never seen anyone haul the hay up that way. You're supposed to run the rope up to the trolley and out the back of the barn. Then when you get the load to the height where you want it, you hit the trip and pull the load into the barn where you stack it. Then the man running the forks pulls everything back so he can grab another load."

The boss said, "You mean the tongs."

"I learned to call them the forks, but that's a small matter."

George spoke to Dunbar. "What do you know?"

"I learned to call them forks, too. And, yes, you have to pull it from the other end. Furthermore, I didn't see a trolley in the harness room or when I was up there. You're going to have to find one somewhere, or none of this is going to work."

"Then what's the pulley for?"

Dunbar shrugged. "For hoisting things up there, I suppose. Smaller things. But not for any systematic method of moving hay up into the loft."

"Why didn't you say something earlier?"

"No one asked." Dunbar put on his coat,

a buckskin-colored canvas work coat, and took a pair of yellowish leather gloves from the pocket. He put on the gloves and assumed an air of waiting.

The boss pulled off his wool cap and slammed it on the ground. "By God, I don't like the way the two of you just waited to make a fool of me."

The boss picked up his cap and stomped away. What thoughts went through Dunbar's mind as he watched, I do not know. As for myself, it occurred to me that the boss would have a much harder time dropping a load of hay on someone from the other side of the barn.

The hay loft went unoccupied, then, and the three wagonloads fit in the ground-floor area as George Clubb had said they would. The boss kept his distance, and once the hay was in, George absented himself by going to town.

Dunbar lingered over coffee and a serving of apple pie I had made. When a feeling of there being only two of us in the bunkhouse set in, he said, "I sometimes wonder about the boss's wife."

"Mrs. Wardell?" I asked.

"Yes. I wonder if they've had children of their own, or if she has taken any kind of interest in the two working girls."

"I've never heard of their having children," I said, "though they might be old enough to have children who have grown up and gone out on their own."

"You say they've been here four or five years?"

"About that. I've been here for two years, so I don't know for sure."

"What's her name?"

"Mrs. Wardell? I believe it's Nancy."

"I haven't seen her."

"She doesn't go out much. Even in two years, I've seen her but a few times. Thinking back to your earlier question, or comment at least, I don't know that she has any maternal interest in the girls. She doesn't turn them out with their hair braided or in cute outfits. They're always rather plain-looking."

Dunbar gave a mild shrug. "It's hard to know about other people."

"They do live out of the way. And even here, they keep to themselves."

"Have you ever talked to those girls?"

"No, I haven't. I'm sure they know how, though they've always seemed silent. Even at a distance, I haven't seen them talk."

"Oh, yes," said Dunbar. "They can talk. He hasn't cut their tongues out, like the king in the story."

"I don't remember his name," I said, "but the girl's name is Philomela. She becomes a nightingale in one version of the story and a swallow in another. And she has a sister as well."

"That's the story I was thinking of. The nightingale."

The wind was blowing as it can only blow in November — cold and bleak and relentless, day and night, whining at the eaves of the bunkhouse and driving bits of dead grass through the air. I was humming a song to myself and thinking that it was no day to be working outside except for the most pressing chores. Yet the boss had George Clubb and Dunbar working behind the barn, on the windward side. At a little after eleven in the morning, the foreman barged into the bunkhouse and told me they needed my help.

I took off my apron, put on a coat and a tight-fitting winter cap, and followed him across the yard and around the barn. There I saw where he and Dunbar had cleared a path by moving old fence posts, coils of barbed wire, scraps of iron, and twisted sheets of metal. The sheet metal was weighted down with fence posts, and I was glad not to have to move it in such a strong wind.

One object remained in the way, a rusty iron structure the use of which I did not recognize. It consisted of a thick frame about four feet high with a shaft and gear wheels mounted inside.

I tipped my head into the wind, holding onto my cap, and said, "What are we doing?"

"This thing's in the way."

"I can see that. You don't expect the three of us to pick it up and move it, do you?"

"No. I want to tip it up and put a skid under it." He pointed to a sled about five feet wide and eight feet long.

I looked up and down the pathway they were clearing. "Has the boss not given up on his idea of putting the hay into the loft?"

"He didn't say."

For a moment I was amused by the thought of the boss trying to save face, as it seemed to me, after having his men pile junk in the way for years. My reverie ended when George said, "Here he comes. You can ask him yourself."

I turned to see Prentice Wardell marching into the wind, dressed, as it had seemed to me before, like a Russian soldier. His face was clouded with anger, and his eyes were hard.

"You!" he shouted at Dunbar. "Get over here!" He made a motion with his arm and pointed at the ground in front of him.

Dunbar did as he was told, carrying a six-foot iron pry bar. He held it upright like a pikestaff as he came to a stop and rested the end on the ground. He was wearing a short-billed gray wool cap instead of his usual black hat, and he looked as if he could have been a vassal to a feudal lord.

"I told you I didn't want you talking to my hired girls."

Dunbar's eyes held steady as he said, "This country has laws and rights. You can't hold somebody in bondage, and you can't restrict other people's freedom of speech."

"Well, aren't you the good citizen?"

"I might be."

"You can do it somewhere else. I want you off my ranch. Now."

Dunbar hefted the iron bar, and Wardell flinched. As Dunbar leaned the tool against the iron structure and turned halfway, the boss pulled an old sock out of his coat pocket. The toe of the sock swung with weight, and I could not believe the boss would try to sap Dunbar with such a paltry weapon.

I was right. He turned to the foreman and handed him the sock.

"George, here's his pay. Give it to him when he's packed and ready to go."

"Can we finish with what we're doing here?"

"I said now, and I mean it." The boss turned and walked away.

"I guess that's it," said George. He hit the iron frame with the heel of his hand. "We'll take care of this son of a bitch some other time."

Dunbar had the blue roan saddled and the buckskin packed in less than an hour. The wind was blowing the horses' tails in strands when he stopped at the bunkhouse door and I stepped out to say goodbye.

He was wearing his black hat and brown overcoat, and he stood in front of his horses, holding the reins and the lead rope in his left hand as he held out his right hand to shake. "So long, Cyrus."

"It's been good to know you," I said. "Keep the wind at your back."

"Can't always." He put his horses into position, and with the lead rope in one hand, he pulled himself aboard with the other. He tipped his head so that the wind would not carry away his hat, and he turned his horses north toward town. The wind blew their tails sideways as they trotted away, and I thought I had seen the last of Dunbar.

I was wrong.

At about ten the next morning, with the wind blowing as before, motion in the ranch yard caught my attention. I looked out the bunkhouse window to see Prentice Wardell hurrying to the barn with the two silent sisters. He had each one by the upper arm, and they showed no resistance. As the three of them disappeared into the barn, Dunbar rode into the yard.

Ah-ha, I thought. *The boss has been keeping a lookout.*

Dunbar had both of his horses. He rode up to the hitching rail in front of the bunkhouse and dismounted. As he tied the horses, I saw that the buckskin had a riding saddle instead of the usual packsaddle.

I opened the door and stepped out.

Dunbar said, "I thought I saw Wardell headed for the barn with the two girls."

"You're right," I said.

"That might make things more difficult." He took off his coat, hung it on the saddle horn, and settled his black hat on his head. He was wearing a gray flannel shirt and a charcoal-colored wool vest, buttoned snug. His dark-handled revolver hung in plain view.

He walked across the ranch yard, and I followed at a distance of ten paces. Fifty feet from the barn, he stopped. The doors to the loft were open, and Prentice Wardell stepped into view. Like Dunbar, he was not wearing a coat and had a pistol at his side. Next to him stood Ophelia, the older of the two sisters, with a rope around her neck. The rope led up to the pulley and back into the barn.

Dunbar spoke loud and clear into the wind. "I've come for the girls, Wardell."

"You'll do nothing of the sort. Take them God knows where and do God knows what with them."

"Your righteousness is noteworthy, but you should give it up. I'm taking these girls to town."

"You are not. If you don't turn around and leave, I'm pushing this one off the ledge." Wardell put his hand behind Ophelia's back, and the girl trembled.

"The law's going to get you one way or the other. Causing a girl's death would not be —"

"I said leave."

"I'm taking these girls, and the law will be

coming for you. You've kept these girls against their will, and you've done things that no judge or jury will tolerate."

Even with a small audience, the public nature of the accusation could be felt. It hung and spread in the ranch yard like a chill.

Wardell's face was bunched in anger, and his voice pierced the air. "I *hate* you!" he shrieked, as he pulled his pistol and fired.

Dunbar drew his gun in a smooth motion as the bullet whistled past him and spat into the ground at my left. Raising and aiming with the hammer cocked, Dunbar fired.

Prentice Wardell dropped his pistol and pitched forward. He fell headlong, like the bad angels who were cast out of heaven in the great poem, and he landed with a thud in the dust.

The story ran through town in no time. Dunbar got the girls settled into the Eureka Hotel. Finding myself without a job or a place to stay, I took up there as well. Within a few days I was helping in the kitchen, and I heard all the gossip.

What a terrible thing it was for a man to take girls like that and use them. And his wife knew all about it, even abetted him. Now she was gone, and she had taken all the money from the bank. George Clubb was gone as well, and as far as anyone knew, he had taken up with Mrs. Wardell.

Unkindest of all was what the townspeople said about the two sisters. How could those girls stay there, the people said, unless they wanted to? They could have walked away at any time. Little Indians.

The girls themselves caught wind of the comments, of course. They had come out of their room and were working for the hotel, sweeping and cleaning as before, as they waited for someone to come for them from New Mexico Territory.

One day as I served them dinner when no one else was in the kitchen, I told them I was sorry for everything that had happened to them.

Ophelia said, "We're through the worst of it, but we've heard what people say. They can't know what it's like. It makes no sense to someone who hasn't lived in a situation like that. He had a strange power over us, a bond that we couldn't dare to break. At the same time that he forced us to be loyal, he held us in fear. People say we could have left, but it seemed impossible. Too big. There was the fear of what he would do if he caught us. And there was the fear of what people would think, that they wouldn't believe what we said, or that they would look at us as if it was our fault. As it turned out, we were right."

"I'm sorry they've said all those unkind things," I offered.

The girls looked at each other, and Ophelia said, "They just don't know what it's like. They don't want to believe that we couldn't leave on our own. Or maybe they just don't want to think about what it was like to live that way. The only person who listened and believed us was Mr. Dunbar."

"I believe you, too. But credit goes to him. And he has sent word to New Mexico Territory. You told him your last name, didn't you?"

"Yes. It's Darling."

"How nice," I said. "And did you come from Albuquerque?"

"No," said Ophelia. "We lived in a small town named Polvadera. We'll know it when we go back."

John D. Nesbitt lives in the plains country of Wyoming, where he writes western, contemporary, mystery, and retro/noir fiction as well as nonfiction and poetry. His recent books include *Dark Prairie, Death in*

Cantera, and *Destiny at Dry Camp,* frontier mysteries with Five Star.

■ ■ ■ ■

PIMPLE
BY JOHN NEELY DAVIS

■ ■ ■ ■

Sometime in the past, a cowboy riding across these vast unmarked plains had observed, "This place ain't never gonna amount to more than a pimple on a skinny dog's ass." He was mostly right.

Once a week, a stagecoach came through heading south to Oneida. Three days later, and traveling in almost the same ruts, the identical stagecoach passed through northbound. Twice each week a train came through — once, westbound toward Santa Fe, and a day later, eastbound toward St. Louis. Other than that, only the relentless wind visited — starting thirty minutes after sunrise and ending thirty minutes after sunset — and that was as dependable as the train engineer's watch.

Pimple started and ended with one building, a combination general store/saloon, depot, and stage station, with living quarters on the second floor. It was visible for ten miles in any direction, sitting there in a sea of blue grama and buffalo grasses. The smoothness of the grass surface was marred only with an occasional island of juniper or clump of mesquite. Not counting antelopes, coyotes, and prairie dogs, permanent residents consisted of Bill Rayburn and his daughter, Louise.

Three ranch headquarters were within a fifty-mile radius: the Slash Q, the Rocking V, and the Box Seven. Cowboys dreamed of visiting Pimple and, using flimsy excuses, would gladly ride twenty-five miles in hopes of visiting with Louise, even if only under the ever-watchful eye of crotchety old man Rayburn.

His ornery disposition was constructed around protecting Louise. She was a beauty with blonde hair and fair skin not yet defiled by the High Plains wind, a woman-child, one of those females who had developed winsome curves while her mind was still unaware of her effect on men. She would have stood out in the highest society and fanciest ballrooms of Denver or Dallas, but out here in a land where the next woman might be fifty miles away, Louise was quickly reaching legendary status.

"Well, looky there at what the wind blew

in," Louise said. "Yesterday it was three tumbleweeds; today it's Mick Warren. Box Seven fire you?"

"No'm, nothing like that," Mick said. "I was sent to buy a pint of horse liniment, big bottle of chloroform, camphor, and a bucket of axle grease."

"Sent or volunteered?"

Mick looked down at his boots. "Guess you could say I volunteered. Somebody had to do it."

"Second time this month," Louise teased.

"Guess I was the easiest spared."

Mick just told his first lie of the month. The Box Seven foreman had appointed Slim Harrington to make the hot and dusty ride down to Pimple. However, Mick had offered Slim a day's wages, eight bits, and the promise to ride night herd for him next Saturday night in exchange for the rights to run the errand. Because Slim was always broke and always sleepy, he cut the deal with Mick. Slim left money on the table 'cause Mick would have given him more.

"Well, I'm glad. You're my favorite from the Box Seven. At least you bathe."

Mick blushed. "That ain't saying much. But I reckon it beats nothing."

Louise saw Mick's embarrassment. "Really, I'm glad for the company. Dad left

195

before daylight for Sweetwater. Trying to buy some cattle from a widow woman over there. It's his third trip. Dad said she's harder to deal with and more cantankerous than a croker sack of cockleburs. Truth be told, I believe he'd rather look at her than at the cows. No telling what time he'll get home."

Mick stood by the window, hiding his uncontrollable smile and looking down the railroad tracks. "Train to St. Louis comes today, don't it?"

"Yes. The southbound stage will be here in about thirty minutes, too. Sometimes, it doesn't even stop for more than a blink. Drop off mail or pick some up. Sometimes it don't stop at all. But the train always stops. I fix a beef sandwich for Mr. Kemp, the engineer. He gives me six bits."

"Whoa! Six bits! Why, I don't make much more than that in a day."

Louise laughed. "Maybe I'm a better cook than you are a cowboy. That's why I'm paid that much. But, if you don't tell anybody, I'll make you one for nothing. It's just meat and bread and a sour pickle. I wouldn't pay two bits for it myself."

The north wind picked up and sent tumbleweeds racing southward across the prairie. They stopped on the windward side of the building, huddling up like exhausted travelers waiting for more energy before continuing their headlong flight.

The squeak of the leather strap coach-braces, the jingle of trace chains, and the rumble of steel-rimmed wheels against the pitted road brought Mick and Louise out onto the front porch. The coach, enveloped in a furious cloud of dust, thundered toward them, the four horses dripping with sweat and spotted with foam and fighting against the bits.

The man riding shotgun pulled against the rope line attached to the brake pole as the driver tried to impose his will on the horses. The guard bounded down from the seat as the coach came to a stop, jerked the left-side door open and reached inside. "Come outta there, you sorry son of a bitch," he said, as he dragged a large man out into the dusty road and flung him to the ground as if he was no more than an unruly child. "Don't you never book a ride with us again, even if'n it's fifty years from now. You hear what I'm sayin'?"

He glared at the man he had just forcibly evicted, then put his foot on the metal step and swung back up onto the bench. The dust hadn't even settled when the driver lashed the leather lines against the horses' backs, and the coach resumed its frantic trek toward Oneida.

Louise turned to Mick. "Well. I believe now I've seen it all."

Mick jumped off the porch and vaulted the hitching rail. He leaned forward and helped the still stunned man to his feet. "You all right, mister?"

The man stood, dusted his clothes, and reshaped his hat. Standing, he was larger than he appeared while sprawled in the dirt. "Young man," he said, looking down on Mick, "I've had rougher treatment from more genteel folks and common criminals. It was a misunderstanding — nothing more, nothing less. I am scheduled to catch the train here," he pulled a silver-cased watch monogrammed with a cursive O from his vest pocket and inspected the timepiece, "at one forty-five."

"That's about an hour from now," Mick said. "You got time to rest a bit. Maybe Louise can fix you something to eat. She makes real good sandwiches but they are priced pretty steep."

The big man looked at Mick. "What's your name, cowboy?"

"Warren. Mick Warren. What's yours?"

"You can call me Mr. Olive," the man said and pulled his black satin vest down over his more than generous stomach.

He studied Mick. Freckles. Unruly red hair. Sweat-stained shirt and hat. Patches on both knees of his pants. "Hmmm. I believe I'll call you Bumpkin. You know what a bumpkin is?"

"No, sir, I don't. I'd druther be called Mick. That's what my folks named me, but if you want to call me Bumpkin, I guess that's OK."

Mr. Olive looked at the woman-breasted girl. "And you, young woman, I believe your name is Louise. That's what Bumpkin called you. Is that correct?"

Louise, flushed-face, turned away from his embarrassing stare. "Yes, sir. Louise is my name."

The plain print dress did not hide her shape. Mr. Olive looked at her from heels to the top of her blonde hair. "I could call you Lou. That's sweet. However, you remind me of a lamb I once owned. A ewe. A young female sheep, you know. I believe Ewe fits you very well. Innocent. Sweet. Ripe." He nodded, "Yes, Ewe, fits you."

Mick did not understand this game and it confused him. "Louise is a nice name. That's what everybody calls her."

"Well, mayhaps I'm different from everybody else. Perchance I see something you don't see. Maybe I'm not satisfied with just looking." Mr. Olive did not look away from the young woman.

"I've got to fix the engineer's sandwich," Louise said. She hurried across the porch and went inside, leaving the two men out in the dusty road.

"What do you do, Bumpkin?" Mr. Olive asked.

Mick shrugged. "Just regular cowboying. Fix fences. Breaking horses. Help with the calving. Branding. Castrating young bulls. Doctoring calves. Stuff like that."

"Well. A really talented fellow. You can throw a calf to the ground. All by yourself?"

"Yes, sir. If there ain't nobody around to help me."

"And doctoring and castrating. You handy with a knife?"

"Well, not too good. But I'm a good whittler."

"A good whittler! Wonderful." Mr. Olive leaned across the hitching rail, arms hanging loosely. He let his tongue dangle from the corner of his mouth and eyes roll back in their sockets. "This the way the calf looks when you throw it to the ground?"

"No, sir, mostly they don't do their eyes like that," Mick said. "Maybe sometimes, but mostly, not."

Mr. Olive pushed his hat back on his forehead and chuckled. "You are too much, Bumpkin, just too much. Are there more like you where you come from?"

Mick could not understand why Mr. Olive was laughing. "Yes, sir. But I'm the youngest."

Inside, Louise busied herself behind the grocery counter slicing beef for the engineer's sandwich.

The two men entered from the porch and Olive stopped to watch Louise slicing the bread.

"Bumpkin, you ever notice how smooth Ewe's arms are? Wonder how they'd feel around your neck?"

Mick moved to a table in the saloon part of the building and sat in a worn chair. "No, sir. I never noticed. I figured they was just normal."

Mr. Olive moved to the table and sat across from Mick. "Bumpkin, man as observant as you, why, I'd bet that you are a helluva card player."

"No, sir, my folks didn't believe in playing with face cards. I'm a pretty good Forty-two player."

Mr. Olive laughed. "I've seen that game. Played with dominos. Children's game. I'm

201

talking about a real game. A man's game. Blackjack!"

Mick shook his head. "Never played that. Saw some fellers over at the fort playing it once. 'Spect I'd better not try to play it. 'Specially since I don't know how."

"Oh, don't worry about that," Mr. Olive said and shoved his bowler hat back from his forehead. "I'll teach you. All you need to know is how to count to twenty-one. You can count to twenty-one, can't you?"

Louise paused, holding the butcher knife away from the piece of beef. "Let him alone," she said. "You've not got a cause to talk to him that way."

Mr. Olive took a deck of cards from his inside coat pocket. "I'm just going to teach him a game," he said. "Mayhaps I'll teach you a new game. Something I bet you don't know."

Louise frowned, turned quickly, and went back to slicing the beef.

"How much money you got?" Mr. Olive asked Mick.

"A dollar two-bits of my own."

Mr. Olive studied the cowboy's face. "Well, that ought to get us started. Course, I'm not accustomed to such high-stake games. And you may have to bear with me or mayhaps help me with the counting.

Once I get past ten, I run out of fingers and can get confused."

Mr. Olive fanned the cards across the table in a perfect arc, scooped them together, divided them into equal halves, and riffled them. He formed a bridge with the combined deck and the cards cascaded like a waterfall into a neat stack. He split the deck into halves, riffled them at the corners, and squared the cards into a perfect pack.

Two minutes later, Mick was broke.

"Thanks for teaching me the game," Mick said and pushed away from the table. "I believe I'll walk around a bit, go outside, see if the train is coming."

Mr. Olive leaned across the table and grabbed the cowboy's arm. "Just a minute, Bumpkin. You said you had a dollar and a quarter of your own. You got more money on you?"

Mick looked at Mr. Olive's hand clutching his shirt. "Yes, sir. Nine dollars. But it ain't mine. Ranch foreman gave it to me for the supplies."

"Well, what do you think the foreman would say if you brought the supplies back — and still had a pocket full of jingle to boot? Bet he'd be impressed with you."

The cowboy shook his head. "Wouldn't be right. Ain't my money. Can't take no risk with it. I'd be up a creek if I came back broke and without the stuff he sent me after. He'd probably take it outta my hide."

"Oh, I wouldn't worry about it," Mr. Olive said. "It looked like you were starting a hot streak before you lost the last hand. Why, I'm not sure I'd be a smart man to keep playing with you."

Louise cut four slices of bread and put the knife back into the slot of the wooden block. She moved to the table where the two men were sitting and wiped her hands on her apron. "Why don't y'all stop playing and let me fix you a sandwich?"

Without looking at Louise, Mr. Olive snapped, "Why don't you mind your own damn business? He's a grown man. Don't need a woman bossing him around. Do you, cowboy? You are a man of your own, aren't you?"

Mick looked at Louise. "She's not bossing. She just knows that it wouldn't be right to waste any more money in a game. 'Specially, money that ain't mine."

Mr. Olive pulled the silver timepiece from his pocket. "Twelve fifteen. Haven't got more than thirty minutes. What say, Ewe? Ready to go upstairs and learn a new game. Cowboy here will watch the store. Look at it this way, I teach you and when he grows up, you can teach him."

Mick pulled his chair closer to the table and dragged a cloth sack from his pocket. He reached in, pulled out nine one-dollar bills, and spread them on the table. "There," he said. "Now let's play blackjack. I start as the dealer."

Mr. Olive smiled. "Wonderful. Ewe, I wonder if you might make some fresh coffee. And if you will, sprinkle crushed eggshells in it; kinda takes the edge off it. I've got a sensitive stomach. Can't tolerate harshness in coffee or people, far as that's concerned." He cut the cards and laughed. "In fact, I'm a very sensitive man. After Bumpkin cleans me out of money, I'll show you just how sensitive I can be."

On the second deal, Mick busted and the deal passed to Mr. Olive. He hit four blackjacks in a row; Mick busted twice, drawing a face card to a ten and three each time. Then Mr. Olive hit twenty-one twice, and Mick was down to a single dollar.

"You bringing coffee?" Mr. Olive shouted over his shoulder.

Louise came from behind the counter and put two cups on the table. "Be right back."

Mr. Olive turned in his chair and watched Louise move toward the kitchen. "My, my, a good shearing will do that young woman fine. And do me better."

Mr. Olive took a .44 derringer from his coat pocket and laid it on the table. "Bumpkin," he said, "I don't expect you to carry a gun. Or, at least, I haven't seen one. I just wanted everything to be out in the open. Card playing buddies need not keep secrets. You're not hiding a gun in that coat, are you?"

"No. I don't have a gun. Sometimes when a sick cow needs shooting or we get a polecat under the house, I borrow one from the foreman. I never had need for a gun."

Mr. Olive nodded. "Splendid. Splendid. I didn't take you for a gun-toting man, but I just need to have everything in the open." He turned toward the kitchen again. "Ewe, if we're going to have any special time together, you best hurry with that coffee. Don't want you missing out on the fun."

Louise walked from the bar to the table, holding the enamel coffee pot, careful not to splash the contents on the floor.

Mr. Olive looked up at her and smiled. "What a sweetie you are. The train just may have to wait a couple of minutes for me. Or make that, for us." He smiled again and cupped his hand around Louise's breast.

She emptied the pot of steaming coffee onto his upturned face, and Mick swept the table aside as if it was no more than a dried mesquite leaf.

Two steps forward and Mick wrapped his arm around Mr. Olive's head and twisted. It was not as difficult as throwing a calf to the ground. The gambler lay on the floor in much the same position as he had taunted Mick earlier — tongue dangling from the corner of his mouth and eyes rolled back in their sockets. He twitched once and did not breathe again.

Neither Mick nor Louise spoke. A gust of wind shook the flimsy building. In the distance, the train's whistle moaned. The wind gusted again, and this time peppered the window with sand and small pebbles.

On the day Mr. Olive died, Louise made the engineer's sandwich and took it out to him. When she came back into the store, the chairs and table had been uprighted, and Mr. Olive's body was not in sight. Only shards of eggshells and an irregular shaped damp spot sullied the floor.

A year and a half later on a fine spring morning when the High Plains sky was the color of a robin's egg and a north breeze ushered winter tumbleweeds toward Oneida, the population of Pimple increased by one — Louise and Mick Warren's son,

Ellison, came into the world.

Two days after baby Ellison's arrival, St. Louis railroad detectives closed the file on the death of an unidentified man. The man had arrived at the rail yards approximately eighteen months earlier in a cattle car with forty steers. The corpse was trampled to a condition that his own mother could not have recognized him. A silver-cased watch monogrammed with a cursive O was found near the remains, and a still-loaded .44 derringer, fouled with straw and manure, lay at the opposite end of the cattle car.

John Neely Davis, a writer of western and Appalachian fiction, lives in Franklin, Tennessee, with his wife, Jayne. His most recent western novel, *The Chapman Legacy,* was released by Five Star in June of 2018.

BULLWHACKER
BY ROD MILLER

The woman muttered under her breath, using words she would never say aloud. She cursed the oxen that had wandered off in the night. She cursed the rain that made the trail up Little Mountain a boggy mire, more stream than road. She cursed the tattered wagon sheets through which water seeped and dripped, fouling the scant supplies that must see her through the winter in the valley she hoped to reach this day, and cursed again the storm hindering that arrival.

And she cursed the man who, months ago, way back on the Elkhorn River, had done his best to prevent her joining the migration, declaring her wagons unfit for the road, her oxen not up to the trail, and a widow woman with a passel of children a burden on the company.

In a fit of ire, she had told the wagon master she would not only make the trip to the distant valley without his help, she would get there ahead of him. But now, the storm, the scattered stock, the muddy trail gave lie to her promise.

June, 1848, Elkhorn River, Unorganized Territory

Cornelius Lott tugged the seat of his pants out of his backside cleavage. He wadded his floppy felt hat and raked his fingers through scant hair. He scuffed a foot through the dust, walked over to the biggest of the animals, and slapped it on the shoulder.

"Ain't no way, Mary," he said. "These here critters is the sorriest bunch of cattle I've ever seen. This one here's the onliest one looks like he can pull his own weight, and that not far. Rest of these ain't no good. How do you expect to get these wagons across the plains when you ain't got but four oxen barely worthy of the name yoked to half-growed steers and a cow?"

Mary Smith said nothing.

Lott slapped the ox on the rump in disgust. "And speaking of wagons. These of yours ain't in no better shape than the cattle. 'Specially this farm wagon. Damn thing'll fall apart 'fore you've gone half a mile. And what about that rattletrap ambulance hitched to the back of it? Which of these useless cattle you expect to pull *two*

212

wagons? And that other'n ain't much better
— looks ready to collapse just standin'
there."

The sorry state of her means of convey-
ance was not news to Mary. The twenty-
seven-mile trip from Winter Quarters to the
Elkhorn where the wagon trains were as-
sembling revealed the weakness of her
preparation. Already, a wagon axle had
cracked climbing a creek bank, a bow on a
yoke split, and a spoke had shattered on a
wobbly wheel. And it was true the teams
were mismatched and poorly trained. Even
the loose stock — two milk cows with
calves, and half a dozen sheep — seemed
more prone to wander than submit to herding.

"Land sakes, Mary! You ain't even got a
man to run this outfit!" Lott blustered, tuck-
ing plump thumbs behind his braces and
giving them a tug.

John, at fifteen, and the oldest male in
Mary's "family," stepped forward. Nine-
year-old Joey threw his hat to the ground
and, with doubled fists and red face, started
for Lott. Mary grabbed the back of his collar with one hand and placed the other on
John's chest.

With another tug at his galluses, the
wagon master blustered on. "That there

pimply boy ain't growed up enough to lead, and that hot-headed runt ain't worth a mention."

The boys strained forward, but Mary kept them in check.

"Them, and them three girls, that half-witted woman, and them two old women you brung along ain't gonna be nothin' but trouble. Never mind what the brethren say, I'm damned if I'll let you-all hold this company back."

Now it was Mary's face that flushed red. She studied the small crowd gathered to see what the commotion was about, then spoke.

"I will have you know, Cornelius Lott, that me and mine will be no burden to you. How do you suppose my Hyrum and I got from Kirtland to Far West? How do you suppose I got from Far West to Nauvoo, with Hyrum locked in jail? And how do you suppose I got from Nauvoo to Winter Quarters with Hyrum dead in his grave?"

Mary punctuated every sentence with a determined step in Lott's direction. She stopped a scant foot from the man and raised a pointed finger to within an inch of his nose.

"Do not be attempting to school me in the ways of wagon travel, Cornelius Lott. You are not to worry one iota about me or my family or my wagons or my livestock. And if what you mean by a 'man' to take charge is anything like the likes of you, I will happily take my chances with me and mine alone."

She emphasized the point with a thrust of her finger into the man's chest, then turned on her heel and walked away. Lott, flushed and flustered, sputtered for a response but found none.

Mary turned again to face him. "Know this. I will make the trip to Great Salt Lake City with this company, and I shall do it without your help. Not only will I arrive there in good order, I shall do so ahead of you!" She stood her ground and the crowd parted as Lott walked away.

The family Mary spoke of was no family in the traditional sense of the word. Joseph — Joey — was her son by Hyrum, and Martha Ann, just turned seven, also resulted from their all-too-brief marriage. The other children, John and his younger sisters, Jerusha and Sarah, were the three youngest of Hyrum's children from his first wife, who died from complications following Sarah's birth. Two older girls from that union were married and gone.

In addition to the children, Mary had inherited three other women upon marrying Hyrum. "Aunty" Grinnels and Maggie Brysen, spinsters in their fifties, were part of the Smith household before Mary's arrival, helping to care for the children. The third woman, Jane Wilson, was a distressed soul, prone to fits. Hyrum, being a charitable sort, had taken responsibility for her care.

Now that responsibility was Mary's. And, later on the emigrant trail, that obligation would give Cornelius Lott yet another reason to confront Mary.

Jane was fond of taking snuff. And, noticing her supply diminished late one afternoon as the wagons circled for camp along the Platte River, she walked the mile or two up the trail to another wagon camp in the expedition to visit a friend and replenish her snuff box. Jane told Mary she would spend the night there, and rejoin her come morning.

Lott walked among his charges in the gray light of dawn, assuring all was in order before giving the command to roll out. After his customary dismay at the state of Mary's stock and equipment, he asked if all was well.

"That it is, Mister Lott."

With a snort, he grabbed his galluses and leaned toward the woman.

"All well? You tell a lie, Mary Smith. I have it on good authority that a woman of your party is missing! Jane Wilson is gone, likely wandering alone in the wilderness. And who can say what tragedy may have befallen the poor woman? No thanks to you, this train will be delayed until she — or what remains of her — can be found!"

In his ire, he chose not to hear Mary's explanation.

"Well, then, Mister Lott, you may stay and search to your heart's content. But as for me and mine, we shall take to the trail and Miss Jane will join us in good time."

With a poke from her prod, Mary the bull-whacker "hawed" her team around the parked wagons waiting ahead of her. John and Joey followed with the farm wagon with the trailer hitched behind, and the girls shepherded the loose stock along after. No one paid any attention to the florid-faced wagon master's hollering and stomping — save a few members of the company who turned to tightening the lashings on wagon sheets, checking the keys on ox bows, and finding other mundane tasks behind which they could conceal their amusement.

As Mary predicted, Jane rejoined the train and plodded along the Platte Valley with the rest of the Smith caravan as the days stretched into weeks.

It was somewhere in sight of Chimney Rock that one of Mary's uncertain draft animals finally failed her. But it was not a cow called to service under the yoke that faltered, nor one of the half-grown steers. For no apparent reason, one of the strongest of her oxen, the offside wheeler on her lead wagon, staggered and collapsed. The hulking beast gasped its last, tumbling to its side, and Mary watched in horror as the reflected sun faded in its glazed-over eye.

The woman dropped to her knees and sat with head bowed, whether in prayer or despair the members of her family could not say as they gathered. The other wagons in the train creaked to a stop and the circle of onlookers grew. Barely a breath was drawn among the bystanders until the wagon master elbowed his way through.

Lott pulled off his misshapen felt hat, wiped a palm over sweaty forehead and pate, then dried the damp hand on the seat of his pants.

"Mary Smith, I warned you about this very thing. Here we sit idle on account of your poor preparation. That we have made it this far before you fulfilled my prophecy is the only surprise here."

Mary rose to her feet and brushed the

dust from the skirt of her dress.

Lott pitched in. "Now, woman, unless you have a better idea, drag this animal out of the way and yoke up a milk cow, or one of those sheep if you'd rather. Be quick about it and you may catch up to our camp by nightfall. But we'll not wait."

No member of the company spoke up, but Lott heard much mumbling and muttering as his charges shuffled and scuffed.

"Well?" he hollered. "Get a move on!"

"Wait," Mary said. Her voice was soft, but reached every ear.

"What is it, woman?"

Mary studied the faces in the circle. She stepped closer to Lott. "I have a better idea."

Lott's only response was a furrowed forehead and arched eyebrows.

"You said, 'unless I have a better idea.' Well, I do," Mary said.

The furrows in Lott's forehead deepened and his lips tightened and turned down.

Mary's eyes locked on Lott's without blinking. "I want this ox healed."

The wagon master's eyes widened and his jaw worked at a reply, but none came.

"You hold yourself up as a pious man, *Brother* Lott. Lay hands on that ox and command him to rise."

Lott stammered and stuttered and sputtered and spit as crimson crept upward from his collar, coloring his entire visage. "I will not!" he finally managed. "It is sacrilege! It is blasphemous!"

"It is the Lord's will." Mary looked around at the stunned faces around her. "Does He not say, 'Ask, and it shall be given you'?" She again fixed her gaze on Lott. "I believe you will find that in Matthew, *Elder* Lott. And does not James tell us, 'Is any sick among you? Let him call for the elders of the church; and let them pray over him'? And does he not go on to say, 'the prayer of faith shall save the sick, and the Lord shall raise him up'?"

"It don't say nothing about no ox! It is an outrage to even suggest it. Besides, that critter ain't sick, he's dead!"

"Do you lack faith, Mister Lott? Surely the Lord's mercy extends to animals. I cannot quote chapter and verse, but there is a Proverb that reads, 'A righteous man regardeth the life of his beast.' Are you not a righteous man?"

Lott's hat hit the ground. "Enough of your spouting scripture, Mary Smith. We're burning daylight here. Now, the rest of you, get a move on!"

Nobody moved.

Mary again scanned the faces in the

crowd. "Josiah Fielding," she said, settling on the face of her cousin. "You are the closest this family has to a man at present. Will you lay hands on my ox?"

Josiah hemmed and hawed, nodded sheepishly, and looked to a friend who likewise signified his willingness.

"I forbid it!" Lott said.

The men ignored the wagon master and walked slowly toward the ox, removing their hats as they went. Lott followed, tugging at their shoulders and remonstrating them with every step. The crowd drew closer, forming a tight semicircle around the fallen ox, shushing Lott. Fielding and his friend knelt beside the prostrate animal, laid hands on its horny head, and prayed fervently for the Lord's blessing. The prayer ended with a command to the ox to rise and walk and an "amen" repeated by the onlookers.

Only Lott failed to voice the benediction, instead emitting a derisive snort.

The ox responded with a snort of its own, drew in a long wheezing breath, rolled to its stomach and tucked its legs, hiked up its hind end, then the front, rattled the draw chain with a shake of its head, and looked for all the world ready to pull.

Mary, a smile teasing the corners of her mouth, said, "Well, why are you people standing around? You heard Mister Lott — get these wagons rolling."

Never mind Cornelius Lott's difficulties with Mary Smith. The man enjoyed a long — and deserved — reputation as a competent, capable leader. His assignment as wagon master of this train in the larger migration was neither surprising nor undeserved. Almost without question, the emigrants in his charge valued his leadership, followed his orders, and held to his advice. His malice toward Mary Smith was viewed as a curious and atypical oddity.

Given Lott's orderly approach to all things and attention to detail, it was a wonderment to all that while Mary's inferior draft cattle slogged along day after day and mile after mile, it was Lott's oxen that next delayed the train.

It happened in the gray light of dawn one morning along the Sweetwater as the company approached Independence Rock. When the cattle were roused from their bed grounds and herded into camp to commence the day's work, several of the wagon master's oxen were not among them.

Expecting his teams had wandered away in search of greener grass, Lott assembled a party to search the surrounding plains. The oxen were soon located, dead on the ground.

No clue as to the cause of their demise was evident. Perhaps it was a bellyful of alkali-tainted water. More likely, the bull-whackers thought, in their grazing through the night the animals happened onto a patch of poisonous plants.

Lott was having none of it.

"Mary Smith!" Lott hollered as his mount slid to a stop next to her wagons. "What have you done, you infernal woman?"

Wide-eyed and open-mouthed, Mary had no answer, and could only shake her head.

"Well?"

She slid the kitchen box the rest of the way into the wagon and dusted off her hands. "Pray tell, Mister Lott, whatever are you talking about?"

"You know good and well what I'm talking about! What I want to know is how you did it."

Lott dismounted and moved toward Mary with long strides. She backed away, but bumped against the back of the wagon. John and Joey heard the ruction and came running, but Mary signaled them to stop short. Others stopped their chores and gathered round. With little attempt to contain his anger, Lott told how his oxen — and only his oxen — had died in the night under circumstances he saw as suspicious.

"How, Mary?" he said. "Was it you, or did you send these boys of yours to do it?"

"I ask you again, what do you think we have done?"

"Don't play the innocent with me! What did you-all do to my cattle?"

Mary only stared at him. She looked to the boys, but both looked bewildered. She looked back at Lott and shook her head.

"Dammit, woman! My patience is wearing thi—"

"I will thank you to bridle your tongue, Mister Lott," Mary said as her ire rose along with the flush in her face. "We did nothing to your animals. To even think so is absurd. If no oxen belonging to others were so afflicted, it must be that they had better care in herding."

Mary paused to catch her breath, then, in a voice so soft most strained to hear it, she offered Mister Lott the use of some of her cattle, poor and trail-weary and unfit for service though they may be.

The wagon master shook a finger in Mary's face, but despite his working jaw, he could find no words. He turned and strode away, stopped to again waggle his finger at Mary from a distance, then walked away again. Realizing he had left his horse, he hove to and ordered a boy standing nearby to fetch it. Jerking the reins from the boy's hand, he yanked on the bit and dragged the startled horse away with him.

Winding up the trail toward South Pass, the company, following Lott's wagons, which were drawn by the few oxen he had left yoked to animals borrowed and bought from fellow travelers, plodded through meadows, sand dunes, rocky ridges, and sage-covered plains, and crossed, time and time and time again, the Sweetwater River. All along the way, the trail was littered with cast-off goods from earlier emigrants, with dead cattle ranging from bloated corpses to whitened bones, and with graves — a seemingly endless parade of graves lining the wagon road. Some were covered with heaps of stone to keep varmints at bay; some displayed headboards pulled from wagon boxes and crudely carved with a name and date; some marked only with sticks lashed together to form a cross. Others were unmarked, their presence made known only by disturbed earth; still other, older graves by a depression where the ground subsided as the corpse beneath moldered away.

The presence of trailside graves was so

common an occurrence by then that they went all but unnoticed; as ever-present as the dust and the wind. But the reality of it all came home to Mary one evening as she watched Jane Wilson perched upon a wagon tongue writing in her journal. This, too, was commonplace, but this evening it piqued Mary's curiosity.

She gathered her skirts and sat beside Jane on the tongue. "You are a staunch keeper of records, Miss Wilson."

Jane nodded, and closed the book, her place marked with her stub of a pencil.

"I do not mean to pry, but what is it you write?"

The woman blushed, and, head bowed, looked upward at Mary. "It is nothing," she said. "Just a few notes. Numbers, mostly."

"Numbers?"

Jane nodded. "I keep track of things. Keep count."

"May I see?"

Jane's flush increased as she handed the book to Mary. Mary paged backward through the entries. The notations were much the same.

July 19 — 14 miles, passed 2 graves
July 18 — 16 miles, 4 graves
July 16 — made 15 miles, 7 graves passed

July 12 — 15 miles, 5 graves
July 11 — 13 miles, 15 graves
July 6 — 9 miles, passed 6 graves
July 5 — 18 miles, 9 graves
July 4 — 12 miles, passed 2 graves
July 1 — 16 miles, 3 graves
June 30 — 14 miles, 3 graves

And so on, all the way back to the Elkhorn River.

"You have a lovely hand, Miss Wilson."

"Thank you."

"But why keep such a dismal count?"

Jane again bowed her head, and Mary waited for an answer.

"If I . . . without someone . . . if no one takes note of those who died on this trail, I fear they will be forgotten. If their passing goes unnoticed by those who followed them, will they have died in vain?"

Mary gently closed the book and handed it back to Jane.

When the Oregon and California Trails diverged from the Mormon Trail at Fort Bridger, the Utah-bound emigrants knew they were on the home stretch of their thousand-mile trek from Winter Quarters to Great Salt Lake City. The wagons crossed the Bear River and creaked and crawled down Echo Canyon before facing their last obstacle before reaching home.

Although Big Mountain was a barely noticeable ridge among the peaks of the Wasatch Mountains, climbing it put the train at its most elevated point on the entire trip. A scant twenty miles from their new home, the Salt Lake Valley was within sight from the summit. But getting down off the top of Big Mountain proved one of the toughest trials on the trail.

Mary, John, and Joey unyoked the lead teams on their wagons and rough-locked the rear wheels by chaining them together. The wagons slipped and slid and skidded one at a time down the hill as John poked, prodded, geed, and hawed the wheelers around the stumps of cut trees frequenting the track. After getting the Smith wagons down safely, he did the same a dozen times more, helping other wagons in the train negotiate the steep course. At the bottom, with wheels unlocked and lead teams back under yoke, the wagons made it another mile or two along the road to make camp on the banks of Brown's Creek.

"A long day for you, John," Mary said when the boy plopped down in the dusk on a log. Where his ragged clothing wasn't sweat-stained it was saturated with dust.

"And this your sixteenth birthday."

John shrugged. "Wagons all down safe," he said between mouthfuls of boiled rice and raisins. "Should be out of these mountains by tomorrow."

"So they say. But the ridge we have yet to cross — Little Mountain, they call it — to reach the canyon down to the valley looks much the same as the one we crossed today. The climb is steep, and the descent as well, they tell us." Mary dusted flour off her apron as she studied the fading sky. "I do not like the look of the weather. I fear there is a storm in the offing."

"Joey out with the critters?"

"That he is. Off there in the woods somewhere," Mary said, pointing with her chin in the direction the boy had taken, as she hefted an oven of biscuits from the fire and set it aside to cool. "I expect he will have them bedded and be back soon."

And so he was. The fire burned low and glowed to ashes as the Smith camp slept. With the ribbon of dawn barely discernible in the east, Mary shook the girls and women awake, and rousted out the boys to fetch the stock.

But someone — Cornelius Lott, they expected, or someone under his orders — had been there before them. None of the

Smith cattle were anywhere in sight. After reporting the loss, the boys set out to search farther afield.

Mary stood forlorn beside her packed wagons. Lined up beside her like so many tenpins were Jane Wilson, Aunty Grinnels, Maggie Brysen, and the girls — Jerusha, Sarah, and Martha Ann.

The wagon master did not bother to tell Mary the train would not be waiting for her. Lott merely looked back and smiled as his lead wagon, first in the caravan on this last day of the journey, rolled past.

In keeping with Mary's prediction, the sky had clouded up overnight. Rather than the morning brightening as it should, it dimmed as heavy black clouds rolled over the crest of the Wasatch, threatening to boil over. And they did. With wagons strung out along the steep trail up the ridge, oxen bearing down under the load and bullwhackers urging them on, the storm broke.

Lightning flashed, the bolts raining down in overlapping arcs. Thunder cracked and rolled and boomed and echoed off the mountainsides. Rain fell in sheets, pouring onto the dusty road up the ridge and turning it into a quagmire. Panicked oxen thrashed and kicked and bucked and bolted, threatening to overturn wagons as the wheels slipped and slid and sank into the mud.

Fetching logs and rocks in a near terror, men, women, and children chocked wheels so the wagons wouldn't roll backward down the mountain. Drovers tugged and wrenched and jerked on draw chains and clevises and oxbows and yokes to free the panicked animals in an attempt to keep the wagons on their wheels, rather than toppled and tipped over. Once free, the uncontrollable cattle stampeded down the ridge and disappeared into the tempest.

The storm passed, the clouds thinned, and rays of sunlight sliced through, illuminating the chaos on the ridge. Curses, wailing, and cries of despair tumbled down the hill to where Mary and her charges crawled out from under dripping wagon covers.

They did not wait long before John and Joey, soaked and sodden, followed the Smith cattle and livestock out of the woods and into the campsite. Sheltered somewhat in groves of quaking aspen and patches of scrub oak, the animals had weathered the storm better than the hitched oxen exposed on the bare ridge.

"The brindle milk cow and her calf are missing, Miz Mary," John said, hat in hand. "And two of the sheep."

"That is as it may be. Once we reach the valley, we will come back to find them. Are these animals fit to work?" Mary said with a nod toward the cattle, ready to resume her duties as a bullwhacker on the emigrant trail.

"Yes'm," John said, and they set about the business of yoking the draft cattle to the wagons.

The oxen, the young steers, and the unlikely cow, long since accustomed to the yoke, huffed and grunted their way up Little Mountain, finding enough firm ground beside the rutted track to ease past the mired wagons.

Reaching the head of the train and Cornelius Lott's conveyances, disabled and helpless, Mary Smith did not return the wagon master's loathsome stare. She marched on by with all the dignity an unfit widow woman could muster, leading her unsuitable wagons, useless animals, and hodgepodge of a family, her eyes fixed on the trail ahead, the end of which she would reach by nightfall.

Rod Miller has won four Spur Awards from Western Writers of America, twice for short stories as well as for a novel (*Rawhide Robinson Rides the Range,* from Five Star) and a poem, and has also been a finalist in the same categories. His latest Five Star novels are *Rawhide Robinson Rides a Dromedary* and *Father unto Many Sons.*

■ ■ ■ ■

Ih-tedda's Son
by W. Michael Farmer

■ ■ ■ ■

Geronimo rolled a cigarette in an oak leaf. He lit it with a splinter from the iron stove's fire, smoked to the four directions, and then passed it to Ih-tedda. She smoked to the four directions, feeling the smoke bite the insides of her mouth and nose, but was pleased that her husband honored her this way. She handed the cigarette back, and waited with her hands folded across her belly, patient and ready to hear his serious business.

He finished the cigarette and tossed the remains into the low yellow flames flickering just inside the stove's open door. Outside, the winter wind swished through the tops of the tall pines, sounding like the surf at their last prison, Fort Pickens, on Santa Rosa Island. Here at Mount Vernon Barracks north of Mobile they at least had more privacy in their own cabins, but the air was still thick and wet like that at Fort Pickens and more and more of their friends and children were dying from mosquito bites and the worms the White Eyes called tuberculosis.

Geronimo spoke in the thin whispery voice of a vigorous old man. "Ih-tedda, I have decided you and Lenna must go." He waved a hand toward the door. "Leave me. Return to your mother and father in Mescalero."

Geronimo's words made no sense and she felt as if he were beating her. Ih-Tedda glanced at the slits of the old man's eyes, and the words from his thin, pitiless lips filled her mind with darkness. Only determination, the same unbending will that had carried him across many wars and the killing of many enemies, showed on his face. She stared at the dirt floor, her heart racing. She spoke slowly to keep her voice from wavering.

"Why do you say this? I had no man before you. You stole me from my people. I hated you then but learned to love you. I have been a good wife for you. Our place is always clean. You never have to wait to eat. I submit to you in our blankets when it's proper. Our daughter is a delight, whole and perfect and filled with laughter. Have mercy on us. I beg you not to send us away."

The pitiless lips said, "You must go. The Blue Coats may change their minds any time and kill us all. They plan to free the Mescaleros they took to Florida, but not the Chiricahuas and Mimbreños. You are Mescalero. I should be a Mescalero because I married you, but the White Eyes will never let me go. There is no reason for you to lose your life. I took you without courting you. Now you have a chance to be free. Take it! You are a fine wife. I never beat you much or hard. You nearly always please me. Our daughter, Lenna, is a good child, but if she stays in this bad air, this place of White Eye sickness, she will soon make the journey to the Happy Place and you will not be far behind her."

"Please, husband, I want to stay with you."

"Woman, you must go. That is all I have to say."

Ih-tedda hated the train. Black grit in its smoke made her dirty and its clank and rattle pounded against her ears all the way from Mobile to El Paso. The train arrived late and the wagons from Mescalero didn't have much time for the return drive before the sun began disappearing in a brilliant golden haze.

The light nearly gone, the little group

parked the wagons in a circle and made a cooking fire near a water tank filled by a creaking windmill. Charlie Smith, the old Mescalero scout, who was their leader, said to eat and rest. It would be a long drive to Mescalero the next day.

Ih-tedda's mother brought dried slices of baked mescal, blue juniper berries, and mesquite flour bread for them to eat. The mescal, sweet and sticky after it was warmed over the fire, filled Ih-tedda's memory with the good years she had at Mescalero. *Perhaps things will be better even without Geronimo. Maybe I can find a good husband at Mescalero to take care of Lenna and me.*

Her father took a bite of the mescal, chewed, and sniffed before saying, "Daughter, it's good my eyes see you again. Your husband has freed you from the Blue Coat prison. You come back to us without bride presents and have Lenna to care for because he stole you away. You must have a husband soon, one who can care for you. I think I know the man."

She frowned. "A husband so soon, Father? Can't I wait a little while? Who is this you know?"

A coyote yipped and was answered. Hearing the Trickster, source of many childhood stories, once more and smelling the burning

240

piñon cedar made her happy, but her father's words filled her with foreboding.

Staring into the dark, her father glanced at her and looked away. "Yes, it must be soon, or a bad reputation comes quick. You have come back to us and are now a rejected woman with a child. Few men want such a woman. I'll find you a good man when we reach Mescalero. You must accept him. I don't think there'll be others. That is all I have to say."

Coyote howled again, nearer and louder. In her despair, Ih-tedda wanted to answer him, but dared not. It would not be proper.

The wagons left their camp in the gray light of dawn. Gold poured on the mountain edges as the sun peeked above the horizon and then floated higher into the cold morning air. Ih-tedda, holding Lenna, sat between her mother and father, neither saying much as their wagon bounced along the road ruts to Mescalero. Seeing the desert again in the bright sunlight, even seeing it at the end of the Ghost Face Season, when the creosotes were thin, the mesquite had few leaves, and the yucca stalks stood tall and dry and shaking in the wind, stirred Ih-tedda to happiness. To again see the mountains in the gray distance and to smell the sage and dust after four years in the piney woods was a blessing from *Ussen*.

Night had settled cold and black when they reached her mother's tipi. After they unloaded the wagon, her father took the horse to rub down, feed, and water. Her mother built a little fire in the center of the tipi and began making them a meal.

The smoky smell of the tipi's interior, seeing the old blackened coffee pot and heavy iron stew kettle hanging over the little orange and red flickering fire, and touching the furs and tanned skins folded, stacked, and ready for use filled Ih-tedda's mind with a flood of memories from the good days in Mescalero when she was still her namesake, Young Girl.

Since leaving the train, Ih-tedda had not been alone with her mother to speak heart-to-heart about private matters. Her mother said, "I cried out to *Ussen* when they told me you had been stolen. I thought I would never see you again. Now you are here and *Ussen* has blessed us with your child. I think soon you will have a new man. Did the man who took you treat you well? Did he break any bones when he beat you?"

Lenna stirred in Ih-tedda's arms, yawning and chewing at her fist, then went back to sleep. "No, he never really beat me. The first time he took me he was gentle. I liked my man. But, to his enemies he showed no mercy. I have seen him smile and never look back after killing Mexicans. He sent me away because he wanted us free before the Blue Coats changed their minds and killed us all."

Grease dripping in the fire made a pleasant sizzle and its smell made Ih-tedda's mouth anxious for a piece of the beef her mother roasted. Of course, she and her mother couldn't eat until her father returned and had his fill. She hoped he would come soon, but memory said he never hurried.

"Why is Father so anxious to find me a man, any man, who will take me? I want to be free of a man for a while."

Her mother never lifted her eyes from her cooking. "Be quiet, Daughter. You have returned to us without a man. You have no husband. Now you must do as your father says."

"But my moon time is late. What if I carry another child? No one will want me."

Her mother smiled as she turned the meat. "Then all the more reason to take a man sooner rather than later. He won't know if the child is his or not as long as you are quiet." Ih-tedda opened her mouth to answer, but her mother shook her head. "Be quiet and do as I tell you."

The falling sun turned the rippling western clouds to purples, reds, and dark orange. Shafts of bright light flew through the tops of the tall pines to strike the far ridges in pools of yellow as a shadow appeared by the tipi door and a cough announced a visitor. Ih-tedda saw her father smile. *So, the one man on the entire reservation who will take me comes.*

Her father said in a loud voice, "Come. Our fire is warm and we have food. Join us."

The blanket over the tipi door lifted. A head covered in long gray hair and a face shadowed with many deep wrinkles pushed into the tipi, nodded at the women, and moved to sit down in the place of honor to the left of Ih-tedda's father. The man had crossed eyes, a broad nose, and thick smiling lips. Ih-tedda felt her stomach roll as though she had eaten bad meat. *No, Father. Please, not Old Cross Eyes.*

Old Cross Eyes and Ih-tedda's father smoked and made small talk about reservation politics and how hard the Ghost Face had been. At their first long pause in conversation, Ih-tedda, at her mother's nod, said,

"Does our guest have hunger? Will he eat now?"

Old Cross Eyes grinned. "Hmmph. Woman, you have light behind your eyes. My belly is empty."

Ih-tedda filled a gourd with a big slice of meat, wild potatoes, chilies, slices of mescal, mesquite beans, and crunchy acorn bread and handed it to Old Cross Eyes. Her mother handed a gourd to her father. Ih-tedda rocked Lenna in her arms while she and her mother sat back to wait until the men finished.

Old Cross Eyes emptied his gourd and handed it back to Ih-tedda. "Will our guest have more? There is plenty."

He shook his head. "My belly is full. You cook good. I like a woman who can cook."

Ih-tedda stared at Lenna sleeping in her arms. "My mother taught me well before I was taken." He wiped the grease from around his mouth and rubbed it on his boots with his blue-veined hands. From his Blue Coat scout jacket, he pulled tobacco and papers, rolled a cigarette, and with a twig from the fire, lighted it, smoked to the four directions, and then handed it to Ih-tedda's father, who smoked and returned it.

Old Cross Eyes crossed his arms and studied Ih-tedda and Lenna like they were a mare and filly he might buy or trade. "So, your divorced daughter, who cooks good, has left Geronimo? Her child is a girl? She is ready to take a new man?"

Ih-tedda's father looked at her with raised brows, his signal for her to answer. "Yes, I left Geronimo before the Blue Coats changed their minds and killed everyone. Yes, the child is a girl. She has two harvests."

"Did Geronimo beat you often?"

"No. Not much and not hard."

"I think you must keep your tipi clean and as I know already, cook good."

"I do."

"What is your child's name?"

"Lenna. Soon she will be off the cradle-board."

"Hmmph. The child looks well-cared-for despite being in prison with you and Geron-imo."

Old Cross Eyes turned to Ih-tedda's father. "I like your daughter. I see she already has a tipi set up near you. She has courage to leave the warrior Geronimo and come here with her child. She is divorced. Still, I offer you a good pony and a rifle for her. Every moon the Blue Coats give me eight dollars because I'm too old to scout anymore. Eight dollars every moon is enough for us to live on, if she doesn't waste it. I'll treat her with respect and we'll stay in her tipi nearby to be close to you and serve you. Will you accept my offer, Father of Ih-tedda?"

Ih-tedda knew her father's answer before he opened his mouth. He had not expected to get anything for her. Old Cross Eyes was smarter than he looked. Ih-tedda wanted to take Lenna and leave, go anywhere, do any work, do anything not to be tied to this old man with ugly eyes. Only her late moon time stopped her from leaving. She should not be alone in the mountains, even in the Season of Large Fruit, to birth a child. The risk was too high that it would die if she had no help. After the child was born, she would have two children to care for. She needed to stay near her mother.

As it was proper, her father thought for a while. He then crossed his arms and looked across the fire at Ih-tedda, and seeing nothing to discourage his answer, said, "I accept your generous offer. I give you Ih-tedda to be your woman."

Up the ridge a wolf howled in the cold darkness and was answered by another. Ih-tedda kept her face a mask of indifference, but she wanted to howl, too.

Old Cross Eyes grinned. "Good. I have horses I have promised to sell in Tularosa.

247

Ih-tedda, I will come to your tipi in three suns as the sun goes into the mountains and we will begin our life together."

"I will welcome you in three days. Your evening meal will be ready."

Old Cross Eyes nodded, "*Ussen* blesses me."

Ih-tedda waited. The shadows outside were growing long, the light from the fading sun dimming. Her first meal for her new husband was ready, her acceptance complete of the inevitability of becoming the woman of Old Cross Eyes while expecting her second child by Geronimo. Old Cross Eyes had taken her just in time. She might fool him into believing the child was his and puff him up in his assumed virility to ensure he took good care of her. Ih-tedda smiled and shook her head. *Men are so strong and powerful, but like saddled ponies, are so easy to guide — all, that is, except Geronimo.*

A shadow by the door appeared with a throat-clearing cough.

"A tipi and your new woman are ready. Come and eat." The door blanket raised and Old Cross Eyes stepped in to stand across the fire from her. He wore new canvas pants. His Blue Coat jacket looked freshly brushed and clean, and he held his ancient campaign hat between his hands.

"Woman, I have come. Will you take me?"

"I will take you. Come, sit by the fire and I will serve you the good things I have cooked for our first night together."

He unbuttoned his coat and, pulling it off, handed it to her. She folded it and laid it at the top of their blanket. He stepped around the fire and with a groan caused by stiff, arthritic knees, eased down beside her. "Hmmph. I have found a good woman. It is warm in her lodge when the wind is cold and her lodge smells of fine food." His eyes followed her every move as she filled his gourd with venison, berries, chilies, potatoes, and dried mescal slices that she had carefully steamed back to their original cooked sweetness. She handed the gourd to him and sat back to wait, but he shook his head and waved a hand toward her. "Woman, join me in your feast. I've thought about you every day since your father told me you were leaving Geronimo. Your mother taught you good cooking, and I can see Geronimo has trained you well as a wife. I'm a lucky man to have you. Come, eat with me."

Ih-tedda filled her gourd, poured them both cups of coffee, and sat down beside him, demurely folding her legs under her fine, beaded buckskin shift. She had to admit Old Cross Eyes had manners. He made very little sound eating.

After they finished and she had cleared her cooking fire, he rolled a cigarette, lighted it from a fire twig, smoked to the four directions, and gave it to her, and she too smoked to the four directions. She returned the cigarette back to him. He took another draw and tossed what was left into the fire.

He looked at her with his rheumy old man eyes and smiled. "Now that you're my woman, the People will want to call you a name so everyone knows you are mine. I think a good name for you is Katie, Katie Cross Eyes. Since I have given you my name, I think the People should just call me Old Boy. Do you agree?"

Yes. Everyone must know that by taking me, you no longer have ugly eyes. It is I, your woman, who will carry them with your name. "Yes, I agree. Call me Katie Cross Eyes. Old Boy is a good name."

He took a swallow of hot coffee and nodded toward Lenna's cradleboard. "Lenna sleeps peacefully. Good. Does she do this often?"

"She is a good child. She never cries. I think we left the prison camp before its cold, wet air could make her sick."

"Good. I'm glad she's healthy. Tell me again how many harvests has she?"

"Two. By the Season of Large Leaves she will be off the cradleboard. She can already walk, but she does not balance good enough to be on her own without me for support."

"Hmmph. When she leaves the cradle-board, you will have much training for her. It's important that she be taught Apache ways while she's very young. Then she won't forget when she's grown."

Katie looked at her hands in her lap. *Every woman knows this, old man. Why do you tell me?* "My man is wise. This I will do."

Old Boy rolled another cigarette and lighted it for the pleasure of a smoke. He offered Katie a smoke, but she shook her head and looked away. "Too much smoke makes the inside of my nose sore." Taking a long draw, he looked up and blew his smoke toward the top of the tipi.

"I'm not too old to make a child. I would like for us to have one. Will you give me a child?"

Katie looked at her hands in her lap, her heart thumping with relief. *Ussen is good to me. I thank him.* "I am your woman. It is proper for a woman to give her man chil-dren, and I will give you yours."

He smiled and nodded before he took another draw and blew it out the side of his mouth. "I have a good woman. When can we begin? When Lenna is off the cradleboard, will you be ready to make another child?"

Katie stared at the fire as though deep in thought before she turned to Old Boy. "Geronimo did not lie with me after Lenna was born. He preferred his other wife, Zi-yeh, even when I was ready for him to come to me."

The breeze in the treetops paused and on a near ridge, Coyote, the Trickster, yipped to his brothers.

"My moon time passed just before we left the prison. I'm ready to make you a child. Will you come to me this night?"

A smile stretched across the face of Old Cross Eyes. "Truly, I'm a blessed man. I will come to you this night and many others. First, I must see about my horses. I will be back."

Katie smiled and nodded. "I wait for you." She knew Old Boy just wanted to find a place to make water. She checked Lenna, and then pulled off her beaded moccasins and buckskin shift, rolled them up, and laid them by his Blue Coat before sliding under their cold blankets trembling not from the cold, but worry that Old Boy might not be able to consummate their marriage or might somehow learn she already carried a child, feel cheated the child was not his, and treat her in a bad way.

By the time Old Boy returned, the fire had burned down, and glowing orange coals cast dim light in the tipi. He held his hands over the fire's heat before he undressed and slid under the blanket with her. The shock of his cold body reminded her of the ice-rimmed creek where she had bathed early that morning. "You are cold. Lie close to me for a while. The blanket and I will warm you."

"Katie Cross Eyes, you are very good to your man. Soon I'm warm enough to come to you."

He held her in his arms for a while, neither of them moving. She noticed he had the same old man smell, only stronger, as Geronimo. He was gentle with her and she thought they had a good first night. It took him three or four days before he was ready to come to her again, and for this she thanked *Ussen*. After half a moon together, she told him her moon time was late and that she believed she carried their child and must wait for further intimacy until after it was born. Hearing this, Old Boy strutted around like a White Eye rooster, his chest out, saying to the young men that they should hope they were as much a man as he when they were his age.

Katie Cross Eyes had a son, born early, she said, in the Season of Large Fruit. She went to the agency to register the child as her son so they qualified for more rations as a family. The agent smiled at the little girl holding on to her long calico skirt and motioned Katie, carrying the baby on its cradleboard, to a chair across from his desk.

The agent verified she lived with the retired scout named Old Boy, that her name was Katie Cross Eyes, and that Geronimo was the father of her daughter. Then he said, "When was your son born?"

Katie looked him in the eye. It was a custom the White Eyes followed to show they spoke truth even if the Apaches believed it was rude to stare at someone. "My son was born in the Season of Large Fruit in the moon I think you name August."

The agent made tracks on an agency paper with his little spear dipped in black water. He paused a moment, scratched at his chin, and said, "You were here seven months before the child was born. Are you certain the child is Old Boy's and not Geronimo's?"

Katie stared in his eyes and nodded. "I am certain Old Boy is the child's father."

The agent nodded. "And what will be the name of the child."

She swallowed and again stared at the agent's eyes. "My son's name is Robert . . . Robert Cross Eyes."

The agent made marks on the paper and then read the tracks back and asked if what they said was correct. Katie nodded. He laid the paper on the desk in front of her, pointed to a place near the bottom, and said, "Make your mark like when you draw rations." She made her mark and he made his tracks beside it.

"Congratulations, Katie Cross Eyes. Your son is now officially on our records as Robert Cross Eyes and he will count in your family's ration allotment."

She smiled and nodded and walked out into the bright sunlight under a brilliant blue sky.

Robert was a bright child and did well at the agency school. When he was fifteen, the agent, a kind man who understood Apache culture, asked Katie if she would agree to let him send the boy to the advanced Indian school at Chilocco, Oklahoma. Katie told the agent she had to discuss it with Robert before she could agree. She knew feeble Old Boy would want whatever she wanted.

That afternoon as Katie prepared her evening meal, she thought back over the years. When sitting by the evening fire, Lenna and Robert heard Old Boy tell of his scouting days. Their eyes had grown big the first time they heard the story of how the feared and famous warrior Geronimo had stolen their mother, carried her off, and married her when she was Ih-tedda. Katie told them that Geronimo was Lenna's father, but Old Boy was Robert's father. Robert's frown showed his disappointment that the famous Geronimo was not his father also, but a sharp look from Katie kept him from saying anything that showed any disrespect for Old Boy.

Katie smiled and shook her head, remembering how excited Lenna, who yearned to meet her father, had become when they let her go as a Mescalero representative to the Apache Village in the Indian Exhibit at the 1904 Saint Louis Exposition two years before. Geronimo would be there to represent the Chiricahuas. Lenna, a grown woman of fifteen, quiet and beautiful, was in high spirits when she returned from Saint Louis. She told Katie how thrilled she was to meet her father and he to see her. He was surprised when she told him Ih-tedda had given birth to a son the same year she returned to Mescalero. Unknown to Katie, Lenna, counting the months, told Robert when she returned that he might be Geronimo's son but begged him not to say anything to Katie or Old Boy. Within a week he told Katie that Lenna had said Geronimo was his father and wanted to know if it was true. Katie, feeling her face flush with anger, swore Old Boy was Robert's father and told the boy not to ask her about it again, but she saw the same outrage in his eyes she had often seen in an angry Geronimo's years ago. *It is a hard thing to lie to your child, but harder still to lie to a husband of fifteen years.*

Katie and Robert ate their evening meal alone. She picked at her food, and then laid her fork down. "I spoke with Agent Carroll today and need to make a hard decision. Carroll says your mind is bright and that you should go to the advanced school at Chilocco in Oklahoma, and maybe later go on to the Carlisle School. He asked me to let him send you there. I told him I would speak with you first. Do you want to go to Chilocco?"

Robert, his eyes sparkling, nodded. "Yes. I want to go to Chilocco. I would learn much there, and I have looked at maps. Fort Sill, where Geronimo lives with the other Chiricahuas, is only about two hundred miles south of Chilocco, about half a day's train ride. He goes as a famous man to be seen at national expositions and shows. He even rode his fine horse in the inaugural parade of President Theodore Roosevelt. I could visit Geronimo during a weekend by riding the train. Despite what you say, I believe he's my father. I don't look anything like Old Boy. I look like Lenna. I look like my sister, daughter of Geronimo. I feel the pull of his life force. Please, Mother, tell me if Geronimo is my father. I want to know. I have to know."

Katie felt as if a knife had plunged into her heart. She bowed her head and shook it. Water lay at the corner of her eyes, but the dams held.

She knew Robert had seen the edge of her tears when he slapped the table so hard it rattled the tableware, and he shouted. "I knew it!"

Katie raised her face and stared at him with a look she knew would be burned forever in his memory and making his moment of truth feel hollow. "I have not told you it is true. You still do not know. Keep your opinions to yourself in this place. Do not shame Old Boy with your wishing."

She watched him. Defeated once more, he slumped back in his chair staring at her, certain knowledge of his true father so near and yet so far away.

In August Robert told Katie and Old Boy goodbye and climbed on the wagon Agent Carroll drove to the train station in Tularosa, there to begin the long, meandering trip to Chilocco, Oklahoma.

A few weeks later, Katie stood at the door of Agent Carroll. Smiling, he motioned her in to a chair. "Hello, Katie. How's your family? Robert liking Chilocco?"

She folded her hands across her belly and looked out the window. "My family is good. Old Boy still can walk with his stick and is strong for a very old man. Robert writes us nothing since he left."

Carroll smiled and nodded. "He's busy learning many new things. He'll write soon. How can I help you?"

She looked him in the eye. "I need to correct an error in your records."

Carroll raised his brows. "Oh? And what might that be?"

Her eyes stayed locked on his. "Robert

Cross Eyes should be Robert Geronimo."

He winced. "Is there anything else?"

She nodded. "Yes. Please send him tracks on paper that say your records now show he is Robert Geronimo."

"I will, but . . ."

She stood. "That is all I have to say."

W. Michael Farmer has published short stories in anthologies, and award-winning essays. His novels include: *Killer of Witches,* 2016 Will Rogers Medallion Award winner; *Mariana's Knight,* 2017 New Mexico–Arizona Book Award winner for Historical Fiction; and *Blood of the Devil,* 2017 New Mexico–Arizona Book Award finalist for Adventure–Drama and Historical Fiction.

■ ■ ■ ■

ACES AND EIGHTS
BY MICHAEL R. RITT

■ ■ ■ ■

No one had struck it rich in Nuggettown for some time now. I always figured that the name must have been somebody's idea of a joke. Nuggets weren't exactly jumping out of the ground, and any resemblance between this place and something as civilized as an actual town was purely accidental.

The Lady Belle Mine was the only one in town that had produced any significant quantities of gold. The rest of the outfits were small claims, like the one belonging to me and Pete, using rockers and sluice boxes that barely showed enough color to keep the owner of the claim in grub and liquor money on a day-to-day basis.

To be fair, I guess that the town wasn't all that bad. It was young and it was rough, but it had a future. There was talk of the Colorado Central Railroad building a spur line up the mountain to haul the ore from the Lady Belle. We had four saloons, a blacksmith, the assay office, a general store, and three eating houses. We also had a hotel being built, which, when finished, would be the biggest building in Nuggettown. We even had a Methodist circuit rider come through once a month to preach a sermon to the miners and sing hymns.

The street that ran through the center of town wasn't anything more than a mud-filled, rutted path that the freight wagons used to haul ore down the side of the mountain to Denver, and haul supplies back up. An overnight soaker had left about six inches of mud that sucked at my boots as I waded from one side of the street to the other. I had checked out most of his usual hangouts, but I hadn't found my buddy, Pete, anywhere.

Sloshing through the mud, I made my way across the street to Otto's Saloon. Being constructed of rough-hewn lumber, Otto's was one of a dozen buildings in Nuggettown. The rest of the town's dwellings were old Army tents sold as surplus to prospectors after the war. Otto's was currently the largest building in town, having a second story of rooms that were mostly rented out for an hour at a time. It was a nice day out, being early June, and someone had propped open the door with an old wooden beer crate with "Schueler & Coors" painted on the side.

There is a particular aroma that is characteristic of anyplace that men congregate to socialize. A strangely inviting mixture of beer, smoke, unwashed bodies, and horses hung in the air. A saloon was a damned fine place and I took a deep breath as I stood in the doorway for a few seconds to let my eyes adjust to the dim light inside.

I heard him before I saw him. That is, I heard the commotion, and where there's commotion, Pete Canfield is usually right in the middle of it.

"You heard what I said, you damned cheat. I want my money back." The guy sitting across the card table from Pete pushed his chair back suddenly and stood to his feet. The other two gents at the table hurriedly gathered their winnings and stepped back out of the way. Pete sat where he was, his chair tilted back, calmly looking at his accuser, who had a .44 caliber Smith & Wesson Russian tucked into his belt.

Pete let his chair fall forward. Resting his hands on the edge of the table he started to laugh. "You think I need to cheat to beat you at cards, you sorry sack? We all knew you only had a pair of sixes! You're the one who called the bet. Consider your loss the price of a poker lesson."

I had seen this guy around a few times before. His name was Kenny Bassett, but he went by the name of Bass. He was maybe a couple years older than Pete, who was twenty-five, which would have made Bass about my age. He didn't work any claim that I knew of. He just hung around town playing cards and drinking and running his big mouth. He fancied himself some kind of tough guy and liked to flash his gun around, but, to be honest, I never saw him use it for anything other than decoration. Sometimes all it took was some tough talk and the butt end of a gun sticking out of your belt to bully people into submission. Pete wasn't one of those people.

I heard Bass say, "I'll give you 'til the count of three."

Where did this guy come from? He must be reading too many of those dime novels.

Bass stood there with his arms hanging loosely at his sides, poised, as though he were about to do something stupid. Then, sure enough, he did it.

"One . . ."

Pete pushed out with his arms, causing the table to smash into Bass's legs. The sudden impact forced Bass off-balance, and he wound up sprawled facedown across the table. Cards and chips and beer glasses were strewn everywhere. Pete, who was still in his chair, stood up, grabbed Bass by the collar, and dragged him off of the table.

Bass hit the floor and rolled onto his back. That's when I saw the look in his eyes. It was the same look that I had seen once before when this fellow I knew down in Texas miscalculated the amicable nature of a horse he had just mounted. That horse jumped up and arched his back, then took to bucking and kicking like a grasshopper on a hot griddle. The guy wound up backside-down in a water trough with a "what-in-the-hell-just-happened" look on his face. That was how Bass looked now. Things had not gone as he had expected them to.

Pete bent over and grabbed Bass by the shirt front. He was kneeling with one knee pressed into Bass's stomach, which made it difficult for Bass to take a breath.

"Here's another lesson for you. There's no such thing as a fair fight, you damned idiot." With that said, Pete drew back his right arm and pounded Bass in the face three times in rapid succession, then stood up and waited for him to get to his feet. But Bass was out of it. He laid there, dazed and moaning, blood flowing from his nose and a split in his lip.

"Are you about done here?" I asked as I walked up behind Pete.

He turned and flashed a smile that would have made Lilly or any of the other girls in Otto's melt. I'd seen it happen many times. Pete was young and lean with weathered features that made him look a little older than he actually was. He had dark hair and brown eyes that he said he got from his mother. She was half Mexican. He cut quite a swell with the ladies.

"Oh, I think that school's out for the day." He reached down and yanked the gun out of Bass's belt. Bass flinched a little but he didn't make any other move. Pete walked over to the bar and dropped the gun into a brass spittoon that was in desperate need of attending to. Then the two of us headed outside.

We stood on the boardwalk in front of Otto's while Pete rolled a cigarette and struck a match to it.

"You know," I said, "you could at least make an effort to go twenty-four hours without getting into some kind of trouble. He could have shot you, and you're not even wearing a gun."

"No, but you are," Pete said with a grin. "I saw you walk into the bar."

268

"So you were counting on me, once again, to pull your sorry butt out of the fire."

"Hell, there was no fire there to speak of," he said with a shrug. "One of these days, Bass is going to get his self or someone else killed. He should be thanking me for schooling him in the manly art of pugilism."

"Where did you ever learn a five-dollar word like 'pugilism'? Are you fixing to start a school and be a schoolmarm?"

Pete smiled and threw a playful jab that knocked the hat off of my head. I returned a couple punches of my own that nearly caused him to stumble right off of the boardwalk and into the muddy road.

Picking up my hat, we found a relatively shallow place in the mud and started across the street. We were almost to the other side when Pete, who was leading the way, turned suddenly and grabbed hold of my arm like he had just remembered something that couldn't wait.

"You know, Ben, they hung McCall a few months ago."

"You mean Jack McCall, the coward who shot Hickok last year up in Deadwood? Yeah, I heard about that. What of it?"

"Do you remember the cards that old Wild Bill was holding when McCall shot him in the back of the head?"

"They say it was two pair . . . aces and eights. All black."

Pete looked around to make sure no one could hear. He took on a serious expression that was a rarity for him. If I hadn't known Pete any better, I would have guessed that something had spooked him. He lowered his voice to a whisper. "Those are the same cards I was holding in my last hand. What do you suppose that it means?"

I must have looked a little fearful because he laughed and gave me a wink and a slap on the shoulder. "I'm just joshing with you, Ben. You know I don't believe in any of that nonsense."

"Then you weren't holding aces and eights?"

"Oh, I had them all right. I just don't believe that 'dead man's hand' superstition stuff." He turned and took a big step across the last rut, and stood there on the other side of the road.

People had gone to referring to aces and eights as the "dead man's hand" on account of Wild Bill Hickok holding those cards when he was killed. I don't mind telling you, I was a little spooked by the whole thing. My ma used to read to me from a book of Shakespeare when I was a kid. There was this one line from a play where this guy named Hamlet says to his friend, "There are more things in heaven and earth, Horatio, than are dreamt of in your philosophy." That line always stuck with me. There are some things that we just don't know. There are connections between people and events, causes and effects that we don't see. Pete, on the other hand, didn't go in for any of this "superstitious nonsense," as he put it.

I exhaled a deep sigh and joined Pete in front of the assay office. "I wish you hadn't of told me that. It makes it all the more difficult to tell you what I know."

"What are you talking about?"

"It's why I was looking for you. I've got some news you need to hear."

"What news?"

I kicked the toe of my boot against the side of the boardwalk to loosen some of the mud; then I repeated the process with the other boot. "I just got back from Denver with a load of lumber for the Lady Belle. I saw Parker. He's on his way here."

Pete looked as though I had slapped him right across his face. "Parker is coming to Nuggettown? Today?"

"Yep. Wasn't very far behind me. Should be here anytime."

"What the hell is he coming here now for? He's not supposed to be here for another week!" Pete sounded aggrieved, as though Parker had jumped the gun and cheated him somehow. I wasn't sure if his question was rhetorical or not, so I ignored it.

Suddenly, the color kind of drained from Pete's face as another thought occurred to him. "You don't suppose that Sam knows Parker is on his way, do you?"

"That's what I mean to tell you. Sam is with Parker. They're both on their way here. They said that they had given you plenty of time, and since you weren't coming to Denver, they were going to come to you. They said to tell you that your time is up."

Pete started shaking. He sat down on a bench that was there in front of the building. Resting both elbows on his knees, he hung his head and sighed. A long moment of silence followed while he let the news sink in.

After a while, he sat straight up and took a deep breath. He turned to look at me with eyes wide and a sarcastic grin on his face. "Damn it all, Ben. You're a veritable fountain of good news today, aren't you? Anything else I need to know? Has my horse been snake bit? Am I dying of consumption? You might as well get it all out in the open."

I never did like being the person to carry

bad news to another, especially when there wasn't any way to help share the burden. "Don't shoot the messenger, Pete. You knew this day was coming. The two of them have been looking forward to this ever since you shot off your big mouth to Sam."

Pete jumped up like he had sat on a burr. "What was I supposed to do? Sam had me in a corner and called me a coward. I had to say something."

Pete started pacing the boardwalk. Then, in an all too characteristic show of drama, he threw his arms up into the air, a look of bewilderment on his face. But that was Pete. Everything was a theatrical production with him. He'd scratch himself on some barbed wire and he'd be sure that he'd need to see the doc to get it stitched up. If he got in a fight with one guy while playing cards, the next day it would be three guys that he "whooped," and whooped soundly. To talk to Pete, he always had the fastest horse in the territory, could play cards better, drink more, and shoot straighter than anyone else.

"What was I supposed to do?" he repeated.

"Well, there's no way to beat the devil around the stump now. You don't say those kinds of things to Sam unless you intend to follow through with it."

273

Pete looked hurt by my words. "I have every intention of following through with it. I just thought that I would have a little more time. You know . . . a little more fun."

That was the thing with Pete. He never really took anything seriously. I was always the responsible, level-headed one. It was pretty much the pattern of our relationship. Pete would do something reckless and get himself in trouble. Then I would come along behind him and clean up the mess. Before the dust had even settled, Pete would land in trouble somewhere else, and I'd bail him out again. But he was my friend.

My folks hailed from Tennessee but moved to Texas when a neighbor of theirs, Davy Crockett, told my pa that fighting Mexicans would be a heap more exciting than plowing up rocks. Crockett had just finished serving six years as a United States congressman, so he probably figured that it was time to go somewhere where he stood a chance of actually getting something done.

Pa had more farmer than fighter in him, but he did like the idea of moving to Texas. So in the spring of 1836, my ma and pa settled on a little farm near Nacogdoches in the eastern hill country. I was born in 1850, the youngest of four boys and two girls, all born and raised Texans.

At the age of fifteen, I left home and drifted west and south, working on some of the biggest cattle spreads in Texas, including the Allen and King ranches.

I met Pete three years ago while pushing cattle from Waco to Abilene. We hit it off right from the start. Everyone on the drive liked Pete. You could never get a lick of work out of him. He was irresponsible and a bit of a braggart, but he always had a joke or a story handy. He was never dull to be with and he was generous to a fault. He would spend his last nickel to buy you a drink.

We wound up in Colorado because Pete had the notion that he might strike it rich prospecting. We told folks that we worked our claim together, but the reality of it was that at any given time I would be the one busting rocks or panning or shoveling gravel into the sluice. Pete would be lying on the ground chewing on a stem of grass with his hat pulled down over his eyes to keep the sun out. He'd lie there, oblivious to the work that I was doing, regaling me with stories of his exploits with the women he had known or the scrapes that he had been in.

Eventually, I gave up the claim and went to work as a freight hauler for the Lady Belle. Pete manages to get by with his card playing, horse racing, or whatever other diversions he can concoct to help separate Nuggettown's miners and prospectors from the fruits of their labor.

Pete stood there with his hands on his hips, looking east out of town along the muddy road that wound its way through the aspen and white pine, down the mountainside and out onto the eastern plains. He looked the way a man looks when something that he has been running from is about to catch up to him. It wasn't fear. I had seen Pete scared before. This wasn't it. It was more like resignation.

After a minute, he turned to me again. "If Sam and Parker are coming here today, then I guess this is as good a day as any to get it done with."

We had taken about three steps, turned the corner of the assay office, and there he was. Ezra Parker stood there in front of us, casually leaning against the corner of the building as though he had been there for some time. He held a cigar in one hand and a lit match in the other. Instead of lighting the cigar, however, he let the match fall and then ground the toe of his boot into it to extinguish the flame.

He spoke conversationally, as though the three of us were standing at the bar in Otto's, sipping beers together and talking about the weather. "Hello, boys."

Parker was an imposing figure in his mid-fifties, with keen, cold gray eyes that contrasted sharply with his all-black ensemble; from his low-crowned, flat-brimmed Boss Stetson, to a pair of knee-high cavalry boots. A black frock coat covered his six-foot, two-inch frame, and beneath the coat was a Colt .45 Peacemaker that had been broken in years earlier while scouting for General Crook. He had been with Colonel Reynolds up on the Powder River in his campaign against the Northern Cheyenne and had gotten a Sioux arrow in his leg during the Battle of the Rosebud. The arrow had left him with a slight limp that, on anyone else, might make them appear frail. But on Parker, it made him look seasoned, like a hard-earned battle scar.

He held up his cigar for us to see. "I know it's a nasty habit. It's one I've been trying to free myself of." He placed the cigar into an inside coat pocket. "But I admit; sometimes I miss the smell of them."

Pete hadn't moved an inch.

Parker took a step closer and addressed his remarks directly to him. "You've got a nasty habit too, son. It's the habit of not taking responsibility for your actions and your words. That's a pattern of behavior that needs to end now . . . today. I aim to help you out with that."

He took another step closer so that he was within arm's length of Pete. His gray eyes had a way of burning into you like ice on your skin on a hot August day. "Sam and I will meet you at the peach orchard outside of town. You've got one hour to ready yourself. It will be Sam's show, but if you don't show up, it'll be me coming to look for you."

Anyone who figured that this might be a good time for Pete to hightail it out of town and hide out in the mountains for a few days didn't know anything about Parker. He had been one of the army's top scouts, and folks said that he could track a butterfly through a heavy fog. Running wasn't an option.

Pete stood tall and spoke calmly. There was no malice in his words. No fear. No bragging, haughty spirit. Instead, there was a maturity and an acceptance of the way things were that was foreign to the way that Pete usually handled himself. He looked Parker square in the eyes. "I'll be there, but I'll need a couple of hours to settle up a few matters."

Parker pulled his watch from his vest

pocket to check the time. "All right, then. One o'clock at the peach orchard. I'm gonna take you at your word, son. Don't disappoint me."

The two of us stood frozen in our tracks as we watched Parker turn and walk away. The sound of his boots on the wooden boardwalk was accented by the "ta-THUMP, ta-THUMP" of his game leg.

I got to thinking about those aces and eights. "What are you going to do, Pete? Are you sure that you want to go through with this? You know what it means, don't you?" I think at this point I was even more worried than Pete was, and I wasn't the one with the prospect of having Parker gunning for me. More than one man had found out the hard way that Parker's gun wasn't there as a fashion statement.

"I know what it means, Ben. It means that I face up to Sam, or I will have to face Parker. Either way, it'll never be the same after today."

"I'll back whatever play you make, but you gotta be sure it's what you want." I waited a moment longer for Pete to make his decision. When you're stuck having to make a decision that you don't want to make, sometimes it's best to let your instincts take over and not give it too much thought.

Thinking a thing to death can drive a man crazy, especially a man like Pete Canfield, who generally acted first and thought about the consequences later — if at all.

The whistle over at the Lady Belle blew, signaling the shift change for the miners. Up the street somewhere, a dog started howling in protest to the shrill of the whistle, making for an eerie kind of symphony that echoed off of the mountain and disappeared down into the valley.

Pete looked at me and I could see in his eyes that he had made up his mind. "I should have taken care of Sam months ago. I should never have let it get this far. It's time I did the right thing."

He removed his hat and ran his fingers up his forehead and through his hair. Then he used his hat to brush away some of the dust that had settled on his pants. "I've got some goodbyes to say down to Otto's, to Lilly and some of the girls. Then I'm gonna put on some clean duds so I'm looking my best. Why don't you meet me out at the claim in a couple of hours?"

He put his hand on my shoulder and smiled. "Don't worry none about it. Things will work out. They always do for me, right?"

Pete and I agreed to meet at the claim at a quarter of one to ride out to the peach orchard together. Then he turned on his heels and headed back to Otto's.

The time came and I met Pete where we had staked our claim along the river on the outskirts of town like we had agreed. I sat there on my horse and watched as he came out of the tent all bathed and clean-shaven and wearing a new suit. Where in the world he had gotten a suit I couldn't imagine, but he did it. Around his waist he had a fancy Cheyenne styled Mexican Loop gun belt with a floral design worked into the leather. Protruding out of the holster was a pearl-handled Colt.

He came out brushing the dust from his hat. Slicking his hair back and placing his hat on his head, he asked, "How do I look?"

"Like the guest of honor at a funeral," I joshed.

In his best dramatic fashion, Pete clutched at his chest as though in pain. "Well, thank you kindly for those words of encouragement. I guess I don't need Parker slinging lead at me with a friend like you around."

Untying his horse from the aspen limb he had been hitched to, he grabbed hold of the saddle horn and threw his leg up and over, landing in the saddle without touching the stirrups.

"I am your best friend, Pete, and I'll ride

with you down to the peach orchard or up into the mountains if that is what you want. But, truth be known . . . I'm proud of you. You're doing the right thing."

The two of us rode side by side on our way to the peach orchard, which grew on the southern end of town. Neither of us said anything, but we both noticed how empty and quiet the streets seemed. By this time, everyone had heard what was going to happen and folks were making their way to the orchard to see the show. I wondered what it was about a situation like this that brought out the perverse curiosity of people. The same thing would happen at a hanging. People would drive for hours and make a holiday out of watching a man get his neck stretched. We passed several people on the way who, for whatever reason, had decided to stay in town. Each one waved and shouted, "Good luck, Pete," as we passed by. Some just laughed.

Approaching the livery on the edge of town, we saw a man dipping his bandanna into a horse trough and washing his face. He looked our way as we rode past. It was Bass. He had a nasty black eye that was almost swollen shut, and a split lower lip. He glared at Pete. "I hope you get everything you have coming to you, you son of a bitch." Pete rode by without acknowledging his remark or even his presence.

We could see and hear all of the hullabaloo while we were still a ways off. Some of Lilly's girls were decorating the little orchard with flowers and hanging streamers from the limbs of the peach trees, which were in full bloom. The saloons in town had hauled out some of their chairs in a wagon, and they were being unloaded and set up for the people who were there to witness the occasion. There were tables with food set out, and Silas Gant was tuning up his fiddle for the dance that was to follow.

Parker stood there waiting. His coat was unbuttoned and the sides were pushed back. The sun glinted off of the cylinder of the Peacemaker that hung in the holster at his side.

Pete and I brought our horses to a halt and dismounted. I saw Pete's legs buckle a little when he stepped out of the stirrups. I thought about reaching out to steady him, but I didn't want to cause him any embarrassment. I've got to give him credit. He composed himself, stood up tall, took a deep breath, and puffing out his chest, walked right up to Parker.

Parker gave Pete a quick once-over, noticing the way that Pete's gun belt was rigged for a cross draw. "Are you ready for this?"

"I'm ready," Pete replied. "I should have taken care of Sam months ago."

A smile lit the face of the Reverend Ezra Parker, as he held out his hand. "That's what I wanted to hear, son. That's exactly what I wanted to hear."

Samantha Ann Murphy stood under a little impromptu archway that someone had made and painted white and hung with wildflowers. She wore a store-bought, white chiffon dress that she must have picked up in Denver. Her red hair hung loosely over her shoulders and made me think of lava flowing down the sides of a snow-covered mountain. She was already four months along but had barely begun to show.

Sam's father, Thomas Murphy, owned the Lady Belle, along with two other mines between Denver and Colorado Springs. He hadn't approved of Pete courting his little girl, but when he found out that she was with child, he changed his tune, pushing for a wedding so his grandchild wouldn't be born a bastard. He even offered Pete a job as a foreman in the Lady Belle to make sure that he could provide for Sam and the baby. For the past three months, he had been trying to get Pete down to his mansion in Denver so he and Sam could tie the knot, all to no avail. It was actually the Methodist preacher Ezra Parker who came up with the plan to take the wedding to Nuggettown.

"Isn't she a sight?" Pete was transfixed.

"That she is." I agreed.

"I don't know why I dreaded this so much — even if she did goad me into proposing, calling me a coward. All I've ever had to worry about is me. A wife and family is a big responsibility."

Pete and I joined Parker and Sam beneath the little archway. Pete took Sam by the hand. "You sure are beautiful. I'm sorry that it has taken me so long to come to my senses. From this day forward, I won't disappoint you ever again. That's my promise."

Sam struggled to hold back the tears that gathered in the corners of her eyes. Smiling, she placed her hand gently on the side of Pete's face. "I love you, Pete, but I don't want you to have any regrets. If you are not committed to this all of the way, then walk away now. No one will stop you."

Pete bent down and kissed her. "My only regret is not marrying you sooner."

Reverend Parker opened his Bible. "Are the two of you ready?"

Placing his hand on Sam's stomach, Pete answered, "The *three* of us are ready."

"Let's get started then. Dearly beloved . . ."

The reception that followed the wedding was a real shindig. The couple was well liked in the community, and the whole town was happy to see Pete finally do the right thing by Sam. Everyone was dancing or milling around, conversing and enjoying the mountain air, the clear skies, and the June sunshine.

I was leaning against one of the wagons with a cup of cider in my hands when Parker approached. "It was a real nice service, Reverend."

Parker flinched a little at the title and then chuckled.

"I'm not quite used to that yet. I have been called 'Captain' for so long, this 'Reverend' stuff is pretty new to me."

"I never really thought much about it," I said, "but I guess a lot of preachers were something else before they took up preaching."

"That's true. Preaching is a calling, but not everyone gets the call at the same time in their lives. For me, it was a pretty late development . . . and an unexpected one. It might be a cliché, but it's true that the Lord does work in mysterious ways. This was my first time officiating at a wedding."

"Well, I think you did a bang-up job."

"Thank you, Ben. I appreciate that."

"I'm curious, though, if you don't mind me asking. What would you have done if Pete hadn't of decided to do the right thing? Suppose he had hightailed it out for the hills?"

The Reverend Parker got thoughtful for a moment. "The Bible talks about the man of faith actually being two men. There's the old man with the old habits and old way of doing things. Then there is the new man that is being remade into the image of Christ. I'm not sure which man would have gone after Pete, but I'm pretty sure that it wouldn't have worked out very good for him either way."

The newlyweds finished greeting their other guests and made their way over to where Parker and I were talking. I shook hands with Pete and gave the bride a kiss on the cheek.

"How's the old married couple doing?" I asked.

"Hell," Pete remarked. "If I'd known that there was going to be drinking and dancing, I'd of gotten married months ago."

Sam gasped and gave Pete a playful pinch on the arm.

"Ouch! What was that for?"

"You enjoy your drinking and dancing while you can, Mr. Canfield," Sam scolded, "because tomorrow you start your new job as a foreman at the Lady Belle. You have responsibilities now."

Pete answered with exaggerated seriousness. "I assure you, Mrs. Canfield, that I will execute my responsibilities with the highest degree of earnestness and industry."

That led us all into a round of laughter that was suddenly interrupted by a gunshot. I saw Pete spin around and fall to the ground, followed by Sam's scream. Two more shots rang out, fired almost at the same time. The first one was fired by Parker, whose gun seemed to appear out of nowhere. The second shot was mine.

It had all happened in a matter of seconds, as so many life-altering events do. Kenny Bassett had made his way to the wedding reception and mingled in unnoticed among the other guests. After fortifying his courage on hard cider, he waited for his chance to even the score with Pete. Now Bass lay dead on the ground with two widening circles of crimson staining his chest.

I hurried over to Pete to see what kind of condition he was in. The bullet had spun him around so that he landed facedown. Sam was crying, trying to roll him over.

Parker pulled her away gently. "Come on, Sam. Let Ben have a look."

I rolled Pete over onto his back. I could see a hole in his jacket on the left side of his chest just over his heart. I started to undo the buttons on his jacket.

Suddenly, Pete opened his eyes and grabbed my wrist. "Careful there, partner. This suit ain't all the way paid for yet."

I jumped back, shocked and not a little confused. Sam ran over and threw her arms around Pete's neck as he sat up.

"Careful, Pete," I warned. "You've been shot."

Pete got to his feet, albeit slowly, brushing the dust from his new suit. "I'm fine."

"How is that possible?" I exclaimed. "You have a bullet hole in your chest."

Pete reached up to feel the breast of the suit jacket he had on and probed the bullet hole with his fingers. He then reached into the breast pocket and pulled out a deck of cards that he had stuffed inside. Embedded in, but not penetrating, the deck, was a .44 caliber slug.

Now, I honestly don't know what to make out of what I witnessed that afternoon in that peach orchard on the outskirts of Nuggettown. Maybe there was something in the curse of the aces and eights — the dead man's hand — and maybe it was just superstitious nonsense like Pete said. Or maybe it was like the Indians would say; that Pete's medicine was stronger than the curse. Reverend Parker had a different take on it. He said it was the providence of God that wouldn't allow Pete to be taken before his time.

One thing I do know for sure. I could go to a thousand different weddings where everything goes off without a hitch. But let my buddy, Pete, get married just one time and there's a commotion. And where there's a commotion, Pete Canfield is usually right in the middle of it.

(SDG)

Michael R. Ritt lives in a small cabin in the mountains of western Montana with his wife, Tami, their Australian shepherd, Lucky, and their nameless cat. He enjoys studying history, theology, and natural science, and has published several short stories and poems in anthologies and magazines. He is a member of American Christian Fiction Writers, Western Fictioneers, and Western Writers of America.

■ ■ ■ ■

JERICHO SPRINGS
BY MAX McCOY

■ ■ ■ ■

A rabbit screams when it dies rough and that sound was still in my head as I peered through the dirty windshield at the mountain of black dust. It must have scoured the topsoil from a million acres of farmland in Colorado and New Mexico and God Knows Where Else because it looked like a tumbling wall of dirt, topping out here and there like a thundercloud and elsewhere pouring down in cataracts.

I was somewhere south of Boise City and had I been paying more attention to the road, maybe I could have seen the roller in time to pick somewhere safe to ride things out, but damned now if I can think where that might have been. There isn't much north of Dalhart on State Highway 78, just hardpan and heartache. What the drought didn't take from the farmers, the banks had, and the rabbits ate what was left, down to the bark on the occasional tree. I hadn't passed a single occupied house in ten miles, and I was unsure if I was on the Oklahoma side of the line yet or still in Texas. I thought about trying to outrun the roller and make it to Boise City, but I didn't know if I was close enough to town. Besides, the sedan tended to run hot, and in the dust, she was sure to burn up.

So I took the first side road, a crooked and narrow scar across the barren fields leading away from the storm. A faded, hand-painted sign with red letters said *Jericho Springs AME, 3 mi.*

Go to Dalhart, my editor had said while chewing on the stem of a long-cold pipe. *The bank was robbed Thursday by an old cowboy who left a letter behind expressing remorse.* That's not a big story these days, I told Art. Lots of people are robbing banks, and some of them are sorry. His eyebrows semaphored behind his pop bottle specs. I asked: Remorse for what? *That's the story. The cops aren't saying. Keep it on the down-hold, but go there and find out what's in that letter.* I asked why the Dallas bureau didn't want it. *It's about the same distance from them as it is us.* Was anybody hurt? *Not by the cowboy. One of the locals came out of the hardware store across the street with a bolt-*

action deer rifle and winged our man. There was blood on the street. I sighed. How am I supposed to get the cops to let me see the note? *Use your girlish charm, Frankie. Oh, and the good people there are having one of their rabbit drives. Get me a thousand words on that, too, so we get two yarns for one trip.* Why not make it three, I had quipped — the remorseful cowboy, the rabbit roundup, and the one where I'm charged with soliciting a cop.

And that moment, with the easy joke still on my lips, was when I decided Dalhart would be my last assignment for the wire service. The Texas panhandle was 500 miles from the United Press bureau at Kansas City. I had been trying to escape to California for the past year, to leave the misery that was Kansas and Missouri behind, to not ruin another pair of shoes in the blood of another gangland killing. And Dalhart was in the right direction. I owned one thing of value in the world, and that was the old Model A, and I intended to put it to use. After filing the stories, from a booth in a hotel lobby or after slipping a few bucks to a farm family to use their phone on the kitchen wall, I would just keep going. I was starving on the pay from the United Press, the world's second-best wire service, and we'd been *on the downhold* — an order to cut expenses to the bone, which had been in effect since 1921, long before I became a Unipresser — so I figured I might as well starve someplace warm and bright.

On the road behind me, the storm was rolling down like all ten plagues. The air had a peculiar feel to it. The fine hairs on my forearms and the back of my neck stood on end and, as things grew darker, I could see wisps of lightning run from post to post along a wire fence on the north side of the road. The wind began to pick up, pushing at the boxy rear of the sedan, and driving tumbleweeds across the road ahead.

The dust shrouded the afternoon sun, and soon I could barely see the radiator cap at the far end of the hood — or the road beyond, for that matter. The dust and sand skittered over the car with a sound that reminded me of a boat in shallow water. Up ahead, on the south side of the road perhaps two hundred yards away, I caught a glimpse of a weather-washed steeple. A steeple meant a church, and a church meant shelter. I drove on, slowly, afraid of running into another car or perhaps into the wire fence to the north. When I finally could see no more of the road, I eased the sedan over to the right, felt the wheels cross the shallow ditch, and let it roll to a stop at the edge of the barren field. Then I grabbed my coat from the seat beside me, opened the car door, and stepped into the storm. I pulled on the coat and turned up the collar against the sand.

It had been warm and calm earlier in the day, but now the temperature had dropped by twenty degrees. I crawled around the fender to the front of the sedan and, fighting the wind, put my hand on the canvas water bag hanging there. I unhooked the rope from the chrome. With my eyes shut tight against the wind and sand, I drew a red bandana from my pocket, uncapped the bag, and held the cloth beneath it as I spilled some water. I wiped my eyes with the dampness, tied the bandana over my nose and mouth, capped the bag, and slung it over my shoulder.

I kept my eyes mostly shut as I made my way down the road, trusting my feet to feel the edge. Every so often I would dare a glance, but the dust stung my eyes. I could feel the grit in my ears, taste it on my tongue, and feel it grind away the enamel on my teeth.

When the feel of the road changed beneath my shoes, I thought it might be the driveway into the church, so I cautiously turned right.

The wind blew even harder, and I went down on my knees, choking and spitting, and crawled until I bumped into a corner of the building. Another couple of feet to one side, and I would have missed it.

I felt my way along the weathered clapboard, past a window to the entrance, then hunched against the door and felt for the rusty knob. I turned the knob and pushed, but the door didn't move. I put my shoulder into it, but still the door remained firm and clearly locked. I hollered, hoping somebody would hear me, but even if there had been somebody inside, my voice wasn't strong enough to overcome the roar of the wind. I kicked and pounded, trying to force or maybe break the door, but it was oak and weathered and rugged as the proverbial cross. I leaned my head against the door for a moment, wishing I had the breath to curse properly, and knowing I had to get inside or be choked by the storm.

So I slid down the wall to the window. The sill was about chest high; I turned my back and aligned my right elbow with the middle pane, then drove my elbow sharply backward. The glass shattered, scattering pieces inside. Then I reached in through the jagged edge, undid the hook from the eye, and slid the window up. I brushed the glass away from the sill, tossed the water bag inside, and pulled myself up and over. Once on the other side I slammed the window shut — but dust spewed in from the broken place like it was being shot from a firehose. It was dim inside the church, but I could see the back of a pew within arm's reach, and a little rack that held hymnals and testaments. I snatched up one of the Bibles, broke its spine so it would stay sprung open, and jammed it into the space where the pane had been.

Then I picked up the water bag, walked around the end of the closest pew, and sat down. As my eyes adjusted to the gloom, I could see the dust swirling like stars in the vaulted ceiling above.

Then I saw the coffin.

It was still bright enough in the east to throw a shaft of sunlight through a window, illuminating the coffin at the business end of the church, where the preaching took place. The light made brilliant the coffin's occupant, a girl of perhaps seven or eight; her face shone with unnatural warmth and her neatly combed blond hair seemed a tender fire. The effect could have come right from a Caravaggio painting, perhaps "St. John the Baptist." I'd seen a print of it once in a book at the Kansas City Public Library.

I stood up and moved closer.

The coffin wasn't store bought, but a bit roughshod, woven by hand from willow strips, like a basket. The child's dress, which was clean and pressed, was made out of flour sacks printed with an animal cracker design — monkeys and ducks and rabbits. In her clasped hands was a spray of wild-flowers.

"Good day for a funeral," said a rough voice.

I hadn't seen the man slumped in the shadows, sitting in a pew on the west side of the coffin.

"Pardon?" I asked.

"It's Sunday," he said. "Some days seem better for buryin' than others. I know, because it's the day I put my Astrid in the ground last November. Married fifty-one years, would have been fifty-two this sum-mer."

He had not turned to look at me as he talked. The back of his bare head was a tangle of white hair above a frayed denim collar.

"I'm sorry," I said. "The child there. Is she related?"

"No," he said. "Don't know who belongs to her."

Then what are you doing sitting here in the

dark with her? I thought but didn't ask. The old boy clearly didn't want much conversation, and I was getting a queer feeling because he hadn't even yet turned to look at me. Then he coughed, a wet hacking cough, his shoulders shaking with pain.

"I have water. Would you care for some?"

He held up his left arm until the coughing stopped, the hand shaking in the air as if he were busting a bronc.

"Yes," he said. "Feels like I'm dying of thirst."

I carried the water bag up the aisle. Outside, the wind rattled the door and beat against the north and west walls of the church, and I could hear sand slithering down from the place in the broken window-pane that wasn't covered by the testament.

"That's far enough," he said.

I stopped a couple of paces behind him, and he held out a gnarled hand. I placed the bag in it, and he flipped off the cap and took a long drink. Then he poured some into his kerchief and wiped his face.

"You always carry water with you?"

"Only a fool travels without it," I said.

The old man laughed.

"That's for damned sure," he said. "And I'm proof of it."

Outside, the wind keened a death song.

301

"You can sit," he said, motioning to the near end of the pew across the aisle.

"All right," I said, taking the seat.

I could see his face now, and it looked as if he had just about worn it through. His yellow skin was blotched and tight over the cheekbones, his nose was crooked from a bad break many years ago, and his cloudy blue eyes swam in watery sockets.

"The door was locked from the inside," I said.

"Yep," he said.

"Why?"

"Didn't want company," he said. "But, you managed to bust in."

"One of my charms," I said.

He glanced my way, then shook his head.

"You dress like a man."

"Not really," I said. "A lot of women wear pants these days. Practical, with my job."

"A girl with a job," he said. "Still can't get used to it, other than bookkeepers and schoolteachers and . . . well, some ladies that do their business at night. What kind of work do you do?"

"I talk to people and type and use the telephone."

He snorted.

"My Astrid loved to talk," he said. "It didn't matter about who or what. She woke up talking and went to sleep talking. Used to drive me half mad, but now I can't think of any sound that would be half so nice."

Then there came the sound of scrabbling at the front of the church; there were some low voices, and the door rattled against the lock. The old man did not move.

"They'll die out there," I said.

He didn't answer, just cocked his head a bit as if he were listening to somebody besides me. Then he reached beneath his coat, and I caught the glint of something deadly in his right hand.

"All right," he said. "I'm ready. See who it is."

I went to the door, slipped the bolt, and opened it to a blast of dust that blew in a gaggle of refugees. A mother and her children came first, all three dark-headed and looking stray and hungry. They were followed by a young couple in clean but modest city clothes, the girl carrying a picnic basket, and, judging from the way they hung onto one another, sweethearts or newly married. The boy had short hair and thick glasses, and his girl had long blond hair. Last came a black man who seemed neither young nor old, wearing a black suit jacket over coveralls, and who did not seem to hurry even though hell itself howled outside.

"Why was the door locked?" the black man asked. "I've been deacon here for twenty years and never knew the latch to be set."

"The wind," I said, putting my shoulder against the door until I heard the latch. "Where you all come from?"

"Met up on the road," the black man said. "All running from the storm, so I brought 'em here. Who are you?"

"Call me Frankie," I said.

"This is a black church?" the young man asked.

"This is the African Methodist Episcopal Church of Jericho Springs," the ageless black man said. "Been here for more than fifty years, founded by my Exoduster grand-folks. But you all are welcome just the same."

"Hell," the young man said, and the girl gave him a look.

"Excuse us," she said. "We're grateful for the shelter, deacon. We'd have choked to death for sure out there on the prairie. It was such a lovely day, and we thought we'd have a little picnic lunch, then the storm blew up so sudden. We got caught walking halfway home and would have been smothered for sure if you hadn't found us."

"Call me Bascom," the deacon said, and

his voice sounded like a sermon laced with whiskey. "Omar Bascom. And you're welcome, miss."

Then Bascom's eyes went to the broken window, and back to me, and then to the old man sitting in the pew up front.

"That his Ford out there?"

"Mine."

"What kind of business you have to break a window to get in?"

"Survival," I said. "He was already inside, with the door latched. I'll pay for the window."

"And the good book," the deacon said.

"Oh my," the mother said, pulling her children closer. "Is that a coffin?"

"You all better come up here and sit down," the old man said. He had found a folding chair and turned it around to face the pews. He held the ancient blue six-shooter in his right hand, resting easy on his right thigh. Blood seeped from the tail of his blue shirt, down his left pant leg, and was spreading on the floor. Tucked beneath the chair was an old brown satchel.

"Come on up," the old man said, motioning with the gun. "Sit where I can see you. We're going to ride the storm out together."

"You don't look like you're in shape to ride anything out," Bascom said, easing into a front pew. "Put down the gun and let us tend to you. When the storm passes, we'll send somebody for a doctor."

"Past tending," the old man said.

The mother sat with one child on her lap and the other beside her. They were perhaps two and five, the girl older and sitting on the pew, and the boy reaching for the front of the woman's thin smock, and each time the mother gently moved the hand away. I noticed that the mother's own hands were small, scarcely larger than her little girl's.

"Whose child?" the mother asked.

"I don't know," Bascom said. "We found her after services this morning, on the wooden steps out front. Somebody had just left her. Probably a family bound for California. Died of dust pneumonia, I reckon. My wife cleaned her up and we put her in the basket, but with the storm coming, there was no time today to dig a grave in the cemetery out back. We'll use a couple of fruit boxes to put her in the ground tomorrow and save the basket for next time."

"What's her name?" I asked.

"We found no clue," Bascom said. "But her name is known to God."

"Amen," the mother said.

"And where did you come from?" the old man asked.

"Joplin," the mother said. "That's over the state line way east in Missouri. I'm Florence, and this is Finis Junior and Pearl. Our truck is down the road three or four miles, with a rod through the side of the block. Damn that man who sold it to my man, Fin."

"I know those lots on West Seventh in Joplin," I said. "You're lucky you got this far."

"Lucky?" Florence asked, then laughed. "We've never been lucky in our entire lives. Just once, instead of being the ones got took, I'd like to do the taking. I'd just like to know how it feels."

"Where's your man?" the old cowboy asked.

"Finis Senior is with the truck," Florence said. "He sent us along toward Boise City, knowing that somebody would more likely give us a ride if we was alone. Nobody wants to give a man a ride these days." She pronounced Boise like the locals do, not like the city in Idaho, but *Boyce.* "If you don't mind me asking, mister, why do you have that gun on us?"

"You don't seem scared," the old cowboy said.

"What's there to be scared of now?" Florence asked. "This is the end of the world.

307

It's been coming for some time, we all knew it. The sky has turned to ashes and we're all going to be buried in dust."

"Now, we've had dust storms before," Bascom said. "It doesn't mean the end times, not yet."

"Just look outside," Florence said. "It's still hours until sunset, and yet it's dark as midnight."

"I'll get the lamp," Bascom said. "And some newspapers to stuff the cracks in the door and the window sills. And that broken pane."

"Do you have a telephone?" I asked.

"Sister, we don't even have electric," Bascom said. "What do you think?"

"Don't go where I can't see you," the old cowboy said.

"Where would that be? There ain't but one room here."

"You didn't answer the question," the young man said. Now that I was closer to the couple, who were sitting just across the aisle, I could see rings on their left hands, so they must be bride and groom. "Why do you have that gun on us? We haven't done nothin' to you."

The old man didn't answer.

"He robbed the bank at Dalhart," I said. "That's my best guess, anyway. Got shot making his getaway, and from the look of him, it was a gutshot. He's lost a lot of blood and thought he'd hole up here until maybe he could travel again. If I'm wrong, mister, tell me now."

"You've got it all figured out, don't you?"

"No, I've got a few questions left."

"Save them," the cowboy said. Then he turned to the girl with the picnic basket. "Any food left in that?"

"A little," the bride said. "But it's got dirt in it."

"Don't matter."

She gave him the basket, which he picked through while the deacon and the groom went about sealing up windows with yellowed newspapers. The deacon placed a low stool between the pews and the chair where the cowboy sat and adjusted the wick beneath the fluttering flame of the kerosene lamp to give more light. The old man's eyes swam in the yellow glow.

He took a bite of a bread and cheese sandwich, but he couldn't seem to swallow, so he ended up spitting most of it on the floor. "I don't think I should have drank all that water," he said.

"It's your insides," Bascom said. "They're all busted up."

"I reckon."

He passed the basket over to Florence, who began to brush the dust away so her children could eat the scraps.

"Give me the gun and let me help you," Bascom said.

"We'll just wait," the cowboy said.

So we sat in the circle of light, with the dead child beyond us at the altar, listening to the wind and feeling the dust settle on our skin and hair. Bascom motioned for the water, and the old cowboy handed it over, but before he could flip open the top, the groom snatched the bag from his hands.

"What?" Bascom asked.

"You should let us drink first."

"Why?"

"You know why," the bride said. "That's just the way it's done."

Bascom looked to some point beyond the groom's shoulder.

"This house belongs to the Lord," he said. "Here, we are all equal."

"Oh, for Christ's sake," I said, and snatched the water bag from the boy's hands, so roughly that the edge of the bag knocked the glasses from his face. "It's my bag. If this man is good enough to bury our unclaimed dead, he's good enough to drink my water. You'll drink, too, when you get thirsty enough."

I handed the water back to Bascom, who said nothing, but drank.

The bag went around, and each drank their share in a rough kind of panhandle communion. The groom had recovered his specs, now with one shattered lens, and even though his face was as red as my bandana, he drank like the rest.

In time, Florence's youngest child squirmed uncomfortably beside her.

"Junior needs to make water," she said to us in a whisper.

"There's a bucket in the cabinet toward the back, with the brooms and other things," Bascom said. "Draw the cloth aside and you'll see it."

The mother herded both of her children to the far corner.

With nothing to do but sit and watch, I began thinking about the rabbit drive earlier that day. There had been hundreds of families — men and women and all their children big enough to walk — who drove them across several sections by shouting and banging pans, herding them to a place where two long chicken wire fences met to form a sharp corner. The rabbits streaked across the land, faster than I could have imagined, darting in straight lines to one point or another, seeking shelter. But, inexorably, they were funneled to the killing corner. Soon there were a thousand or more rabbits trapped there, hopping over one another and crying, and the townsfolk approached with ax handles and other clubs. The rabbits just gave up, allowing themselves to be snatched up by their hind legs while the clubs came down on their skulls. The rabbits not killed by that first blow screamed, and the sound was like that of a small child screaming in pain. When one rabbit screamed it would get the others going, even the ones that hadn't been snatched up yet, but were shaking and cowering against the fence, and the sound was like a chorus from hell.

You couldn't eat the rabbits after because of the rabbit fever, and it was impractical to skin a thousand dead rabbits, so even the fur went to waste. I understood why the rabbits were killed, because the crops were more important, but the people went about it with a purpose that was beyond it just being a chore. Some of them clearly enjoyed it, and others — the ones who ended up killing the most — beat them to death with a manic zeal that made it clear that they were not just killing rabbits but were trying to beat their way out of their troubles. Perhaps they were imagining the banker down the street, or their neighbor who was just a little better off, or the wife who had left. Some, I'm guessing, were imagining God.

In my head, I had been working on the lead to the story for hours, knowing I would have to phone something in to Art, but I couldn't get past the sound of the rabbits dying. Every time I thought I had something I could use, something about the plains people defending their land from a pestilence that might have come straight from the Bible, there was that sound in the back of my head, mocking me.

"I grew up here," the old cowboy said, bringing me back to the church.

"Tell me about it."

Bascom and the newlyweds were asleep in the pews.

"Not here, exactly, but close enough," he said, his voice dry with pain. "Across the next ridge, where the Springs are. It used to be some beautiful country. My father brought us out here from Iowa after the war. There were bluebells everywhere. And grass. Plenty of grass back then, before we plowed it all up. But my mother loved the bluebells most."

"Did you meet Astrid here?"

"Oh, no," he said. "That was much later,

313

after my time on the cattle trails north to the railheads in Kansas. My God, what a time that was. I was younger than you, back then, and I was tall in the saddle. We would hit Ellsworth or Dodge City or Abilene and it would be hell on a hot plate until our pay was gone. Women and cards and whiskey. I ran with the Texas boys, seeing as how I was just about a Texan, anyway, having grown up so close to the line. This was all in the seventies. I was plenty rough, and got in some fine scrapes, but I never killed anybody, and I'm glad of that. All I have left of that time is this."

His fingers brushed the revolver beside him.

"Funny how we age but guns don't," he said. "Take care of them and they last forever. This is a Colt double-action Lightning. Looks about the same as I bought it, at Dodge City back in '77. Back then, freedom meant a good horse and decent piece of iron. Hell, most of us didn't even keep them on our hips, like you see in the moving pictures. Kept mine in my bedroll, behind the saddle. Plenty handy enough. But my God, I never felt as free as I did then."

"And Astrid?"

"She was keeping the books at her father's

mercantile at Caldwell when I came in to buy a can of coffee. I had never seen anyone so beautiful. It took me two years to convince her to marry me, but she did, in 1884. Because I had stopped hell raising, I had enough money to buy a place, just across the line in Texas. I thought I was going to miss the freedom I found on the range and the cattle towns, but I didn't. I wasn't free, exactly, but I was — hell, I don't know how to explain it. I was where I belonged. And Astrid loved it there, and she loved bluebells, just like my mother. We lived there for fifty years."

"Until the bank took it," I said.

"It wasn't the bank's fault," he said. "It was mine. Like everyone else, I thought the good times would last forever. Twenty-six was a great year. Bought more land on credit. Plowed it all up to plant wheat. So, like just about everyone else, I went broke. It was a kindness the cancer took Astrid before the bank took the house."

"Do you have kids?"

"Among the sorrows of living to be eighty-five is burying your children," he said. "Outlived both our boys. One was killed in the Great War, the other died of the sepsis after he cut his arm while mending a fence twenty years ago. All my family are gone now. Time has made an orphan of me."

Bascom was awake now. He sat up and leaned forward to stare at the cowboy.

"So, you ended up with nothing and nobody," Bascom said. "Is that why you robbed that bank? To take something back before you died? How much you got in that old valise between your legs?"

The cowboy laughed weakly.

"Deacon," he said, "You'd be surprised at just how much."

Then the old man slumped back in the chair. The blood beneath him had pooled and then run, streaking the boards behind him as it sought the earth.

"Let's all be quiet now," the old man said, and placed the revolver in his lap. "I'm talked out."

Then there came a tremendous whack on the back of the old man's head, and he gave one of those pitiful rabbit cries and his body pitched forward to the floor. Behind him stood Florence, the handle of a broom held in her hands like a baseball bat. She must have unscrewed it from the head of the broom when she took her children to the corner. Her dark eyes were wide and shining, and her children clutched at the back of her thin dress. She smiled broadly, then threw the broom handle aside and snatched up the revolver where it had fallen.

"Damn," Florence said. "It feels good."

"Just hold on," Bascom said, half out of the pew.

Moving slowly, I knelt in the blood on the floor beside the cowboy. He was making no sound now.

"Get back up there," Florence said, motioning with the gun.

"You killed him," I said.

"He was dying already," said the groom, pushing the broken glasses back up to the bridge of his nose. "I say good riddance."

"I said get back," Florence told me.

"You can't shoot me," I said.

"I will," she vowed.

"I mean you can't, not that you wouldn't," I said. "That's a double-action. It's not like the hardware the gangsters carry now, the automatics and the Tommy guns. It's an old-fashioned gun, you have to squeeze the trigger hard every time you want to shoot."

"I don't know what that means," Florence said, the barrel wavering.

"You could also cock it each time," I said. "Pull the hammer back."

"What?" she asked.

"Use your thumb."

"I can't reach it," she said. Just the tip of her right index finger was touching the trigger; her hand wasn't broad enough to hook her thumb over the hammer.

"Then you'll have to squeeze, and hard. Those old guns have a trigger weight of fourteen or fifteen pounds."

"Now, why did you have to tell her that?" Bascom asked.

"I dislike incompetence."

"And why the hell do you know so much about guns?" the deacon asked.

"I'm a Unipresser, a wire service reporter," I said. "Crime is my beat."

"Let's think about this situation a minute," the groom said. "The old man got what was coming to him. Justice was served, right? And now we have this valise that is stuffed full of God knows how much cash. I say we divvy it up."

"I have the gun," Florence said.

"But no way to escape without us."

"What about the body?" the girl asked.

"There's already a grave to dig," the groom said. "The old man can go in the hole beneath the girl."

"Please," Bascom said. "Let's not do this. Justice is mine, says the Lord."

"Shut up," the bride said. "We'd like to own a house. Who wouldn't?"

"Eating regular would satisfy us," Florence said, lowering the gun. "I'm holding

318

on to this, but let's see what's in the valise."

"We divide it even?" the bride asked.

"Sure," Florence said. "Let's see inside."

"Count me out," I said.

"More for the rest of us," the groom said. "How about you, deacon?"

The black man shut his eyes.

"I've been poor all my life," he said. "Lord, why must You test me so?"

The groom motioned for the bag, and I grabbed a corner of it and slid it from beneath the chair. It was heavy, and I had to use both hands to lift it up to the groom.

He undid the buckle, took a deep breath, and opened the bag.

"What the heck?"

He withdrew a meager handful of green bills.

"There's not thirty dollars here," he said. "The rest of it is . . . junk. Horseshoes, tins of tobacco, clothes. Some rotten apples."

"But the newspaper said he got five thousand," the bride said. "There must be more."

I shook my head.

"How would you know?" the girl asked.

"Like I said, I'm a reporter. The banks lie all the time about how much was taken," I said. "It's part of the racket, because the federal insurance pays off, or they use it to cover embezzlement."

The groom cursed.

I took my notes from my jacket pocket and unfolded the one on top.

"The old cowboy left a note after robbing the bank," I said. "One of the cops at Dalhart let me copy it after I slipped him a five-dollar bill."

"Can I see that?" Bascom asked.

I handed it over to the deacon.

"Sorry to cause so much trouble," he read, turning the paper toward the lamp. "Hope nobody got hurt. The county is auctioning my place off at the end of the week, as they have a right. That's fine, as I am old and sick and have no more use for it. But there's a horse in the barn named Bluebell. She's a good horse, but old and sick like me, and her ribs are showing. I'm afraid whoever buys the place will put her down, rather than pay to feed her. So, I just need enough to buy a few bags of feed, just to see her through to the end. P.S.: She also likes apples."

The deacon handed the note back to me.

"Well, that's it," the bride said. "No house."

"No nothin'," the groom said.

"Still poor," said Bascom.

But Florence brought the gun up again,

and this time she used her left hand to brace the revolver while she pushed her right hand forward and hooked the first joint of her index finger around the trigger.

"I want the money," she said.

"No," the groom said.

She pulled the trigger and there was a muzzle flash and the sound left our ears ringing. The bullet had gone past the groom and put a hole in another window.

Florence giggled as if drunk.

Her children began to cry.

"No, hush," she said. "That was fun. Want to do it again?"

"Careful," Bascom said. "Let's not put any more holes in anything — or anyone."

"Give her the money," the bride said.

"This is better than a month's pay," the boy protested.

Florence adjusted her two-handed grip to get more purchase on the trigger.

"I missed you the last time," she said. "But now I think I got the hang of it."

The groom looked down but held out the money.

"Nuh-uh," Florence said. "You'll jump me if I take a hand off the gun."

"Then what am I supposed to do?" the boy asked.

"Oh, for crying out loud," I said.

I took the wad of money, tied it up in my bandana, and motioned for Florence to turn toward me so I could put it in the pocket of her smock. Her children were still clustered and crying behind her.

Instead, she pointed the gun at me.

"Your car," she said.

"You have to be kidding."

"Do I look like I'm fucking kidding?"

"No," I said, digging the keys out of my coat.

Trying to avoid the barrel of the gun, I crouched and gingerly tucked the bandana and the keys into Florence's pocket.

"Tends to run hot," I said. "Don't forget to add water or she'll burn up."

"We're going now," she said. "You all stay put."

"Do you understand?" I asked.

"Yeah, water," she snapped. "Now shut up."

"But the storm," the bride said.

"It's been hours," Bascom said. "The wind's died down. She might make it, if the car isn't buried too deep in the sand."

Florence opened the door, and just a bit of dust swirled in. She pushed her children in front of her, and the last thing out was the hand holding the gun. In a few minutes, I heard the familiar sound of the engine clatter to life, and then the whine of the gearbox as it pulled away.

We sat there in silence for a moment, looking at one another.

"Now what?" asked the bride.

"I have to pray for forgiveness," Bascom said. "And come light, I have a couple of graves to dig."

"Shouldn't we wait for the sheriff?" the groom asked.

"The old man is home," Bascom said. "Let him stay here."

I stood, wiping my bloody palms on my pants.

"How far is town proper? I need to phone the bureau."

"A couple of miles down the road," Bascom said. "You'll find a public phone at the little post office there. It won't be open for a couple of hours yet."

That was all right, I told myself. I needed time to think. It wasn't just the new lede for the story I would phone in to Art, but the realization that I was trapped just the same as the other people in the church. How long would it take me to save up to buy another car? How would I ever get to California? For that matter, how was I going to get back to Kansas City? I'd have to hitch back to Dalhart, and then ask Art to wire me the money for a train ticket back. It wasn't the end of the world, but, of course, it never comes with a bang, as Eliot said, it just whimpers. It's everything together, the whole damn weight of it, that drives you down a little farther every time until your mouth is filled with dust and all the light goes out. How much more could I stand before I decided to be the club and not the rabbit?

Max McCoy is a multiple Spur Award–winning novelist and native Kansan. He's the author of the *Hellfire Canyon* trilogy and the novelization of Steven Spielberg's epic TNT miniseries, *Into the West.* He teaches at Emporia State, in east central Kansas.

■ ■ ■ ■

Buryin' Ruby
by Greg Hunt

■ ■ ■ ■

Jeb hardly slept all night, just thinking about Ruby out there in the woodshed. It felt so empty inside the cabin, almost haunted, without her over there in her narrow little bunk beside the stove, snoring louder than him sometimes, and tossing around trying to get comfortable on her pine needle tick. In the deep, dark dead of night, he actually considered that she might be silently floating around someplace close by right now, although he hadn't seen any sign of it yet.

He had been away hauling a load of lumber up from Bradshaw's Post, and was glad he wasn't there to watch her die without being able to do anything to help her. He found her body lying twisted on the ground where she'd writhed in her last death throes, and the bug-eyed, terrified expression on her face was testament to the pain she had suffered in those last moments. One of the first things he'd done was tie his neckerchief over her face, not wanting to carry that spooky image around in his mind for the rest of his life.

But if there was even a little piece of luck in this, it was that the rattlesnake was big, one of the largest Jeb had ever seen, and his bite was deep into the meat high up on her left shoulder, close to her heart. She must have gone fast. The snake lay only a few feet away, headless and as dead as Ruby. She had always been quick with a blade, and it didn't surprise him that she had managed to kill the critter that had killed her.

Damn her for being so careless, Jeb thought as he cataloged all the chores and woman's work Ruby had taken up when she came to stay with him. It wasn't just her cooking he'd miss. She'd kept the cabin picked up and swept out, washed his clothes and bedding, brought in the wood, and a dozen other things. Plus, she put in a pretty good day at the sluices, working shoulder to shoulder dawn to dark with Jeb. Of course, it was no more than she owed him for taking her in during the dead of winter, and probably saving her life, but still . . . Now he'd have to do all that for himself again, just when he'd grown used to settling back with a pipe and a cup of coffee after a long day. Not to mention the quiet that had already settled in like a thick fog. He even missed her snoring and thought the absence of it might be one of the reasons why he couldn't get to sleep. Damn that woman for dying.

What was she doing wandering around up there in the rocks above their diggings anyway? And why was she down on the ground, which she must have been for the snake to strike her where it did? She should have been working. Just a couple of days before, they'd come across rich new colors in a patch of sand and gravel higher up on the hill, and she should have been hauling wheelbarrows of the stuff down to the sluice.

He got up at the first hint of light, pulled on his clothes, and stoked up the stove to reheat last night's coffee. Breakfast sat waiting in a tin plate on the table — last night's leftovers of cornbread and fried salt pork, which he just hadn't been in the mood to finish. He was as tired this morning as he usually was after a hard day's work, and his mood was surly.

Of course, he'd have to bury her before she started stinking, but on this rocky hillside it would take a full day, maybe two, to dig a decent grave. Maybe he'd just lay her out and cover her up with a pile of stones, he thought, someplace a decent distance of the cabin. She was past having a say in the matter and wouldn't know or care. It was a common way to treat the dead in this wild country, if they got even that.

He went out to the woodshed and peeled back the canvas he'd wrapped her in, staring at her for a while with that sense of wonder people felt when they looked at the corpse of someone who had so recently been alive. Ruby had been more than average tall, but thin and lean like most people who lived the hard life out here in the mountains. She might have been pretty once when she was a young girl, but her face and arms were leathery and wrinkled now. Once, after she'd asked Jeb to remind her what year it was, she told him that made her thirty-seven, which was getting on up there. Jeb pulled the fabric of her dress down to cover her ankles because he knew how modest she could be, then combed her frizzy, sun-bleached hair back with his fingers. He started to raise the neckerchief off her face for a final look, but decided he'd rather remember her the way she looked before she was dead. She had a fine smile that made a man feel downright good, he recalled, although he hadn't seen it all that often.

He wrapped the canvas back over her and

carried her a few dozen steps away from the cabin, thinking that would probably be far enough to keep the stink down until nature had done its work. Laying her down, he tried to cross her arms on her chest, but she'd gone stiff already. He arranged her worn old brown dress so it looked decent before he started piling the rocks on her. To cover her up, he chose the heaviest rocks he could lift and carry so that even a grizzly would have trouble clawing its way down to her. He didn't know any words to say, except an awkward "So long, Ruby." He thought he'd make a cross later, and maybe carve her name on it.

He went back to the sluice, planning to put in a regular day's work, but after a few hours, he knew his heart just wasn't in it today. Besides being worn out from the sleepless night, the high country that surrounded him somehow seemed more empty and lonely than it ever had before. He couldn't keep his eyes from roaming over to the pile of rocks, and his brain filled with a strange sort of mortal confusion at how a person could be walking, talking, and so alive one minute, then become just a pile of dead meat the next. It wasn't like him to have thoughts like that, but today he couldn't put them away.

It was only Thursday, two days before he and Ruby usually rode down to Elkhorn Springs, but he decided to go anyway. Maybe a few shots of old man Bradshaw's firewater would wash away this sour mood that seemed to infest him.

Ruby had shown up half-dead at his cabin door just ahead of a hard winter blizzard last December. She told him that Bear Quincy, the man she'd been holed up with at a neighboring claim, had been killed by a band of renegade Sioux. She had barely escaped herself and was too scared to go back to Bear's cabin. A group of miners went over a few days later and found Bear's frozen corpse just outside his cabin door, a single arrow still deeply embedded in his chest just below the breastbone They made a half-ass try at stirring up the trail of his murderers, impossible, of course, in the fresh deep snow, and while they were there, they went ahead and searched his cabin in case he had hidden his stash somewhere inside. They found nothing, and a broader search of the claim would have to wait until the spring thaw. Ruby herself made one trip back to pack her meager belongings into a worn carpetbag so she could take up house-keeping with Jeb.

With his body half-buried in snow, frozen to the ground and stiff as an oak trunk, none of the visitors could do much for Ol' Bear in the way of burying, so they just left him there, a feast for the first winter-starved beasts that happened along.

It wasn't until weeks later that Ruby quite unexpectedly told Jeb the real story of Bear Quincy's sorry demise. Jeb had been down to Bradshaw's, came back surly drunk, and slapped Ruby across the face for not having coffee made and a hot meal waiting. He woke the next morning to find a hatchet on the pillow beside his head, and over breakfast Ruby spelled it out for him.

Bear Quincy had been one of those men who thought women had been put on earth for a man to whale on whenever he took a notion, but Ruby said she never had seen anything in the Bible that said a woman had to abide such treatment. Finally, after fair warning that Bear ignored, she had slid her sheath knife up under his rib cage one day as he stormed at her with a stick of kindling. Afterward, she was worried that the locals might hold it against her if they found Bear's body stabbed to death and thought maybe she did it just to get her hands on his stash. So she took one of the arrows from a Sioux quiver hanging on the cabin wall, one of Bear's souvenirs from an Injun fight, and stuck it down deep into the knife wound. Then it was easy enough to wrap a story of an Indian attack around that.

There was no missing the message, and by the time she was finished, Jeb understood that there was only one tolerable way to ensure himself a good night's sleep as long as he shared his cabin with Ruby.

A cold drizzle was falling as Jeb rode his mule down the mountainside to Bradshaw's Post. It served to further darken his mood, and he was more than ready for that first shot of firewater by the time he reached his destination. Norman Bradshaw, proprietor of the supply post at Elkhorn Springs, measured out an ounce of gold flakes from Jeb's poke while his wife, a mostly silent Crow woman with long, graying braids that hung halfway down her back, tipped a jug and poured whiskey into a clay cup. Bradshaw wrote Jeb's name on a piece of paper he kept on the bar and marked an X under it.

"Are we in for it, Jeb?" Bradshaw asked.

"Naw, I don't think so. The clouds are too thin, and there's still blue sky up north of here." Jeb tipped the cup up and took a drink, wincing at the bite of it. The only resemblance this stuff had to real whiskey was that it burned going down and scrambled a man's mind just as well.

"What brings you down again in the middle of the week?"

"Thought I'd raise a glass to Ruby," Jeb said, actually raising the cup. "She passed on yesterday. A rattler bit her while I was down here picking up that load of lumber."

"Now ain't that a shame?" Bradshaw said. He looked over toward his wife. "You hear that, Meadow? Ruby's dead." The woman gave him a silent nod and her face became more dour, if that was possible. Some of Bradshaw's customers had never heard the sound of her voice.

"Damn careless fool of a woman," Jeb complained. He shoved his cup over for a refill, and Bradshaw put another X under his name. "I just got used to tolerating her out at the claim, and now she's laid out under a pile of rocks. She'd wandered up the mountainside, prob'ly picking flowers or some other such female nonsense. Everybody knows the rattlers are out all over the place this time of year. She should've been more careful."

"I liked that woman from the start when Bear Quincy brought her up the Bozeman. She was too good for him, but you and her seemed to get on fine."

"She wasn't much trouble. A hard worker and didn't talk a man's ear off all day long. I got used to her," Jeb said again. He could feel the whiskey doing its work on him. He choked back the second cup, let Bradshaw fill it again, and moved off to sit at a table against one wall. Most of the place was filled with the goods Bradshaw stocked to sell to the miners, but there were a few tables and chairs on one side that served for a saloon.

Maybe if I just get drunk enough, Jeb thought. But drunk enough for what? He'd been fine before that lanky, homely woman showed up. He'd taken care of himself, obliged to nobody, and was used to the solitary life out there in the mountains. After all his hard work, the claim was starting to yield a decent amount of gold, and he was beginning to see the promise of a good life ahead if he was able to work his claim for just another year, or maybe two. Nobody was sure the Sioux would let them stay out here on their tribal lands that long, but there was no good thing in life that didn't involve some risks.

But now he couldn't seem to steer his mind away from that dead woman out there under the rocks, and back to the reason he had come here in the first place. "Doggone it," he muttered under his breath, before realizing that he wasn't sure in what direction the complaint was aimed. The whiskey wasn't helping, but he didn't protest when Meadow came over and refilled his cup.

Ruby wasn't as jabbery as some women Jeb had known, but she did reveal bits and pieces of a hard life back in Weston, Missouri, first as the rebellious daughter of a country Methodist preacher, and later as the common-law wife of a riverboat man who met his end during an Indian attack somewhere in the northern reaches of the Missouri River. Leaving her young daughter behind with her widowed mother, Ruby had lit out west seven years before, thinking she might marry again, or make some other kind of new start on the frontier, and then bring her child out to live with her. But, instead, she had run into nothing but hard times and bad luck, with no shortage of men glad to use and abuse a woman trying to make it on her own.

Coming up the Bozeman Trail with Bear Quincy, out into gold country, but also into wild Indian Territory, had been pretty much her last desperate roll of the dice. If they found gold, as Bear was so sure they would, and he shared some with her, as he promised, she might have enough to get on back home and make a new start in Missouri. By then she had given up on the idea of settling somewhere in the West. Life was too cruel and dangerous on the frontier, and she'd had enough of it.

But, instead, from any side you looked at the thing, now it was snake eyes for Ruby.

"Sorry to hear 'bout your woman."

Jeb looked up and saw a man approaching, whiskey jug in hand, backlit by the sunlight coming in the open front door. His face was in shadow, but Jeb knew who it was. Silas McGhee was the last man hereabouts that Jeb would have picked for company today, but probably the one most likely to be encountered in Bradshaw's this time of day, or any other time for that matter. It seemed like every time McGhee panned out more than an ounce or two at his claim, he started down the mountain to drink it up.

"It's a hard way to go," McGhee said. "An' a terrible waste of a woman with plenty of use left in her."

Jeb gave him a hard look, but that didn't stop the man from sitting down across the table. "So, was you there when it happened?" McGhee asked. "Did you try to save her?"

"Nope. I was hauling lumber to shore up the sluice, and she was dead when I got back," Jeb said. "But it wouldn't have made no difference even if I was there. The bite was high and deep, a big ol' rattler maybe eight feet long."

"Naw, they don't grow that long."

"All right, maybe six feet then. Doesn't matter. I was always warning her to be careful. Keep looking down when you're walking, and never reach under nothing without checking it first. It was most likely her own durned fault, but that don't make a difference to anybody now. I was always telling her to carry something around, like a shovel or a stick, because those rattlers are mean as the devil when they come out in the spring."

"Water under the bridge," McGhee said, as close to being philosophical as he was ever likely to get. "Did you find her stash?"

"Nope, I haven't looked yet. Pretty sure it's not in the cabin. When she went out for wood at night, I think that's when she tucked it away someplace."

"So you shared with her, then? Bear told me once that he never did."

"A third. And we split the expenses. I thought that was fair. She worked as hard as I did, but it was my claim. Wasn't much to share anyway, though." It was normal and expected for a man to play down his take.

"Maybe she carried it on her."

"Naw, I'd of known." Jeb was uncomfortable talking about his or Ruby's gold stashes to a man like McGhee. There was the hard way to get your hands on gold, which was to dig it out of the hillsides and pan it from the streams, and then there was the easy way, by just taking somebody else's. So he felt compelled to add, "We never did trust each other about that. And I can tell you this much. She could have searched that mountainside from now 'til doomsday and never found where I had my take tucked away. Her or anybody else."

McGhee positioned his jug in the crook of his arm, raised it up, and took a long drink. Jeb signaled the Indian woman for another, and Bradshaw announced, almost conversationally from the counter, "Two left on account, Jeb."

"You and Ruby could have made some good money other ways if you ever took a notion," McGhee said with a drunken grin. Jeb gave him a hard look that didn't seem to take. The whiskey owned McGhee now, and there was no telling what was likely to come out of his sorry mouth. "In a place

340

like this, with plenty of colors coming down from the hills, she could of got top dollar."

Jeb put the whiskey away with one angry gulp and leaned forward so there was no mistaking that he was getting heated up. "You best quit talking about Ruby that way," he warned. "She wasn't that kind."

"Hell, ain't every woman?" McGhee laughed, trying to invoke some kind of masculine camaraderie that he thought every man shared. "Why, I bet when she was up there in that cabin with Ol' Bear Quincy, why he'd . . ."

Jeb didn't even bother to stand up before launching his fist across the table toward the middle of Silas McGhee's face. It landed hard and solid across McGhee's mouth and nose and McGhee went down backward in the chair, his head ricocheting off the edge of the table behind him. He lay on the floor for a moment, snorting and drooling and shaking his head, trying to gather his wits. When he finally did start to clumsily stand up, it was clear that his brain wasn't working too well just yet because one hand was fumbling to draw his sheath knife, and the other went to work pulling his handgun out of its holster.

Jeb picked up the jug from the table and threw it at McGhee, finishing up the damage to the man's face that his first punch started. McGhee toppled back again, clipping his head on the table behind him again, and ended up limp and still on the floor like a sack of potatoes.

Jeb stood up, glancing down at his scratched knuckles and wiping the blood on his pants. He looked over at Bradshaw and said, "You seen it, didn't you, Norman?"

"I seen and heard it all," Bradshaw said. "He was begging for what he got." That was how justice worked out here in the badlands.

During the ride back to the cabin, Jeb began to reflect on the fight. After a couple more drinks, he had left without checking to see if Silas McGhee, still crumpled on the floor, was alive or not. *It would be easier if he was dead,* Jeb thought. Then Bradshaw and his wife could simply bury him out back of the Trading Post with a few other unfortunate pilgrims and take whatever he had on him as payment for their trouble.

But if Silas McGhee recovered and got back to himself again, then Jeb knew there would be some sort of reckoning to pay. Until this was settled, he'd be working with his Army Colt strapped on and his rifle in reach, his eyes keeping on the tree line in daylight and the shadows at night.

But Jeb felt right about what he done to McGhee, dead or not. There was no call for him to say the things he said about Ruby. She wasn't that kind of woman, Bear Quincy or not. She never had told him much about the goings on over there, but Jeb did know that sometimes a person did what they had to, and not what they wanted. Jeb himself had never forced anything on her, not the extra chores and woman's work, or his own manly needs.

But he still recalled those frigid winter nights when the brutal winds and snow blew in from the northwest, howling like ghostly wolves, making the log walls of the cabin tremble and creak. Sometimes on such nights, he woke up to find her standing by his bed, wrapped in her blankets and nearly frozen from the cold. And she would say the words that at the time were as welcome as a mother's hug. "Move over."

There were a lot of ways that people found to survive in this hard, dangerous old world, and who could say which ones were more important than the others?

The snarls and growls and yips of the wolves outside woke Jeb at first light. Without even dressing, he carried his shotgun outside and loosed a few shots up in the direction of

Ruby's grave, too far away to do much damage, but scaring them away with the noise. Then he raised the muzzle up and let go a couple more times at the circling buzzards high above. The wind shifted, and he caught a whiff of Ruby's decaying flesh.

He dressed, then started up the hill toward Ruby's grave, still carrying the shotgun in case he had to discourage the wolves again. *This wasn't going to do,* he thought, as he looked down at yesterday's handiwork. First of all, he had picked a spot too close to the cabin, and he'd be smelling Ruby's sad remains for days or weeks if he didn't do something about it. Some critter had already started digging in the dirt along the edge of the pile of rocks, and a few of the smaller stones he had piled on top were clawed away. There was food under there, and eventually the wild animals from all around, large to tiny, would show up and connive to get their share.

This just wouldn't do at all. Ruby needed to rest in peace, with what dignity he could provide, and Jeb began to realize that he wouldn't have a clear mind until he gave that to her.

With pick and shovel, determination, and back-breaking labor, he managed to get a four-foot-deep grave dug beside where

Ruby lay. He didn't want to have to move her far because he imagined that after two days dead, whatever remained inside that canvas was not something he'd want to pick up off the ground and carry around the hillside or get an unintentional look at if the canvas fell away. Later, he'd rather bring to mind the way she looked that last morning across the breakfast table, sipping her coffee and smiling slightly at him as they laid out their day's work. In the sunlight spilling through the open cabin door, she had looked rested and ready, pleased with the little leather bag of gold he had given her earlier as her share of the week's take, maybe even pleased to be here where she'd ended up, and satisfied to be with him for the time being.

When he thought about her that way, he realized that she wasn't so much trouble to have around. There were a lot worse things to see in the morning than a woman's smile.

As he plodded down to the cabin for his midday meal, Jeb realized that he had been so intent on getting his project started that he hadn't had breakfast. After eating, a wave of exhaustion overtook him. He stretched out on his bunk and was asleep in seconds.

In the dream he had, Ruby was there in the cabin again, rolling out biscuit dough, looking over at him as he came in the door. "You can stomp that mud off your boots before you come in, mister. And you might as well bring in an armload of wood and a bucket of water while you're at it. No reason I should have to do it all the time myself. You haven't lost any arms or legs since I showed up and started doing the chores, have you, Mister Jeb Parkerson?" But it wasn't like nagging. Her eyes twinkled, and she talked to him like he was a youngster that had to be reminded of every little thing. In the dream, Jeb didn't mind it at all.

He spent the afternoon building a coffin for Ruby from the lumber he'd brought up from Elkhorn Springs to use on the sluices. He never had built one before and did his best to make it neat and tight. He put her tick and blankets inside and laid her pillow at one end. Soon Jeb had Ruby settled inside the coffin, down in the grave, with the lid nailed on tight. He thought he would feel better when he got things to that point, with only the grave to fill in tomorrow, and a cross marker to make later.

But standing there beside the grave, knowing she was down there in that box, dead and gone for good, he had an empty feeling inside, and there was an unfamiliar knot in his throat that he never would have expected.

Guilt swept over him, though he knew that there was nothing more he could have done to keep her safe, no way to save her life even if he'd been right there when the snake struck, and no better burying than the one he was giving her now. Maybe he could have treated her better when she was still alive, he conceded. But he hadn't wanted her there in the first place, and a few times, had wished that that she'd just go on off and leave him be. He already had a plan that didn't include her. Once he'd dug whatever fortune he could out of these stony hills, he'd go down out of the mountains and put together a brand-new life for himself. There would be women enough to choose from then, prettier than Ruby, younger and more agreeable, and glad to do their best to make him a happy man. All that was still out there waiting for him, but he had a notion now that sometimes, right in the middle of all those good times, he'd still think about poor old Ruby, buried alone up here in the middle of nowhere.

He'd read over her, Jeb decided. That would have made her happy and might bring him some peace of mind, or at least give him the feeling that he'd done all he could for her in this bad situation. Back in the cabin, he rummaged around in her scant belongings until he found the Bible he knew she kept there. It was worn and ill-used from being carried along through the hard circumstances Ruby had lived through. She didn't read it much, explaining once that too many things in there made her feel bad about the sinful life she'd lived and the sorry choices she'd made. It seemed like every time she opened its pages, it brought to mind something that she should have done differently.

Jeb hadn't had much truck with the Good Book since he was a boy and his daddy used to read to them after supper. He figured he hadn't laid eyes on a Bible in ten years or more, and his reading was rusty, but he hoped he could find something in there that would fit the occasion.

Back at the graveside, Jeb sat down on the edge of the hole with his feet resting on the lid of Ruby's coffin, which didn't seem to him to be any kind of sacrilege. He was worn out from all the hard work and badly needed something to eat and a good night's sleep. But it was dusk now, with the light starting to fade, and he wanted to get this over with while he could still make out the words in Ruby's Bible.

He opened the book and began to thumb his way through, trying to find a few words that he could use to send Ruby off with. But he couldn't find anything that made much sense to him. As the light faded, he decided to go to the beginning and do the best he could. He ran his finger down the pages, finding verses that triggered old, old memories from his boyhood. Finally, he began to feel like he had stumbled onto solid ground. At least he remembered Adam, the first man.

. . . but for Adam there was not found an help meet for him. And the LORD God caused a deep sleep to fall upon Adam, and he slept: and he took one of his ribs, and closed up the flesh instead thereof; And the rib, which the LORD God had taken from man, made he a woman, and brought her unto the man. And Adam said, This is now bone of my bones, and flesh of my flesh: she shall be called Woman, because she was taken out of Man.

Jeb halted the team in front of Bradshaw's Post and looped the reins tight around the wagon brake. In a minute Bradshaw stepped out onto the wooden porch, still sipping his morning coffee from a metal cup. Meadow came as far as the doorway, pausing in the shadows just inside.

"Mornin', Jeb," the store owner said. His eyes scanned the canvas-covered load in the back of the wagon, and he looked puzzled. Usually, the prospectors drove an empty wagon down the mountain and went back up with a load.

"Good morning to you," Jeb said. "Right pretty day, ain't it?" A light coating of frost still blanketed the pasture behind the store, but the sky was clear and the rising sun was warming things up nicely.

"Yep. Now that I'm an old man, I like to see the spring come because my bones stop creaking."

Back behind her husband, Meadow's gazed was fixed on the back of the wagon, her nose crinkling. Jeb had heard that Indians had a sharp sense of smell, far better than white folks.

"What's the word on Silas?"

"He was still breathing after you left, so I left him on the floor where you put him. By the time Meadow and I got up the next morning, he was starting to come around. Couldn't remember much about what happened."

"That's good. I wouldn't have taken no pleasure in knowing I'd killed him. Espe-

350

cially over a woman already dead."

"He left out of here kind of woozy and one eye swolled up like a sweet potato. If I was you, I'd keep a sharp eye out, Jeb."

"No need," Jeb said. "I decided I've had enough of this life up here in the high country, and I'm heading out."

"And you're taking her with you?" From the smell, it had become obvious to Bradshaw and his woman what cargo Jeb was carrying in the wagon.

"I've got her in a box back there, and I need to salt her down good. I'll buy all you've got. Turns out she's got a daughter back in Missouri, and an elderly mother, if she hasn't died. I decided last night that I'd take her home to be near her kinfolks."

"And what about your claim?"

"You can have it. I'll sign it over. You've been a good friend to me, Norman, and I'd like to see you do well. There's still gold to be dug out of those hills. But I'm just tired of it."

"Did you find Ruby's stash?"

"Never even looked for it. Maybe that'll be the icing that will help you get a good price when you sell the claim."

"That'll be downright entertaining," Bradshaw said with a chuckle. "Miss Ruby's Treasure. Fools from a hundred miles around will be crawling all over those hills, turning over rocks and ransacking the cabin. Should be good for business, too."

While they were talking, Meadow had gone into the store, and now she came back carrying as many cloth sacks of salt as she could handle. She dropped them on the ground beside the wagon, then went to work on the ropes securing the canvas covering.

Jeb climbed down from the wagon and turned to her. "Meadow, I'd sure be obliged if you'd take care of this for me. I hate to ask, but I figure all her clothes are going to have to come off to do it right, and she had her pride. There's a pry bar in back to loosen the lid of the coffin."

The Indian woman nodded her head and fell to work as the two men went inside.

Within an hour, Jeb was back on the trail south, which meandered across rolling hills and endless sprawling prairie land that seemed to stretch on forever. He felt good about the decision he made, and only wished she had known before she died that this was what he would end up doing.

That morning before he left the claim, he had walked up the hillside to the spot where she and the rattlesnake had crossed paths and died. The snake's fat, headless carcass was gone now, dragged away and eaten by some other mountain creature. While he was standing there, thinking that he would hold this spot in his memory, he saw a curl of string just visible under the edge of a flat slab of rock. He knelt and pulled at the string, drawing out the small bag of gold, her share, that he had given her that morning.

Forgetting his own rules of survival, he thrust his hand under the flat rock, and pulled out the rest of Ruby's hoard. It was too much, more than he had ever given her as her share, and he wondered for an instant if she had been stealing from him. Then he realized that it must be Bear Quincy's gold, not his. She might have killed him for it or gone back and found it after he was dead. Either way, it didn't matter. All the time she was with him, she had the gold she had come here for, and could have gone on home like she talked about. But she stayed on instead.

That would give him plenty to ponder over during the long journey back to Missouri.

Greg Hunt is the author of over twenty Western and frontier novels. His latest novel is *The Carroll Farm Fight* (Five Star, 2017). He is a native of Missouri, and now lives in Memphis, Tennessee. In an earlier life, he might have been a resident of New Orleans.

A Grave Too Many
by Preston Lewis

Would this feud ever end, Parson Martin Gentry asked himself as he watched Tom Blevins push the edge of the kitchen curtain back enough to peek outside into the fading evening light of a late November day. Blevins patted the butt of his revolver as he looked for the trouble that stalked him. The War Between the States had ceased almost eighteen months earlier, but the killing in their part of Texas had continued as old grudges remained and new ones emerged in the aftermath of defeat. Gentry believed Blevins, a known Union sympathizer, had been more sinned against than sinner in the turmoil that had sent four men to early graves and disabled another seven. Doing most of the sinning, in Gentry's mind at least, was John Wesley, a rabid warrior who had returned from the conflict embittered rather than chastened, but the truth of the vendetta remained as elusive as the peace

357

most folks craved. Gentry feared the feud would never conclude as long as both Tom Blevins and John Wesley survived.

Too old to fight for the Confederacy, Parson Gentry had remained in north Texas, but four of his five sons had taken up the same cause as John Wesley. Three sons returned. One did not. Samuel, his fifth son, had been too young to fight, but now verged on manhood. Standing by his mother near the stove, Sammy stared across the kitchen table at Blevins, the target of so many of the county's unreconstructed citizens. Blevins released the edge of the curtain and turned to face the family, forcing a smile and nodding at Gentry's wife, Susannah, who stirred a pot of stew on the cast-iron stove in the corner. Susannah nodded gently, then placed the spoon in a stovetop cradle and lit two more candles to counter the room's growing gloom as darkness crept up outside.

"Sorry, ma'am, for the intrusion," Blevins apologized, "but today's my boy's birthday. I promised him a present, and I intend to deliver it. Must be hard on you Gentrys, living next to my place, me being the most hunted man in the county."

"Being sought by the law," said Parson Gentry, "is the work of God. Being hunted by the lawless, like you are, is the work of the devil. My place is a refuge from the killing for everyone. I'd do the same for the other side."

"I know you would." Blevins nodded and drew the back of his gun hand over his dry lips. "And, I know you wouldn't tell a soul of my comings and goings, or me of theirs."

The parson nodded slowly, sadly. "Only God can sort the good from the evil, Tom. I'm called to minister to everyone, whether it's you or John Wesley."

Blevins's parched lips tightened, and his hand dropped to the grip of his revolver. "His name grates on my ears, Parson. He and his bunch started it all."

"I won't deny that, Tom, but he's a creature of God."

"So's a rattlesnake," Blevins shot back, "but that don't keep one from biting me."

Susannah stepped toward Blevins and motioned at the kitchen table. "You're welcome to join us for supper, Tom. There's enough stew to share."

Parson Gentry smiled at his wife, proud of her hospitality, even though he knew the servings would be smaller with the added guest, and prouder still that his wife knew when to interrupt his theological discussions when he had no satisfactory answer.

Blevins again peered outside the window. "It smells mighty fine, Mrs. Gentry, but I'm just a mile from the house, and I've a hankering for Emma's cooking. I didn't want to approach home in the daylight so I appreciate you letting me stay and hide my horse in your barn."

"The Gentry place is a refuge for all until God can straighten this county out," the parson added.

Stepping back from the window, Blevins nodded. "I just want it safe for my Emma and my boy." He nodded at Sammy, still standing by his mother. "I want my boy to grow up like Sammy there and be able to ride the roads without worrying about getting shot in the back by his father's enemies."

Parson Gentry glanced from Blevins to his youngest son. "Samuel's turned out fine for the runt of the litter."

Sammy grinned. "I'm his favorite."

"That's true," Gentry responded. "Of course, he's the only one at home with me and his momma now so we don't have many to choose from anymore or to help us with the chores. How old's your boy now, Tom? Jacob, isn't it?"

"Jake's nine today."

"I bet you got him a fine gift."

"Bought it in Fort Worth, I did. A tin whistle."

"What about a gift for yourself, Tom? Have you accepted the greatest gift of all? How are you with God?"

"I've been baptized, Parson, if that's what you mean."

"Baptized, not sprinkled, right?"

Blevins grinned. "Yep, full Baptist, Parson. Got baptized and a bath at the same time."

Gentry smiled. "That's the way it should be done. You sure you won't stay for a bowl of stew? Mrs. Gentry's a fine cook."

"I know that to be true, but I want to ride on as soon as it's full dark." He glanced out the window again. "It's getting close. Give me a few more minutes, then I'll fetch my horse and get out of your hair."

"I'll have Samuel get your horse, Tom, so you can stay inside until it's a little darker."

"That's neighborly of you, Parson, assuming Sammy don't mind the extra chore."

Sammy nodded and grinned. "I'm glad to do it. I can say I helped Tom Blevins in his feud with John Wesley."

Parson Gentry stomped his boot on the plank floor. "You'll say no such thing, Samuel! We don't mention the comings or goings of any visitors to our home, not with this vendetta still burning hot as a branding

361

iron. We don't take sides, and we don't brag about helping one side or the other. We help everyone. Do you understand?"

Sammy bowed his head. "Sorry, Papa, and Mr. Blevins. If you'll excuse me, I'll go to the barn and get his mount."

"Wait just a moment," Gentry said. "Let's pray before you go."

Blevins removed his hat as Susannah and Samuel stepped to the parson. Sammy took his mother and father's hands, then Gentry and his wife extended theirs to Blevins.

"We hold hands when we pray in this house," Gentry informed him.

Blevins nodded, then placed his hat on the table and gently grabbed the proffered hands of his hosts.

After everyone bowed, Parson Gentry began. "Oh, God, see Brother Blevins safely to his family and let this be but the first of many birthdays he will share with his son, Jacob. Protect his son and his Emma from the dangers of the lawlessness that pervades this county. Help him and his enemies see the errors of their ways and come to lie down together like the lamb with the lion. For these blessings we beseech Thee and would be eternally grateful for your gift of them. Amen."

"Amen," repeated the others as Parson

Gentry opened his eyes and released Blevins's hand.

"Okay, Samuel, fetch Tom's horse. Make sure he gets some water so Tom won't have to tend to that when he gets home."

"Yes, Papa."

As Sammy walked out the back door, Blevins picked up his hat and placed it atop his head. "Thank you for your hospitality and your prayers, Parson. I feel safer now."

"Just the same, Tom, you keep your eyes and ears open. I think there's more right than wrong on your side in this vendetta, but God is the ultimate judge of all men's affairs. Ride with God as you leave here."

"I will, Parson. Thank you both for your hospitality in spite of my intrusion, and thank you for your blessings on my safety." Blevins stepped to the window and looked outside again. "It's plenty dark now, so I'll be on my way once Sammy returns."

"I've a couple of cold biscuits from lunch you can take with you," Susannah offered.

"That's mighty kind, ma'am, but I bet my Emma's baked some fresh ones for Jake's birthday," Blevins replied. "I've missed her cooking while I've been on the run."

They heard Sammy approaching, humming a song with each step as he neared the back of the house. Parson Gentry grimaced as he realized his son was humming "Dixie."

"Pay no mind to Samuel's music," Gentry apologized. "He means nothing by it."

Blevins cocked his ear toward the door, listened, and smiled. " 'Dixie,' isn't it?"

Parson Gentry nodded.

"It's a fine tune. I heard tell the night Robert E. Lee surrendered that our martyred President Lincoln had a band serenade the White House with a rendition of 'Dixie.' I figure if he was forgiving enough to request 'Dixie,' I can listen to it without rancor. I just wish John Wesley was as forgiving."

As Sammy neared the back porch, Blevins shook the parson's hand and tipped his hat to Susannah, then opened the door and stepped out into the night. He took the reins from Sammy, mounted his horse, and rode cautiously around the house, then angled toward his own home. Sammy came inside and closed the door behind him. Susannah stepped to the stove, stirred the stew, and announced that supper was hot.

Gentry looked around the room at the four burning candles and blew out the flames of the two farthest from the table. No sense burning more candles than necessary to eat as they were expensive, and money was tight, especially for a parson.

Preaching put little food on the table, so he had to farm as well to eat. He wished not only for enough to feed his wife and son, but also for enough to barter for their other needs and an occasional luxury for his dwindling family.

Sammy fetched bowls and spoons, placing the utensils on the table and carrying the wooden dishes to Susannah so she could fill them with the steaming stew. The aroma of beef, potatoes, and tomatoes tickled the parson's nose, and he wished he could provide greater fare for his family, but he had a calling as a preacher that always overrode everything else. Despite his successes and failures, he always seemed to have enough of everything, but never too much of anything. At least he didn't have to ride around the county fearful of being shot in the back or having his family or home attacked. In that way he was certainly richer than Tom Blevins.

As Susannah filled the three bowls with stew, Gentry seated himself at the head of the small table, propped his elbows on the surface, clasped his hands beneath his chin, bowed his head, and said a silent prayer for Tom Blevins, Emma, and Jacob. His own son sat down to his left as Susannah placed the bowls in front of each, then sat to

Gentry's right. The parson mouthed "amen," then lowered his hands to those extended to him by wife and son. As his fingers clasped theirs, he dropped his head and blessed the meal, then gave his wife's hand a tender squeeze, a sign of affection he always shared with her after a mealtime prayer, his way of thanking his partner for assisting him with God's work.

They ate silently, their meal lit by the two flickering candles. As he chewed, Gentry felt as inadequate as the candles that fought the nighttime gloom of the room. Just as the candles were too weak to cast the darkness aside, Gentry felt impotent to dispel the wickedness that had tainted his slice of Texas since Appomattox. But how could one man, a modest preacher who eschewed violence at that, bring peace and justice to a land that thirsted for both? If the Union troops assigned to bring order to the region had failed, how could Gentry become a peacemaker? Questions such as those tormented his conscience every day as a man of God in a godless land. In such moments of weakness as this, Gentry always turned to his Bible. Even if the Holy Book couldn't provide answers to all his questions, its wise words would soothe his conscience and fight his self-doubts.

As he finished his thoughts and his supper, he heard a noise muffled by distance. He feared it was the dying boom of a shotgun, likely both barrels. Silently, he looked to his wife and son, their anxious eyes widening. They, too, had heard it. One, two, three, four more delicate retorts carried from the distance, and Gentry took them to be shots fired from one or more pistols.

"I fear Tom Blevins is dead," Gentry said softly. "I failed in my prayers."

Susannah reached toward him, took his hand, and squeezed it tightly. "You did your best, Martin. You can't torment yourself over it. What a terrible birthday for his boy."

Gentry nodded and squeezed his wife's hand. "Thank you, Susannah, but I failed."

"Papa," Sammy whispered, "are we safe?"

"I don't know anymore, son, I don't know."

"I suppose you'll handle his funeral, Martin, won't you?"

Gentry stared at the table. "I think not, Susannah."

His wife yanked her hand from his, shocked by his answer. "But, Martin, you —"

Gentry raised his hand for silence. "You don't understand, woman. If his friends came, John Wesley and his ruffians might ambush them as well. So, his friends'll stay away for their own safety. A funeral without guests honors no man. I'll not conduct his funeral, Susannah, but I'll bury him." Gentry grasped his wife's hand again, feeling a tremor in her fingers.

"I'll go with you, Papa," Sammy volunteered.

Gentry pushed his chair back from the table and stood up. "No, son, I must go alone. What I would like you to do is to hitch the team to the wagon and throw the shovel, pick, and axe in the back so I can dig the grave. Come morning, I'd like you to make a cross for a marker."

"Yes, Papa," Sammy answered as he arose and walked to the back door.

The parson watched his youngest son step outside into the darkness to attend to his task. As the door closed, Gentry arose, eased to his wife, and hugged her. "I think I'll retire to our room and read the Bible until the wagon is ready."

Susannah returned his embrace, then gently pushed herself away far enough to grab each arm and look into his eyes. "Are you are okay, Martin?"

"I failed Tom, Susannah, I failed him. My prayer went unheard and unanswered."

"You can't blame yourself, Martin."

Gentry kissed Susannah on the forehead. "I'll do better once I've had a few minutes to read the Bible and ask forgiveness." He slipped from his wife's grasp, picked up a candle, and carried it into the modest bedroom he shared with Susannah. He placed the candle in a holder on the tiny table by his reading chair, sat down, and picked up his Bible, thumbing the well-worn book to the third chapter of Ecclesiastes. "To every thing there is a season, and a time to every purpose under the heaven," he read. "A time to be born, and a time to die; a time to plant, and a time to pluck up that which is planted." Gentry knew the whole chapter by memory, but it soothed him to read the printed scripture aloud. He read the entire chapter twice, stopping in between to say a prayer for Tom Blevins, his soul, and his family. When he heard Samuel pull the wagon up out back, he said a final prayer, asking a blessing upon himself for what he knew he must do. He placed his Bible back on the stand, stood up, retrieved the candle, and returned to the kitchen as Sammy barged in and hurriedly shut the door behind him.

"What is it, Samuel?" Gentry demanded.

"A rider's skulking out behind the barn,"

Samuel answered, his lip trembling.

Gentry blew out his candle. "Susannah, kill the other."

His wife complied quickly. Gentry eased to the back window, moved the curtain aside, and peered into the distance as Tom Blevins had done less than an hour earlier. Gentry thought he could make out a dark form approaching, but the darkness was thick and his worries thicker. His muscles tightened when Gentry heard the sinister call of a man on horseback.

"Hello the house," came the cry. "Is Parson Gentry home?"

Susannah gasped. "Don't answer him, Martin!"

"Who wants to know?" Gentry called back.

"It's your friend, John Wesley," came the answer. "I need you to do something."

"I only follow God's orders, John Wesley."

"Get out here or you'll be seeing God face-to-face in a minute. I'll burn your house down, if I have to, and shoot your family like varmints when you run out," Wesley replied.

"Keep my family out of this, John Wesley."

"Then get out here."

"No, Martin, no," cried Susannah.

"Don't, Papa, don't," Sammy begged.

Gentry shook his head. "I've got to. I can't let him harm you."

"And we can't let him harm you," Susannah retorted.

"I've got to trust in God," Gentry replied as he brushed past his wife.

She folded her arms across her bosom. "He didn't answer your prayers with Tom Blevins!"

"Hush, woman! No more blasphemy!" Gentry stepped to the door and eased it open. "I'm coming out, John Wesley. I'm unarmed, save for the armor of God."

Wesley laughed. "His armor won't do you much good against a forty-five slug."

"He'll protect me when I need it," Gentry said, slipping outside, closing the door behind him, and stepping off the porch. "What is it you want, John Wesley?"

"I got some news for you, Parson," Wesley sneered. "It seems Tom Blevins had an accident between your place and his. Best I can tell he was trying to load his shotgun when it went off and hurt him bad."

Gentry looked up at Wesley's gaunt figure on his skittish horse, just making out the killer's eyes in the darkness. As Gentry took a step toward the feudist, Wesley's horse nickered and backed away.

"Easy, boy," Wesley said, leaning over and patting his mount on the neck, then describing the accident. "Seems the pain was so bad from him shot-gunning himself that he pulled out his pistol and shot his brains out."

"Did it take him four shots to do it?" Gentry answered.

"Can't say, Parson, as he was dead before I could ask him. Point is, I know you do preaching and undertaking and even some doctoring as well, Parson. You need to know he's beyond doctoring, and preaching won't do him any good now. As for undertaking, you just leave him be, let the wild hogs and varmints take care of his remains, what's left of them."

Gentry shook his head. "I can't do that, John Wesley. Every man's entitled to a decent burial. I've had no part in this feud and haven't taken sides."

"That's a lie, Parson. You hid him this evening."

"He asked for shelter, and I gave it to him. I'd do the same for you or your accomplices. I'd even bury you, John Wesley, and give you the final respect every man deserves."

"I've told you once, and I'll tell you again, Parson. Don't bury Blevins! I want to come back in a year and see his bones bleaching in the sun. If I return and he's not where I left him, you'll've taken his side in this feud."

Gentry shook his head. "I do what God tells me, not man."

"If God tells you otherwise, he must not like you because I *will* kill you."

The parson stepped suddenly toward Wesley, whose horse shook his head, snorted, then danced away from Gentry. "Then do it now, John Wesley!"

Gentry heard Susannah gasp from behind the door.

"Go ahead, John Wesley, shoot me now and save yourself a trip."

Wesley spat at Gentry's feet, then yanked the reins on his horse, which spun around. The murderer looked over his shoulder at the parson. "I'll be checking on you, Parson, and on Blevins and he better be where I left him or someone'll have to dig you a grave." Wesley nudged his horse in the flank, and the animal trotted away into the darkness.

Instantly, Susannah and Sammy burst out the door, racing to Gentry. Susannah flung her arms around her husband. "Oh, Martin, what are you going to do?"

"Bury Tom Blevins," he answered.

His day of reckoning with John Wesley

would come as sure as the sun would rise in the morning, Parson Gentry knew, but he had done what was right, what God led him to do. He worried not for himself, but for Susannah and Samuel, for he had dug a hole and then made a grave for Tom Blevins the very night he had died, contrary to John Wesley's orders. Gentry had spent twice as much time as he usually did in preparing the final resting place for a deceased. Gentry had found Blevins's body a bloody pulp from the shotgun blast, likely to the back, though it was hard to tell in the darkness. He searched Blevins's pockets and found a few greenbacks and the tin whistle he had planned to deliver as a birthday gift for his son. Gentry regretted he had not taken one of Susannah's old quilts with him so he could have wrapped the feud's latest victim before lowering him into the earth's dark embrace. But the night was cold, and Gentry had too much work to do in decoying Blevins's grave so that his body might rest in peace. After he had lowered Blevins into the earth, Gentry placed the dead man's hat over his face, said a silent prayer, and then shoveled dirt over the body.

When he had finished filling the grave, Gentry climbed into his wagon and directed the team over the pimpled spot several times to help disguise the site. It was a feeble effort, Gentry knew, because freshly turned dirt was hard to disguise, but he did it in the hope that Blevins might rest peacefully. Then he had ridden to the Blevins cabin and informed Emma that she was a widow. She and Jacob sobbed, and, despite his efforts, Gentry could not console them. He fished the tin whistle out of his pocket and offered it to Jacob, identifying it as a gift to him from his father. He gave the inconsolable widow the greenbacks her husband had carried in his pocket. As if the death of their husband and father wasn't sorrow enough to face, Gentry told them he feared for their lives, the vindictiveness of John Wesley and his gang likely unsatisfied by Blevins's death. Gentry helped them hurriedly pack what clothes and belongings they could, then tossed those possessions in the back of his wagon. After the last load, Emma boosted Jacob into the wagon seat, turned around, and retreated to the door, kissing it and her home goodbye, likely forever. After she climbed into the wagon, Gentry drove them toward the freshly turned dirt on the grave where Tom Blevins would spend eternity. Emma sobbed and Jacob blew his tin whistle, but Gentry did not stop for them to pay further respects as evil men might be watching and might return to desecrate the grave.

Back home Susannah and Samuel had welcomed Emma and Jacob, promising them they could stay as long as they needed. Gentry ran the wagon into the barn without unloading their belongings, then saddled a horse and rode off to find a trustworthy neighbor who could take Emma and Jacob out of the county to a place of safety. That very night the sorrowful journey of Emma and Jacob Blevins continued as a reliable neighbor drove them in Gentry's wagon to a safe haven thirty miles west of Fort Worth. The next morning, Gentry rode back to the mound of freshly turned dirt, leaned over in his saddle, and stuck Samuel's makeshift cross into the still soft ground at the head of the upturned soil. He mouthed a prayer for the safety of Tom Blevins's family and for an end to the county's wickedness.

The next evening after supper, Gentry and his family heard shouts and gunfire from the direction of the Blevins place. Gentry slipped outside and in the distance saw a glow like a yellow tombstone on the horizon. John Wesley or his allies had returned to the Blevins place to murder his wife and son, then burn the cabin to the ground. They, of course, had failed to kill Emma and Jacob, which was God's blessing, but now Parson Gentry feared he had thrust his own family into the feud simply by doing the right thing. Might he wake up one night with his own home aflame? The fear tormented him for the following week. He prayed harder than ever and yet nothing allayed his apprehension. During that week, he relieved Samuel of all outside chores so his son might not be seen or ambushed by a cowardly sniper. Then he waited for the day that John Wesley would return.

That moment arrived on a crisp morning as Gentry exited the barn carrying the pail of milk he had just squeezed from the family cow. Halfway between the barn and the kitchen door, Gentry observed John Wesley approaching on his black gelding. The murderer cradled a double-barreled shotgun in the crook of his arm. His vindictive eyes burned with the rage of revenge.

Gentry felt fear coursing through his veins, but he walked, firm and steady, determined to hide his fears, even when John Wesley leveled his shotgun at Gentry's stomach. The parson took solace in Romans 8:31: "If God be for us, who can be against us?" Surely God was for him. The thought gave him a dose of courage. He thrust out his chest and strode proudly forward.

"Morning, Pastor. You didn't pay no mind to what I told you on my last visit."

"I follow God's commands, not yours, John Wesley." The parson stepped toward Wesley.

The killer's horse nickered, then backed away. "Damnation, Pastor, even my horse don't like you."

"Don't use that kind of language on my place, John Wesley."

The kitchen door swung open, and Susannah rushed onto the porch, gasping in fear. "Martin," she cried.

Sammy came out behind her, his jaw set in defiance, but his eyes jittery and nervous.

"Morning, ma'am," John Wesley mocked. "Just wanted to visit your husband and take him for a stroll. Seems he doesn't take to instructions well."

"He takes to God's instructions, not man's," she shot back.

Proud of his wife and her defiance of evil, Gentry smiled. "It's okay, Susannah. God will protect me."

Wesley laughed. "We'll see if God can protect you from a shotgun blast, Pastor."

"Not in front of my family, John Wesley. Surely, you are not so evil as to do that."

"Nope, Pastor. You and I are going for a little walk. I told you not to bury Tom

Blevins, but you went ahead and did so."

"I'd do the same thing for you, John Wesley. The deceased harbor no vendettas."

"But I do, Pastor. Now have your boy fetch your shovel, and let's go visit Tom Blevins."

Gentry stepped to the porch and sat the milk pail at its edge. "Samuel, would you run to the barn for my shovel." He nodded, jumped off the porch, and raced to the barn. "Susannah, would you retrieve my Bible for me?"

"Oh, Martin," she said, "I'm scared for you."

"The Bible will be my shield."

John Wesley laughed as Susannah retreated into the kitchen. "You place a lot of faith in that old book. It ain't gonna save you now, not after you sided with Tom Blevins. I intend to settle our score."

"Vengeance is God's, not yours or mine," Gentry replied as Samuel came running from the barn, carrying the shovel. Gentry took the tool from his son, noticing a quiver in Samuel's lower lip. "It'll be okay, son. God will look after me." He patted Samuel on the shoulder as Susannah, tears streaming down her cheeks, burst from the house, bounded down the steps, and thrust the Bible in her husband's hand. As soon as he took the Bible, she threw her arms around him.

"Oh, Martin, I don't want to lose you. Tell me what I can do?"

"Just pray, Susannah. That's all any of us can do."

"Okay, Pastor, it's time for us to go." Wesley scowled and waved his shotgun at Gentry.

"Let me saddle my horse first," Gentry replied.

Wesley shook his head. "It's not that far, Pastor, and you won't be returning."

Susannah bawled and hugged her son.

"God'll decide that, John Wesley, not you."

Wesley looked up at the cloudless sky and snickered. "I don't see your God anywhere, Pastor. And if he's a Yankee God, I don't want any part of him." Wesley waved the shotgun for Gentry to start walking, then turned to Susannah and sneered. "Say goodbye to your man of God. If I hear you or the boy've told the law about this, I'll come back and kill the both of you."

With his right hand Gentry placed his Bible against his heart, then took the shovel mid-handle with his left and smiled at his wife and son. "I'll be back by noon. Have a good meal for me," Gentry said, strangely confident of his return. As he started toward the Blevins place, Gentry said a silent prayer for God's grace over his wife and son to ease their worry until he returned. He felt no need to pray for himself. His faith assured him he would survive, even though the sobs of his wife told him otherwise.

As he walked around the corner of the cabin, John Wesley trailed, riding a gelding as black as his own heart. The horse seemed as skittish as John Wesley was wicked. Perhaps a nervous horse favored a man on the prowl, sensing danger before a rider's instincts kicked in.

"Where are we headed, John Wesley?"

"To the grave I found where Tom Blevins died. You even put up a cross to spite me."

"I did what God told me."

"So you speak to God, do you? Have him say something to me, Pastor."

"Your heart is too hardened to hear, even if he spoke."

"My ears are listening, Pastor, and I don't hear a goddam thing."

"Don't blaspheme God, John Wesley, or you'll tempt fate." The pastor extended the Bible toward Wesley. "The Holy Book will save me."

"Nothing can protect you now, Gentry, and save your breath 'cause you'll need it to dig up Tom Blevins."

Gentry pressed his Bible against his heart and walked silently toward the crude cross Samuel had fashioned from a pair of weathered boards. The pastor walked slowly, taking a half hour to reach the site. John Wesley relished the walk like a tomcat toying with an injured mouse before the kill.

When they reached the cross beneath a stand of live oaks, Gentry ignored his accuser and stared at the earth, gratified that he had taken twice as long as usual to give Tom Blevins a proper grave, not just a hole in the ground.

"Quit stalling and start digging," Wesley ordered. "I want his body removed and scattered to the four winds."

Gentry smiled at the command, even if the task was repulsive and ungodly. He removed his coat and hung it from the stub of a broken tree branch, then placed his Bible on the rock at the base of the tree. After rolling up his sleeves, Gentry stepped to the mound of dirt and attacked it a shovelful at a time. He worked slowly and deliberately, tossing the dirt in a pile that grew taller as he dug deeper. The digging was easy compared to the first time he had excavated the hole. He had thought a lot that dark night about how to provide Tom Blevins a grave beyond John Wesley's reach.

As the pastor shoveled dirt, John Wesley circled him on his horse, never getting down, likely so he could dash away if anyone approached. Gentry doubted that possibility as no one else but him and the dead man's wife and son knew where Tom Blevins lay buried. Gentry kept digging, confident that Tom Blevins would rest in peace in spite of John Wesley.

Finally, when the hole was about three feet deep, Gentry hit hard, unturned dirt. "I'm at the bottom," he announced.

"Then throw out the body."

Gentry shook his head. "Can't do it."

"I don't care how disgusting the chore is, throw out the body."

"It's not here!"

"What do you mean, it's not here? Don't tell me Tom Blevins arose from the grave!"

"Well, he's not here. Come see for yourself."

Wesley yanked the reins on his black gelding and steered him to the shallow pit where Gentry stood. The gelding shook his head and blew his displeasure as Wesley forced him to approach the hole and the pastor. Standing up in his stirrups to inspect the hole, Wesley pointed the shotgun at Gentry.

"There's nothing here but me," Gentry said.

Wesley's face reddened with rage. "What's your play, Gentry?"

"I dug two graves the night you ambushed Tom Blevins."

"Then you dug a grave too many, Gentry. Take me to the other and dig him up."

"Won't do it, John Wesley. Your hatred ends here, ends now."

"My hatred will simmer until every carpet-bagger and Yankee-lover like you is dead in Texas." Wesley twisted the reins and directed his horse to the foot of the hole, all the time aiming the shotgun at Gentry. "Take me to his grave or die here, Gentry."

The pastor shook his head. "The feud's over for Tom Blevins! You'll not drag him back into it."

"Then, Gentry, you just dug your own grave."

The parson unrolled his sleeves, then buttoned the cuffs. "I'd like to die in my coat with my Bible in my hand."

"Nothing doing," Wesley answered, pointing the shotgun at Gentry and backing his horse away from the foot of the would-be grave.

Gentry stared at the shotgun's twin black eyes, looking into the darkness of eternity. His faith gave him courage as he stepped to the foot of the hole and used the shovel to push himself out of his grave, pulling the implement with him. He straightened to his full height, then stepped away from the edge of the pit, his hand gripping tightly the shovel's handle.

The gelding tossed his head and snorted. Wesley struggled to control the animal and keep his weapon aimed at Gentry.

"You plan to shoot me in the back like you did Tom Blevins, John Wesley, or can you look me in the eyes when you pull the trigger?"

"Damn right I can, Pastor. Prepare to meet your maker, you son of a bitch."

Gentry nodded, vowing to die as a man, not a coward. He thrust his chest out and flung the shovel aside.

The abrupt movement frightened the fidgety gelding, which suddenly reared on its hind legs as John Wesley tugged the reins to control the animal. The rider cursed God as the gelding landed on his hooves.

Gentry flung his hands in the air and jumped at the horse, screaming shrilly.

The frightened animal bucked and reared on its hind legs again.

Wesley yanked the reins with his left hand, while his right hand flailed to control the shotgun.

Gentry kicked the shovel at the bucking mount.

The whining gelding reared again, kicking the air with his forelegs, as Wesley lost his balance.

Boom! The shotgun exploded, then fell from Wesley's hand.

The black hide of the gelding's neck turned red, splotched with blood.

Wesley tumbled backward, just as the dying horse collapsed on its back, the gelding's legs twitching uncontrollably. Wesley disappeared beneath the horse, which thrashed about momentarily until death overtook the gelding.

Wesley screamed in agony, first at the pain and then in horror as he realized he was pinned between his dead mount and the cold earth. He fought against the carcass to free himself, panicking at the futility of his exertions, then glancing about to find his shotgun.

Realizing Wesley's goal, Gentry dashed around the slain horse and grabbed the shotgun. He stepped to Wesley, thrashing on the ground, his right arm flopping helplessly at his side, evidently broken in the fall. Desperate, Wesley reached with his left hand for the pistol pinned under his right hip, but he could not reach the sidearm, the pain from his broken bones pulsing like molten lead through his body. He screamed. Gentry stuck the shotgun at Wesley's ear and stepped on his broken arm, drawing more shrieks and curses from his former captor. The pastor bent over and yanked the revolver from Wesley's holster, then backed to the rear of the horse, pulling Wesley's carbine from its scabbard.

"I can't use my arm," Wesley cried. "My leg feels broke. Help me! Please, Pastor, help me!"

Gentry carried the weapons to the tree where he had hung his coat, dropping the rifle and revolver, then breaking open the shotgun's breech to make sure both barrels had been fired. They had. He then snapped the barrels back in place, grabbed the business end of the weapon, and beat it against the tree until the stock broke.

All the time Wesley screamed in agony. "Help me, don't shoot me," he cried.

Until then, Gentry had never considered shooting John Wesley, so he picked up the carbine and pointed it at the feudist.

Wesley begged for mercy. "Please don't, Pastor, please don't shoot me. I'm not ready to die."

"Neither was Tom Blevins," Gentry answered, then aimed at Wesley's hat a couple feet behind the wounded man's head. He pulled the trigger. The gun exploded. The hat flew backward. Wesley flinched, then begged for mercy.

Gentry fought the devil's urging to shoot John Wesley and put him out of his misery like he would a wounded animal, but animals didn't have souls. John Wesley did, no matter how dark it might be. Instead of shooting over his antagonist again, Gentry turned to the hole he had twice dug and then he fired, emptying the gun into the pit that John Wesley had planned to make the pastor's grave. When he had levered the final hull out of the weapon, he grabbed it by the barrel and beat it against the tree until it, too, shattered.

Once the carbine was useless, he picked up the revolver and took it over to Wesley, whose eyes widened as he whimpered in pain and fear. Wesley fought against the gelding's body to free himself, but the excruciating pain of his crushed hip and broken leg left him breathless and grimacing as tears of agony drained from his eyes.

In an ungodly moment, Gentry squatted by John Wesley and stuck the revolver barrel in his ear. "The devil in me says I should pull the trigger. What do you think, John Wesley?"

"No, no," Wesley pleaded.

Gentry nodded. "Maybe you're right." He stood up, then stepped to the gelding's head. Bending over, he shot the animal in the ear, not to ensure the gelding was dead as much as to terrorize John Wesley. It was an ungodly gesture, Gentry knew, but one that seemed appropriate nonetheless. Then he shot the pistol in the air until it was empty, broke it apart, and tossed the parts in the directions of the four winds, just as Wesley would have had him do with Tom Blevins's body.

Gentry retreated to the tree to retrieve his coat, which he grabbed and draped over his arm. He picked up his Bible, held it against his heart, and offered a silent prayer of gratitude to God.

"Please, Pastor, please!" Wesley sobbed, "Help me! Don't leave me trapped here!"

Gentry finished his prayer and turned to his tormentor.

Wesley pleaded, "Give me a chance!"

"Like the chance you gave Tom Blevins or planned to give me?"

"I was funning you, Pastor," he cried. "It hurts, it hurts bad. Please help me."

Gentry nodded. "Okay, I'll give you the best medicine I can, the Word of God." He opened the third chapter of Ecclesiastes and read to John Wesley about a season and a time to every purpose under heaven, a time to be born and a time to die. When he completed the chapter, he closed his Bible and looked at John Wesley, helplessly trapped beneath his horse. "I think, John Wesley, you need some time alone with God. May he have mercy on your soul for I have no more to spare today."

"Don't leave me, Pastor, don't. I hurt so."

"No more than the families you've wounded with your meanness. Good day, John Wesley. You need to have a long talk with God about all your sins."

"Please don't go."

"I promised my family I'd be back for my noon meal," Gentry said, "and I promise you I'll be back tomorrow." Gentry turned his back on his tormentor and walked away. He was halfway home before the sound of Wesley's screams and cries died away in the distance.

As he came within sight of his modest home, the front door flung open, and Susannah and Sammy bolted out toward him, shouting and crying as they ran. He raced toward them, opening his arms for them. They ran into his embrace, and he grasped them both.

"We heard shots, then feared you were

dead," Susannah sobbed.

"Are you okay, Papa?" Sammy asked. "What happened?"

"God decided not to call me home, son."

"But John Wesley," Susannah asked, "what about him?"

Gentry pulled himself from the grasp of his wife and son, then put his arms over their shoulders as they walked back to their humble place.

Sammy echoed his mother's question. "What about John Wesley?"

"He's contemplating his relationship with God."

"And what about you?" Susannah asked.

"I'm fine, just hungry. In the morning, though, I'll need to retrieve my shovel and see if I dug a grave too many."

Preston Lewis is the Spur Award–winning author of thirty western, juvenile, and historical novels. He is best known for his comic western series, *The Memoirs of H.H. Lomax.*

FRANK & JESSE
BY BILL BROOKS

They were hired to go up to the summer range and watch over Mr. Flaver's herd of shorthorn cattle for the season and then bring them down to the valley before the snow fell.

"You boys think you can handle that?" Mr. Flaver asked over whiskey at the Two Queens there in Askin.

"We've been watching over cattle a lot," Frank said. "Rode all the trails before them Kansas grangers put the kibosh to the herds and starting putting up bob wire."

"You boys in the war too?"

"Was, ain't no more," Jesse said. "I reckon you heard that, though."

"I reckon I did, seeing's how it's been over ten years. What you boys been doing in the meantime?"

"Knocking around, mostly," Frank said.

"Knocking around," Mr. Flaver said, as if he didn't see that as much of an accomplishment. But he needed two men to ride up into high country and take over from the two that was there. Or, make that one. Blevins had come down two days ago asking for his pay.

"I'm sick," he said.

"Sick of what?" Mr. Flaver asked.

"Sick of them goddamn stinking cattle and sick of that one-eyed son of a bitch Morrisey. He can't cook worth a damn and I sure can't neither, nor will I. So let me collect what I'm owed for the past month and good luck to you."

"Well, that is a hell of a piece of news," Mr. Flaver said, getting out his checkbook and scratching a month's pay on it with a nib pen he dipped into ink; then he tore it out of the book, handed it over, and said, "I sure hope you ain't lookin' for no work 'round Askin no more, 'cause nobody's gone hire a quitter."

"That's fine, they ain't, 'cause I'm quittin' this country and headed for the gold strikes up in Colorado. Georgette Mims is going with me."

"You mean that crib whore works out behind Winegrove's lumberyard?"

"I reckon you met her, then?"

"I reckon I heard of her. She's diddled ever'thing that walks or talks, you included, must be."

"Well, she's officially out of the whore business. We're going to get married."

"Sounds like you two will make the perfect couple. Don't let that door hit you in the pockets."

So that was it and Mr. Flaver needed a hand to hire to go on up to the summer meadow and help out Morrisey, the leftover man. He ran into Frank and Jesse there in the saloon and judged they looked like hands the way they were dressed in faded blue shirts with large kerchiefs draped around their necks, dungarees rolled halfway up the shafts of the worn boots, and those Stetsons that had seen better days notched back off their white foreheads and weathered faces.

They were as lean and hard as fence posts but stood relaxed with one foot resting on the rail and elbows propped on the bar slavering over a nice cold beer and a shot of good whiskey before them.

Jesse smoked a cigarette and Frank stared up at a mounted buffalo head over the bar and muttered, "Big son of a bitch, ain't it?"

Frank looked, and said, "Yeah. Wonder who got that and where they got it at. Ain't seen a buffalo anywhere in Texas no longer or nowhere else for that matter I know of."

"Me either," Jesse said, lifting his beer and swallowing half down, then swiping his long sable mustaches with thumb and forefinger to get the beer foam out. "I knew an old boy in the war claimed he hunted buffalo with Custer in Kansas. Said that son of a bitch missed and shot his own horse out from under him, and this was in Kiowa country, I do believe."

"Jesus, he was that bad a shot, huh?"

"I reckon. Must have surprised the shit out of that buffalo."

"His horse too, I reckon," said Jesse.

They both laughed at that.

They were just getting around to that other thing cowboys talk about, women, when Mr. Flaver approached them.

"Stand you boys a drink?"

"I won't stop you," Jesse said.

"I won't neither," said Frank.

Mr. Flaver circled a forefinger in the air and the barman brought over a bottle.

"Whyn't we walk this over to a table," Mr. Flaver said.

"Sounds like a capital idea," Frank said and the three took the bottle and found an empty table and propped themselves into chairs. Flaver poured, then they drank, then he refilled each of their glasses.

"I was wondering if either of you is looking for a job maybe?"

Frank looked at Jesse and Jesse looked back. Frank usually did most of the talking because Jesse didn't care much for discussing business of any kind. He'd talk you to death if it was talking horses, dogs he'd owned, which was the best of the cattle trails he and Frank had ridden — Jesse was partial to the Goodnight-Loving while Frank thought the Sedalia-Baxter Springs was the better, but that was only because he met a strawberry blonde chippie who'd taken his virginity in Baxter Springs, and a man's first time is something not easily forgot or let go of.

But neither Frank nor Jesse missed too much about trailing them damn mossy horns that would hook, or stampede, in the middle of the night, and you go racing after them on the deck of a hurricane pony praying to the Lord it don't step in some damn gopher hole and pitch you headlong just to be stamped into ground meat by those hooves.

A cattle drive was, in fact, how Frank and Jesse first met, going up the Western trail.

Frank and Jesse had both fought in the War Between the States: Frank for the Union, and Jesse for the Confederacy. But once the war was over, they put it away because a man just can't keep fighting a war forever is the way they both looked at it and that's what struck a chord of friendship between them. They were just young men who were lucky enough to survive getting shot or bayoneted and came home with all their limbs attached.

They'd both taken up droving for the time being. It was an adventure — kinda like the war, only not so terrible.

And besides, they got to do it from the back of a horse and they both admired and appreciated that species of animal a great deal.

"The onliest thing can match a good horse for beauty is a woman," Frank often opined around the fire or in a saloon.

"Except if the woman is ugly like some I seen," Jesse offered.

"Listen to me, old son," Frank would as likely say. "You turn out all the lights and they're as beautiful as you like them to be."

"True enough."

"A woman and a horse has a lot in common," Frank would say.

"And you can ride both."

"True too."

"And you can talk sweet to 'em and they'll listen."

"Well, you can't marry 'em."

400

"I know a feller who tried — up in Liberal, Kansas, once. Rode straight into the justice of the peace's office and said he loved his horse so much he wanted to marry it, official."

"Do tell."

"That justice got down and looked and said, 'Well, you can't marry this damn horse, it's a gelding.' "

Frank chuckled at that, but another hand sitting around the fire that night listening — a dull boy who'd once been kicked in the head by a cow he was milking — leaned in and said, "A geldin', why gol-dern. Dint he think a mare would be better?"

They all laughed so hard coffee ran out of their noses.

"So, what is it you're hirin' for?" Jesse asked the man wearing a sugarloaf hat. He looked like he had money but he talked simple.

"Need me a man to go up to the high pastures and help my other man watch a herd of cattle I got up there, then bring 'em down end of autumn, before it snows and traps 'em up there. Either you boys interested?"

"What's it pay?" Frank said.

"What's a feller expect to do, just watch over 'em?" Jesse asked.

"Who's your other man you got up there now?"

"How come just one?"

"One what?" the man said.

"One man up there now, seeing's you're needing another'n?"

So Mr. Flaver explained about the hand that quit and the one who didn't and poured them another shot. He liked these boys. They seemed just dumb enough to babysit cows.

"I don't know," Frank said. "Me and Jesse here is saddle pards. Been together now . . . how long's it been, Jesse?"

"Almost seven years."

"Why hell, you're practically married sounds like," Mr. Flaver said, attempting humor. Jesse and Frank looked at him without smiling.

"Some might think that an insult, mister," Frank said.

"Oh, I didn't mean nothing by it, was just trying to . . ."

"No, sir," Jesse said. "We work as a team, me and Frank does. You ever rope and heel a cow, Mr. Flaver?"

"Sure, plenty of times when I was your age. Grew up ranching. My daddy was a rancher who had to fight the Comanche and the Apaches and Tonks, too."

That kind of impressed Frank and Jesse, but they didn't know why. Maybe it was the good liquor they were nipping sitting there with a man wearing a sugarloaf hat.

"I don't knows as I could afford to keep three men up there," Mr. Flaver said, rubbing the knob of his chin.

"Well, then," Frank said. "I reckon we thank ye kindly for this fine whiskey and the job offer, but here's the deal: Jesse and me weren't exactly looking for jobs. We were just passing through. Thinking of going on down to ol' Mexico and find us a couple of plump señoritas till winter passes."

"Why, winter is still a time off," said Mr. Flaver. "It's a long time to lay around and do nothing."

"True enough," Jesse said. "But we won't exactly be doing nothing, will we, Frank?"

Frank waggled his head.

"Not if'n we find them señoritas, we won't."

Jesse reached for the bottle, two thirds empty now, and Mr. Flaver watched him with eyes that were miserly now that it looked like he wasn't going to hire either one of these rounders. Lots of the men of Askin had fled for the gold strikes in Colorado and California, so help was hard to come by, least anybody who could be trusted to watch cattle and bring 'em down before winter took hold.

"All right then," Mr. Flaver said, "you boys are holding all the cards and I got spit. Sign a contract to stay and bring my beeves down and don't lose too many in the doing and I'll pay you one hundred sound dollars each when you get back here."

"Hundred and fifty," Frank said.

"Why don't I just sign over my place and wed you my daughter in the doing?" Mr. Flaver said sarcastically. "I look rich to you?"

"You don't look none too poor," Jesse said. "Does he to you, Frank?"

"Not wearing that fancy hat, he don't."

"One twenty-five and that's as high as I'll go. I'd as soon let them cattle freeze for the outcome of my profit will be the same I pay you two waddies three hundred dollars just to sit up there and eat beans and cornbread and laze around."

Frank looked at Jesse and Jesse nodded slow.

"Looks like you hired two rootin'-tootin' sons-a-bitches," Frank said with a grin. Now how 'bout we celebrate with another bottle."

"And we'll need a small advance," Jesse said.

"For what?"

"Well, it's gone be at least three months up there in those mountains with nothing but our hand. So me and Frank would like to get in one last poke before we go, assuming you'll want us to leave tomorrow?"

Mr. Flaver could not but shake his head. But on the other hand, he had been young once himself and knew what it was like. Now, he had a young wife, about half his age, and as much as he liked diddling, she about wore him to a nubbin after the first year by wanting it almost every night. She didn't seem to understand that men's plumbing was different than a woman's and that the older a man got, the more the old faucet got creaky. He envied those boys their youth. He'd have given everything to be one of them again.

He pulled out his wallet and slapped twenty dollars on the table.

Jesse and Frank looked at it, then at each other, then at Mr. Flaver.

"That sure won't buy much in the flesh department," Frank said.

"Puncher, in this town that will buy you all the pussy there is twice around. We got but one crib whore left on account of the preachers and married women prodding the town marshal to run them off. Between them and these waddies running off to the gold fields and needing the company and somebody to cook and clean and wash their clothes, the flesh pot has gotten mighty slim. And if you don't hurry, even she might be gone. You'll have to take turns, of course, but she's a good ol' gal and will do right by you. Name's Alice Shadetree and you'll locate her just east of the town limits living in a Sibley tent some soldier gave her in trade. Can't miss it. Have fun and come 'round to the café seven sharp in the morning and I'll meet you there."

"This other man you got up there," Jesse said. "What's he gone be doing if me and Frank go to tend the cattle?"

"He's a cook and all-around hand. Do whatever you ask him to. Real nice fellow. Just got one arm, but a worker nonetheless. Sort of felt sorry for him. He's my wife's uncle. Charlie Morrisey's his name."

"He does the cooking and cleaning around camp?" Frank said.

Mr. Flaver nodded.

"You boys stumbled across a real sweet deal, damned if you didn't. See you first light then."

Mr. Flaver watched them mount their horses tied off at the hitch post — a dun and a bay with double rig saddles, Winchesters in the boots. They rode easy, confident, talking to each other. He figured they were discussing who'd get first crack at Alice Shadetree. And he wasn't lying about her sexual skills or appetite. For a fifty-year-old, she screwed like her back had no bone.

Then he smiled and headed home, already thinking that with all that talk and remembering his youth, he might just take a bath, then haul Minerva up to the bedroom. It had been two months and she'd been after him and after him. Well, tonight she wouldn't have to.

He'd be after her.

II

The next morning, Mr. Flaver was out front of the café sitting high in the saddle, a fancy English thing, and holding the lead rope of a big jack mule loaded with supplies.

He could see Frank and Jesse'd been drawn and quartered by Alice Shadetree by their tired looks when they rode up.

"See you boys had a good go-round or two with Alice," he said gleefully.

Frank grunted. Jesse did the same.

"You didn't mention she was somebody's grandma," Jesse said.

"Maybe great-grandma," Frank said.

"Well, did you or didn't you. My money

is on you did."

"It ain't nobody's business," Frank said. "Let's get going."

They rode behind Mr. Flaver with heads that felt like rocks and feeling a might uncomfortable in the saddle after their adventure with Alice Shadetree. They couldn't hardly stand to think about it, but that is all they did. That and the whiskey they consumed. But they had to admit, too, that despite Alice being long in the tooth, she had an amazing body and an amazing way of using it, so after one or two bottles of ol' blabbermouth, they didn't much care her age or looks in the throes of passion. In addition to which she played a concertina and danced for them and wore red pantaloons in the doing.

Up all night and had to force themselves to go and meet Mr. Flaver when they'd much preferred sleep.

"What'd you think of that lady?" Jesse said quietly to Frank as they rode along, ever climbing into the higher elevation of the mountains that lay directly ahead.

"How do you mean, what did I think of her?" Frank said.

"I mean what'd you think of her?"

"Well, hell, I don't know what you're asking."

"I have to spell it out to you?"

"I reckon maybe that would help."

"I mean, did you feel bad diddling her seeing as how old she was?"

"No, not overly much, not after I got some liquor in me and she stopped dancing around and playing that damn squeeze box and turned out the lights."

Jesse stayed silent.

"Why, what'd you think of her?"

"Same, I reckon."

They both rode along silent for a time, then Frank said after he rolled a shuck and started to smoke it, "I admit it was kinda strange all three of us in the bed together. I never done nothing like that before."

"You ain't?"

"No. You have?"

"No."

"Bullshit. I know you did by the way you said you didn't."

"You couldn't hardly calm her down, could you?"

Frank shook his head, the cigarette dangling from one corner of his mouth. They got into the trees and could smell the vanilla, the smell of the pines, and the cooler air was welcome from what it was down in Askin.

"It was damn near a rodeo," he said, "and

here I thought when she first answered the door there wasn't no way she could . . . would. Hell, you know."

"There you go again asking me to read your mind when all it is, is but a single page scribbled with nonsense. Would what?"

"I thought at first it was somebody's mama and the daughter was inside. So when we found out that *she* was her, I thought was we to go ahead with it, we'd kill her first try and it scared me some, I do admit."

"You mean when you went to do it to her?"

"Yes. You?"

"Maybe, somewhat. That's why I let you go first. Figured she died, I wouldn't have to bother."

"I bet you was surprised when she didn't."

"I bet you was too. Figured anybody'd kill her off diddling her, it would've been you."

"Well, you can't say I didn't try. I mean not to kill her, but just in the course of action, you know."

They stopped for lunch by a gurgling stream and drank of its water and it was cold and sweet. They ate cheese and liverwurst sandwiches with slices of onions.

"My Minerva made these," Mr. Flaver said. "She knows I like a good liverwurst

410

sandwich, but says it makes my breath bad."

Jesse and Frank sniffed them but were too hungry to not eat and they proved to taste better than they smelled, but soon as they devoured them, they lay back in the grass with their hats over their faces and fell fast asleep, exhausted and wishing now they hadn't agreed to the job. For jobs, as they'd come to learn, required commitment to another and they weren't the committing kind, so much having been ruined on the subject from being in the war and often under command of fools.

They had often discussed getting their own spread and being their own bosses, but that required money for a down payment and the only way that could happen was to work for someone and save their earnings.

Robbing banks and stages and trains was an option, but the very idea of getting locked up in a jail or prison put them off such notions. Once, while discussing this, Jesse said, "What do you suppose them fellows that get locked up for a long time do for the lack of female companionship?"

"You don't want to know," Frank answered.

"Oh." Suddenly it dawned on Jesse.

Then there was the aspect of possibly getting shot by lawmen or irate townsmen, or worse, bespectacled bank clerks. No, they agreed they weren't ready for the owlhoot trail.

Seemed like they'd hardly closed their eyes before Mr. Flaver shook them awake, saying, "We best get going. We're lucky we'll make the pasture before dark. Some of this trail is tricky in the dark. Once saw a man ride his cayuse right of the edge a little farther up. I guess he had a hell of a ride for about five, six seconds before the rocks ended his nonsense."

He tapped heels into his horse's flank and tugged the lead rope on the pack mule.

"Wonder if we did the right thing taking this job?" Jesse uttered so that Mr. Flaver couldn't hear them.

Frank just shrugged his shoulders, letting his horse follow along as he fished out his makings and rolled himself a shuck.

"It is kinda pretty up here," he said after exhaling twin streams of smoke through his nostrils.

They rode along the rest of the day at a slow steady climb, and as the sun sank low beyond the trees, they came out of the forest into a valley of grass like a green bowl full of grazing cattle.

Off in the near distance stood an old log and chink cabin with a stone chimney and shake roof and a cottonwood corral. A lean-to for horses butted on one end of the cabin. There stood an old gray mule the color of unwashed linen watching them approach. It whickered at their horses and the pack mule whickered back.

"Must be old lovers," Jesse said, ever the wit.

"Must be," Frank agreed.

"Air up here's a might thin, ain't it?"

"You just ain't used to air ain't in a saloon or cathouse is all."

"I reckon."

As they rode up to the cabin, an older man with hair white and scattered as a pullet's feathers stepped out of the cabin door, a thumb hooked in one gallus, raising it over his shoulder while the other hung loose. He had a long face with muttonchops that were just shy of a beard, and a squint eye. The way he stood, he looked like a mis-struck nail.

"That's my other man, Charlie Morrisey, the one I'd have preferred to quit if one was going to. But, of course, God would not be so kind."

"Hidey," Morrisey said as they rode up. "I guess you know Bob done quit."

"I know," Mr. Flaver said, arching his back from the ride.

The hand looked Frank and Jesse over as they dismounted, looked them over with his only eye.

"Who're these fellas?" he asked Mr. Flaver.

"They'll be here the summer, help bring the herd down come fall."

"Where's that leave me, Mr. Flaver?"

"You'll do the cooking and cleaning and whatever else these boys need you to do."

"Well, now, yes, sir, Mr. Flaver. I half thought you was going to let me go."

"Normally, I only keep two men for the herd, but I'll make an exception this time. You help these men unpack the mule, and get settled in."

They set about unloading supplies and putting them in the cabin with everybody taking notice of the demijohn of whiskey that was packed. And, among the packed supplies, was a fair-sized two-man tent.

Mr. Flaver walked out a ways and looked off toward his grazing herd, took off his hat, and swiped his forehead with his shirtsleeve. It pleased him to look at his holdings.

When they'd finished the unloading and turned the animals out into the corral, Mr. Flaver had Morrisey cook up some grub. He would stay the night, then head back down in the morning, he said.

The grub was hellacious — some sort of stew — but the biscuits were very good, and afterwards, Morrisey fished for a compliment on his cooking but got none.

Mr. Flaver took one of the two chairs outside and set on it, letting the nightshade come down around him, and Morrisey set with him on the other chair.

Jesse and Frank went for a walk, saying they'd like to get the lay of things but really just to talk about their situation.

"I don't know about you," Jesse said. "But that old boy seems like something escaped from a madhouse or something the way he watches everything out of that eye."

"Let's not judge too quick," Frank said. "After all, we're stuck with him for at least two months. It ain't that long, then we'll run these beeves down and collect our wages and be on our way."

"Well, least we got a little whiskey and tobacco and a deck of playing cards to keep us from getting bored."

"That's the spirit."

Mr. Flaver spent the night and was gone in the morning, leaving the three men to watch over things.

"Usually the other man rides out and camps, overlooking the herd," One-eye said, a nickname they'd already tagged him with.

"And the other'n?" Jesse said.

"Stays here, cooks, brings you'ns out grub."

"We'll that sounds fine with us," Jesse said. "Don't it, Frank?"

"I reckon."

"That's what the tent's for, you'ns to live in."

"Why is it us has to live in a tent when there is a roof and walls here. Why ain't it you?"

One-eye shrugged, said, "I'm the senior man is why."

Frank said, "To hell with it, Jesse and me will go. Fix us up some grub to last us a day or two till you bring us more. And we'll take half that whiskey too."

So it was agreed that Frank and Jesse would ride out to watch over the herd from wolves and possible rustlers.

They were saddling up when Morrisey came out, and said, "You boys ever shoot anybody?"

"Not yet, but there's always a chance," Frank said sarcastically, his meaning obvious.

"They's rustlers come 'round sometimes and me and Bob had to run them off with gunplay. I think Bob might've nicked one on account we found a blood trail."

Neither of them said a thing but rode off on toward the grazing ground and set up the tent when they got there, then set out front and smoked and looked on at the grazing herd of shorthorns, what some called baldies.

"Tell the truth," Jesse said as they smoked, "I'd just as soon live out here than in that stinking cabin with that old coot."

"You say that now but if it comes bad rain and wind and lightning, you might wished you was back in that cabin, stink or not."

They flipped a coin to see who would ride out and check on the herd just to satisfy their duties. Frank lost the toss.

"I'll be back in the mornin' and we'll swap turns," he said.

And thus it was and thus the first month of their work began.

Mr. Flaver came up with more supplies at the first of the next month and didn't say too much, glad that the men had stuck and threw his bedroll down on the spare cot and went straight to sleep.

He'd brought more coffee and another demijohn of whiskey as well as other necessaries.

And thus it went until near the end of September, at the end of which, they planned on bringing down the herd because the weather had turned cold and the skies threatening.

"We'll be shed of this place soon," Jesse said as they huddled in their coats against a stiff wind howling up through the valley, stiff enough to threaten to collapse the tent.

"I am ready to say so long to this place and go find us another, hopefully more interesting."

"One with young whores, too, I hope," Frank said. "Not like that granny down in Askin."

So they got started on a conversation about whores they'd known and which was best and which worse and in what towns they'd known them.

"You reckon she is yet alive?" Jesse asked.

"I reckon she could be. That old gal had some grist to her. Why, you thinking of going to see her again we get down?"

"Hell, no."

Frank laughed, said, "Pass on that bottle." And: "Goddamn, it's cold, ain't it?"

All night the wind hammered the sides of the tent, the canvas popping so loud they could barely sleep for it and the cold. In the morning, they awoke to a foot of snow on the ground and more falling fast.

"You best get out here," Frank called to Jesse, who had been having ragged dreams about old whores.

Jesse climbed out and stood looking at the wonderland.

"Well this is a hell of a note," he said.

"We waited too long."

"Hell, no. Let's ride back to the cabin and get that old bastard and have him help us round up that herd and get them down."

They couldn't even see half the herd for the whiteness and maybe some of them had climbed up into the tree line.

The old man was snoring and they shook him from his blankets.

"Get up!" Frank ordered.

"What? What is it?"

"It's snowing and it don't look like it's going to quit neither. We got to get Flaver's cows down."

The old man rose stiffly and went to the door in his long handles and looked out. Scratching his rear, said, "You ain't lying."

"Get dressed."

"Fer what?"

"Round up the herd."

He cackled, and said, "Shit, I ain't going out in that."

"We do it now or we don't get 'em down," Jesse said.

"Not my concern."

Frank grabbed him up, and said. "You

damn well better make it yours."

Morrisey grabbed at Frank's wrist with his hand, which was more like a claw with long uncut horny fingernails.

"No, sir. I done quit. I'm staying put."

"What do you mean, you quit? How'd you quit?"

"I just quit, is all. Can't a man just quit something? That's what I did. Quit."

Frank released his grip on the old man's throat and turned to Jesse.

"I guess it's up to us to get that herd down."

Jesse glared venomous at the old bastard.

"You tell Mr. Flaver you quit?"

"I will, come the spring when I go down."

They turned and went out and mounted their horses, their saddles already covered with three inches of snow. With the heavy wind-driven snow, it was hard to see even as far at the outhouse.

"I don't see how we're going to accomplish anything in this," Jesse said.

"We got to try."

"We could get lost easily."

Frank didn't answer but turned his horse back to the camp with Jesse following.

The storm's fury increased, seeming to double in intensity, and they barely found their way back to the tent.

420

"They's no way we can go on till it slacks up, Frank."

Frank solemnly agreed. They dismounted, removed their saddles, ground-reined the horses, and climbed inside the tent, grateful to be in out of the raw cold wind.

"Damn it to hell," Frank said inside his blankets. "Damn it all to hell."

All day and night the storm raged and finally buckled the tent with wind and snow buildup and they had to burrow their way out during some night hour, shivering and cussing their fate.

In the outer darkness, the sky was red and the world below was glowing white, and it seemed like they were standing in a beautiful nightmare of something they didn't want to be part of.

The horses were gone. They'd broken free and fled. But for all its fury, the storm had then abated and left the world in silence but for Frank and Jesse's cussing. There was only one thing to be done — trudge back to the cabin in snow to their knees.

By the time they arrived, they were nearly frozen and could feel neither feet nor fingers. They barged in through the door and stood as close to the wood burner as possible.

The old man was sitting on the side of his

bunk as if expecting them.

"Tried to tell you boys," he said. Rising, he went and prepared a coffee pot he'd earlier melted snow in, tossed in some Arbuckle, and set it on one of the stove's plates to cook.

"You'ns hungry?"

They simply shivered and warmed their hands until they could feel their fingers and their feet by removing their boots and wet socks and holding their feet against the stove's heat.

The old man shrugged when they didn't say anything and set about cutting pieces of a smoked ham and opening a can of beans. He prepared three plates and placed them on the small table, which had just two chairs.

"There it is, when you're ready," he said and laid down in his cot again and covered up with blankets and went to sleep.

A short time later Frank and Jesse, exhausted by the trek from tent to cabin, flipped for the leftover cot. Jesse won and laid down and was stone asleep in minutes. Frank took the floor and followed suit.

Morning came too fast and hard. Both of them awakened to the sense they were crawling out of a grave.

When they checked, the snow was halfway

up the side of the cabin and they had difficulty pushing the door open.

"Son of a bitch," Frank said.

"It's the way of the mountains," the old man said from his perch at the table. He was nursing a cup of coffee laced with near the last of the whiskey.

"We're screwed royally," Jesse said.

"True enough," the old man agreed. "Might as well set and eat you something and get some of that coffee."

As much as they hated to admit it, the old man was right. There wasn't a damn thing they could do. They'd become trapped.

The days went by with little change. Sometimes it snowed and added to what was on the earth, and some days it was sunny and blindingly bright. They worked hard to shovel a path to the privy. A small comfort to be sure.

"Wonder where it is our horses got off to?" Jesse said.

"Let's hope they found refuge," Frank said. "I hate to think of Nel getting froze to death. She was a real good horse."

"I know it," Jesse said.

All the while, the old man listened and shuffled about the cabin and tinkered with a clock that didn't work and they asked him what he cared about time and he said he didn't, that it was just something to do. They played stud poker for matchsticks and the old man won almost every hand and cackled like a laying hen.

They took turns watching out the window at the ever-falling snow, which alternated with sunshine and the purest blue sky, and off in the distance, they could see the dark line of trees but that was all. Just white and blue and blackness became the color of their collective world.

Soon enough they grew short on food and the stockpile of chopped wood for the stove that lay outside the cabin grew dangerously low. The old man produced a pair of snowshoes from under his cot.

"One of you is any good, you can put these on your feet and set forth to see if you can kill somethin' to eat."

Frank and Jesse were weary of the entrapment, knowing they wouldn't be freed from their log and chink jail until spring.

They talked it over outside the cabin, bundled in coats with scarves tied around their ears. They were sick of the smell of the old man, his watching them and cackling, his loud snores.

The fresh air, even frozen, smelled good and they breathed it in deeply.

"Tell you what," Jesse said. "I ever get off

this mountain, I'm going back to Texas where it don't ever snow — that part."

"I'm of a mind to go with you," Frank said.

"I do believe that old man is becoming crazy."

"Crazier, you mean."

"Well, you're the better shot," Jessie said. "You take the rifle and hunt us something."

"I'll do my best."

The old man and Jesse watched Frank trudge off across the snow, rifle in hand, walking awkwardly with the snowshoes until he disappeared over a ridge; then they went back into the house.

"Poker?" the old man said.

"Why not."

They played for hours on end until the light began to dim and Jesse stood away from the table, not for the first time, and went to the door and looked out into the gloaming and sure enough he saw a figure darkly coming toward the house.

"He's carrying something," he said over his shoulder.

The old man came forth and stood in the doorway, and said, "I don't see nothin', my eye ain't that good. I hope it's more'n beans."

"Beans?"

425

The old man hocked and spat into the snow that, on the wind side, reached near to the roof. Every passing day, Jesse was more sure the old man was losing what little mind he had. *Beans.*

Jesse waited until Frank reached the pathway they'd shoveled, then dropped what was in his hand.

"I hope you can cook a badger better'n you can a beefsteak, Morrisey," he said.

The old man nodded, spat again, went in and got his butcher knife, and came out again while Frank took off his snowshoes and entered the house and set in front of the stove's fire.

He was shivering and his hands were blue. Jesse poured him a cup of Arbuckle, weakened some because they were running low on coffee like everything else, and handed it to him.

"You got any whiskey you can add to this?"

"The old man drank the last drop while I was out in the privy; otherwise, I'd have you some."

"That badger was the only living thing I seen and I must have hiked five miles, ten to and fro. It's like nothing's living no more, all this snow set in."

"Well a badger beats a raw potato, that's

for sure."

"You think he can make it eatable?" Frank said glancing over his shoulder at the door.

"I don't know. How good can a body cook a tasty badger?"

"Damned if I have any idea."

That night they ate a rank badger stew with the last of the winter potatoes and the last of the onions tossed in, lots of salt and pepper. They ate with trepidation at first, all but the old man, who dug in like it was a Delmonico steak, and soon enough their hunger overrode their wariness and they, too, were shoveling it down.

Later that night the cramps got them and they rushed outside to relieve their bowels and puke and straggle back inside. But the old man slept solidly, as if immune to whatever it was that had doubled Frank and Jesse into misery.

Whatever had sickened them passed within a few days but left them weak and lethargic as children. More snow fell during the night, carried by a raging wind that howled along the eaves.

The next morning, they found the old man's mule dead in the corral, glazed over with ice, its neck and head stretched forth, its large yellow teeth bared as if it had fought the storm with all it had only to lose the battle.

"Well, least we got something to eat besides badger stew, of which we have none anyway," the old man said without sentiment.

He spent the better part of the day butchering the animal with a hand axe and knife, tossing its parts up on the roof with the help of Frank and Jesse, in order that wolves wouldn't come along and steal it.

And for a few weeks, as long as the mule lasted, at least they contented themselves with food. But the fuel was low and they had to start tearing down the lean-to for the boards and the corral for the wood to burn.

"I wonder if Mr. Flaver even cares about us or his goddamn cattle?" Jesse said.

"I think he's no way of getting through with this snow," the old man said.

They ran out of coffee, then flour to make any sort of biscuits. They sucked marrow from the bones of the mule and dreamt of things no longer available, with women being lowest on that list, for a man's hunger overrides everything.

They began to quarrel a good deal, usually provoked by the old man's grousing, saying if they hadn't come and he'd gotten trapped, he'd have had plenty to tide him over, but with three mouths there wasn't enough. Saying they'd surely all end up dead by the time spring caused the snow to melt.

They took umbrage at his accusations, and even between Frank and Jesse, they quarreled over the least little thing, for they felt hemmed in, cooped up, worse than a prison or jail.

They had little to occupy their lives but quarrel and when the last of the mule — neck flesh and bones — came to bear, their dark mood only got worse, their quarreling more until there seemed no peace.

The old man slept soundly in his cot more often than just at night. Frank and Jesse took turns sleeping in the spare cot, the other on the cold floor.

Finally, the wood from the shed and corral was burned up, so Frank and Jesse set forth to the nearest trees to see could they fell some wood. It was a hard go with Jesse using the snowshoes and Frank trudging and struggling through the near waist-deep snow.

By the time they reached the tree line, it was nearly dark but the moon was full and they could see plainly enough to pick an aspen and hacked away at it until it crashed earthward, then chopped off limbs to make a fire and lay down in their blankets beside it, exhausted and addle-brained.

Lying there with the fire between them, Jesse said, "What we gone do, Frank?"

"About what?"

"About this situation."

"I reckon I wished I knew. Horses gone, mule et, no other food. I reckon we've hit near to the end of the trail, partner."

There was silence for a time, but for the crackling of the firewood.

"I hear freezing to death isn't so bad," Jesse said. "They say you just lay down and go to sleep."

"Who says? Surely not them who have done it."

"Would you take your own life, Frank? Put a bullet in your brain, if you had to?"

"I reckon I won't know until that time comes."

"Well, it surely seems to be coming and soon."

"Go to sleep."

"I'm trying."

"Try harder. We got to haul as much of this tree back down as we can manage."

"Okay, then."

Finally, they managed a few hours of fitful sleep but it did not feel like rest whatsoever. And, in the morning, they chopped the tree into manageable pieces they could get a rope around and pull.

After more hours of struggle, they reached the cabin again, dropped the wood as it was, and went with frozen limbs into the cabin.

The old man was sitting there in a chair with a shotgun pointed at them.

"What the hell are you about?" Frank said.

"Running low on victuals," the old man said. "Got me to thinking what was I gone to eat, and it come to me. You two fellers are somewhat rawboned and not much fat, but I figure together you'll get me through the winter."

They didn't have to say anything to each other. Frank and Jesse had been partners for too many years to not know what the other one might do in a desperate situation.

Together they rushed the old man and his scattergun boomed loud enough that a deaf man could have heard it.

The shot caught Frank in the middle and carried him off his feet and slammed him down on his back. A few of the pellets caught Jesse, but not enough to slow him down. He yanked the shotgun free from the old man and used it like a club to beat him until he no longer moved or spoke, his skull broken open like a melon hit by a sledge.

Jesse was blindly incensed and might have kept clubbing the old man had he not heard

Frank moan. He dropped the shotgun and went to his partner's aid.

The coat Frank was wearing was already soaked through with blood, and worse when Jesse opened it and saw the grievous wounds.

Jesse lifted him with unknown strength — for Frank was the larger man — and carried him to the bunk and laid him gently upon it. Their eyes met and Frank's were asking questions Jesse had no answers for.

Jesse found a clean shirt among his things and used it as a bandage to try and stanch the blood, but almost as quickly it too became soaked.

"I'm dying . . ." Frank uttered. "Killed by a goddamn crazy man . . ."

"You ain't dying. Stop that sort of shit. I'm gonna save you like I did a lot of them soldier boys in the war. I never told you but I was a surgeon's assistant. Shit, I saved plenty shot worse'n you."

"You're . . . you're a piss poor liar," Frank said, struggling with the effort to speak. "Why you never was no good at cards."

"Well, you'll see. You'll damn well see. Now be quiet till I can get you patched."

Frank raised a hand and let it fall on Jessie's arm and weakly shook his head.

"Just roll me a shuck. I'd like one more

before the passing . . ."

Jesse rolled a shuck and lighted it, then went to put it between Frank's lips, but his mouth was slack, his face ashen, his eyes half lidded. He was gone.

Jesse drew the blanket up over him, for he never wanted to see Frank looking like that again, then stood and went to the doorway and opened it and smoked looking out at the great white wilderness.

Maybe now it was time. It wouldn't take much. Just place those shotgun barrels under his chin and pull the trigger. Die quick or die slow, he told himself.

III

Spring came and Mr. Flaver was finally able to get up to the summer range and see what happened to his hired hands, and more, to his herd. He'd worried all winter when they hadn't come down in the fall. From his window he'd seen the snowfall up high.

He came upon Jesse sitting in a chair out front smoking a cigarette, patches of snow still clinging to the ground in places. The corral was gone and so was the shed, and so was the privy.

He dismounted and came forth but Jesse didn't seem to acknowledge him, like he was

433

in a spell.

Mr. Flaver couldn't remember which one was which, their names, so he said, "Frank?" Jesse looked up. His beard was thick. He looked gaunt and hollow-eyed and almost uncomprehending of who Mr. Flaver was.

Mr. Flaver reached into his coat and pulled out a silver flask of whiskey and held it forth. An unsteady hand took it and drank from it and lowered it.

"I reckon you boys had it pretty hard lasting out the winter up here," Mr. Flaver said. "Where's the others?"

Finally, Jesse stood, said, "There ain't no others. Just me. And I'd kindly like to ride down off this mountain, you don't mind."

"You mean they're dead?"

Jesse just stared at him.

"Well, what about my herd?"

"I reckon some is out there somewheres," Jesse said. "But they ain't my cattle and this here ain't my job no more."

Mr. Flaver could see that the young man had gone nearly mad by the stare and voice. He determined that Frank or Jesse or whichever one it was, was lost in the head and no point fooling with such a man.

They rode back down the trail together. Mr. Flaver wondered what the young man had done with the bodies, knowing no grave could have been dug in such frozen ground. But he did not deign to ask. When they reached Askin, he wrote a check for two hundred and fifty dollars, keeping in mind they'd both been up there all winter. The young man took the check and put it in his pocket and walked out. Mr. Flaver watched from his window as the hired man headed for the railroad station, then heard the evening flyer's whistle signaling its arrival. He knew the train would only stop for ten, fifteen minutes before pulling out again.

He'd send some men up to find his cattle, what was left of them, and ask they search for the bodies of the two men. And when the hands returned with a few dozen of the baldies that had somehow survived, they reported finding no bodies, but did find what looked like some human bones.

Mr. Flaver shook his head at the report knowing then why the young man had the look of madness about him. Desperate men with nothing to eat, it made sense they'd only find bones.

Mr. Flaver drank a whiskey and then another and told his young wife that night he was getting out of the cow business. She asked why.

"I just am," is all he said. "I just am."

Bill Brooks has written more than forty historical novels and is a full-time writer these days. He lives in Florida.

436

■ ■ ■ ■

Barquette of
the XP
by Tim Champlin

■ ■ ■ ■

January 1861
Nebraska Territory

Today would be Neal Barquette's last ride for the Pony Express. Only one more long dash on a series of ponies from his home station northwest to Fort Laramie — just over eighty-five miles — and then he was done.

As soon as the decision was made last night, he felt the tension snap as if he'd tripped the trigger on his cocked Colt. He slept soundly for the first time in more than a month.

Swinging open the door of the Mud Springs station, he stepped out into heavy cold. *Whew! Must be around ten below,* he thought, blinking away tears the bitter wind stung from his eyes.

He squinted east down the beaten trail that snaked through brown bunch grass. Two hundred yards away, it disappeared into a swale in the prairie. "Huh! Empty as my belly," he muttered. "Five hours late already. What's holding you up, Johnny, m'boy?" *Even if I could leave right now, I'd be past midnight getting to Fort Laramie.*

"Ah, but this day it makes no difference," he smiled, fingers pressing against the envelope inside his deep shirt pocket that contained his carefully crafted letter of resignation. He'd be handing it over to Division Superintendent Jack Slade by this time tomorrow. What a relief to lay down this burden and free himself to look for another job where no one knew him and he could start afresh. Months of being ridiculed and ostracized by his fellow riders would be over.

One wrong move had proved his undoing. Late last spring, Neal refused to take the mail on his assigned route when it was learned Indians had massacred several horse tenders and the keeper and had burnt the next station in eastern Utah. To him, it made no sense to risk his life for a bunch of letters that could just as easily be delivered a day or two later when the danger was past.

But the incoming rider, Rod Finley, had snorted his disgust at this fear, grabbed a fresh horse, and continued east, carrying the mochila of mail past the burnt buildings and dead bodies. He arrived on a lathered pony four hours later at the next home station, having outrun a half-dozen Indians.

But word of Neal's cowardice had quickly spread along the route and his life with the Central Overland California Pikes Peak Express Company turned sour from that day. He was reassigned east to the Mud Springs station near the North Platte River.

"If the Paiutes make your knees knock, you'll get the willies for sure when you run up on the Sioux," Finley had taunted him. "Not only will they lift your hair, they'll flay you alive and practice other nasty tortures I can't even describe."

Two other riders later failed this test of honor as well. One had been fired, and the other quit three weeks later after his life had been made miserable by ridicule.

The riders Neal didn't know well simply ignored him once he began riding back and forth between Mud Springs and Fort Laramie. He was treated as if he didn't exist. Most station keepers dealt with him only when it concerned work.

Hostlers were usually friendlier. On the whole, they were a pretty rough bunch, some former outlaws. But perhaps they accepted him as a social outcast, similar to themselves. Neal was fairly sure Ramon Diego, the half-breed hostler at Mud

Springs, mistook Neal's weathered face and black hair as belonging to another mixed-race youngster who'd only gotten the riding job because he was short, wiry, and athletic. In conversations, Neal revealed he was of Basque origin and had grown up on a grassland sheep ranch a day's ride from Mud Springs. But he was certain Diego had no idea what a Basque was. Diego, himself, Neal learned, was the son of an Arapaho father and a captive Mexican woman.

Neal took a last look down the trail. With no rider in sight, and shivering in his shirtsleeves, he retreated to the warmth of the Mud Springs station and latched the door behind him.

"It's mighty near dinnertime, Al," he said to the broad back of the stocky station keeper who was bent over the hearth poking up the fire. "I expected to be outa here before daylight. Reckon I'd best get some food in me before I leave." He didn't favor starting a run on a full stomach; the rhythmic surging of a galloping pony tended to make him queasy. Considering he was already an object of derision, motion sickness was not something he admitted to.

Alonzo Smith only grunted as he continued jabbing the coals with an iron poker. Sparks showered up the clay chimney. The mixture of dead cottonwood and dried buffalo chips made for a hot fire but gave off a strange odor in the low-ceilinged room.

Smith stood, red-faced, and leaned the poker against the wall. "I wrapped up a bacon sandwich for you." He nodded toward the table. "This here antelope stew is about done." He swung the iron pot back over the fire and lifted the lid with a thick glove to stir the steaming concoction.

The aroma made Neal's stomach growl. But he ignored the invitation to eat. As far as he knew, nobody at this station had been able to go hunting for antelope recently. His nose had caught the tang of chili peppers. The fiery pods were a staple in Smith's cooking — especially when he wanted to disguise the flavor of groundhog.

"What time is it, anyway? Johnny shoulda been here by daybreak at the latest."

"Hell, Neal, after eight months, you know all the things that can bust a schedule," Smith retorted. "The Pony doesn't run on a timetable like the New York Central."

"Maybe not, but the weather's dry, and there ain't nothing betwixt here and Julesburg that would slow him down. The trail's froze hard and no hills from the South Platte up this way. No hostiles out in January. The Sioux likely gone into winter camp . . ." His voice trailed off as Smith turned his back and busied himself washing some dirty pans in a bucket of water.

If the Central Overland California and Pike's Peak Express was going to move the mail from St. Joe to Sacramento in a flat ten days, Barquette and his fellow riders would have to somehow make up for every hour wasted here. But then, he realized again, it was irrelevant to him.

Smith turned around, wiping his wet hands on a dirty towel. "Could be anything," he continued the conversation — "a rider stopping for an hour at Fort Kearny to thaw out. Maybe one heaving his guts out after downing some bad grub. Could be a pony threw a shoe or stepped in a prairie dog hole. With stuff like that going on all the time, it's a wonder Russell, Majors, and Waddell can keep any kind of schedule at all."

To take the edge off his hunger, Neal helped himself to a thick slice of drying bread and plucked a limp piece of greasy bacon from the skillet on the stove.

He was wearing long johns under his heavy canvas pants and chaps, and a wool shirt. The blazing fire was making it uncomfortably warm, so he stepped outside again without his coat to clear his head of smoke and to examine the weather. The wind had subsided a bit, but the low pewter-colored overcast and the heavy cold jangled a silent alarm in his head. Growing up on the northern plains, he'd seen it all too often. If he'd been paid recently, he'd bet a month's wages snow would begin before dark.

Fidgeting, he reentered the building, anxious to be off ahead of the coming weather. Smith didn't seem concerned. He was snug here where it was warm and dry. With plenty of food and firewood, he could ride out any blizzard. Melting snow or breaking the ice in the nearby spring would provide water. As a middle-aged man in charge of this lonely home station at Mud Springs, Smith didn't have to bother with hazards of the trail. The station keeper and hostler could fort up in this log and sod shelter. Their job was to focus on supplying food and a spare bunk, keeping the horses healthy, grain-fed, and ready for the riders from east or west who could arrive at any hour of the day or night.

The heavy door burst open and Ramon Diego entered, admitting a gust of brittle air that stirred the smoke in the room. "Unsaddled the pony for now while we wait." The hostler shoved the door closed and strode to the plank table, his shiny, greasy buckskins trailing a miasma of woodsmoke and horse sweat. Swinging a leg over a low bench at the table, he rubbed his calloused hands. "Al, gimme a bowl o' that stew. The hawk's on the wing out there today, for sure."

"Hell, get it yourself. Your legs ain't broke."

Diego looked up sharply but didn't reply. He simply got up and dipped up a bowl. "I smell bread."

"Five minutes," Smith said, opening the slide of the small oven built into the side of the brick fireplace.

How these two disparate characters managed to get along for months on end was a mystery to Neal. At least they had overnight riders bunking with them to provide a diversion from their own prickly personalities. And Neal knew from experience that Diego, a dark, whip-thin man, was one of the best hostlers on the line, who had a knack for handling horses — almost as if he were one of them. On occasion, he even earned extra money gentling wild mustangs when the company ran short of good horseflesh. His tangled black hair was held in place by a blue headband; a whiskerless face showed his Indian heritage. It mattered not that he bathed only in warm weather in the nearby springs and trailed a perpetual nose-wrinkling odor on the air behind him. He was a valued employee.

On the other hand, Alonzo Smith, former clerk at an Arkansas land office, managed to maintain some decorum of civility in this wilderness. At least weekly, he heated water, stropped his straight razor on an old surcingle, and scraped off graying whiskers. He even washed his clothes whenever possible.

"Better warm up your belly with some o' that hot coffee," Smith said, gesturing at the blackened pot that hung by an iron hook just inside the fireplace.

Neal gave a dismissive wave. "I'm wound up enough already." Truthfully, without something to cut it, the black stuff was like drinking acid. Al never made a fresh pot; just added to it day by day as needed.

Neal popped the last of the bread and bacon into his mouth and then dipped up a gourd of drinking water from a bucket near the wall. It was cold and tasted faintly of algae.

"Al," he said, changing the subject, "how long's it been since we got paid?"

The station keeper's broad face went blank. "Hmm . . . if I recollect, it was the first or second week of October." Then, he arched his eyebrows at Neal. "You gonna start complaining about *that* again?"

Neal shook his head. "Just wondering."

"What've you got to spend it on out here, anyway? There's plenty work to keep you busy, roof over your head when you need it, and food."

"I'm grateful for that, sure enough," Neal said, hastily. "It's just that . . . well, my father thinks I'm having a grand old time off riding for the Central Overland California and Pike's Peak Express and making good money. I haven't been able to send him anything for weeks. He's likely wondering what's become of me. That sheep ranch will be mine someday, and if I don't help him keep it, well . . . there won't be nothing for me to go back to." Neal didn't repeat the name other riders were beginning to dub the company — the COC&PP stood for "Clean Out of Cash and Poor Pay." Smith, loyal to his employer, thought the name disrespectful.

"I figured you joined the Pony to *get away* from tending all those smelly woolies."

"Well, I . . . ." He stopped suddenly and cocked his head. A faint drumming of hooves on hard ground could be heard. He sprang to the door and jerked it open. Diego was right behind him.

A horseman could be seen in the distance,

448

rising and falling, coming on at speed, urging his mount down the home stretch like a jockey — exactly what Johnny Frye had been before hiring on with the Pony. Neal grabbed the field glasses from a shelf just inside the door. The undulating figure snapped into focus. It was Johnny's small frame hunched over the animal's neck and flying mane.

Neal bounded back into the room, shrugged into his hip-length sheepskin coat, and wrapped the long wool scarf around his head and neck, then jammed on his wide-brimmed hat. Lastly, he pulled on his lined leather gauntlets and went back outside.

Ramon was already leading the saddled pony out of the stable.

Neal ran a hand over the *XP* brand on the dun's flank. The animal quivered with excitement, muscles rippling under the smooth hide. Diego held the bit as the pony fiddle-footed, apparently knowing what was coming.

An explosive clatter of iron-shod hooves on frozen ground, and the bay came plunging in, distended nostrils snorting steam like a locomotive. Johnny Frye slid lightly to the ground while the horse was still moving. He yanked the leather mochila off his saddle and tossed it to his relay.

"What happened?" Neal yelled, grabbing the reins of the dun and flinging the mochila over the small saddle. Horn and cantle thrust up through slots in the leather to hold it in place.

"Train was late from Saint Louie to Saint Joe. Busted a cylinder head. They had to wait on another engine."

Neal nodded. "Figured it was something like that." Johnny was too good a horseman to be the cause of the delay.

Diego had snatched up the loose reins of Johnny's exhausted bay and was walking to cool him down while Frye headed for the door of the station.

Neal grabbed the saddle horn with both hands. With a quick hop-step, he vaulted into the saddle without benefit of stirrups. He knew this pony; the dun needed no touch of spur. As soon as the animal felt his weight, he bolted ahead as if shot from a giant spring. He was at full gallop within a few strides.

Neal's toes sought the stirrups and he settled into the surging motion. Next swing station was Courthouse Rock and then on to Chimney Rock, the giant spire that was a landmark for wagon trains.

Long hours spent tending his father's flocks with a border collie on the upland

450

summer pastures near the Black Hills had strengthened Neal's natural affinity for solitude and nature. Carrying the mail also provided hours of solitude to contemplate a variety of things. Riding a fast horse on a beaten trail didn't require much concentration, and his mind wandered.

But today his thoughts were jerked abruptly to the here and now by the breathtaking cold. The pony's speed was whipping a twenty-mile-an-hour wind directly into his face, bending his hat brim upward. He looped the reins over the horn and, balancing easily to the rhythm of the galloping pony, adjusted the wool scarf to cover his nose and lower face, then jammed the hat down, pulling the cord tighter under his chin. Breathing through his nostrils without the scarf made his nose feel stuffed up. But it was only the hairs inside his nose freezing. When it was that cold, he had to protect his lungs.

Growing up on the Great Plains, he'd come to respect winter — a grudging respect only, such as the cavalry gave the warlike Sioux. Winter and the Indians were both mortal enemies who tendered no quarter.

The sheepskin coat covered his upper body, hips, holstered Colt, and part of the saddle. In place of boots, which became stiff and hard to pull on and off, he wore mid-calf moccasins. This footgear was one of his prized possessions. He'd traded two new stag-handled knives and a spavined horse to a Cree woman for this pair of handmade moccasins. The insteps were decorated with a pattern of green and white stained porcupine quills, while the soles were double thicknesses of buffalo hide. The insides were lined with wolfskin harvested in winter so the pelt retained the downy undercoat of fur as well as the tough outer guard hairs His toes were usually the first of his extremities to be bitten by frost. But the fur lining, and the hooded stirrups that cut the wind, effectively warded off the insidious cold during the several hours it took his mounts to dash from swing station to swing station on his eighty-five-mile run.

Thus armored against the elements, he was reasonably comfortable, except for his fingers inside the gauntlets. They still hurt with such cold he had to pull off the gloves and blow on his fingers every twenty minutes to keep them from going numb and useless.

Neal considered what he was leaving behind. He loved the riding. It was the people who never let up on him. Good things never outlasted the bad. At seventeen, he was still growing, and might eventually get too heavy to be a rider, even though he was only one-hundred-thirty pounds on a five-foot, seven-inch frame. Everything was designed to cut the amount of weight a pony had to carry. Even the small, slotted saddle was merely wet rawhide stitched over a wooden tree. With only stirrups and necessary rigging added, it weighed no more than ten pounds. It was the mail stuffed into the four pouches of the mochila that counted — the mail was what paid the way for the whole operation.

There were other factors beyond his control. He couldn't go indefinitely without receiving his salary. The owners of the express were in financial trouble.

It appeared the country was rushing toward a civil war that would likely disrupt the Pony.

And how long would it take the backers of the telegraph to begin planting poles and stringing lines across these vast open spaces and even the Rocky Mountains? The end was in sight for this job, and he'd better prepare for it. Even trains were destined to replace stagecoaches in a few years.

His future was probably in sheep ranching. But the thought of fighting off greedy cattlemen for public grazing didn't appeal to him. *Forget the future; it's a blank.* It was time to go where he could be respected. The company would fail soon. He would get away before he was fired, he rationalized. *But the company might fail even sooner without you. Where's your sense of loyalty and responsibility? Your parents taught you better. You're not a quitter. You signed on to carry the mail. You have to at least give them some notice,* a voice within him argued. He gritted his teeth. Conscience had no logic. He had to plan ahead and get on with his life. It was time to start looking for other work.

The bare buttes of Jail Rock and Courthouse Rock loomed ahead, thrusting up several hundred feet above the prairie. He saw them as through a fog, but then realized it was snowing a couple of miles away. Big flakes began to fall, melting on his eyelids.

An hour later it was snowing heavily when he made a flying exchange at the swing station. Galloping out on a fresh pony, he was surprised how quickly the station and the two hostlers vanished behind him in the whirling flakes.

On to Scottsbluff. As long as the spire of Chimney Rock was visible, he could keep the trail. The dry snow was already fetlock deep and piling up fast on a northwest wind.

Thirty minutes out, he spotted the Indians.

Something dark and moving caught the corner of his vision. He swiveled his head. From the bouncing back of his galloping mount, he saw at least five braves through the gauzy curtain. His heart gave a leap and began to pound. He slitted his eyes against the stinging ice crystals. Very likely Sioux, he guessed. *Where the hell did they come from? Maybe riding out of the Black Hills following migrating buffalo?* Winter meat was crucial. But it appeared they were traveling light. The plains tribes hated whites for intrusion into their lands and for decimating buffalo herds just for sport. The Indians took every opportunity to strike back. *I'm the only game available.*

Normally, the best tactic against hostiles was to outrun them on the faster, grain-fed express ponies. He leaned over the pony's neck and touched its flanks with spurs. The animal tried, but apparently had nothing in reserve.

The Sioux had seen him and were coming fast out of the blizzard to head him off. Already they were well within pistol range.

Even though the blowing snow obscured it, Neal knew the surrounding terrain;

maybe the Sioux did not. He slowed his mount to guide him off the trail.

THUNK!

Something like a club struck his left thigh. A feathered shaft was suddenly protruding from the front pouch of the mochila. Before he could react, another arrow deflected off the saddle horn and ripped his gauntlet.

Neal guided his mount directly away from the hostiles to present them with the smallest possible target. Apparently, their skill with bow and arrow was greater than their prowess with firearms — especially from the backs of moving horses.

He made for the row of cottonwoods that grew along the base of Courthouse Rock near Pumpkin Creek. How far away was that shelter? Two miles? More?

The wind was scouring the ground almost bare in places and drifting the powdery snow in others. The pony galloped free for a hundred yards, then stumbled into a drift and floundered, knee-deep for a distance.

Neal had no time to look back. All his concentration was focused on attaining the limited protection of the trees. His heart was thudding in his chest, and his breath steaming like that of his laboring pony. He leaned low over the saddle horn, expecting every moment to feel sharp flint of an arrowhead bury itself in his back.

He thought he heard two shots, but the heavy snow deadened sounds. He could only hear his pony's heavy breathing and the soft thudding of hoofs in the snow.

After what seemed like hours, the wind and blinding snow seemed to ease. Neal looked up and saw he was in the lee of giant Courthouse Rock, which was sheltering him from the blast.

He twisted in the saddle and glanced over his shoulder. The dark figures against the white background seemed to be more distant, but he couldn't be sure. But one thing he could be sure of was that his pony was tiring and slowing. He slid out of the saddle into knee-deep snow and led the horse, stumping along on stiffened legs. It was a losing race. They would have him for sure within a few minutes.

Suddenly his right foot plunged down a steep incline beneath the snow and he rolled headfirst into a drift, icy particles going down his neck and up his sleeves. He staggered to his feet and clapped his hat back on his head. Gasping, he took hold of the reins and walked slowly ahead. It was still daylight, but the blowing snow was creating a false twilight. He'd reached the sloping bank of Pumpkin Creek near the base of

Courthouse Rock. Dark trunks of gnarled cottonwoods stood yards apart and ahead he could see a flat white sheet that appeared to mark the frozen creek.

He'd have to find a good spot and make a stand. His right hand felt under his coat to make sure the Colt hadn't fallen from its holster. It dawned on him that he and his horse were now below the sight line of the pursuing hostiles. If he could somehow find cover before they saw him again, maybe he could hide. He looked for fallen timber. The snow was not as deep among the trees and he led the pony as quickly as he could stagger along. Something was wrong with his left leg. Numb from cold? He could feel a slight stinging sensation he hadn't noticed before. He glanced down and saw the chaps were stained with dark blood all the way to his foot. The arrow had gotten him before it embedded itself in the mochila pouch. A thrill of fear stabbed his stomach. That much blood probably meant an artery had been severed. The way his heart was pounding, he could very well pump out his life's blood in a short time.

Ah, there's what he needed — a giant cottonwood that had fallen across the creek, its thick trunk and tangled roots providing a place to shelter from pursuit. The tree lay along a ridge of snow the wind had piled up on the lee side. Even though he and his pony were out of sight, there was no actual hiding with his tracks plain in the snow. Would this be the end of the trail for him? Even though he was still breathing heavily from exertion, he felt strangely calm.

"Well, fella, I'm sorry I got you into this." He pulled off his gauntlet and stroked the animal's nose. The pony snorted, still winded.

For the first time, Neal realized the second arrow that ripped the glove had raked a raw cut across the back of his hand. The pony would fare better than he would. As soon as the party of Sioux disposed of him, they'd take the uninjured pony along with them.

He looped the reins over a broken branch but was certain the fatigued animal wasn't going anywhere. Then he hunkered down, half-sitting in the thigh-deep drift behind the thick bole. He made no attempt to bare the wound in his leg. At best he had only minutes before pursuit caught up with him, so he pulled his Colt and slowly turned the cylinder, making sure it was capped. The heavy sheepskin coat and holster flap had protected any snow from wetting the powder. He leaned his elbows against the tree, laying the seven-and-a-half-inch barrel atop the horizontal trunk. He kept a gauntlet on his left hand but gripped the icy gun butt with his bare right hand since the forefinger of the torn glove wouldn't fit through the trigger guard.

He could only await the outcome. It wouldn't be long.

For the first time he was aware of the profound silence. Only a low moan of wind sounded now and then in the bare branches far overhead. Thin skeins of snow were whirled from the tops of drifts, emphasizing the loneliness of nature in its winter sleep. For some reason he thought of wolves and buffalo and lynx, and all the animals who did not hibernate in warm dens. Theirs was the tough life, finding prey or forage in such an environment. Many of the weaker, older ones would perish.

His left leg had begun to throb, either from the wound or the cold. The rest of his lower body was comfortable, insulated by the deep snow. His face and one hand were freezing. He'd removed the long scarf from his head to facilitate hearing, and his ears and nose were numb.

Predators and prey. The same tableau was being played out here and now by humans — men who did not act on instinct and should have known better.

Very likely he'd never see another sunrise. How strange was Fate, or the workings of Providence. He chuckled with ironic humor. Had he resigned yesterday, none of this would have happened.

Long, early dusk was settling in under the trees.

He heard a voice.

Getting a grip on his Colt, he removed his hat and ducked lower behind the tree trunk. He heard horses snorting and ventured a peek through the tangled roots. Three riders were leading the others down the snow-choked slope of the creek bank, apparently following the tracks.

Holding the Colt under his coat to muffle the sound, Neal double-clicked the hammer to full cock. The pistol was of the latest design — a .36 caliber 6-shot revolver with a long barrel for accuracy.

All five of the riders drew up and Neal heard them in conversation. No doubt they'd seen blood in the snow. Did they think he was mortally wounded and going off to die? One of the braves gestured around at the grove of thick cottonwoods. Neal wondered if he might be suggesting this was a good place for an ambush. Their voices rose in argument.

Neal held his gloved hand over the nose

of his pony, praying the animal would not answer the whinny of one of the hostile's ponies. But his hand slipped off and the express pony snorted loudly. Neal jumped behind the log, pistol in hand, as the Sioux walked their horses toward him in foot-deep snow. Three had arrows nocked and two were holding rifles. They were no more than fifteen yards away.

Heart pounding so that it shook his body, Neal rested the barrel on the log and took careful aim, holding his breath.

Boom!

The rider in the lead threw up his hands, dropped his bow, and toppled backward off his horse. The others let fly quickly but their horses were plunging at the blast, and the arrows whistled overhead.

Neal fired again at the two holding the rifles. But their panicked ponies were whirling in circles trying to bolt and the riders could get no aim. A rifle bullet chipped dead bark from the tree trunk. Neal fired twice more, quickly, yellow flame stabbing out from the muzzle and clouds of white smoke obscuring the Sioux. He could barely make out one of the Indians leaping down and grabbing his wounded companion and flinging him across the back of his horse.

Neal had only two shots left. Gasping, he

gripped the Colt, determined to sell out for the highest price.

But the Sioux had had enough. Yelling, they kicked their mounts into motion and lunged away through the trees and up the bank.

Neal waited. Several minutes passed, and his heart rate began to subside. He pulled on his right glove and waited, eyes and ears alert. A long quarter hour dragged by, and his hopes rose. Had they vanished into the blizzard with their wounded or dead companion? Finally, satisfied they were gone for good, he leaned his head against the tree trunk, sweat beginning to chill his body.

When he holstered his Colt, his hand brushed the lump bulging an inside pocket. A bacon sandwich. He wasn't hungry, but knew he needed fuel to ward off the intense cold. He brought out the food and ate it, washing it down with handfuls of snow; his canteen was missing from the saddle.

It was nearly dark when he finished and he wondered if he should try to examine his wound. He'd have to strip off the chaps, canvas pants, and long johns. Instead, he examined the snow and blood-caked leg on the outside. He flexed it slightly. The blood was frozen solid and he felt no wetness underneath. With luck the arrow had missed an artery. If so, the intense cold would stop the bleeding, he knew, but the wet blood turning to ice next to his skin could freeze the tissue. He knew he had to get up and move on to try for Fort Laramie where he could get help. Walking would keep the blood flowing to his extremities and generate some warmth. It would also keep the leg from stiffening up.

He decided to wait a little longer to be sure the Sioux were gone. He wrapped the long scarf around his head, ears, and neck and put on his hat. Meanwhile, he'd just rest here awhile in this soft drift. His pony was nibbling the snow and moving around a bit, lifting one leg and then the other. The animal did not appear to be in acute distress, so Neal leaned his head back against the trunk, tucked both hands inside his sheepskin coat, and closed his eyes, warm and comfortable.

He jerked awake to something wet and warm smothering him. A big tongue was licking the dried salt off his face. When he moved to one side, the pony whickered.

"Thank God, you're on the job," he said aloud, struggling to his feet. "I'd just settled in for a long winter's nap — from which there's no awakening."

He realized the danger and brushed the snow off his saddle, wondering if he had the strength to mount. He hooked an arm around the saddle horn and urged the pony forward. After dragging him several yards, the pony stopped in snow only a few inches deep.

His left leg didn't work well enough to reach the stirrup, so he awkwardly mounted from the right side.

Then began an ordeal that seemed to go on forever. The bitter night cold had settled in, but the wind had died and only steady snowflakes fell straight down. The pony found the trail again and plodded onward. At times, only half conscious, Neal thought he saw figures materializing out of the darkness on either side of him. They seemed so real he sometimes put up a hand or yelled or tried to reach for his Colt. But they were only spectral visions that vanished. At other times he awoke, startled, to realize he'd been asleep in the saddle. Now and then he would pull up and get down to lead the pony, to give them both some relief. He stumped along, beating his gloved hands against his sides until sharp pains in his fingers and then in his toes announced circulation was returning. When that happened, he jogged ahead to pump the blood even faster.

He had to make the next station at Torrington, a few miles this side of Fort Laramie. When he felt too fatigued to walk, he again struggled into the saddle and let the pony carry him.

Without moon or stars, there was still some vague visibility because of the whiteness all around. The pony seemed to sense the trail and held to it.

Neal was unaware when the snow stopped. But once, opening his eyes and rousing himself again, he noticed the grayness of coming day. The light gradually grew, even though a heavy overcast persisted. Then he dozed again, and only snapped awake when the pony stopped.

Someone yelled and two men were lifting him down from the saddle. He was at Torrington. Neal felt himself being carried inside a brightly lit room with a wood fire crackling.

"See to that pony. He saved my life," Neal mumbled, sounding drunk since his jaw was nearly frozen.

"Don't worry. He'll get a rubdown and plenty of oats," a deep voice said. "Let's have a look at you."

"Water," he gasped.

A strong arm lifted his head and shoulders

while a canteen was put to his lips. He gulped down a long drink, and then lay back with a sigh on the blanket in front of the fire. He felt his clothing being pulled off, and rough hands rubbing his arms and legs. Then he passed out.

When he awoke some time later, he didn't at first know where he was. He smelled coffee and meat frying. He was lying naked under a blanket in a bunk, his left thigh snugly wrapped with bandages.

"By God, you're awake!" Neal recognized the voice of big Harvey Wilkerson, then saw the walrus mustache as the station keeper came into his line of vision.

"How long have I been asleep?"

"Four hours, give or take. It's about eleven o'clock."

"At night?"

"Morning."

"Did the mochila go on to Fort Laramie and Horseshoe Station?"

Wilkerson jabbed a thumb at the mochila hanging on the back of a chair. The Sioux arrow still protruded from the mail pouch, telling its mute tale. "Ain't no riders here to take it."

"My run doesn't end until I deliver the mail to Fort Laramie." Neal sat up on the edge of his bunk and his head spun for

467

several seconds. He closed his eyes to keep the room from tilting.

"You ain't going nowhere for a while. When the eastbound rider comes in later — if he comes in — I'll have him backtrack and take it."

"That's not his job. Gimme a mug of coffee with some blackstrap molasses in it and saddle a pony." He staggered to his feet and had to grip the upper bunk to keep from falling.

"I can't let you do that."

"You got a clean pair of pants I can borrow?"

"Sure, but . . . that leg . . ."

"Is it okay?" Neal did not feel feverish, but his leg throbbed.

"Yeah. Arrow cut a deep groove across your thigh, the cold kept the swelling down before you got here. The hostler poured some whiskey in it and sewed it up. Glad you weren't awake for that." Wilkerson smiled grimly. "It should heal okay, but you'll have a good scar."

Neal was trying to gulp down the hot, sweetened coffee without burning his mouth. Then he sat and pulled on his high moccasins, which were still damp. A pair of pants that were too long followed, then his wool shirt. He saw his Colt had been reloaded and shoved the long pistol into the holster.

"Has the storm passed?"

"Yep. Left a couple feet of snow on the level."

He shrugged into his sheepskin coat. Something crinkled in his shirt pocket. He drew out his letter. The envelope was bent and partly stained with bacon grease.

He walked to the fireplace and flipped it into the flames.

"What was that?" Wilkerson asked.

"A letter parting ways with an old love of mine. She hurt me." He shrugged. "But we're both young, and maybe I was partly to blame." He jammed on his hat, slung the mochila over his shoulder, and limped to the door. "I think she deserves another chance."

Tim Champlin is the author of forty-one books and more than three dozen articles and short stories. Retired from the U.S. Civil Service, he remains an avid sailor, bike rider, and tennis player.

■ ■ ■ ■

RUNNING IRON
BY ROBERT D. MCKEE

■ ■ ■ ■

The colonel knew that the man who pulled his buckboard next to the Model T was Wiley's son.

Don't look at him. Look toward the cotton-woods.

Once the wagon had rolled to a stop, Wiley's son said, "Get out. I'm taking you home. Albert can fetch that contraption of yours later."

The colonel didn't move.

"Goddamn it, Cooper, get out of that automobile. Climb in the wagon. And get in back. I won't have you sitting up front with me."

When the colonel still didn't move, Wiley's son set the brake and jumped to the ground. He grabbed the colonel's thin upper arm and screamed, "Get out of that thing, you son of a bitch, and do it now." He jerked the colonel from the runabout's seat and dragged him to the rear of the buckboard.

473

He dropped the tailgate and shoved the colonel onto the wagon bed.

Jabbing a finger in the colonel's face, Wiley's son shouted, "I may've had to put up with you everywhere else for the last thirty years, but not out here. If I ever see you on my place again, I'll shoot you. If that don't kill you, I'll toss a rope around you and drag you behind my horse." He leaned in closer, and between clenched teeth, he whispered, "I'll drag you 'til there ain't nothing left." The colonel didn't respond. "Are you hearing me?" It seemed important that the colonel was listening.

When the colonel still made no acknowledgment, Wiley's son spit into the prairie grass and returned to his seat.

The buckboard lurched, and as they pulled away, the colonel looked again toward the cottonwoods in the distance.

The colonel realized Albert and Suze wanted to take the morning train to Cheyenne because they thought he was crazy. But they were wrong. Sure, he was getting absentminded. And there were times the fog came in thicker than others, but, hell, he'd turned seventy-two on his last birthday. What did they expect?

He told that to the pup Cheyenne doctor

they went to see. "I dare you to show me another seventy-two-year-old," he said, "who's not forgetful on occasion."

"So, you're seventy-two, are you?" asked the young doctor.

"That's right." Hadn't he just said that?

"By your appearance, Mr. Cooper, I'd put you at no more than sixty." The doctor grinned a dimply faced, childlike smile. To the colonel, the doctor looked no more than twelve — thirteen tops. Even so, he was an arrogant little shit.

"His hard work keeps him fit," said Suze. Suze was the baby in the family — ten years younger than her brother, Albert. "He still works on the ranch as hard as anyone," she added. The colonel appreciated his daughter's exaggeration.

Suze usually took his side. She'd been against visiting a doctor at all, but Al insisted. The colonel figured it had something to do with what happened with the tin lizzie two or three days back. That whole business had been embarrassing, and it had riled his son. Al had used that against him to convince Suze they needed to take their father to their hometown doctor, Bennett Sloan. Sloan was the only physician in Douglas, Wyoming, and a quack, as far as the colonel could tell. That was what the

475

colonel had always counted Sloan to be. But when Sloan said he couldn't find much wrong, the colonel's estimation of the man shot up. For thirty seconds, anyhow. It dropped again when Sloan suggested they take him to see this young fool in Cheyenne.

At first, the colonel had refused to go. "I won't leave right in the middle of calving," he had shouted at his son.

And Al, who, at thirty-three, was way too big for his britches, said in his usual, soft-spoken, pain-in-the-ass way, "Pa, calving's been done now for more than a month."

"So," said the Cheyenne doctor, who looked like a baby, "I hear you were in the army. Is that right, Mr. Cooper?"

Mr. Cooper. Charles Cooper had not been *Mr.* Cooper since July 2nd of '63 when he'd been promoted to Lieutenant Colonel. It was a brevet promotion, but, still, he'd been a mere twenty-two at the time.

"I also understand part of your service included the big fight in Pennsylvania. What can you tell me about that?"

The big fight? Who *was* this bonehead?

The doctor offered a wink and a condescending smile. "I'm a bit of a history buff." The tone of his voice implied confidence that the colonel gave a damn. Which he did not. But, since he could see the stern

476

scrutiny on Albert's face, he answered the question.

"I served with the great John Buford." The colonel felt the same twinge he always felt when General Buford's name was mentioned. The general was a hero who passed much too soon. "We picked the spot where the battle would be fought, and we held them Rebs there by the McPherson place until reinforcements arrived. Most folks'll tell you it all began on the first. But the boys in John Buford's Cavalry Division know it really started on the thirtieth day of June when the general ordered us to set our entrenchments on the high ground south of town."

The colonel saw Albert's scrutiny fold into a grimace. The kid was no doubt tired of Gettysburg stories.

The doctor turned to Al and nodded toward a sitting area with a sofa, a cocktail table, and a couple of wing chairs on the far side of the large room. "If you don't mind, Mr. Cooper, perhaps you and Miss Cooper could allow your father and me the chance to have a visit."

When Albert didn't respond, Suze said, "Of course," and gave her elder brother's sleeve a sharp tug. With a frown, he followed her to the couch.

Even though the distance allowed some privacy, the colonel knew the kids could still hear what was being said. He expected this whippersnapper doc wanted it that way.

The doctor stood — what was his name? Had anybody said? — and came around his desk. He took the chair Albert had vacated, scooted it over, and placed it in front of the colonel.

"Do you remember, sir, an incident two weeks back when you drove your automobile off the ranch?"

The colonel wasn't sure what the doctor was getting at. "I'm always driving the tinner off the ranch. That's what I bought 'er for."

Had he driven it off the ranch two weeks ago? Could be, but, so what?

The colonel assumed the whole mess began a couple of days earlier in the barn when he couldn't get the Ford started. Albert was furious. No matter how hard and often the colonel cranked the damned thing, the motor wouldn't catch. Though he'd gone through the routine a thousand times before, on that day, for some reason, the colonel was unsure if the spark retard and throttle were supposed to go up or down — or, he wondered as he sat in the doctor's office, had it been that he'd forgotten to flip the magneto switch? Whatever it was, it had been something stupid. He had admitted that, and, in the colonel's opinion, Al's over-reaction was uncalled for.

"Yes, of course," said the doctor, "I know you purchased the auto for transportation around the ranch and for trips into town, but I'm told this time when you drove away, you hadn't mentioned leaving, and you were gone for more than fourteen hours before a neighbor brought you home. Do you recall that, Mr. Cooper?"

"It's not Mister. It's Colonel." Voicing the difference sounded petty, but he didn't care.

"Sorry, sir, of course. Do you recall being lost for more than fourteen hours, Colonel?"

Lost? When was he lost?

"I remember I couldn't get the motorcar going." Wasn't he still in the barn on the ranch when it wouldn't start? Even if he was out and about when the Model T stopped, he sure as hell couldn't believe some neighbor brought him home.

He ran a shaky hand though his still thick and mostly brown hair. "What neighbor are you talking about?" he asked.

"That isn't important," said Albert from across the room.

Just as the colonel figured, his son could hear every word.

If he did drive off without telling anyone, he could understand how Al might be upset. But it was still no cause to haul him a hundred and thirty miles to some know-nothing pip-squeak of a doctor.

"When the neighbor found you, you were stopped in a pasture." The doctor spoke with slow deliberation, as though speaking to a child. "He found you in the automobile, staring into the distance. You would not respond when he spoke to you. What had you been doing, Colonel, for all that time? And why didn't you go home?"

"The lizzie wouldn't start." The colonel cringed at the old-man inflection that had crept into his voice. "But that was in the barn."

"No, I'm sorry. Two weeks ago, you were off the ranch. As I understand, a couple of days ago, your son found you in the barn trying to start the auto once again without telling anyone you were leaving. But the time I'm asking about occurred two weeks ago. You were trespassing. A neighbor brought you home. And the automobile was working fine, sir. It started easily enough when your son retrieved it. Tell me, Colonel, what were you doing at the neighbor's?"

As the pushy pup kept firing questions, the colonel's throat constricted. He stiffened and gasped.

"Colonel?" the doctor asked, leaning forward.

With difficulty, the colonel swallowed away whatever clogged his throat.

"Colonel, are you all right?"

The colonel dug a kerchief from his hip pocket and blew his nose. "Yes," he lied but doubted the doctor was convinced.

"Why . . . were . . . you . . . in . . . the . . . pasture?"

And with that, the fog slithered in.

Had he *really* been at some neighbor's?

The fog thickened. Answers to the doctor's questions were there. He could almost see them. They hung in the mist, dangling just above the ground.

"Oh, God," he whispered, suddenly terrified. The feelings of panic came more often now. And here, in this strange place, he couldn't fight them anymore. "Oh, God," he repeated, and to this baby — this fool — the colonel admitted the truth. "I can't," he said, his eyes burning with tears. "I try and try, but I can't remember."

He was asleep in the hammock behind the house when he again dreamed of the cottonwoods. The dream was a frequent visitor, but this time it was so real he could hear the wind soughing through the upper branches.

The voices in the trees called him.

He first heard them long ago, but for years he shoved them aside. Now he heard them often. They refused to be ignored.

With effort, the colonel escaped the tight arms of the hammock and made his way to the barn.

Once inside, he noticed the phaeton was gone. During the week, Suze kept it and the horse she used to pull it at the colonel's house in town. Suze stayed at the house when she was teaching. The sorrel Al usually rode was also gone. With the warm weather, perhaps Al and a few of the boys were moving cattle to higher country. His son was a busy man, and the colonel never knew where he was.

Smoke billowed from the cookshack chimney. Albert had assigned Lester, their cook, the task of watching the colonel during the day. But Lester was a poor nursemaid, especially at times like now, when he was busy throwing together chuck for the boys who were not trailing cows up the hill.

The runabout was in the back of the barn. Its top was down, and the colonel admired the machine's lines. What a remarkable thing it was. How much the world had changed since his boyhood.

Who could've dreamed of such changes? With a smile, the colonel answered his own question. Maybe Henry Ford, and that Edison fella. And those two bicycle makers from Ohio, who, of all things, learned how to fly.

Yes, sir, all those boys dreamed of a new world, all right, but the colonel hadn't. The old world was good enough for him.

He could, though, appreciate the wonders the dreamers produced. For now, at least some of the frightening clouds that so often filled his head were gone, and he was certain he could start the T.

Set the magneto. Lift the timing stalk to retard the timing. Push the throttle down — slightly — to set the idle. Pull the hand brake to neutral. Go 'round front and give her a crank.

Again he smiled.

And hope she doesn't backfire and break your arm.

But the colonel would not take his lizzie. Lester, even as he banged his pots and pans, could not miss the louder bangs and pops the flivver would make as the colonel drove it through the yard.

Instead, he crossed to a stall holding Ginger, his old strawberry roan. She huffed a greeting. "Hey, ol' gal," he said, rubbing the horse's pink nose. "Let's get outta here. What d'ya say?"

When he saw the distant cottonwoods, he clicked his tongue and put Ginger into a lope.

On this late spring day, the trees had already leafed out nicely. Soon the air would be thick with their floating cotton. The stuff would pile up in the tall grass like snow.

Why was he drawn to this stand of trees? The festering answer had been with him for years, but now it was lost. Part of him was glad. Relieved. But another, larger part could not let it go.

As Ginger took him closer to the trees, the fog began to lift.

The colonel, having once been a cavalry officer, enjoyed the sounds behind him when he led a group of riders. The hooves pounding the earth. The musical jangle of bits and spurs. The snickers and snorts of horses. To the colonel, these were all grand sounds, whether he was leading men to battle or merely to right a wrong.

At a quarter mile from the ranch house, the colonel lifted his right hand, and the fifteen riders behind him slowed to a trot.

He turned in his saddle and gestured for Benjamin Jeffers to come forward.

"Ben," he said, "go on ahead. Take three men and search the barn."

Jeffers nodded. He motioned to Clark Hughes, his hired man, and two others. The four gigged their horses, rode past the cottonwoods along the creek, and toward the barn.

Chickens scattered as the colonel led the rest into Alexander Wiley's yard.

When they stopped in front of the house, the low afternoon sun cast the group's thick shadow all the way to the corrals.

The colonel turned to Rick, his foreman, and said, "Call him out."

The foreman stood in his stirrups. "Wiley, come out of that house."

A window curtain moved, but there was no response.

The foreman raised a hand to the side of his mouth and called again. "Wiley, Colonel Cooper needs to visit."

The colonel waited for the door to open — or, he thought, with a touch of foreboding — a rifle barrel to poke from a window. But neither of those things happened. Instead, a small, shirtless man carrying an axe came around the side of the house.

"What do we have here?" the man asked.

He wore no hat, and the sweat on his bald head gleamed even in the dimming, late-afternoon light.

"What you have, Mr. Wiley," answered the colonel, "are some concerned citizens."

"Concerned about what?" Wiley hefted the axe over his shoulder and slammed it into the ground, burying its head. "I hope it won't take long, Colonel. As you can see, I'm busy out back chopping our wood."

"It won't take long, sir." *Sir.* It never hurt to show respect to a man you were about to ask uncomfortable questions.

The colonel dug a small pipe from his vest pocket. The pipe was already loaded with short-cut tobacco. He popped a match alight with his thumbnail and took a full minute to get the pipe going.

It also never hurt to make the man wait.

"I'll ask you again, Colonel. What's this about?"

Before the colonel provided an answer, Ben Jeffers rode from the barn and toward the group. When he saw Wiley, he looked down at the man and asked, "You been stealin' any water lately, Wiley?"

The colonel smiled. The summer before, Alex Wiley had been caught diverting water from a no-name trickle that fed into the La Prele. The La Prele was a creek that Jeffers took much of his water from, and Jeffers's water-right preceded Wiley's by fifteen years. When Jeffers noticed the La Prele's flow was lower than normal, he and a couple of his boys followed it upstream and discovered a dike on Wiley's creek. They destroyed the dike and beat the hell out of Wiley. As far as most folks were concerned, Wiley was lucky a beating was all he got, and that was the end of it. But Ben Jeffers wouldn't let it go. Every time Jeffers's path crossed Wiley's, Jeffers would ask Wiley if he'd been stealing any water lately.

The colonel found it amusing.

When Jeffers asked his question this time, as usual, Wiley provided no response.

"Did you fellows run across anything in the barn?" asked the colonel.

Jeffers shook his head. "The boys're still lookin'."

"Do I understand correct," asked Wiley, "that you got men rummaging around inside my barn?"

The colonel nodded. "Yes, sir, you are correct."

"What gives you the right to trespass on my property?"

"Well, Mr. Wiley, I'd say that *right* gives me the right."

"What the hell's that supposed to mean?"

Rick, the foreman, aimed a finger at Wiley's bare chest. "Watch your tone when you speak to the colonel."

The riders behind them moved in closer and lined up before the small man.

"It's okay, boys," said the colonel. "I understand why Mr. Wiley wouldn't want folks digging around in his possessions."

" 'Specially," added Jeffers, "if he's got somethin' to hide."

"I'm missing some cattle, Mr. Wiley, that've been grazing down along the river. Do you know anything about that, perchance?"

Wiley's protruding Adam's apple bobbed a couple of times when he tried to swallow. "No," he said. "I don't know what you're talking about." The colonel noticed that staring up into the stony faces of a dozen armed cowboys made Wiley's eyeballs bulge.

The door to the house opened, and a boy of about twelve ran onto the porch. "Pa, what's happening? What're these men doing here?"

Wiley called back over his shoulder, "Sheila, get the boy inside. Now."

Wylie's wife, a woman in her late twenties, rushed through the door and grabbed her son. "Billy, get in here this second." She dragged him into the house.

"And no matter what, both of you stay put," shouted Wiley. "It'll be all right."

"Maybe not," said Jeffers with a smile. A few of the men chuckled.

"Mr. Wiley," said the colonel, "I had some men ride about your place the last day or so and do some counting. It seems your small herd has grown."

"I'd say that's none of your business." Wiley's words were strong, but below the surface, they held a tremor.

"You could be right."

"If you're saying I stole some of your cattle, you're mistaken. Check 'em. They all carry my brand."

"Is that so?"

"It'll be dark soon, but, if you like, come back tomorrow. I'll ride out with you and you can see for yourself."

"Well, sir, I might do that."

"You're more than welcome to, Colonel. All of them cows is wearing the Circle W."

"That's your brand, the Circle W?"

"It is. Always has been."

"The W standing for 'Wiley,' I suppose."

"What else?" said Wiley.

"Could be," offered Jeffers, "it stands for 'Water.'"

Everyone, except for Wiley, had a good laugh.

As the colonel and his men enjoyed the joke, Hughes and the other two riders Jeffers had checking the barn came out leading their horses. Hughes carried something in his right hand.

"Looky what we found." He lifted a metal rod and handed it to Jeffers.

"Well, my word," said Jeffers. "Ain't this interestin'." He handed what he held to the colonel.

The straight steel rod had a narrow end that curved into a semicircle. "Looks to be a running iron," said the colonel. "What do you think, Mr. Jeffers?"

Jeffers nodded. "Yes, sir. That'd be my guess." Jeffers looked at the shirtless man. "What'd be your guess, Wiley?"

"I ain't never seen that thing before." Now the tremor in his voice had risen to the surface.

Jeffers seemed to be enjoying himself. "What was it you said your brand was?" he asked.

"I believe he said the Circle W," answered the colonel.

"By golly, that's right. I believe he did. And refresh my recollection. What is your brand, Colonel?"

"I have a couple of them. But the animals

that've gone missing are carrying a Rocking C."

"Rocking C. That was the brand you registered when you first came into this country. Am I right?"

"That's right."

"You know, sir, I'm not sure I ever heard what the C stands for. Is it Charles or Cooper or Colonel?"

"Well," said the colonel with a shrug, "I'm not sure myself. Could be any of the three, I suppose."

"I wonder," said Jeffers, pointing to the running brand in the colonel's hand, "how hard it'd be to use that thing to turn a Rocking C into a Circle W. What are your thoughts on that, Hughes? I know you to be a fella handy with a branding iron."

Hughes and the other two who had searched the barn were again in their saddles. Hughes took off his hat and brushed a hand through his thin blond hair. "Well, Mr. Jeffers," he said, biting the edge of his lip as though trying to contain a smile, "I'd say it'd be an easy task. You could use the curve there on the end to bring the Rocker at the bottom of the Rocking C around into a half-circle and connect it with the curve at the top of the C. Then you could use the edge of the curve on the brand to burn a W into the circle's center."

"By gosh," said Jeffers. "That does sound easy." He turned to face the group. "Don't it, boys?"

To a man they voiced their agreement.

It seemed Ben Jeffers was having too much fun with what the colonel considered to be a serious matter.

"Mr. Wiley," said the colonel, "this looks bad. As you know, men get hanged for such activity."

"I know it, sir. I know they do." The man's sweating from chopping wood had not lessened. He used a forearm to blot his brow.

"What do you have to say about it? I'm glad to listen."

"I don't know what to say. 'Cept I swear to you, Colonel. I have never seen that iron." The tremor in his voice was joined by a tremor in his legs. "Never. If my small herd looks bigger to your boys, it's only 'cause we've been lucky this year. The calving went well, and we're doing fine." He looked at the ground. "I do admit to branding a couple of mavericks down by the Box Elder. Them critters was unmarked and motherless. And, like I say, that was way down at the Box Elder, miles from your place. So, yes, sir, I've done me a little maverickin', but I have no reason to steal, sir. And even if I did, Colonel, I'd never be fool enough to rustle from you. I swear it."

"Could I toss in my two cents?" asked Jeffers.

The colonel nodded.

"The way I see it, this situation is not complex. We have you, Colonel, who, in the last month or so has come to possess fewer animals than you did before. And we have this fella who, in that same time, has come to possess *more* than before. I'm not saying that's proof that what he's now got once was yours, but we know this highbinder. He ain't cow savvy. We also know he's a stealer of water, which, to my thinking — in this dry country — is a crime as bad as rustling. Now, I'm not trying to make cattle thievery less than what it is. It's a harsh crime, deserving of a harsh punishment." He pointed to the running iron. "On top of it all, we now have that." To Hughes, he asked, "Where did you find that exactly?"

"Hid behind a sack of oats. He has a couple of Circle W brands hanging on the wall, but that there iron was hid."

Jeffers looked again to the colonel. "I hear out on the Sweetwater, the mere possession of a running iron's a crime — a crime that often warrants the severest penalty. Now, sure, them fellas in Sweetwater country are a rough bunch, quick to sling a rope over a sturdy branch, but when it comes to brand changers, I believe they've got 'er right."

He jerked a thumb at Alexander Wiley. "This man is a known thief. It is my belief he is also a liar. And I ain't the only one to think it. He steals water, and to my eyes, it appears he steals cattle. Who's to say what else such a man might do?"

With Jeffers's every word, Alex Wiley seemed to shrink. He now stood with his head down and his hands clasped in front. His body shook as though the warm day had magically turned to December.

Looking again at the iron he held, the colonel said, "This instrument is of no use whatever except to alter brands." He tossed it to Jeffers and turned his gaze to the prairie grass that stretched all the way to the distant sky. "You know, Mr. Wiley," he said, "we are all struggling in this rough country. You, me, and every man among us. We must fight the elements —" He looked down at Wiley. "Lift your head and look at me, sir." Wiley's head popped up. "We fight freezing winters and scorching summers. There's blizzards and tornadoes. Blowing winds that never seem to stop. We have coyotes, bobcats, and cougars killing our livestock. We gotta grow our crops in topsoil no deeper than the end of a man's thumb. Until recently we had to worry about savages not only stealing our cattle and horses, but stealing our very scalps. Ours is a difficult life, Mr. Wiley, and in addition to everything else, what we do not need, sir, is some avaricious man of low character diminishing our chance of survival."

The colonel exhaled a long, slow breath, as though the chore of talk was an arduous one.

"But, Colonel, I swear I never rustled nothin'. I took some water. And I branded a couple of mavericks, but them animals wasn't yours. I swear."

"They belonged to someone," said the colonel. "And it wasn't you."

The colonel and Wiley's eyes held for a long moment, and still holding the gaze, the colonel said to Jeffers, "Have someone make a loop."

When the colonel said that, Wiley fell to his knees. "No," he pleaded. "This is wrong, sir. Wrong. Even if I did do what you say, a man deserves a trial. This ain't legal. It ain't *right.*"

Ignoring Wiley's pleas, Jeffers said, "We can do better than a loop, Colonel. Mr. Hughes is capable of making a proper noose." He nodded to Hughes, who pulled the slip knot on his horn string and took down his rope.

When Jeffers said the part about the noose, Wiley began to wail. "No, please, please. I have a wife. I have a son. Don't do this. Don't."

Jeffers turned back to the colonel and asked, "Should we allow this sniveler a moment with his family?"

Wiley, still on his knees, rocked back and forth, beating his fists against his thighs. "Please, Colonel, I beg you, do not *do* this."

"No," said the colonel in answer to Jeffers's question, "I think not." From the corner of his eye, he could see the faces of Wiley's wife and son in the window. "It would be a mawkish thing, making the episode more trying on all concerned."

"Whatever you say, Colonel."

The colonel turned his horse and looked out past the barn. "Have the men bind his hands and take him to the trees. Those cottonwoods look to be a likely spot."

When the bullet knocked the colonel from his saddle, he hit the ground hard. Red geysered from his chest. But that was all right. As the blood flowed out, so did the fog.

He watched as a lone rider approached.

The man shoved a saddle gun into a scabbard and reined in a half-dozen yards from where the colonel lay.

The man was Wiley's son.

He dismounted and came forward carrying a coiled rope. Bending down, he lifted the colonel to a sitting position and slipped a loop over the colonel's shoulders and underneath his arms.

"I told you what I'd do if I saw you on my place again." He snugged the loop tight around the colonel's upper chest. "Truth is, I shoulda killed you many years ago."

Wiley's son stood and returned to his horse. He climbed aboard and made two quick wraps of the rope around his saddle horn. "I feared the shot would kill ya. It would yet, if I left you lay. But that'd be too easy. I'm gonna drag you 'til you're nothing but a bloody piece of gristle." He gave a toothy grin. "When I'm done, it'll be like you never was. Are you hearing me, old man?" Just as on that day a couple of weeks earlier, it seemed important that the colonel was listening.

This time, the colonel acknowledged the question with a nod. And with that, what remained of the fog drifted away.

The colonel looked from the man toward

the swaying cottonwoods. When he did, Wiley's son gave his horse the spur.

Robert D. McKee is an award-winning author of four novels and numerous short stories. His stories have appeared nationally in both commercial and literary publications. He and his wife reside in the Rocky Mountain West along Colorado's Front Range.

ABOUT THE EDITOR

Hazel Rumney has lived most of her life in Maine, although she also spent a number of years in Spain and California while her husband was in the military. She has worked in the publishing business for almost thirty years. Retiring in 2011, she and her husband traveled throughout the United States visiting many famous and not-so-famous western sites before returning to Thorndike, Maine, where they now live. In 2012, Hazel reentered the publishing world as an editor for Five Star Publishing, a part of Cengage Learning. During her tenure with Five Star, she has developed and delivered titles that have won Western Fictioneers Peacemaker Awards, Will Rogers Medallion Awards, and Western Writers of America Spur Awards, including the double Spur Award–winning novel *Wild Ran the Rivers* by James D. Crownover. Western fiction is Hazel's favorite genre to enjoy. She has been reading the genre for more than five decades.